OUR FEELINGS HAD NOT BEEN ROMANTIC . . .

On that Saturday night of our first date, I stayed all night at Judith's apartment but when we finally went to sleep, I slept on a cot in the front of the apartment. Judith was in the habit of sleeping alone.

Judith was a sensuous creature and frankly so but she had been fearful of falling in love because of her work and her career. And she had been hurt by her first marriage. She was afraid of too much intimacy and proximity.

The first time that we made love, it was as though we both had expected it to happen, as though we had known without being fully aware that it would happen. There had been immediate interest when we had met; and desire had been awakened. But our feelings had not been romantic.

Books by James T. Farrell

YOUNG LONIGAN: A BOYHOOD IN CHICAGO STREETS

GAS HOUSE MCGINTY

THE YOUNG MANHOOD OF STUDS LONIGAN

CALICO SHOES

JUDGMENT DAY

GUILLOTINE PARTY AND OTHER STORIES

A NOTE ON LITERARY CRITICISM

A WORLD I NEVER MADE

CAN ALL THIS GRANDEUR PERISH?

THE COLLECTED SHORT STORIES OF JAMES T. FARRELL

NO STAR IS LOST

TOMMY GALLAGHER'S CRUSADE

FATHER AND SON

ELLEN ROGERS

$1,000 A WEEK AND OTHER STORIES

MY DAYS OF ANGER

TO WHOM IT MAY CONCERN

THE LEAGUE OF FRIGHTENED PHILISTINES

BERNARD CLARE

WHEN BOYHOOD DREAMS COME TRUE

LITERATURE AND MORALITY

THE LIFE ADVENTUROUS

THE ROAD BETWEEN

A MISUNDERSTANDING

AN AMERICAN DREAM GIRL

THIS MAN AND THIS WOMAN

YET OTHER WATERS

THE FACE OF TIME

REFLECTIONS AT FIFTY AND OTHER ESSAYS

FRENCH GIRLS ARE VICIOUS

AN OMNIBUS OF SHORT STORIES

A DANGEROUS WOMAN AND OTHER SHORT STORIES

MY BASEBALL DIARY

IT HAS COME TO PASS

THE COLLECTED POEMS OF JAMES T. FARRELL

BOARDING HOUSE BLUES

SIDE STREET AND OTHER STORIES

SOUND OF THE CITY AND OTHER STORIES

THE SILENCE OF HISTORY

WHAT TIME COLLECTS

WHEN TIME WAS BORN

LONELY FOR THE FUTURE

A BRAND NEW LIFE

NEW YEAR'S EVE—1929

CHILDHOOD IS NOT FOREVER

INVISIBLE SWORDS

JUDITH AND OTHER STORIES

Judith

and other stories

James T. Farrell

MANOR
BOOKS
INC.

A MANOR BOOK

Manor Books, Inc.
432 Park Avenue South
New York, New York 10016

Library of Congress Catalog Card Number: 70-180073

ISBN CODE 0-532-22113-3

"Judith" was published by the Duane Schneider, Press,
©, 1969 by James T. Farrell.

"Mr. Austin" appears in *Works in Progress*, Vol. 2
copyright ©, 1971, by James T. Farrell.

"On a Train to Rome" copyright, 1953, by *New World
Writing*.

"On the Appian Way" was published in *Thought*, May 3,
1969.

* * *

"Anne Rutledge" from *Spoon River Anthology*, by Edagar
Lee Masters. Published by The Macmillan Company.

"Anne Rutledge" from *Spoon River Anthology*, by Edgar
Lee Masters. Published by The Macmillan Company.

Contents

Judith   *1*

Mr. Austin   *75*

On a Train to Rome   *97*

On the Appian Way   *105*

The Old-Timer   *111*

Episodes of a Return   *131*

Exiles   *155*

A Night in New Jerusalem   *231*

Only Tomorrow and Tomorrow   *249*

Tom Carroll   *261*

Sister   *339*

Introduction

I am writing this introduction from the Hotel Chelsea on West Twenty-third Street in New York City. Almost twenty years ago I lived here. And Eddie Ryan, who tells the story of *Judith*, is meant to be living in this hotel. In Front of the Chelsea Hotel there is a plaque put up by the Mayor's Committee. My name appears on this along with the names of six dead men who, at one time or another, lived here—O. Henry, John Sloan, Arthur B. Davies, Robert Flaherty, Thomas Wolfe, and Dylan Thomas.

In a sense the stories in this book are of time. Here there are other times, other places. There are characters and events strung over a panorama of time. As such, this work is a continuation of my lifework. I have attempted to create out of the life I have seen, known, experienced, heard about, and imagined, a panoramic story of our days and years, a story which would continue through as many books as I would be able to write.

I shall not presume to tell you, the readers, what these stories are about, thereby conditioning your judgment and impressions. I release the stories with the hope that they will strike some chords of memory, of thought, of interest—and that they will have some effect in infecting those who read them with feelings of different characters, times, places, dreams, and experiences. For this is why an artist works.

James T. Farrell

Part One

I

Teresa wrote saying that Judith had been a sensational success in London, that she was very happy, and that she had bought a house in Kensington.

I hope that Judith is happy.

I remember the last time I saw her. It was a hot summer afternoon in June over three years ago. She was planning to sail at midnight for London. We had sat talking in a big, almost empty, restaurant. Judith was wearing a low-neck summer dress. She looked beautiful. That inner discipline which was so much a feature of her personality was not evident. Her face was soft. She was eager to go to London, yet there was a certain sadness in her.

Finally we had to part. I was scheduled to make a tape for a radio broadcast on baseball and Judith had to return to her sister's apartment for an appointment.

We knew that we could not be alone at her sister's, that it was too late for that afternoon, possibly forever. Judith revealed her sadness more than I did; not by direct admission but by the tone of her voice, the brightness of her eyes, the tenderness of her gaze. I felt the sadness in her. It was in me. It was in life.

I was planning to remarry Marion. It was not until after Marion and I had resumed living together that Judith had realized that she loved me. This fact shadowed our farewell.

"It's all over with . . . ?" I snapped my fingers, "I'm sorry dearest, I can't remember his name."

"Andy. Andy Catlin. He's very good."

"Poor guy; he's too good."

We laughed, but not unkindly.

"I told him that he was. I hated to hurt him but I had to," Judith said.

"He was bound to be hurt and he'll love you all his life as an ideal."

"I'm afraid so."

"Don't be so concerned, Judith, he won't suffer acutely. He'll only suffer from frustrated devotion."

"He can be hurt, Ed."

"Everybody can. But it won't change his love. That will burn with the purest flames because he's the loser."

Judith thought for a moment.

"Yes, I know what you mean. Of course you hurt him, Ed."

"I didn't mean to."

"But you knew that you would."

"I can't help it, dearest, I won't step aside in such matters."

"He was sweet, Ed, even after that night when you hurt him. He doesn't like you."

"I haven't anything against him."

"You shouldn't," she laughed quietly.

"He's a good technician in physics but he doesn't have much imagination."

"I know you're right, Ed. I don't love Andy. I never did. He gave me a feeling of comfort. He was so devoted to me."

"Maybe you need that."

"I did. But not any more. That's how much I've changed during these last three months."

I leaned over and kissed her. She didn't protest even though we were in a public place.

"I'm sorry you have to leave so soon."

"So am I, Ed."

"I'm not making any promises about what I'll do when I see you again."

"And I can't say what I'll do."

"You mean whether you'll have any defenses?" I asked.

She laughed.

I ordered another beer.

"Have a farewell drink, Judith."

"All right. I'll go overboard and have a daiquiri."

I ordered it.

"I'll miss you—sometimes."

"Will you?"

"You know I will, Judith. We love each other."

Her silence was assent, I was certain of it.

"Yes, Ed," she said pensively.

"I don't know that we made a mistake."

"Are you making a mistake now, Ed?"

"No." I thought for a moment. "No, dearest."

For a few moments, we were silent. The waiter brought our drinks. I held my glass out and we touched glasses.

"To you, Judith, and to wonderful things for you."

"Thank you. And to you, Ed."

We drank.

"Now to absent friends."

"To absent friends, Ed."

I was referring to mutual friends in London, friends to whom I had introduced Judith. One of these was Teresa Lasser.

"You're glad to be going, aren't you, Judith?"

"Yes I am. I'll be happy in London."

"I might get over; but I don't know when."

"I hope you do."

"I'll think of you often, Judith."

"And I'll think of you."

I held my slender beer glass out and she touched it.

"You know, we're funny."

"How?"

"Our time schedules; they are at tragic and comic variance. Time. Time and your piano. Your piano has always interfered with your emotions."

"Perhaps. I had to go to a psychiatrist after my divorce and during the last two years. And I took a rest. I was utterly exhausted. But I don't want my work to interfere in the future. That's what I've decided. That's how I mean I feel different. I believe my playing will be better."

"I remember the night you were perfect. That was your great triumph; you never played better."

"I did in Europe."

"I mean when I heard you. I was proud."

"Why?" she asked, a bit coyly.

"You were playing for me."

She didn't speak immediately.

"Yes, in a way."

She toyed with her glass, then took a drink.

"I've never felt so free. Now I feel that I can live. I feel that the world is new."

We finished our drinks and I signaled the waiter for the bill.

"I have to make a radio tape about Babe Ruth as a pitcher."

"And I can't be late for my appointment either."

"Yes, Judith, we've got to say goodbye now."

We left. The sun was baking New York. We both felt the hot air as we stepped outside the airconditioned restaurant.

I waved for a cab.

"I'll drop you off."

Inside the cab, I kissed her.

"We can't Ed."

"I know; I won't muss you up."

I kissed her goodbye and watched her walk into the apartment building on West Twelfth Street. At the doorway, she turned and waved. She looked beautiful.

I rode uptown to the radio station.

II

I first met Judith eleven years ago. I had not heard of her. I knew nothing about her career and reputation. It was at a small party. She was beautiful that evening and in my thoughts I responded to her. I was married to Phyllis then.

Judith wore a dark dress, a mixture between red and purple. Her hair was thick and curled. I thought how I wanted to see her again, and that I probably would.

Four years later Judith told me that she had noticed me that evening and had also had the passing thought that we would meet again.

Judith's escort was Francis Mirando, a press agent. He was a decent enough person but colorless. He wanted to write but had never succeeded at it. My hostess, a close friend, liked neither Judith nor her piano playing. When Francis and Judith had gone, she said:

"She's pestering Frankie to marry her but he doesn't want to."

One of the guests mentioned her playing.

"She's not a great musician. She plays with no feeling; she's a mere virtuoso."

A few months later, I received an announcement and tickets for a concert that Judith was giving. I went. Judith had selected some rarely played Bach compositions. As a pianist, she seemed cold. But the audience in the theater at Columbia University received her with prolonged applause.

Afterwards, I went backstage to thank her for the tickets. Phyllis had been unable to go with me that night. Judith smiled and asked me to join some of her friends at her home.

She lived in an enormous apartment on an upper floor of a fortress-like apartment building on Riverside Drive. I did not know it at the time but she had been only recently divorced. The aftermath of her divorce had been one of anguish.

Most of those who were at the small after-the-concert party were Judith's coterie. Her playing enthralled them. In Judith they found someone to admire, to regard as a genius. Judith was a fulfillment for them. And she had a need of them. They formed a circle which seemed intimate without any real intimacy.

That evening the devotees sat around admiring Judith, flattering and praising her, asking her questions and listening attentively to everything she said. She told of how she traveled with a dummy keyboard so that she could practice on trains and in hotel rooms. She got out the dummy keyboard to show it to them. She talked about the trivialities of travel—catching trains, sleeping on them, hotels, her routine when she was on tour, audiences in various parts of the United States and Canada. She spoke of the hours that she practiced. The devotees told her that she was wonderful.

I did not think that Judith was particularly intelligent. I sat, said little, and listened. I asked a few questions about the anxiety of performing artists but there was no real chance to talk with her. I left before the other guests. Judith accompanied me to the door, thanked me for having come, and expressed the hope that she would see me again.

A few months later, I received tickets for a concert of hers at Town Hall. I went with a friend, Jenny Nickelson, who was a violinist. Jenny sensed my interest in Judith.

"Eddie, you needn't feel ashamed of your friend. She's very good; she's a musician but she doesn't play with feeling."

"Some people call her a mere virtuoso," I said.

III

Four years passed. Phyllis and I were separated. I was in California visiting my sister, Frances, when I received a notice of a Bach concert which Judith was to give at the YMHA on Lexington Avenue in New York City. I wrote her saying that I would attend. I received a note in reply in which Judith said that she would leave tickets for me. I went alone to the concert and was moved by her playing. Afterwards, I went backstage to thank her and to congratulate her. Judith was tired. She was drinking a cup of tea as she sat receiving people. She smiled on seeing me. She asked me to wait and attend a party being given for her by some of her friends.

I met Andy Catlin that night. He was tall and blond and had an inescapably countrified look. He taught physics and had a good academic reputation. He was moving about the side hall of the YMHA with an air of concern. I put him down as one of her devotees. When the crowd thinned, Judith waved to me.

"We're ready to go now. Will you ride in the car with me?"

"I'd be pleased to."

Andy looked disappointed. But then he turned quickly to duty.

"I'll take your things, Judith," he said.

"Please do. My scores and the bag are in the dressing room. And Andy, could you take the Altmans and Joan in your car?"

"Yes, I have room."

"I'll get my coat and we'll leave," she said, turning to me.

In the automobile of a friend, riding by my side, Judith sank back and exclaimed:

"I'm exhausted."

"Maybe you ought to go straight home, Judith," said Mrs. Rommel.

"Oh no, Helen, I'll feel refreshed after I have another cup of tea."

"You ought to be tired, Judith, you were magnificent tonight," said Mr. Horton, who owned the car.

"Was I? I slipped on one note."

"No one noticed," Helen Rommel said.

"I'm so happy it's over."

"Just relax, dear," Mr. Horton said.

We arrived at the party which was being held in a penthouse overlooking Central Park. It was a large party and there were others there besides the devotees. I met some interesting people. I was able to talk with Judith for only a few minutes when she came and sat next to me.

"Would you like to have dinner?"

"When?"

"When will it be convenient for you?"

She looked at the ceiling.

"Could you call me at home tomorrow? I can't think clearly now after the concert. Do you have my telephone number? I live in the same apartment. Do you remember it?"

"Yes I do."

She gave me her telephone number.

"Do call me tomorrow."

"I will. What time will be best?"

"Phone me at any time. I'll be practicing but I'll answer the phone to be sure I don't miss your call."

"I'll call. We might go to the Matisse exhibit at the Museum of Modern Art before dinner if you'd care to."

"I'd like that very much. I've been intending to see the Matisse show."

I talked with various other guests, among them a charming Indian woman who admired Judith as a pianist. I looked at

Judith from time to time. She no longer seemed tired; she was almost glowing.

I had been attracted to Judith from the first meeting about four years earlier. She had been most cordial and warm toward me. I wanted to make love to her. And I knew that I was going to try.

IV

On the following Saturday, I met Judith downstairs in the Museum of Modern Art.

I regard Matisse as one of the most normal and joyous of painters. I thought of this as I checked our coats. A week before, I had come to the opening of the Matisse exhibit with Olive, an artist. Afterwards, we had gone to her apartment. What was Matisse? A means for seduction. I laughed to myself. This was the kind of situation that Schnitzler might have liked to develop into a one-act play.

I can never see too much of Matisse. His world is swept with rich, luxurious color. He painted canvases with brightness and sunlight. In many of them, I feel something of the sensuousness of the Côte d'Azur and the Mediterranean shore.

"To me, Matisse is one of the most normal of modern painters."

"Yes, I agree. Look at this one, Ed."

She pointed to one of my favorites, an interior scene done with riotous but controlled colors.

We spent an hour looking at the paintings and sketches.

"He's so full of life, so rich, he leaves you with one of the most important impulses you can have stimulated by art—you want to live with more intensity of feeling."

I clenched my fists as I said this.

"He's full of life."

"Come here," I said, taking her arm. "I want you to see some of his early paintings."

After another hour, I said, "I can't look any more; I'm saturated."

"I've seen enough too. But what a happy idea this was."

"I was hoping that you would like Matisse."

"How could I not?"

"I once met a crazy old Irishman in Davy Byrne's Pub in Dublin. I had just come from Paris and I asked him if he liked Paris. He got up from his table and said melodramatically: 'The man who doesn't like Paris ought to be locked up.' You aren't crazy and we'd make a big civil liberties case if they locked you up. Ergo, you like Matisse."

—Schnitzler, I thought.

How often had I wanted to spend an evening like this when there had been no one to spend it with.

"Are you hungry, Judith?"

"Starved!"

"I know a French restaurant near here."

"I'd like that."

We went to a French restaurant on West Fifty-third Street. It was almost full but we got a table in the corner. We ordered.

Judith was easy to talk with. There was no need to hunt for something to say. She could grasp ideas and she was interested in hearing me talk.

While we were eating, I told her:

"I'm glad I'm having dinner with you."

"I'm enjoying it, too. And I enjoyed the exhibit."

"I'm glad for a reason."

"And that is?"

"When I first met you, I liked you. I wanted to know you better."

"I felt the same way."

"You sent me a ticket to your concert at the McMillin Theater."

"Oh yes, I remember that concert. I gave your name to my secretary. I must have thought that you would be interested in coming to the concert."

"I'm glad you did."

"So am I."

She smiled.

Judith was not coquettish; she did not flirt. She was a serious woman but not in a boring and humorless way. She would laugh and occasionally, she commented on the humorous aspects of the situation; but most of the time, her sense of humor was rather passive.

"I believed that I would meet you again, I wanted to," she said.

"It's fortunate for me that I received the notice of your concert."

"I must have given your name to my agent."

We talked about ourselves.

"Oh that was a bad time for me," she said. She was referring to the party at which I had met her. "I had gotten my divorce and I felt somewhat shattered. Even when you want a divorce and know it's necessary, you feel that way. I did. I felt battered around."

"You didn't look it."

"I thought I did."

We talked about many things as we ate. Then we went over to Fifth Avenue and walked toward Fifty-second Street. I took her arm. There was an invigorating chill in the air. I held on to her arm. When you are very lonely, a companion discovered is doubly valued. Walking along Fifth Avenue with Judith, it seemed as if I had entered a different dimension of life.

We went to the Sherry-Netherlands for hot chocolate. There was a three-piece orchestra there that I liked, especially the violinist. They played waltzes, "Dark Eyes," and folk songs. We sat for about an hour, listening and talking. Then we left. I hailed a cab. Inside I put my arms around her and kissed her.

Judith responded.

V

Judith was a very lonely person. She had good friends and she could have had suitors. But her life was in her work. She spent long hours daily in practice, all alone except for her Angora cat. She taught music at the Belenson School of Music and also accepted a few private pupils. She was doing research on Bach with the aim of writing a book about him. And she was an organizer of a series of monthly evenings at which new American composers were played. And she was making a recording of the *Goldberg Variations*.

She had very little free time.

Judith was an ambitious woman but not in a ruthless, careerist way.

I asked about her girlhood. She told me that she had come to New York from the West Side of Chicago to study music on a Belenson scholarship.

Her family had been able to give her only a few hundred dollars. She had had to support herself. She had lived in a small room in a rooming house, paying about five dollars a week. She studied and practiced at the Belenson School until six in the evening. Then she was alone. She could not practice any more until the next day.

"I used to walk along Riverside Drive and look up at the windows of the big apartments."

"What would you think when you did that? What would you dream about?"

"I'd say to myself—'Gee, the people in all those apartments have got pianos.'"

Judith had lived for a piano since she was a little girl. Her family was poor. Her father had been a bakery wagon driver. He was a Turkish Jew from Constantinople who had emigrated to America. He had died when Judith was a little girl.

Judith had given her first concert at the age of six. When she was thirteen, she got a job playing in a moving picture theater. It was discovered that she was too young and she had to give up the job. She had gone to work because the family needed money.

"I didn't have any childhood," she said.

Judith had gotten along well in grammar school and in high school in Chicago. But she had felt set apart from her peers. At home with her mother and sister, she would play the piano as they sang. She was hungrily ambitious to perfect her playing and to earn recognition and fame. But there was more to it than this. The piano had grown into her life. Day after day, she sat at the piano. Her most intimate feelings, her dreams, her capacity for love, for giving, the justification of her life, the fulfillment for those long hours across the years —all of this had gone into the piano. She had early fixed on Bach, studied his life and works, played and replayed and memorized all of his compositions. The discipline that Judith had imposed upon herself was rigid. But this was her life. It was not only what she did but it was also what she lived for.

Judith did not have time for people. Her way of life precluded many intimate friendships. She guarded her time and herself; and yet she had many friends. She enjoyed parties, preferably small ones with conversation about music and the other arts. Considering the amount of work that she did, Judith led a considerable social life. But this did not save her from loneliness. There was a vacancy, a center of emptiness which she felt. Love was absent. But she was loved by Andy Catlin. And I came to love her.

Her schedule prevented her from being spontaneous. She could not give way to whim, act on impulse, or feel free to cater to a sudden wish. She had missed these little indulgences which women need. And she had missed petting and fondling. She had had to protect herself from many of the things which not only give women happiness but which make up the major content of their lives.

VI

On that Saturday night of our first date, I stayed all night at Judith's apartment but when we finally went to sleep, I slept on a cot in the front of the apartment. Judith was in the habit of sleeping alone.

Judith was a sensuous creature and frankly so but she had been fearful of falling in love because of her work and her career. And she had been hurt by her first marriage. She was afraid of too much intimacy and proximity.

The first time that we made love, it was as though we both had expected it to happen, as though we had known without being fully aware that it would happen. There had been immediate interest when we had met; and desire had been awakened. But our feelings had not been romantic.

VII

The next morning, Judith got up and cooked breakfast. She did not keep much food in her refrigerator but there was always bacon and eggs. She enjoyed cooking but she rarely had time for it.

The morning was sunny. I sat at the table in her kitchen

thinking that I did not want to do any work that day. I sat with her at the table talking, feeling an afterglow of contentment from the pleasure of the night before, and enjoying the breakfast, the conversation, my thoughts of Judith, the sight of her, her presence, the morning with the sun outside the window, and the big section of blue sky that I could see through the curtains.

Judith wore a white silk robe which helped keep my attention on her body. Her eyes were full of happiness. And I felt happy with affection. I was relaxed and I was proud of her. Thinking of this, I smiled.

"That smile of yours," Judith said, her voice low.

She was articulate about herself, yet she was shy about expressing her emotions. Her sudden shyness at the breakfast table was charming. For a second, she seemed like a young girl. I watched her. She had a good profile. I noticed her little ears.

I made a move to rise. Judith quickly turned.

"I'll get you more coffee, Ed. Do you want more?"

"Yes, please."

I wondered about her sudden reticence. Last night she had been a prisoner of an intense sensuality. It had not only been passion, it had been a hunger of the flesh. She had had such a feeling of need that it seemed like desperation. She required this violence of flesh in order to retain the clarity and discipline which enabled her to work the way she did.

Judith set the coffee before me and sat down.

"You're very affectionate, Ed."

"Am I? Yes, I guess I am."

I pushed a pack of cigarettes toward her. She took one and lit it.

"Do you like to go back to Chicago, Judith?"

"No I don't. Do you?"

"Yes, now I do. I like my family and many people I used to know have apparently worn out their dislike of me."

"I've played there many times."

"How were you received?"

"Not very enthusiastically except for a few friends and admirers. But once when I was playing in Chicago I decided to go back to the building where we had lived on West Madison Street. When I walked into the hallway of that building and smelled those cooking odors, I couldn't stand it," Judith grimaced. "The smells, the dirt, the noise. I was terribly distressed. I'll never do it again, never."

"I have the notion that we all have to go back."

"Do you think so, Ed?"

"I mean that we need to go back and to face ourselves."

"I don't know if I agree with that."

"I'm not certain myself; it's a notion."

"I had curiosity to see the place again, of course. Maybe it was more than curiosity."

"You were eighteen when you came here, Judith?"

"Yes, eighteen."

"You must have been lovely."

"I didn't think much of that."

"How did your mother feel about your coming here alone? A girl of eighteen? Was she worried?"

"No she was glad because I had a scholarship. They couldn't help me much. Mother couldn't. My older sister Miriam didn't help much. We didn't get along too well. We get on better now. I guess it's better; we don't quarrel."

"You don't feel close to her?"

"No."

"What does she do?"

"She works in an office. Her friend Ely has a little money. He's been her friend for years. I see her partly because of a sense of obligation. And she wants to see me."

"Is she proud of you?"

"Now she is. She wasn't. I don't feel any antipathy toward Miriam but we're not close."

I took off my glasses and unwittingly put one earpiece into my cup.

"What the hell am I eating my glasses for? I've been fed."

"I fed all your needs, didn't I?" she asked shyly.

Our hands reached out in a simultaneous gesture. I held hers.

I wondered, for whom did Judith play? For whom did she work? She had spent her life developing and perfecting her technique. For whom? For what? Probably here was the reason Judith had her coterie of devotees. I continued to hold her hand. She smiled softly.

Love, warmth, closeness. Judith did not have these.

—Neither do I, I thought.

"You look wistful, Judith."

"Do I? I wasn't aware of it."

"Do you know the poetry of Francis Thompson?"

"One or two of them. The famous one, what's the title? *The Hound . . .*"

"*The Hound of Heaven.*"

"Yes that's it. I like it."

"I admire him much more than the contemporary critics seem to. But I just recalled two lines of his I love. That's sloppy."

"What's sloppy?"

"Saying I love the lines. I like them. They run, I think,

> *Go, and too late thou shalt confess*
> *I dreamed thee into loveliness*

That might not be the precise quotation but it's close."

"Yes, it's nice."

"I won't dream you into wistfulness," I said.

She didn't answer but she smiled.

I finished my coffee. I knew that I should leave, it was time for me to be getting back to my hotel.

"I guess I'll have to be leaving now."

I got up, bent down and drew her head against me. I kissed her hair.

"You've been very sweet; thank you, dear."

"Thank you, Ed."

She rose and went to the door with me.

"Goodbye, dear," she said, kissing me.

It was the first time she had used the word "dear."

VIII

It was windy on Riverside Drive. I walked for a few blocks with the wind driving against me. I turned off toward Broadway. I was too contented to think. The long evening with Judith continued within me, lingering in memories that came and went.

Maybe Judith would be permanent, I thought.

On West End Avenue, I hailed a taxicab. Slumped back in the seat, smoking a cigarette, I looked casually at the people on the sidewalk. I thought for a moment that I should have taken the subway, that I was being indulgent. I didn't care.

I'd work all day in my hotel and I would not feel that depressing loneliness which often left me restless and unable to concentrate. I'd feel at ease with myself. I did in the cab.

Sunday morning. I used to take my son, Tommy, out on Sunday mornings before the separation. But now, Tommy was in boarding school. And Sundays were like other mornings except that it took longer to read the newspapers and there was no mail.

Men and women were out walking.

I thought of Judith as the cab shot along.

Back at my hotel, I did not find it easy to work. There had been times when I could not work because I felt lonely, I felt the need of a woman. At such times, I would think that a woman would change my mood, and then, I could go on working without forcing myself, and I would be satisfied to be by myself in my hotel room. But now, I could not work and I had been with Judith. I should have stayed with her all day.

It was difficult to write. I kept ordering coffee. My thoughts were scattered. The day passed slowly.

Several times I thought of telephoning her. Twice I went over to the telephone but I didn't phone. Judith would have her own thoughts and feelings. And perhaps she was trying to work. But I believed she was able to continue with her work more easily than I, and with less strain.

I was convinced that the previous evening had had much the same meaning for her that it had had for me. It had been a response to need, a need that was almost frantic. But with such a need so controlling you, you could not be free. You did not have full control over yourself.

I laughed.

Why should you have full control over yourself?

Judith had not hesitated with me. She had not put up any preliminary resistance. She had not flirted, nor had she been uncertain. But she was not what many men would call "easy." I did not know her well but I could see that she had many little walls protecting her from the dangers of too much intimacy. After all, she had not fallen in love with me. She was feeding herself with an experience in order that she could go on. She was taking, or rather accepting, what she wanted because her body demanded it; and it was good for her and for her work during her long hours alone at her piano.

I knew that this did not explain Judith fully but it explained her in part. But what it did not explain was more important than what it did. I did not know this on that Sunday.

Sunday passed.

On Monday I phoned her and asked her if she were free that evening. She was not free until Thursday evening. I was both relieved and regretful. I would be free to work for three evenings, and I could look forward to seeing her. Yet I would have liked to see her that evening.

Could I be in love with thoughts like these? And if Judith were in love with me, would she not have changed her plans so that she could see me before Thursday?

I felt uncertain. I wondered how Judith felt, whether or not she thought it was wrong for her, not morally wrong, but wrong in the sense that she did not love me and did not want a relationship to develop. Intimacy can lead to shame, guilt, or disgust.

I had no such feelings. I knew that when I saw her next Thursday, I would kiss her at the door of her apartment. And I was sure of her response.

On Thursday, I left my hotel early. I arrived at Judith's apartment at six-thirty, the time we had set. She was wearing a dark suit with a red knit blouse which was very becoming.

"You ought to get in the apartment first," she laughed after I embraced her.

"I suppose so."

"I don't really object, Ed."

"I thought about you all day."

"Why?"

"This is why," I said, drawing her to me.

"Darling, come, don't you want to eat first?"

"No."

"Come, we'll eat a quiet dinner."

"All right, dearest."

We ate on Broadway in a restaurant I used to go to when I had lived in the neighborhood about nine years earlier. It was large and a bit noisy. There was a lineup of people at the bar.

"Just think, Judith, I used to stand up at that bar and drink too much."

"I wouldn't think that you'd drink too much."

"I don't drink at all now, but I've been a damned fool plenty of times."

"Haven't we all?"

She told me about her day. She was faced with the problem of changing agents. And had spent some time recording.

"What did you do on Sunday, dearest?"

"What did you do?" she asked, smiling.

"Not much."

"You were going back to your hotel to work, weren't you?"

"I didn't."

"Why?"

"You."

"I didn't do much either. I thought of you, Ed."

I took her hand.

"Maybe it was Matisse," I joked, and then seriously, "The exhibition was wonderful. He's a great artist. He makes it easy to fall in love."

"Yes he does," she laughed.

We didn't rush; we talked. The conversation just happened. I talked about Baudelaire. I caught myself just as I was going to mention his sonnet *La Danseuse*. I had started to speak of its perfection, its integration, the use of the metaphor. But I thought of the last line

La froide majesté de la femme stérile.

Judith was not a dancer but she was an artist. I didn't want to say anything which could hurt her feelings.

After another hour or so of conversation, I paid the check and we left. It was cold and windy outside. We turned onto 116th Street to walk to Riverside Drive. The wind slashed at us, it felt raw. I took Judith's arm.

"Do you like this wind?"

"God no. I can't even talk in it. Ooooh!"

I stayed later than Judith had intended. She was tired and

had wanted to get to bed by midnight but we sat in her kitchen talking. She made me hot chocolate and I had some cheese and crackers with it. She wore the same white robe. I liked her in it. I looked at her with a sense of possession. I had known the body under that robe, but once she had put it on, she had regained a sense of mystery.

Judith spoke of music. She explained how she played, how she used her fingers. She also said that she wanted to get on with her book on Bach. We talked of other books. She considered Albert Schweitzer interesting on music, but wrong.

"I'm playing so much better, Ed. You'll hear at my concert next month."

Finally, we both were yawning. I thought of suggesting that I spend the night but I sensed that she would not want that. She looked very sleepy.

"And I had planned to go to bed early."

"I'm not sorry I kept you up."

"You're sweet, Ed, but now I must send you home."

"Yes, dearest. I'm leaving."

I rode back to my hotel in a cab. I felt wonderfully sleepy.

—Judith is from Chicago too, I thought.

This pleased me. In a sense, a dream of my youth was being fulfilled. Two artists, falling in love. But the reality was different from my dream. It was not disillusioning but it was different. Judith and I were not depending on each other, growing together, with our work intertwined, living almost every minute in unison. We were quite independent of each other and did not feed on each other's nature for our work.

The cab rolled along. I thought idly. A writer and a concert pianist. This love affair was so different from how such an affair might be imagined by others. But I was thinking of the cliches and banalities of love, which were silly. Things were very simple with Judith.

I fell asleep thinking of her as she had looked in the kitchen.

IX

My relationship with Judith was close to being ideal. She was not demanding or questioning and she showed evidence of a tender feeling toward me. She was considerate and was careful not to offend me even in little things. And she was passionate and responsive. She made love more like a girl than a woman.

Judith never spoke of past lovers. We never asked each other intimate questions. She spoke of her marriage but not of other men. She undoubtedly had had lovers but I was convinced that she had not had many experiences. I knew this without asking. She had not had the time for them; she had lived most of her life for her music. She had dreamed of love, perhaps, just as many others do. But hers had been the girlhood of a prodigy. She had played her first concert at six. Much of the experience that Judith had missed she could well have missed; but she believed that she had missed something; she was catching up with herself.

Judith fit seeing me into her schedule. She was free only two evenings a week and she was frequently fatigued. She was preparing for a concert in Canada and had not been able to practice as much as she would have liked.

I would go to her apartment at about six-thirty or seven. If it were a weekday night, she would be wearing a simple suit. We would go to dinner and then back to her apartment. Neither of us cared for movies. There were some silences between us as there are between any two people but we talked much, and we talked easily and naturally.

Judith had good taste in literature. Whenever she commented about her aesthetic likes or dislikes, she was honest just as she was in everything else. We often talked of books and pictures, and sometimes of music. I would let Judith do the talking about music.

Making love with her stimulated me and I would sit by the side of the bed afterwards presenting what would almost amount to a lecture on literature. I enjoyed speaking like this to her. Most of the people whom I saw talked about politics, trade union problems, and foreign affairs. Judith had read some of my books before we had come together. She liked my writing.

Twice Judith asked me to go to concerts for which she had tickets but I couldn't make it.

One Saturday night, after we had had dinner and had seen a French movie, she said that she wanted to go to a party for a friend of hers, a composer. I suggested that we skip it and go home but Judith said:

"I must go. We won't stay long I promise."

The party was on Clarendon Avenue near Judith's apartment. Most of those there were musical people. I knew a few of them; I was glad that I had gone with her. Judith was well liked. I was a little vain about escorting her to the party. I had a good time. We stayed for about an hour and then left.

We saw a few of her friends and some of mine. But now as I look back, I realize that we spent most of our time alone.

I remember Christmas that year. I had picked out some earrings for her and had also sent her a newly published translation of some of Baudelaire's essays. We couldn't see each other on Christmas day; I was planning to spend the day with my son, Tommy, and Phyllis. Judith had to be with her sister. Another sister had come from Chicago and was staying with her. She was cooking a turkey for a family dinner. Judith complained, saying that there was a strain between her and her sisters, especially the one from Chicago. She was also supposed to be tied up with them on Christmas Eve but she came down to my hotel and we had dinner at a Spanish restaurant on Tenth Street.

"I shouldn't go back with you, dear, I must get home. I've left things undone and I told my sisters that I would be back early. But I want to go back with you."

"I want you too, Judith, my dearest."

"I was delivering presents. I told my sisters I had to deliver a few but that I'd be back by eight o'clock at the latest."

X

Judith was lying in the rumpled bed.

"You were delivering presents?"

"What I brought you is very little, Ed."

Shyly, like a little girl, she handed me packages wrapped in Christmas paper. There was a reproduction of an El Greco, a Leonardo da Vinci, and Cranach the Elder.

"I thought you might get them framed and put them on your wall."

"I shall."

I kissed her.

"I can't stay any longer, darling, I have to go. My sisters are waiting."

Then she laughed.

"They have no idea why I went out tonight."

"I wish your sister hadn't come to New York."

"I do too, Ed. It's a constant tension between her and her husband. You've met Miriam. I get along with her—at least it's a truce. But my other sister," she raised her hands in a gesture of hopelessness.

"I didn't even know about this other sister."

"I never spoke of her. She's making up for something that's frightful. She's trying to be sweet. She feels she must come as a duty because of my career and reputation. I must go, darling."

"Smoke one more cigarette. I won't see you until when?"

"I'll be back in New York on January second. I must get away; I am exhausted. But I'll be back on January second."

"I'll miss you, Judith."

"And I'll miss you."

Her manner changed; she was suddenly shy like a young girl. I could imagine her at fifteen or sixteen on the West Side of Chicago. She would have been thinner and perhaps shorter. Her legs might have been skinny; and she would have been wearing a sweater.

"Whenever I see that smile on your face, Ed, I know you're thinking of something."

"I was thinking of you and trying to imagine what you were like, what you looked like when you were sixteen."

"I was a skinny little girl. I was just beginning to fill out."

"I bet you were a cute *quelque chose!*"

"I don't know. It was a very awkward period. I wasn't happy. I wasn't happy for years before I came to New York. I was happier in my little room here than I was back home. I practiced so much, I didn't have time for play or fun. I remember riding downtown for my lessons, carrying my music. I would think how I would someday play before crowds of strange people, rich and important people. None of the girls I knew would ever do that; but they seemed to have more fun than I did."

"What else did you think?"

"That's about all. I'd tell myself, 'Gee!'"

I embraced her and sank my face into her hair. With her head against my shoulder, I caressed her hair and kissed her ear.

"Darling, I wish I could stay longer with you but I absolutely must leave now."

"I understand."

She dressed. As I sat smoking, I had a feeling of emptiness.

"Do you like Christmas, Judith?"

My mood was the result of the holiday season, not Judith.

"No."

"I usually don't either. We have to bear it, I guess."

I thought of Christmas morning when Tommy was young. He would be so bright-eyed, so lost in surprise and ecstasy as he gazed at his presents under the tree. Those Christmas mornings had been happy.

"Let's have a cup of coffee together before you go back home, Judith."

There was hesitation on her face.

"I can't say no," she laughed.

I put my arms around her.

"Don't mess me up again," she joked, "I'll have the coffee but we truly must hurry."

I helped her with her coat.

"Thank you darling."

We went to the Homestead, a bar and restaurant near the hotel. It was dim and there was a good-sized crowd lined up at the bar.

"I should have been home hours ago. I don't know what my sister will think, I'm seeing her for the first time in four years. God, I'll be happy when tomorrow is over with. In the country I can rest. And I can practice for my Canadian concert."

We drank the coffee and talked about American women.

"Many of them seem confused. They don't know what they are, women or careers. They're thrown into increasing competition with men and this mixes them up."

"It's still a man's world," she said.

"Yes," I agreed.

"And when women have been subservient and imbued with a slave mentality for centuries, they can't erase the effects of it overnight," she said.

"Several generations of women will be sacrificed to the emancipation of women before they can feel fully at home with their freedom. There will have to be confusion, agony and anguish."

"Will it require only a few generations before people are free, free in their souls and spirits? Not only women, but men too?"

"I don't know."

"I wish we could talk. I love to talk with you, Ed, and to listen to you. But I really have to leave. It's after eleven. And darling, you know I wish you a Merry Christmas."

"And you know that I wish you a Merry Christmas," I said, taking her hand.

I held her hand for a few moments; she looked pensive.

"Are you sad, Judith?"

"No, Ed. No, I'm not sad. You are. You're often sad, aren't you, darling?"

"I never liked Christmas, not since I grew up."

The television was playing Christmas songs. I could hear the drinkers wishing one another a Merry Christmas. A bar was one of the gloomiest of places on Christmas Eve. I knew that most of those in the Homestead wouldn't have been there if they had any other place to be.

"I'd like to make you less sad."

"You did."

"That's sweet. It makes me feel good. And now."

We laughed.

"I'll put you in a cab and you can be delivered to the joys of your family reunion."

"It's too painful for me to joke about, darling."

I paid the check and we left. I hailed a cab on Twenty-third Street. I waved after her as she was driven away. I was lonely. I would have been more lonely if Judith had not come to see me.

XI

I knew that I would miss Judith and I did. But in a way, I welcomed her absence from the city. I did not want to become dependent on her. She seemed to feel the same way. We had often spoken of permanence; we both placed our work above all else. And I was sure that when Judith thought about me, she also thought about how her work might go should we remain together permanently.

Judith's career had been the result of hard and lonely work as well as talent. So had mine. We could not help but think in terms of what would be good for our careers, or threatening to them.

Judith wanted love but she was cautious, if not afraid, of any relationship that would subject her to too much strain and tension. Physically, she could give herself fully, but psychologically she held back. The wounds of her marriage and divorce were healing but she was groping. She did not know for sure what she wanted to do with her personal life. She did not want to risk making a mistake.

Love is a need, but one that can go unfulfilled.

XII

I phoned Judith the day after New Year's. Over the telephone, her voice sounded warm and affectionate. Her week away had been wonderful, she was fully rested. Her fatigue was gone. She had needed this rest even more than she had realized. She had seen the snow and had walked in it, drinking in the quiet and solitude.

We planned to see each other the next evening.

Judith had two big concerts scheduled in January—one in Canada and one in New York at the end of the month.

A pattern had evolved between us. We were together two evenings a week, sometimes three, dependent on her schedule. Judith was not free to be in love. Her love affair had to be related to her work. In some ways, she lived like a man, giving her best energies to the pursuit of a career.

Love should have an explosive first period in which other interests are subordinated, or even neglected. But Judith had little free time. Love, which she wanted badly, if not desperately, and which she needed, interfered with her career. She had little time for thoughts about the man she loved. She could not give him the many little attentions which a woman does when she loves a man. Love could not interfere with her plans. Judith could not change. She could not abandon her career to become a wife. Even as a mistress, she was limited in her availability. Rarely could we see one another on an impulse of the moment.

At first, I thought Judith worked this way because she was ambitious and a little unsure of herself as an artist. I believed that she was financially secure and could give up some of her teaching and touring if she wished. But Judith was not at all rich; she lived off her income. She had no large savings. Her way of life was not extravagant. She paid a high rent but she needed an apartment with room enough for her grand piano. She had a part-time secretary, professional expenses, and she ate mostly in restaurants because she did not have time to cook. She bought very good clothes at the best shops in New York but not very often. Judith was careful with her money, but not frugal or parsimonious. She wasted little, if any, of it. She was not trying to become rich. She never sought engagements which would have called for cheapening of her talents. Money was a means to her ends.

When Judith returned from Montreal, she told me that her concert had been a grand success. She spoke of an old teacher whom she had seen. He had been very proud of her. Seeing him had been a joy for her. And after her concert in Canada, Judith was confident that her coming New York concert would be very successful. It would be one of her best. By successful, she did not mean that she would make money; she meant her playing, the responses it would evoke.

I was beginning to realize that permanency would not work out satisfactorily for us. She was planning to go to Europe in about two years, and then she thought that she would make an Australian tour. I knew that I could not travel with her. And I did much traveling myself. I could not take the time from my work. I wasn't jealous of Judith or the attention she received as an outstanding pianist. I was happy about her growth and success. And Judith was growing.

Part Two

I

And there was Moira. Moira was tall and handsome. She worked in an advertising agency. For years, Moira and I had been in the incipient stage of having a love affair. She had had Lesbian tendencies but had been going to a psychiatrist for two years and seemed to be making progress.

Moira struck some deep chord in me. At times I thought I loved her. We had never made love but we had been on the verge of it more than once. The year before, when I was recovering from a severe abdominal attack due to an ulcer, Moira had come to my hotel to see if I needed anything. She had been sweet and sympathic. I was kissing her when my doctor walked in; I had not locked the door.

"You're getting better, Eddie," he joked after walking in to find her in my arms.

This was before my trip to California when I had received the announcement of Judith's concert. After my return from California, and after I had taken Judith to the Matisse exhibit, Moira had relapsed into a shell of coldness.

One evening when Judith was busy, I telephoned Moira and asked her if she had eaten. I used to do this often and we would have lunch together, and occasionally, dinner. I still felt close to Moira even though I had abandoned all hopes of ever making love to her. When I telephoned her, she said that she had plans.

I began reading and decided to eat later at the Homestead. After all, I did have Judith now and it was easier to spend some evenings alone.

A few minutes later, my telephone rang. It was Moira.

"I couldn't stand to hear you sound so sad. Your voice sounded so unhappy, Ed, I couldn't bear it. I've broken my date to be with you."

Moira's remarks surprised me. I was glad that I would be seeing her although I had not been too disappointed earlier when she had said that she was busy. I took a cab to her apartment in Greenwich Village. Moira looked lovely; she did not overdress but her clothes were striking. We sat on the sofa and talked for a few minutes. I put my arm around her and kissed her. I had done this many times before.

But on that evening, Moira responded instantly with open-mouthed kisses.

"Do you want to eat first?" she asked.

I did not think that Moira knew of Judith. I believed that her sudden passion was probably the result of whatever was happening to her through analysis.

II

I met Moira shortly after the end of the War in 1945. She had seemed shy, unsure of herself. She was interested in Irish literature and Irish history. I used to talk to her about these subjects. She did not say much; she listened. I was struck by how good looking a girl she was with her straight figure and long legs. She had straight dark brown hair which she wore simply, parted in the middle. It was becoming. She liked long earrings and said she felt naked unless she had them on. She had fine features but often her face would be expressionless, almost mask-like.

Moira had several voices. They were not always the same. Her voice could be high-pitched and false-sounding; or if she were depressed, it could be very low. At other times, she spoke in meek, whispery tones. With some people, she raised her voice and spoke loudly.

Although she was a highly articulate, sometimes witty person, Moira had difficulty in language when we talked. She would confide in me, using words from psychoanalysis and applying Freudian generalizations to herself. She was not always clear and she would struggle to say something.

She was unsure of her judgment and was often drawn to avant-garde tastes.

Moira was a Village person in the sense that she lived in an atmosphere of Greenwich Village intellectuals and often reacted as though they were watching her, ready to argue if she affirmed the wrong taste or liked the wrong book.

I was not immediately drawn to her sexually. At first, my feeling was sentimental. She was Irish. Then, I began to think of her as a very close friend. She avowed friendship and respect for me. I believe she meant this. But Moira was never the same on two successive occasions. She had periods of gloom, depression, and silence. She would sit across from me at a table in a restaurant, a withdrawn expression on her face. I would talk to her quietly and sometimes her mood would lighten but not always. Other times, she would be gay; and now and then, after I had accepted the fact that there would be no sex between us, she would flirt with me.

Moira was a girl bulwarked with psychological defenses and protective ruses.

Her defensiveness was different from Judith's. Judith was protecting her time and perhaps she was protecting herself from being hurt. But Moira was protecting herself from being known.

Moira's childhood had been unhappy. She had no use for her father, whom she rarely saw. Her mother had died when she was a girl. She had lived with a grandmother, a stepmother, and she and her older sister, Katy, had been sent to boarding school. At first, the girls liked it there because they had been sent away from a home they hated. But in time their feeling changed. Moira began to do odd and eccentric things. Later in college, she studied Hindu thought, took up fencing, and dressed sloppily—in a way her classmates considered bizarre.

After graduating, Moira tried avant-garde publishing. She lost a few hundred dollars before she gave up and went to work at an advertising agency.

I respected both Judith and Moira. To have love affairs with them simultaneously did not seem fair. I did not believe that I was merely looking for sexual relationships. I felt a need to focus my emotions and I was ready to do this.

Or I thought I was.

But why I thought myself more in love with Moira than with Judith is still unclear to me. I had been forewarned about Moira. I knew Gertrude Morgan who had been Moira's girlfriend. Gertrude was a kind of sympathetic girl but somewhat drab and easily dominated. She had been hurt when Moira had ended their affair. I believe that this was Moira's last affair with a woman.

I knew that Moira was given to moods, almost to changes in character. And I knew how she fenced people off from herself.

Judith, on the other hand, was looking for love. She sought to find within herself a deeper capacity to love, to give herself in feeling and emotion. And I wanted to do this. I believed I did.

Moira was looking out for herself. Her personality did not seem coherent.

A few years earlier, she had telephoned me and said that she wanted to come see me. I was still married at the time. Moira needed to talk, she said that there was something. she wanted to tell me. I told my wife Phyllis that Moira was coming over to talk to me and that I suspected she would tell me that she was going back to the Church.

Moira's voice was meek and apologetic that day. She began by telling me she had a surprise.

"You're going back to the Church?"

"How did you know, Ed?"

"I guessed."

She was surprised but this was not a demonstration of any clairvoyant insight on my part. Moira had been a Catholic. Her literary tastes and her way of talking about books suggested mysticism. I knew her well enough to know that she was in revolt against authority. This revolt was not directed toward any goal, nor was it bound up with any desire to change or improve the world or the conditions of life for man. Moira needed authority. She wanted it. Her emotions were confused.

Moira explained why she was thinking of going back to the Church but her explanation was not clear. She spoke of the beauty of the early Christians. There were hidden meanings in Catholicism, she said, and it would be good for her.

I agreed.

This was shortly before her thirtieth birthday. She herself told me earlier that she felt the age of thirty was one of crisis for a woman. It was a time for undergoing analysis. Analysis would be expensive, it would take a good part of her salary; but it would be worth it; she would gain insights.

She asked what I thought.

I did not want to either encourage or discourage her. I told her that perhaps she was making a good decision but that she would know this herself. If she did decide to undergo analysis and needed money, I would lend her some. She thanked me and said she would ask only if she were in a very bad hole. She never did.

Moira went into analysis. At first she was almost euphoric about her experience. And then one day I heard she was ill. I learned that she had cracked up and needed a psychiatric nurse. Her sister and brother-in-law were helping to pay the heavy costs of her illness.

I feared that she would never recover. The nurse was necessary because she was suicidal.

But in eight months, Moira was back at work; at first, part time. Then, full time. She seemed to be recovered and she was continuing with her analysis.

One Sunday morning, after Phyllis and I had separated and I had moved into a hotel on West Twenty-third Street, Moira telephoned and asked if she could come for breakfast. She arrived a half hour later in a mood of deep depression. We had breakfast, walked to Washington Square, and sat there talking. It was a warm and muggy day for January. I talked fairly steadily and her mood lifted.

I left her and returned to the hotel to write.

I had not seen Moira again until the night she telephoned me back to tell me that she had changed her plans in order to be with me.

III

Our love affair began.

For a few weeks, I saw both Judith and Moira.

Moira was sometimes evasive, saying that she could not see me on a night that I would suggest. Instead of setting a date, she would ask me to telephone. There was not the same directness and simplicity with her as there was with Judith.

I did not tell either of them about the other. I felt some twitches of guilt. I would try to rationalize my conduct in my own eyes but then I'd give up.

One Saturday night early in February, Judith and I had dinner and then returned to her apartment. I was lying on the bed; she was sitting on the edge of it. We were talking.

"Ed, do you think you can ever fall in love again?"

I knew the answer to her question.

—Yes.

But I did not give it.

Judith was falling in love with me. This was my immediate thought. That was the moment for me not only to have said yes but also to have told her I loved her. I had the impulse to do this; but I did not follow my impulse. Judith seemed more a stranger to me than Moira. Moira was Irish and so was I. In our background there were feelings, emotions, and needs which would bring us closer together than Judith and I could ever be. I did not think of all this at that moment but these were things that I had thought of during the period when I was seeing them both at the same time.

And there was Judith's career. Her piano. I was not sure what I wanted from a woman. How much. I wasn't sure about Judith and me.

But Judith was ready for a declaration of love. And she was ready to declare her own love. I was not ready. The fact that I did not answer her question had its obvious significance.

I was not ready to say: "Judith, I love you."

I stopped telephoning Judith. I intended to but I kept putting it off. I did not want to tell her about Moira; I did not want to explain that I was breaking off. Even though I knew Judith had been ready to declare her love, I did not believe that she would suffer by my sudden failure to telephone her. Her readiness was experimental. It was a chance she was ready to take. We had been intimate in our self-revelation as well as physically. We had told our thoughts, expressed our feelings. A declaration of love could not have resulted in greater intimacy. It would have meant a building together of our fates. And I was not ready to do this. Neither was Judith. She would have retreated from the consequences of the declaration she asked for.

But I was ready to do this with Moira.

There was something willful in my feeling for Moira. I was cultivating an illusion. It was as though I had summoned all of the yearnings and desires of my boyhood and adolescence and fixed them on her. She served as an object to fulfill lost desires. And yet, I felt no such clarity of feeling with her as I had with Judith. Moira was more interested in herself and more self-absorbed than either Judith or I. In Judith's case and in mine, self-interest and absorption were involved with our work. Moira thought of herself, her emotions. The center of her interest was herself, herself in analysis. She went to her analyst four times a week. Her moods were determined by what happened in those sessions with her doctor. She believed that she was gaining superior insight. Once she told me she thought I should go into analysis.

"No one can know himself without analysis," she said.

Moira was the prey of her moods. I could never be certain of what she would be like when I saw her. She might be quite happy, or very depressed. She would be meek, pliable, responsive and loving; and then she would be cold and almost arrogant. It was impossible to feel assured with her.

With her friends, Moira became still a different person. Among them, she was loud and dominating. She invariably made herself the center of attention. And she seemed a bit coarse. The quality of her humor was commonplace. She had no subtlety and she treated her friends arrogantly. I did not like to go to parties with her; I would be distressed at the spectacle she made of herself. She seemed to be unaware of the way she was acting. Seeing how she behaved with people who admired her for her pathetic vulgarity, I would think that we could never have a permanent relationship. But alone with me, she would change and become loving and responsive. I would disregard the impressions I had had.

Actually, Moira was testing herself. She was trying to be in love with me. She was thinking of permanency, of marriage. The future was a burden to her and she dare not make a mistake.

For a couple of weeks, around the time of my forty-eighth birthday, Moira became more simple. She was not withdrawn when we were together. She was like a woman blossoming in emotions. I felt that she was truly in love. I disregarded any doubts I had had. I was quite happy.

On my birthday, we had dinner, went to a hockey game. I spent the evening with her in her apartment. Moira had started to act peculiar. She complimented me about love-making almost like a cheerleader, or like someone giving encouragement to someone whose ego needed it. This was odd. Actually, Moira was talking to herself. She was making an effort to love as a woman, and to believe in our relationship as one which would be happy and permanent, and good for her.

I was asked to Paris as a delegate to speak at a festival of literature and the arts. Moira congratulated me. I made no plans as to how long I would stay.

"I wish you could come to Paris with me, Moira."

"I couldn't, Ed. I couldn't go until I finish my analysis."

"I want to show you Paris someday."

"I would love it."

I lectured at a school in New Jersey one evening. Moira, her sister Katy, and Katy's husband came with me. On the bus returning to New York, Moira was very quiet. She showed no interest in the conversation. We rode through the night, sitting side by side. I was not comfortable but I knew of Moira's moods; she would change.

Back in Manhattan at the bus terminal, Katy asked:

"How are you two going home?"

"You can take me home," Moira said.

We were all surprised. Moira did not want me to go home with her that evening.

The next Saturday, we went to a play. Moira was much the same as she had been on the bus. We went to her apartment later. I stayed with her. Around dawn, Moira said to me in bed, in the darkness.

"I want to talk to you, Eddie."

I sat up and lit a cigarette.

"I don't want to hurt you; I couldn't bear to hurt you."

"Tell me what you feel, Moira, dear."

"You're older than I. Too old."

I was not hurt, and I was not surprised. I had been expecting a breakup and it was better that she do the breaking. Had I been the one doing it, she could have been set back. I had not thought of breaking up with her, but instantly I knew that I was ready for it.

Moira started to explain why she was ending our affair. She wanted marriage and permanency. I was in no position to marry her; I wasn't free. And I had responsibilities. Then she repeated:

"There's too much of an age difference between us. I'll still be young when you're an old man. I don't want to hurt you, Eddie, but I have to tell you the truth."

"You're not hurting me, Moira, dear."

She did not need to explain more but she did. She spoke of the age difference, of her need for permanence, and of the insight her analysis afforded her.

The scene had its comic aspects. I sat on the edge of the bed, at first naked, and then with my shirt on because of the chill. Moira was nude. She sat up. I looked at her; she was lovely. She explained, talking earnestly with a simplicity that was unusual for her. I smoked and listened; I said little. The effort she was making to be soothing was touching, a measure of affection, and also a sign of how much she feared being hurt or rejected.

"You're almost fifty, Eddie."

"Yes, my dear. There's nothing more to say except thank you."

"It's awfully decent of you to take it this way."

"Moira, it's senseless to try to convince anyone about their emotions. To do so would be manipulation."

She looked down at the sheet on the rumpled bed. Outside the narrow window of her bedroom, the dawn was coming. The air was blue, growing light. New York was silent.

I dressed.

"Moira, here's your key. I'm leaving it on the dresser, right here."

"Yes."

She was waiting for me to leave. Dressed, I bent down to kiss her goodbye. She turned her cheek to me.

"Thank you, Moira."

"Thank you, Ed, for taking it so decently."

I left.

It had snowed during the night. The dawn had come. I walked in the snow on Seventh Avenue toward Sheridan Square. The wind whipped snow in my face. I was relieved; I was lucky, in fact. It did not matter that I had been the one rejected.

The morning was chilly. I crunched the snow under my feet. I could feel the sting of it whirling against my face. People passed me, some with their heads lowered because of the wind and snow. I took a cab to Twenty-third Street and had coffee in the Homestead.

I could not go back to Judith now. It would have been in bad taste. She might never learn of Moira and me; but still it would have been in poor taste. I could telephone her. But what would I say?

This was the middle of March.

Before I left for Europe on April 15, I was deeply grieved. I was leaving my son and I didn't know for how long. One night I wept. I phoned Moira in a mood of desperation. She coldly said that she was busy and could not see me. I felt bitter for a few moments but then I realized that Moira was struggling to find herself. She could not help anyone else bear problems and sorrow.

I telephoned Judith. She was not at home. I was relieved. I knew that I had not been fair to her.

On a lovely spring day in April, I sailed on the *Queen Mary*. Going to Paris would be good.

Part Three

I

I returned from Europe in October. Moira had written me but my answer had been cold. I had written Judith and apologized for not having seen her. I explained that I had been deeply troubled. This had been true, but only part of the truth.

In Paris, I had fallen in love with Jeanette. Her husband was in the Argentine on business. She had spent her vacation in Italy. She had suggested that I go with her. I had.

I had finished a novel while I had been away. I regarded it as my best book.

I returned to New York thirty pounds underweight.

Three weeks after I returned, I went into the hospital for an operation. It was a success. No malignancy was found. Moira did not come to see me during my five weeks in the hospital. Judith did. She also sent a big bouquet of roses.

She came one evening. We talked for over an hour and ate dinner in my room.

"I should have telephoned you, Judith. I'm sorry."

She accepted my apology. We talked as friends. It was accepted that our affair was ended.

"You look well, better than I expected, Ed. I was worried. This is the first chance I've had to come. But I can see that you are going to recover magnificently."

"Yes, there's no reason to worry."

She spoke of her work. She had spent a good summer at Tanglewood. I asked her if she had made any progress on her book.

"No, Ed, I was too fatigued. Now I'm teaching at Columbia and I just don't have the time. I'm moving into a smaller apartment."

"I remember the sound of your slippers in that long hallway. I would wait for you to come to me, hearing your walk."

We laughed.

"I didn't have the energy to move before. I should have. But I've got a cute little apartment now. I'm buying new furniture. I'm anxious to see if you like it."

"All you have to do is invite me."

"You know I will."

I was glad to see Judith and I enjoyed talking with her. I decided that it was best that our affair was ended. We were friends, good friends, with warm feelings for each other. We could not have felt quite as affectionate had we not made love.

We spoke of plans. I was planning to return to Europe.

"I'l be playing in England next summer."

"That's wonderful, dear. Maybe I can get over to hear you."

"I hope so, Ed. It's going to be very good for me. You must hear me play now. I can feel how I'm improving and developing."

I walked to the elevator with her and thanked her for having visited me.

I saw Judith several times that winter. She gave two con-

erts which I attended. And I went to a reception at her apartment after one of them. Andy was there like a man on duty.
When I left, he thanked me for having come. Neither Judith
nor I spoke of our affair. It seemed to me that she, as well
as I, considered it ended. But there was a feeling of warmth
when we saw one another, and a mutual interest in our work.

I went to Paris again in the spring. I had told Judith that
I might see her in London but I got to England in May before
she arrived. And again in October after she had returned to
America. I wrote her a few letters and received a card from
her.

I returned from Europe almost broke and had to take a
smaller room at the hotel. It was a hard time for me. I was
worried and frustrated and I started drinking again. I was
very lonely. I had left Jeanette in Paris; I believed that I loved
her. I had gone back to Paris because of her. But she was married. I couldn't have a trans-Atlantic love affair.

I phoned Judith one evening and suggested dinner. She was
free. We went to an Italian restaurant on Thompson Street
below Washington Square. Judith had been near my hotel
making recordings and had picked me up. We had walked
over to Fifth Avenue and down to Washington Square. It
was an Indian summer night; I was moody and full of
memories.

Judith told me of her success in London.

"I wish you had been there, Ed. I'll show you the clippings."

We took our time eating. I took her hand on the table and
held it a moment. We both smiled. Her smile was a bit wan.

"Do you remember the book you gave me? Baudelaire's
essays?"

"Yes, do you like them?"

"Yes, some; but what a warped idea he had about women."

"He didn't really love them."

"I can believe that."

She spoke again of London, of friends of mine whom s⟩ had met, especially Teresa.

"They were wonderful to me. I don't know how I c⟩ thank you for giving me an introduction to them."

"I'm always glad when my friends like each other."·

"I used her piano."

"Yes, she told me when I saw her in October."

I had almost said "we." Jeanette had been with me. I too⟩ Judith's hand again and held it. I looked at her. I wondere⟩ Judith? Jeanette?

We talked for a long time over coffee. I deliberately d⟩ layed leaving. I enjoyed her company. I wished that I had n⟩ stopped seeing her. I wouldn't have fallen in love wi⟩ Jeanette.

Finally, we left. We strolled through Washington Squa⟩ and then I hailed a cab. We rode several blocks in silence. ⟩ felt tension between us; I was tense. I put my arm arou⟩ her and drew her head to my shoulder. I caressed her chee⟩ I kissed her. Judith clung to me.

"Oh, darling," she exclaimed.

She had moved to a small apartment on York Avenu⟩ Most of the furniture was new. The bedroom had pink p⟩ lows and there was a pink cover on the bed. It was a femini⟩ room, more feminine than any room in the large apartme⟩ on Riverside Drive. She had carefully selected everything f⟩ her small apartment. And her bedroom seemed to have be⟩ arranged with thoughts of love.

We talked. We both avoided saying anything too person⟩ We were shy in the face of all that had happened. Mo⟩ than shy, we were surprised. Several times Judith laughed ⟩ though she were laughing at both of us. We had not ⟩ captured the mood of those first times; but I was awa⟩ fully aware, of how much affection I held for her. I was ve⟩ glad for that night. I sat in a chair smoking while she sat ⟩

in bed. The lights were dim. I realized how soft her voice was. Her cat sat staring at me.

"He doesn't know me any more," I said.

We laughed. I had confused her cat before, when she lived in the other apartment.

"I've got to make friends with him all over again," I joked.

Judith didn't speak. She looked at me, thoughtfully. I knew that she was uncertain about this new development—the unexpected resumption of our love affair.

"He's as surprised as I am," Judith said.

"We're all surprised, dear."

"Yes," she said thoughtfully.

In Paris, there was Jeanette. My affection for Judith could not be undivided. I would have to follow the course of my emotions.

"I thought of you often, Ed," Judith said, speaking very seriously.

"And I thought of you."

I had. I felt badly about how I had let things end with her.

"And that letter you wrote me from France. I was glad you wrote me."

That had been over a year ago.

I went and sat by the bed.

"I'm going to have to send you home now, darling. I'm so tired and I have a long day tomorrow."

"I like your hair," I said, rumpling it.

"I'll see you again, darling. Soon. You'll telephone tomorrow?"

"Yes. What time?"

"After four. Now kiss me good night. I'm not even going to see you to the door. That's how tired I am."

Judith and I began seeing one another much as we had before. I was writing to Jeanette and planning to return to Paris the following spring. Sometimes I was troubled. I believed that I was beginning to really want Judith, and only

Judith. I was agitated. I was in bad financial circumstance and I had heavy obligations. I had written Jeanette and told her that I was not sure that I would be able to return to France in the spring. She had replied with suspicion and accusations. This had happened before Judith and I had resumed our love affair.

I thought of Judith and Jeanette. They were both ambitious, Jeanette's ambition was almost fierce. Judith had none of Jeanette's suspicion and she was warmer although she was less able to express her warmth. But Jeanette was warm and thoughtful also. There was less understanding between Jeanette and me. She was French and I American; there would always be a language barrier.

Then I sold two stories for a good price. I took Judith to dinner to celebrate. We were playful that evening. Judith was not often gay and spontaneous but on this night she was. We walked along lower Fifth Avenue. I kissed her on the street.

On Sunday evening, she was entertaining several friends including Stanton Worthington, the composer. She had asked me to come at about eight-thirty. At a quarter to six I telephoned her and suggested that we have a quick dinner out. I had worked all day in my room and the prospect of eating alone depressed me. But Judith said that with company expected, she simply could not go out. Then, in about ten minutes, she phoned me back.

"Darling, I can't bear to think of you eating alone. Come up and I'll scramble some eggs."

I took a cab to her apartment instantly, happy that I wouldn't have to eat alone and delighted that I was going to eat with her. I could look forward to an ideal evening. After eating, we would talk until her friends came. And when they left, I would take her in my arms. I could look at her from time to time as she sat talking or listening, finding pleasure in the respect and affection in which she was held and I would know that she was mine.

It was slightly difficult for Judith to invite me on the spur of the moment. She could not give easily in little things. She was used to a way of living. She must have realized, as though she were making a discovery, that I was lonely. Grateful as I was, I saw pathos in the incident. There were so many small things which Judith could not know. In matters such as these, she could not give. Doubts came to me. If Judith and I lived together, she would have to learn.

Even though I was happy and grateful, I had doubts again on that Sunday afternoon.

Judith was hooking her dress as I arrived.

"You can't muss me before my guests arrive," she joked as I embraced her.

"I can but I won't," I teased.

She laughed.

"You had better let me go or I can't give you anything to eat."

Judith worked efficiently and quickly in the kitchen. I sat at the table while she scrambled the eggs and made coffee. Then I set the table and we sat down to eat.

"There's lots of time," Judith said, glancing at her wristwatch, "but this is better and more convenient than going out."

"I like it better."

It was my first, my only, meal at Judith's other than midnight snacks or that breakfast on the Sunday morning after our first date.

We talked of ourselves. Judith told me what she had been doing for the last few days and I talked about my work.

"I'll put the dishes in the sink. I have a woman coming in the morning."

"I'll help you."

"Don't bother, darling. Sit on the sofa and I'll be with you in a minute."

I smoked and contemplated my feelings of pleasure.

Wouldn't I have much happiness if I were with Judith? My eyes traveled around the room. I looked at the big Steinway piano which filled one end of the living room.

"Ed, I didn't show you my notices from England, did I?" Judith asked, coming into the room.

"No, I'd like to see them."

Judith got the clippings. I read them, happy and proud for her. The British critics had hailed her as a great pianist, an original but sound interpreter of Bach. They had described the spell she had cast over her audiences. After I had read them and given them back to her, we sat and talked randomly but not intimately. Intimacy could not be taken for granted. These few minutes, twenty or thirty, were rare in her life and mine.

It was not an exciting evening but it was pleasant. It had been twenty years since I had seen Stanton Worthington. I had not realized that he would have aged so. When I had met him, I had thought of him as one of the young composers. But he was now a man well over sixty. He was simple and gracious and he obviously had real respect and affection for Judith. He was a gentle man, modest and serious. He seemed to be growing old well with a feeling for the fullness and the possible ripeness of life. He had come into his own as an artist and a composer and had gained a feeling of mastery over his medium. He was living through his final but best creative period.

The talk was of music, mostly. Time passed. At around eleven-thirty, the guests left. They probably had obvious thoughts when I remained behind. But I was pleased. People don't like to be in love in secret.

Judith spoke of Andy.

"He telephoned. He wanted to come over this evening."

"I wouldn't have been jealous."

"I know that, Ed, but I see no reason for going out of my

way to hurt him. And it would hurt him to leave with you remaining behind to be with me."

"It's not my intention to hurt him, but what am I going to do? I mean, am I going to get out of his way?"

"Are you?"

"No."

"I didn't think that you would say yes."

"Judith, everybody is hurt by love, by being rejected or by losing in love. I don't want to sound cold, but it's true."

"I know," she answered thoughtfully. She was reflective for a few moments.

What was I planning to do? Cut poor Andy out and then go off to Paris and Jeanette, leaving Judith to handle as best she could whatever affection she felt for me? I told myself I would have to follow the course of my emotions.

"I didn't like telling Andy 'no' tonight. I'm sure he knows why."

"You mean he knows about me?"

"Of course he does."

"I'm sorry," I said.

"Sorry for Andy?"

"No, just sorry. I am sorry but I won't get out of his way, darling."

I kissed her.

II

Judith was preparing for her annual concert in New York late in November. She had been complaining of fatigue. We seemed to be going on as we had. But I knew that I would have to decide, that our relationship would have to deepen and become a permanent one, or at least permanent in intention. I thought of living with Judith, even marrying her should I get a divorce. I knew that I would not be jealous of her when she toured and that we would not quarrel. We still had not had a quarrel. We would have our own work and it was sufficiently separate so as to minimize any spirit of rivalry. And together we could afford a large enough apartment for her to practice and me to have a work room. I believed that we loved each other although we were not very demonstrative. We had both been disciplined by work and experience so that love did not interfere with our work. Then I would think of Judith's piano and I would tell myself she lived for it, that everything else took second place in her life. She was tied to her career, she could never escape from it. The needs of her career dictated to Judith, not only in matters of time and how she used it, but also in matters of feeling. And I needed attention from a woman, even to be babied sometimes.

I would think of permanency but then I would have these doubts. I reminded myself that I had allowed my emotions and impulses to carry me away in the case of Moira.

I continued to see Judith. My feeling for her seemed to be growing. I knew I had to make a decision, one that would be difficult and perhaps painful. But I was prepared for this.

My friend, Hendrik Norstrom, came to New York. He was a member of the Dutch parliament and had been sent to represent his government at the United Nations. Hendrik was a civilized and cultivated man of about sixty. He was interested in music and when I told him of Judith's concert, he expressed a desire to attend. Judith was delighted to leave tickets for us.

I took Hendrik to the concert. I was convinced that he would not be disappointed. I did not tell him of the relationship between Judith and me but I believed that he had guessed it. I had spoken too warmly and enthusiastically about her. We had dinner before going to the concert. It was enjoyable but I was looking forward to the concert and to the reception for Judith being given afterwards.

Hendrik and I arrived some minutes ahead of time. I saw

friends of Judith and members of her coterie. I also saw Andy.

Judith looked beautiful.

Judith always insisted that she played Bach as he intended his music to be played even though the piano had not been invented during his lifetime. She sometimes did make the piano sound like a harpsichord. She played with strength and vigor, sometimes more like a man than a woman. Once seated at the piano, she had great poise and an air of authority.

On this evening, she looked out toward me as the applause died down. I knew what her look meant; she was playing for me.

From the first note, Judith held the audience. She had scarcely played a few bars when you felt a concentration of attention all around you. Bent slightly forward, her hands moving expertly back and forth on the keyboard, Judith revealed a new depth of feeling. The music came with strength and a rare sweetness. She created a hushed feeling in her audience. They became lost in the music. It came out like something full of a restrained joy, filling you with a hunger for joy. There was a happiness, possibly a desperate happiness, in her rendering. At the end of each selection, the audience burst into enthusiastic applause which would break suddenly, spontaneously, like rifles going off. The audience was enthralled. While she played, they were as quiet as devout worshippers in a church. Judith was lost in her music and so was her audience. Her playing was liquid and flowing and suggested a great purity, not only of sound, but of feeling.

During the intermission, the people in the audience were quiet. The spell she had cast still held them. Hendrik nodded his head approvingly and said:

"I like it very much."

When Judith finished, the audience applauded her wildly. I was sorry it was over. I had been away from the world, alone in a world expressing something beyond words. I had been there, not with Judith, but with her playing.

She played two encores, again to wild applause. She made her last bow and disappeared. It was over. The lights on the stage were dimmed. People rustled and moved to the rear. They were still half-enthralled.

Judith had come into her own. She had acquired another dimension. All of her years had been a preparation for these last two hours.

III

A larger crowd than usual waited to congratulate Judith. They gathered in a room to the side of the main hall. I waited in a corner with Hendrik.

"Yes, that was fine," he exclaimed.

On the stage, Judith had still looked fresh at the end of the concert. When she came out and took a chair at one end of the large room, I could see that she was very tired. People lined up and slowly went forward as one person after another shook her hand and spoke to her. We stood back. I saw Andy hovering around her. When the crowd had thinned out, I approached with Hendrik. She gave me a tired smile. I introduced Hendrik; he shook her hand and congratulated her. She was gracious in thanking him.

"You look tired, dear," I said.

"I feel exhausted."

"You were really quite wonderful."

"Was I?"

"Yes."

"I'm almost too tired to go to the party, Ed."

"Don't. I'll take you home."

"I must. Wait and ride with me."

We moved off and stood in a corner. More people spoke with her and extended their congratulations. As the last few began to talk of leaving, I turned to her.

"Are you ready to go, Judith?"

"Just about."

"I'll get your coat and your music, Judith," Andy said.

"Thank you," she said tiredly.

He went back to 'her dressing room. She stood up, shook her head sadly, looked bewildered. She said to Hendrik:

"It was exhausting."

"It was very fine."

"Thank you."

She looked at me and smiled wanly.

"I'm too tired to explain to Andy; he has his car."

"I'll take you in a cab, dear."

"All right, we'll leave in a few minutes," she said.

Andy brought her coat. We left in a group. I took Judith's arm and hailed a cab. I opened the door for her. She hesitated a moment, then turned to the group and told them that she would see them all at the party. She got in, I followed with Hendrik behind me. Andy stared at us, blank.

The party for Judith was being given by Harry Traubman, a lawyer. He owned a brownstone on West Twelfth Street. Judith did not say much in the taxi. I put my arm around her and she sank back, remarking on how exhausted she was.

"It must have been very tiring," Hendrik said.

"It was. I'm so glad it's over."

Others were arriving just as we were. A group gathered on the sidewalk in front of Harry's house. Judith lagged back with me, took my arm and said:

"Andy is expecting to take me home. I hate to hurt him, Ed, he's so sweet to me."

"I know that."

"Shall I let him? It's just taking me home."

"I'll take you home, Judith."

"All right, I'll have to tell him. Poor thing."

Her voice was weary.

The party was large and noisy. There were about seventy-five guests. Several of them did not know Judith or know of her concert that night. I was surprised that Harry Traubman was giving the party. He was a successful lawyer and many of his clients were theatrical and literary people. He was a big man and had a handsome face, but it was a weak face too. Harry was over sixty and seemed to be growing sad with age. I had always had pleasant relationships with him. He acted glad to see me but was surprised to notice me entering his home with Judith.

"Jesus Christ, Ed, why don't you leave the music world alone!" he said.

"I have to protect them from you."

"You old son-of-a-bitch. I'm glad to see you. And my congratulations to you, Judith. I have already heard that your performance was magnificent."

"Thank you, the audience seems to have liked it."

"Liked it? They're raving about it."

"You're kind."

"Now, what will you have to drink? I know this old so-and-so will drink anything," he said, pointing to me.

"No, Harry, I'm not drinking."

He looked at me with a startled expression.

"I don't believe it. What'll you have?"

"It's true; but Judith needs a drink."

"We'll open the champagne now."

"If it's champagne, that's different," I said.

"See, I knew it," he said, laughing at me.

"I'd prefer to sit down with a sandwich and a drink, darling, but I must circulate and see these people," Judith said.

"Yes, I know."

"You'll take me home?"

"I plan to. If you get tired, tell me. I'll keep my eye on you."

"You're sweet, Ed."

She squeezed my hand. Harry returned with glasses of champagne. I pulled Hendrik to my side and introduced him to Harry. We drank to Judith. I squeezed her hand as she was led off by Harry. She was quickly surrounded by admirers. I saw Andy hovering near her, looking lost. The party was too large to be interesting. There were too many guests milling about. Most of them were successful people, well fixed and settled in life. They regarded themselves as advanced in ideas but they were not culturally serious people. They merely enjoyed the social life of cultivated people. There were lawyers, a sprinkling of businessmen, a few agents. Of course there were some of Judith's friends, some of whom I had tagged in my mind as members of her coterie. With so many people present, it was impossible to converse. Strangers met and didn't know what to say to each other. They exchanged banalities. Men tried to find unattached women to flirt with. The bar was crowded. Guests kept shoving their way through to get drinks. Once they got them, they shoved to get out of the crowds. People who rarely saw each other lamented that fact, agreed to get together for luncheon or dinner soon, really soon. Those who had begun to turn grey were congratulated on how well, how young, they looked. A few guests told jokes. Now and then a loud burst of laughter would break out from a group. Guests kept milling around.

Judith was complimented by those who had and those who had not heard her concert. Some guests apologized for not having been able to attend. A number of the men, and some of the women, told her how lovely, how beautiful she looked. Time passed with most of the people scarcely aware of it. Some of them seemed to be waiting for the party to begin, waiting for something to happen.

I was bored but not unduly anxious to leave. This was Judith's night and she was enjoying it. She had earned the praise being lavished on her.

I was introduced to people whose names I didn't catch or else forgot the moment they were uttered. A number of conversations began but did not end. I introduced Hendrik to some people I knew. He stood talking to several of them. I stood, sometimes in a corner or on the side, looking. The steady explosion of human voices was numbing. Finally I went downstairs to the den and library where there were fewer guests. I found a seat on a sofa. By that time, my feet were tired. Hendrik soon joined me. Several conversations were going on. One about politics. A second about Judith and music. And a third one about Broadway and the stage. I listened more than I participated. Hendrik sat with me for a while but then said that he had to leave. He had to attend an early-morning U. N. committee meeting on the New Guinea-Indonesian issue. I told him I was waiting to take Judith home. I was proud as I said this.

Judith soon came downstairs.

She was given a comfortable chair. She looked very tired. I asked her if she were ready to leave. She said she would be soon but she felt that she should stay a little while longer and talk with a few of her friends.

Andy sat near her, silent.

"Ye Gods, what a party!" Harry Traubman said.

"It's a lovely party, Harry," Judith said.

"It was too big. Now we've cut it down to size; we can talk *entre nous*. Darling, you look lovely tonight."

Judith thanked him.

"Judith, you touched me here, in my heart," said Ely, her

sister Miriam's friend. Ely was an ordinary fellow who owned a small store. He and Miriam had gone together for years but neither of them wanted to get married.

"It's nice of you to say that, Ely," Judith said.

"I mean it. You hit me here," he touched his chest. "I'm just an ordinary fellow, that's all I am. I'm nothing more than that. I'm an average fellow, not exceptional in any way. But I felt you were playing for fellows like me tonight. You were saying what we can't say for ourselves because we don't know how. That's why you touched me here."

He touched his chest over his heart again.

"That's the sweetest compliment I've received all evening," Judith told him.

"I mean it, Judith."

"I know you do, Ely."

Shortly after this, Judith and I left. Andy walked out at the same time. Judith stopped to talk to him for a moment; I waited about five yards away.

"No, I'm sorry, Andy. It's impossible." I heard her say.

She joined me. Andy looked at us, bewildered and hurt. She had refused to let him take her home.

Judith took my arm. We walked slowly toward Fifth Avenue. I was watching the street for a vacant cab.

Ely, in his simple way, had spoken the truth. Judith had released and reproduced something pure and unspeakable, something which struck at those hidden chords in our nature. She had broken through to a kind of perfection. I felt very close to her as we walked toward Fifth Avenue.

I took her arm.

"Darling, I'm dead tired. I'm simply dead tired, exhausted."

"I'll get you home right away, dearest."

"Yes, please, Ed, take me home," she said like a little girl.

I was able to get a cab. Seated inside, I put my arm around her and she laid her head on my shoulder. I caressed her cheek with my fingers. She didn't speak; she was almost asleep. We rode in silence.

At her apartment, she slumped beside me on the sofa. When I kissed her, she said in a voice of utter weariness,

"Not tonight. I can't. I just can't."

I looked down at her face. She was so tired, so worn out, that she looked like a woman in the depths of despair. Her face was slack; she stared at nothing.

"There's nothing, nothing left in me."

"You feel lonely, don't you, dearest?"

"Yes," her head moved against my shoulder. She continued to stare. "Just sit with me a minute, darling."

"Yes," I said, caressing her cheek and her hair.

"I'm so tired."

"I know, dearest."

"Everything is drained out of me."

"You need to sleep."

"That's all I want now. Sleep. I feel empty, empty."

We sat for a few more minutes, her head on my shoulder. She kept staring blankly. This, this was what she had worked for. This was how she felt after her hour of triumph. There was nothing to say. Words were too burdensome to be uttered; they were a weight upon her tongue.

"I feel nothing," she said.

"Go to sleep now, Judith, dear."

"Yes."

"You must get to bed. Shall I help you?"

"No, I'll manage."

"Good night, Judith, darling."

I kissed her.

"Good night. You understand, don't you, Ed?"

"Yes, Judith."

She walked to the door with me. I kissed her good night and left.

I had never seen anyone more lonely than Judith was that evening. I rode back to my hotel thinking of her.

IV

I dined with Judith on the following Saturday evening. We went to a movie. She appeared to be well rested but she spoke of how totally exhausted she had felt. She was happy because of her success. She knew that her playing that night had been a peak in her career. She had grown. And she was looking forward to the concerts she was scheduled to give in London, Dublin, Amsterdam, and Stockholm.

"I'll be sensational," she said.

This did not strike me as boasting. Judith was an artist.

"I felt myself growing, darling," she said.

When I left Judith, I believed that we were either already very much in love or that we were falling in love. Perhaps our relationship would be permanent. I thought of Jeanette in Paris. I believed that I was more attached to Judith. I washed aside my doubts about the fact that we both had careers.

We planned to dine on the following Wednesday. She was back in her regular routine. But on Wednesday, I received a telephone call from a nurse to tell me that Judith was ill and that she could not see me. She was confined to her bed with a virus infection and she could not speak to me on the phone. I asked if there were anything I could do but the nurse said that Judith was being taken care of and that she should be recovering rapidly. I sent her flowers. I telephoned the next day. She was resting but still could not speak. I phoned every day for six days and spoke to the nurse. On the seventh day, I was able to talk to Judith. She sounded weak. Her voice was tired but she was recovering. She had been so weak that she had scarcely been able to lift her hand. In a few days, she would be recovered and could go out. Then we could have dinner and spend the evening together.

When I saw Judith again, she was well and said that she felt good.

"But I was totally exhausted, Ed, I was so weak. I couldn't read or think. I wasn't able to concentrate. I didn't want to lift my arm. I've never been that way before. I'll be glad when June comes and I can go away. I'm sailing on the *Queen Mary*."

"I might get over to London to hear your concert."

"I hope you can, dear."

The next week Judith was recording not far from my hotel and she was to pick me up there. She came up to my room at about eight-thirty. She sat on the bed, and smiled rather self-consciously.

"Darling, I have something to say," she said, speaking very tenderly.

I guessed immediately what she was going to say.

"Is it Andy, Judith?"

"How did you know?"

"I didn't until this moment."

"Are you angry?"

"No, my dear. I am not at all certain that you and I could be happy. Possibly you need someone like Andy, someone to take care of you and to worship you as he does."

"I think so. You're not angry, Ed?"

"No, Judith dear. I believe that we have both had our doubts."

"Maybe that first time, Ed?"

"The night you asked if I could ever fall in love again?"

"Yes."

"You were falling in love then."

"Yes, I think so. Yes, then it could have been possible. But now, I wouldn't hurt you for anything in the world. But

Andy will be better for me. And it would not be right for me to make love with you and to see Andy."

"Are you going to marry Andy?"

"I think so," she said shyly.

I embraced her, kissed her on the forehead, and told her:

"You know that I hope you will be happy. Very happy."

"Thank you, darling. I was nervous about telling you. I didn't want you to be angry. But I do think Andy will be better for me."

"Perhaps, Judith. I don't know."

We went to the Homestead for coffee.

"Yes, it might have been that night. You weren't ready then. And now, I don't know. I don't feel right, Ed darling."

I was disappointed; in fact, hurt. But without having consciously thought about Judith and Andy, I seemed to have unconsciously sensed what was coming. I was not surprised. I stared at her sadly. We were silent for some moments.

"I can't bear to think of hurting you, dear."

"You're more important to yourself, Judith, than to me or to anyone else."

"It's sweet of you to take it this way."

"No it isn't; it's merely sensible and civilized."

"I began to think of us and the future when I was ill."

"Possibly it was the night of your concert, dear. Remember how you looked out at me from the stage?"

"Yes, and you saw me?"

"I did. And I knew you were playing for me."

"I was, Ed. But I don't understand. What do you mean?"

"The way you played that night; that was your triumph, darling. You probably changed then but didn't realize it immediately."

"Perhaps. I don't believe it would be right for us to go on. Andy is good to me; he's very sweet. And he loves me, Ed."

"I love you too, Judith."

And yet, even though I meant what I was saying, I was not seriously hurt by her decision. I knew that I would miss her, sometimes want her, sometimes feel sad, but I experienced no tearing anguish, no great emotional pain. I was sad. Perhaps we were both losing something important, even precious. I wondered why neither of us had trusted our love, our feeling for one another. We had both hemmed ourselves within our separate loneliness.

"I'll always have affection for you, Ed. You know that, don't you?"

"Yes, my dear."

"I just think this is what I need."

"I understand, Judith."

V

During the holidays, I moved to another hotel. Right after New Year's Day, Judith came to see my new apartment and to have tea. We talked like old and dear friends.

I went to Europe in the spring but I was not able to get to London while she was there. I received a post card from her.

When I left Paris that September, I felt that it was a farewell to Jeanette. I decided that I would not return to Europe the next year. It was not without some anguish that I reached my decision. But my problems in America and my relationship with my son demanded it.

In November, I received a telephone call from Judith's sister, Miriam. She told me that Judith was returning the next day on the *Queen Mary*.

I had thought often of Judith, especially after my return to America. After all, I had not been emotionally free the year before. Now I was. Perhaps now we would really fall in love.

I did not think of Andy.

Judith was surprised to find me waiting among her friends at the dock but she was pleased. She was happy, full of her English and Continental successes. We all went to her apartment. Andy was there too. I left early, after we had agreed to have dinner that evening.

I called for her later. We kissed in greeting. I looked at her British press clippings and then we went to dinner in the Village.

"I'm not returning to Europe, Judith. You must have heard about a French girl."

"Yes I did."

"I'm not going back. I am emotionally free."

"I don't know how I feel, Ed. But I was so pleased to find you at the dock this morning."

"When Miriam called me, I thought that you would guess that I'd be there."

"No I didn't. But I was hoping to see you again. You know, Ed, I'm not marrying Andy. That's all off."

"I thought that it would be."

"It wasn't right. Poor Andy. I told him before I left."

"You know, Judith, I do love you."

She smiled.

After dinner, we walked back to Washington Square. It was an Indian summer night. The atmosphere was almost sensuous. A few people were in the square. The trees were bare through the night haze. My thoughts went out to the universe, much as they had when I had been young.

"I used to be so damned lonesome, the first time I came here to Washington Square when I was young," I said.

"Yes?"

"I wanted a girl but I didn't know how to get one or find one."

"I was lonesome too."

I put my arm around her. We walked on along lower Fifth Avenue after leaving Washington Square.

"This is my favorite part of New York," I said as we passed the new Brevoort apartments.

"I like it too, but it's changing."

We walked on.

I was tense. Judith seemed tense.

"I'll get a cab."

"Yes."

Inside the cab, I kissed her.

VI

For a third time, Judith and I were together and I was able, in every sense except a legal one, to commit myself. We fell back into the same pattern. Judith resumed her work and once again she had a heavy schedule. But we went out to dinner. And I took her to visit various friends. Judith complained less of fatigue.

Two or three times I thought of speaking to Judith about our relationship, the possibility of permanence, but I didn't. There was no sense in discussing permanence; I wasn't free to marry. If we were to remain in a permanent relationship, it would happen. It did not need to be discussed. I was sure that Judith would not favor the idea of living together. She was too accustomed to living alone; her habits were fixed. The adjustments that she would have to make would constitute a threat on her time and her work.

Judith had not made up her mind to remarry, or at least not in any definite sense. If she had, it may have been different. She would have arrived at a fundamental decision about herself. And Judith still had doubts about a permanent relationship with me. She was not ready to give herself unconditionally in emotion, in spirit, and to accept the obligations of marriage. She seemed to believe that she must do this if she were in love. Not being ready to do this, she was not convinced that she was in love.

Judith wanted to be in love and to be loved. The absence of love in her life had left her a wistful creature, a woman more sad than she would admit to herself.

And so, for the third time in less than five years, Judith and I were having a love affair. I had at last declared my intentions in the sense that I would not hold myself back and refuse to go where our emotions and feelings had led us. Judith did not tell me specifically how she felt. She was warm and affectionate. In a number of small ways, she conveyed a tenderness of feeling. But at times, she would fall into silence. I would sense that she preferred to be alone and to sleep. I would kiss her good night and leave. Now and then, she did not respond to a sign of affection. Since we had twice broken off our intimacy, I knew that our feelings must take their own course, and that any efforts to force them should not be made.

I sometimes believed that Judith had something on her mind. She was looking forward to her return to London the next June. When she spoke of her plans, she became animated. In London she would be happy. She had come to like London and to enjoy spending much of her time there. Her successful concerts had something to do with this. She believed that she was more appreciated as an artist there than she was in America.

One Saturday evening, we went to the Italian restaurant on Thompson Street. I called for her that evening. Riding downtown in the taxicab, Judith was silent. As we ate, she was more restrained than usual. Several times she looked off wistfully. I was touched and deeply sympathetic.

—Judith is a sad girl, I thought.

While we were having coffee, Judith looked at me and said with strain in her voice,

"Ed, I have something to tell you."

"I know, dear."

She was surprised for a fraction of a second. She forced a smile and took my hand.

"Ed, I don't think I can continue."

"I know, Judith."

"How?"

"I sensed it coming, dear."

"You are sensitive. You know how I feel, how much respect and affection I have for you. We're friends, I know we are, I feel it, but I can't go on. I don't know why but I don't think it would be right."

I waited for her to go on. She was looking at me sadly, strain in her face.

"I don't want to hurt you. I don't want you to be mad, angry, or to feel hurt."

"It's best to be hurt now, dear. You don't want to make a mistake any more than I do."

"I can't afford to make a mistake, Ed," she spoke quickly.

"Darling, if something doesn't work three times, let's not think of trying to force it," I said.

She looked at me gratefully.

"I'm just not ready, Ed."

We had our coffee and then walked. I was melancholy. Some things cannot be. I had long since learned that there is no victory or defeat in love and that it is better to be rejected, no matter for what reason, whenever there is doubt. But for a moment, masculine vanity rose in me. I felt an impulse to let Judith know. I controlled my impulse.

There was a chill in the air. Washington Square was deserted except for a few stray figures. The trees looked bare against the night. I felt more a sadness of life then because of Judith and me. Perhaps I would suffer more later. Perhaps not. Happiness had long seemed to be an accident and I had given up all ideas of chasing for it.

Judith was silent, walking beside me.

"You have no plans, dear?"

"Yes, I'm returning to England. I'll stay in London at least a year, maybe longer."

"Maybe that will be good for you, Judith."

"Oh it will; I know it. I like the life there. And the audiences, Ed, they're more responsive."

"Maybe I will get over again. I don't know."

"I hope so."

I hailed a cab on lower Fifth Avenue and took her home. We did not say much in the cab. I kissed her good night.

"Thank you, Ed," she said.

I rode back to my hotel. There had been a suppressed sadness in the evening. I had said a kind of farewell to Judith. I could see her again, but even so this had been a farewell. Judith was not ready to do what she felt such a need to do, to give herself fully.

Judith would change.

But still, only the day before, I had wondered if marriage to Judith would mean being wedded to her piano. Had I wanted her? Yes. And I still did. But we both doubted our love. Perhaps we were too much alike in dedication and ambition.

We had not won in our careers because of the inspiration of love.

The cab moved down Second Avenue. Traffic was heavy but the lights were set so that we went steadily at a low speed.

I would be lonely. Judith would be. She would change but then it would be too late. We loved one another but always too late, always out of time.

Would Judith be lonely? I thought that she would. I remembered the night after her concert. She had been lonely and exhausted beyond feeling. She would know this feeling again. It was the price she paid for her art. And it was what she wanted to escape. But she couldn't—not yet. That was the meaning of her second rejection.

I got out of the cab, paid the fare, and went to my room. It was disorderly with books and papers. I sat on the bed brooding. Judith! I wondered what she was doing.

VII

I went to two of Judith's concerts. One Sunday night I took her and Hendrik Norstrom to dinner. We went to the Italian restaurant on Thompson Street. I still felt sad when I saw her. She and I had not gone to the end of our relationship. And now we never would.

Soon after this, Judith again became exhausted. She dropped her work and went to the country. I received two letters from her. She told me how she had been doing nothing, had slept for hours, had allowed herself to relax completely, and was slowly allowing her energy to be restored.

She was not in New York at Christmas but she sent me a telegram. It was long and full of warmth. The tenderness of a woman was in the message.

Restored, Judith gave concerts again; she went on tour.

She was passing through New York to change trains. I was to meet her for dinner. But there was confusion as to our meeting place and I went to the wrong place.

By the time Judith returned to New York, I had already decided to remarry Marion. We attended two of Judith's concerts. Judith was reserved, especially with Marion.

And then I saw her to say farewell on the day she sailed. I have already said that Judith has had new successes abroad. But she went off seeking more than success; Judith went off to find happiness.

I hope that she has.

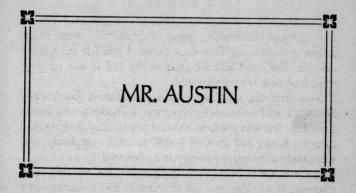

MR. AUSTIN

Mr. Austin was short, less than five feet, five inches tall. He looked Irish but he was of Anglo-Saxon descent.

Eddie Ryan had first met him when they both lived in the Hotel Verve in the early 1960s. Eddie used to see him going out at nights, he often wore a tuxedo, but Eddie had not paid much attention to him. Later, when Mr. Austin had learned that Eddie was the well-known writer Edward A. Ryan, he had started talking to him. Mr. Austin told Eddie that he was a Republican, that he had his own stock brokerage company. Mr. Austin was annoyed that Eddie did not act more impressed than he did.

But Eddie was too concerned about his work and the problems that confronted him. Eddie Ryan was in trouble, serious financial trouble. He did not even notice when Mr. Austin moved out of the Hotel Verve. He thought no more about Mr. Austin.

After months of struggle, Eddie realized that he could no longer afford to live at the Hotel Verve. The rent for his one-room studio was over three hundred dollars a month. But the idea of moving did not appeal to Eddie. He had friends

in the neighborhood; he was used to it. And it was compara-
tively safe, the streets were never deserted. Eddie liked to
stroll at night. Whenever he felt restless or whenever he
came to a block in his writing, he would put on pants and
shirts over his pajamas and walk around for a few blocks.
Eddie himself had never felt fear about walking around New
York City at nights but he had heard enough about mug-
gings and violence to know that he should be careful.

Eddie learned about the Winston Estates through a friend.
The rents were reasonable; it was just one block away from
the Hotel Verve. He would still be in a familiar neighborhood.

Two months later, Eddie moved into a studio apartment in
Winston House. His rent was less than one half of what
he had been paying at the Hotel Verve.

One day, about a week after he had moved in, Eddie was
standing in the lobby waiting for an elevator. When the elevator door opened, Mr. Austin stepped out.

"Oh, so you're coming over to live with the proletariat?"
Mr. Austin jibed.

"No, with the old ladies who drink wine secretly," Eddie
answered.

"Natalie Moirsky told me she had heard that you had
moved here," Mr. Austin said. "She lives here too, but in
another building. I guess lots of the folks from the Verve will
be trying to get in here. They want too much rent over
there."

II

Eddie soon noticed that Mr. Austin acted different at the
Winston Estates. He dressed less formally; he wore turtle-
necked sweaters and knit shirts. There were many ladies,

widows, and maidens in the Winston Estates, and any man who moved into the apartments received attention. Mr. Austin was no exception. Some would smile at him invitingly. Others would get fluttery at the sight of a man on the elevator. Mr. Austin was aware of this and he felt more manly. He would throw out his chest, and his chest was broad and solid. For years he had exercised every morning to develop the muscles. He might not be a big man and he might not be a young man but he was a man with muscle. He was proud of this. He knew that a semi-retired stock broker had no need for muscle. He had had a heart attack, a massive coronary. It had frightened him. That was why he was semi-retired; he was going to take care of himself. And his exercises were good for him; they kept him young.

III

Every night, between ten-thirty and eleven, the New York *Times* for the next day was delivered to the lobby. One night when he could not sleep, Mr. Austin decided to go down to get the paper; he would look over the closing stock prices. He put on a pair of casual slacks, a turtle-necked knit shirt, and canvas shoes. When he reached the lobby, he saw that there were several women standing around. He walked over to the desk.

"*Times* in yet?" he asked.

"No. They're all waiting for it too," the man behind the desk answered, indicating the ladies with a nod.

There were no other men around. Mr. Austin casually joined the ladies and started a conversation.

This became a nightly ritual. Here in the lobby, late at night, Mr. Austin could seem to be what he wanted to be. He could be a stockholder of consequence waiting to see the final closing figures of the market. And this was the role he assumed when Mrs. Thomas, a widow, was there.

A few years before, Mrs. Thomas would not have gotten a second glance from Mr. Austin.

Mrs. Thomas had started out as a secretary in a large cosmetics firm. It was not genius but perseverance that had won for her after twenty-five years of loyal service a salary of more than two hundred dollars a week. Mrs. Thomas had gone to work at seventeen, the year she had finished high school.

After a few weeks, Mr. Austin knew that Mrs. Thomas was ignorant but she was intimidated enough by the illusion of his intelligence to keep silent.

Her salary plus the income from her husband's estate provided Mrs. Thomas with a nice little nest egg. She wore expensive clothes and owned a new mink coat. She had a considerable amount of stock and seemed to appreciate his advice. Mr. Austin also noticed that after they began to wait for the paper together in the lobby, Mrs. Thomas started paying more attention to the way she looked when she came down. She no longer wore a comfortable skirt and blouse with flat shoes; she wore the same kind of clothes she wore to her office. Good suits, tailored dresses with simple jewelry.

Working in the office of a cosmetics empire had taught Carolyn Crosby Thomas about clothes and makeup. And her exposure to the women in this business world had convinced her that she should keep her mouth shut. This and the resulting isolation from the others in her office had given Carolyn a reputation for being close-mouthed, which in her world was the same as being trustworthy. Carolyn's success story was due to nothing more than her own acceptance of her inferiority.

Carolyn Crosby had been thirty years old when she had married Mr. Thomas, a widower in his fifties. He had moved to Winston Estates after his wife had died. He had one married daughter who lived on Long Island. Mr. Thomas did not want another family. He had a heart condition and was afraid to indulge in sex. Therefore he did not allow himself to be tempted. He was polite and pleasant but never affectionate for fear that his passion would be aroused. At first Carolyn had been hurt and confused but then she had retreated a little more into her silent world of withdrawal.

When Mr. Thomas had died, she had cried. She would be alone again. Except for Mama; she still had Mama.

IV

Mr. Austin telephoned Carolyn Thomas at her office twice. Once he had said that he would be in the neighborhood where she worked; maybe they could meet for a cocktail at five. Another time he called her to give her some advice on stock. A development had occurred and he thought she should contact her broker about it.

Mr. Austin knew that Carolyn Thomas looked up to him. He liked this. It wasn't his fault she thought he had more money than he did. He had not lied to her. He wasn't penniless even though he did not have the same financial security that she did. Their combined incomes would be comfortable, very comfortable. Mr. Austin was careful to appear in the role he enjoyed when Carolyn Thomas was in the lobby, that of the successful Wall Street broker.

V

When Eddie Ryan's friend Althea was there, Mr. Austin was the intellectual. Even though he had never heard her say anything profound, he guessed that she was one of those brainy women or else Eddie Ryan wouldn't be her friend. Mr. Austin did not know why he kept trying to get her to notice him. It wasn't as if she were anybody. Hell, she was a Greek. Her father probably ran a hotdog stand somewhere.

Mr. Austin could not understand why Althea did not recognize the fact that even though they were on the opposite sides of the fence politically, they both could use their brains. They were different from the others in the lobby; they could think. But whenever he would try to start a conversation with her, she would watch him for a minute or two, shrug her shoulders, and walk away. At times like these, Mr. Austin would feel enraged. She was rude. And he was being a damned fool to let some half-breed get him worked up. It wasn't good for him. Who did she think she was? Look at the way she dressed. Blue jeans. Hell she must be near forty. No lipstick. He didn't see how Eddie Ryan could be interested in her but then Eddie Ryan was pretty much a has-been. Still, the name Edward A. Ryan impressed people. Sometimes Mr. Austin would be walking through the lobby with a neighbor and they would pass Eddie Ryan with his hair uncombed, his face unshaven, walking along with his head in a book.

—That's Edward A. Ryan, the novelist, the neighbor would say excitedly.

This always annoyed Mr. Austin. Eddie Ryan dressed like a bum. The man never washed his hands; ink was permanently imbedded under his nails. Oh sure, he knew that Eddie Ryan had written a couple of good books but so what? What had they gotten Eddie Ryan? He couldn't afford to live at the Hotel Verve. And the way he bragged about his books.

—My forty-first book is being published.

Eddie had stopped Mr. Austin in the lobby to tell him this. For a moment, Mr. Austin felt no hostility. There was pride in Eddie Ryan's face and a kind of boyish joy. What the hell, Mr. Austin thought, Eddie Ryan wasn't a bad guy.

Just then a young airline stewardess stopped and turned.

"I couldn't help overhearing you, Mr. Ryan. Congratulations to you and good luck on your new book."

Mr. Austin had become enraged with jealousy. He had noticed the girl on the elevator several times. She was a stunner. He had tried to catch her eye but she had ignored him. But she had approached Eddie Ryan. Why? Because Eddie Ryan had written a couple of books about his childhood, his drunken Irish-Catholic family. Eddie had chronicled his rise from a world of Irish booze and Irish ignorance. For this, good-looking young girls pinned medals on him. Well no thank you. Thanks just the same. If Eddie Ryan wanted to go around writing books and telling the whole goddamned world about his lousy childhood, that was his business; but no thanks, not for him. Nobody knew that he was an orphan. His old lady had not even had the normal instincts of a woman. And she had had no imagination either, leaving him on a doorstep. He had never known about a family, or about comforts and nice things, not until he himself had gone out and gotten them for himself. Mr. Austin had made up for many of the things that he had missed. But he could never make up for "Tiny." That's what the other fellows in the orphanage had called him.

"Hey, Tiny, off the field. The game's not for midgets."

"Tiny, how d'ya find your dick? I suppose you have to call it Dicky; it's small, ain't it? It's gotta be."

Oh yes, he had had to take it as a kid but some people don't spent time bawling about things like that and trying to make people feel sorry for them. Some people accepted the world the way it was and accepted the fact that nobody else would do anything for you, that you yourself had to go out and make yourself the life you wanted. And he had done it, by God. From the time he was eighteen years old, he had carried his own weight. And he had not written a book about it either so that the whole world could feel sorry for him. He didn't want anyone feeling sorry for him. Why should anyone? He had made it.

Many people in Winston Estates seemed to be impressed by Eddie Ryan. Althea more than anyone else. Mr. Austin often passed her carrying his shirts to the laundry or carrying large envelopes of typed manuscript to her office.

Neither Althea nor Eddie had much to say to him. Mr. Austin noticed that when he saw the two of them together, they always walked closely, one talking intensely and the other one concentrating on listening.

VI

"I was out with a very unusual girl last night. She was extraordinarily beautiful and, surprisingly enough, intelligent," Mr. Austin said to Althea. He had hoped that she would come downstairs for the paper tonight; he knew that Mrs. Thomas was visiting her married nephew for the weekend.

Althea did not bother to answer him.

"She's a refined young lady, she has more than thirty floor-length gowns," he went on.

"God, she must be refined if she owns that many," Althea snickered.

"Well she is. She knows how to dress. When a man takes a young lady out and spends forty or fifty dollars for dinner at a nice place, he wants her to look right," Mr. Austin declared.

Althea did not answer. She looked toward the door.

"I'll admit that that isn't all that a man's interested in, not unless he's a moron. But as I said before, she's an intelligent young lady. Our conversation was interesting, at times brilliant."

"Come on, Mr. Austin, you never had a conversation in your life and you know it. You give speeches."

"She's a well-known and talented actress."

Althea looked toward the door again. The *Times* was later than usual. She turned toward Mr. Austin.

"And what has this talented young actress played in?"

"You should have seen how the young men in the place looked at her. God, were they jealous of me. You should have seen the envy on their faces."

The newspaper delivery man arrived. He walked toward the desk, the bundle of papers on his shoulder. When he reached the desk, he swooped them off and placed them on the desk. The clerk handed him an envelope with money in it.

Althea walked over and picked up the top one. She handed the clerk some change.

Mr. Austin could feel himself getting annoyed. She had not been the least bit interested in talking to him. Damn her, he would not give her the satisfaction of seeing how much she annoyed him. It wasn't good for him, anyway. The doctor had warned him on his last checkup.

"I may as well buy a copy of this Jewish daily, too," Mr. Austin said, taking a copy of the *Times*.

"Oh Mr. Austin, I always forget about your subtle wit," Althea said. She made no attempt to mask her contempt.

VII

The extraordinary young woman that Mr. Austin had taken out was Natalie Moirsky. Eddie Ryan had seen them, or at least he thought he had but he wasn't sure. It had been dark and the two of them were walking out of the apartment house. They had crossed the street and started toward Hampton House where Natalie lived. Eddie had seen them turn into Hampton House.

VIII

Mr. Austin did not go out as much as he had. And when he did go out, he did not stay out late. He tired easily. He knew that he had to take care of himself. He continued to do his exercises; there was no point in looking sick. After his last heart attack, his doctor had put him on a diet. Mr. Austin knew that a loss of weight at sixty-five could mean flabby skin. He didn't want that. There was no point in having the world feel sorry for you. Besides you couldn't expect clients to be happy with a broker who looked like he was going to kick the bucket at any minute. You couldn't blame clients for wanting healthy-looking young men. He would feel the same way if he were sitting on the other side of the desk. You couldn't get too upset about things like that; all you could do was try to be intelligent and objective about it.

Mr. Austin followed his exercise routine even more religiously. He did not admit even to himself that another reason for this was his fear of shrinking. He knew that shrinking was part of the aging process and he was determined to do everything possible not to lose any height.

Mr. Austin was afraid of dying but he stubbornly fought against his fear.

Autumn was coming on. Mr. Austin was glad. He had difficulty breathing during hot days.

And he had made a killing on the stock market. He was better fixed now. He planned to buy some new clothes, maybe a new tuxedo. Maybe after the weather cooled off a little, he would go to dancing school and pick up some of the latest dance steps. There was no sense in doing it until fall. He became tired too easily in the hot weather.

September passed. October moved on, day by day. The Presidential Election was coming up. The Republicans were going to win with Richard Nixon. He was going to enjoy that. To the ladies in the lobby who spoke of Governor Wallace, Mr. Austin said that he was voting for Wallace too. This was merely gallantry calculated to please the fairer but dumber sex. There were days of that October when Mr. Austin would tell himself that his life was pretty good, shaping up better. On these days, he fought both his age and his heart.

IX

October still was passing.

There was a big, bald-headed man who lived in the building, on the eleventh floor, Mr. Austin believed. Mr. Austin did not know the man's name; he was a big blubber of a fellow but Mr. Austin did know that this big man was an engineer, a Republican, and that he went to Mass every single morning. And he knew that the man had a heart condition. Mr. Austin figured that the man was not long for this earth. He might depart for Henceforth before November 6, and the Nixon-Agnew vote might be reduced by one. Oh well, it was a Republican year and one vote less would not change the outcome of the election.

Mr. Austin was sorry about the old man. It was sad. But he had to be honest with himself; he was glad that it was not his turn.

When the big fellow whose name he could never remember died, Mr. Austin was sorry.

But a man dies. The days pass. Few remember him. The living think of the living.

X

Mr. Austin had looked forward to the autumn. And the fall had come. It was going by, while he continued to plan on this being the autumn of his life. He did not go out very much; it was not that he did not want to, he did. But he tired too readily. He knew this and was pierced by terror. It was the terror of death. It came stalking into his apartment, stalking a sure victim. The color would go out of his face and he would stand, motionless, almost like stone.

Mr. Austin fought this fear.

XI

One night Mr. Austin was reading the newspaper. He had just come up from the lobby. He had not dallied in the lobby tonight. He had bought his paper and come back up to his apartment. He wasn't feeling too good tonight. He had not been feeling too good all day. But it was nothing. He read the newspaper. No, it was nothing. Nothing to worry about.

He read a news account about a speech Nixon had made. The speech didn't seem to say much. But then Hubert Humphrey wasn't saying any more and he was using a lot more words to say it.

Mr. Austin was in too much discomfort to enjoy his own wit.

The pain came.

It came suddenly but when it did he knew that he had been expecting it. He gritted his teeth, his lips closed tightly. His shoulders hunched. He was half-crumpled on the bed. He was dying. It was all over. It was a wordless thought, a feeling more than thought. He was dying and there was no one. Breathing was a struggle; the pain was crushing his chest. He was choking. His head dropped forward on the bed; his right hand was beneath him. His left arm curled toward his head, his fingers twitched.

This is death. Death was pain and gasping. It was choking in a convulsive effort to breathe. The veins alongside his head stood out with his struggle to breathe. They were purple.

—I'm dying, he thought.

XII

Mr. Austin was not dead. He was weak and he was afraid, but he was alive. The pain was still there but it had ebbed, and he could breathe. He was breathing fast but he was breathing. He lay still for some seconds. The seconds became minutes. The perspiration on his face was cold.

Now the pain was mild but his heart was still palpitating. Before, it had pounded like a hammer.

He was all right now. The pain was gone. He could sit up. The pain was gone. It had been nothing more than a little flutter. It was nothing. He would get up now.

But Mr. Austin did not get up. He lay there. The light in the apartment made him blink when he opened his eyes. He closed them again and lay there. Mr. Austin was deciding. He was deciding what to do. Should he call someone? The pain was gone now; he was all right. But the pain had been severe. Maybe he should not dismiss it lightly. And it had lasted a long time. He didn't know what to do. He could not think. He opened his eyes again. He was tired, very tired.

He knew he should telephone the doctor. The pain had been too severe and it had lasted too long. He should telephone.

This was what Mr. Austin decided to do as he sat on the edge of the bed.

He stood up. He felt a little wobbly. He ought to get hold of himself; maybe he didn't even need to call the doctor. It might have been a severe case of indigestion. But still, he felt weak in the knees. He sat down again.

He picked up the receiver on the intercom telephone and dialed Mrs. Thomas' number.

XIII

Mrs. Thomas had hurried to Mr. Austin's apartment. He had not planned to tell her how worried he was but when she had answered the phone, his loneliness and his fear had taken control of him. He told her that he was sick, he needed someone.

In a few minutes, Mr. Austin heard her knock. He would have to get up to open the door. He sat for a few seconds. He could not get himself up on his feet. Finally he got up, went to the door and opened it.

"Oh, Mr. Austin!"

She could not conceal her alarm. Her mouth had opened, her lips quivered. She could not help herself; she had not been prepared for the way the poor man looked. Mr. Austin was a sick man, a very sick man. His face looked grey. He would have to have a doctor and right away.

"Oh, Mr. Austin," she repeated.

He tried to muster up a grin but it was more of a grimace. He was sorry he had phoned her. No, that wasn't true. The idea of being alone had frightened him.

"What happened, Mr. Austin?"

He was slow to answer.

"I've had a digestive upset."

"Hadn't I better try to get a doctor?"

"Will you go with me to the hospital?"

Mr. Austin had not known that he was going to ask this.

"Yes, of course, Mr. Austin."

"You'll have to call my doctor first, his name is Cleary. John Cleary. His number is in that little book over there by the phone."

Mrs. Thomas called him. Dr. Cleary agreed that Mr. Austin should go to the hospital; he would send an ambulance. This frightened Mrs. Thomas but Dr. Cleary explained that he did not want Mr. Austin to exert himself in any way whatsoever; it could be fatal.

Mrs. Thomas was not sure that Mr. Austin would agree to go in an ambulance. She would have to persuade him; he was a very sick man. She remembered her husband, the way he had looked. He had not looked nearly so sick as Mr. Austin looked right this minute. And he had been dead by the time the doctor had reached their apartment.

"What do you want me to pack for you, Mr. Austin?"

"A toothbrush."

The man was woozy. She would have to take over; that was all there was to it. She walked over to the closet. She found a small suitcase on the shelf. She took it out and opened it. She walked over to the chest of drawers. She felt no embarrassment as she opened drawers and took out pajamas. Her own husband had died two years ago. And Mr. Austin looked like a dying man. If there were anything she could do to help him, she would. It was her duty as a Christian.

Mr. Austin was glad that she had taken over. He was too weak to pack but he did not admit this to himself. He told himself that he was glad that he knew a woman who knew what a woman's job was.

Mrs. Thomas packed neatly and carefully. Just as she was

closing the suitcase, the intercom phone rang. She picked it up. It was the desk clerk downstairs. The ambulance had arrived, two attendants were on their way up.

Mr. Austin was carried to the ambulance on a stretcher. Mrs. Thomas rode with him to the East Side Hospital.

XIV

Mrs. Thomas sat in the waiting room. They had taken Mr. Austin into the emergency room.

Dr. Cleary had stripped Mr. Austin to the waist.

Mr. Austin could feel some palpitations of the heart. Sweat broke out on him. But his fear did not completely curb his pride as they bared his chest.

"You can see, Doctor, that I'm in good shape. Not an ounce of flab anywhere."

Dr. Cleary put his stethoscope to Mr. Austin's chest and listened. He did not reply. In a moment he ordered that Mr. Austin be taken up to the room he had reserved for him.

A nurse reported to Mrs. Thomas, calling her "Mrs. Austin." Mrs. Thomas blushed. She explained that she was a neighbor and that her name was Mrs. Thomas.

"I was afraid that the poor man had had a heart attack. He looked the way my husband did. He passed away after a heart attack."

The nurse was sorry but she was busy and she would have to move along. Mrs. Thomas picked up the suitcase she had packed for poor Mr. Austin and handed it to the nurse, explaining what was in it. The nurse thanked her. Mrs. Thomas felt embarrassed again. The nurse was impatient as Mrs. Thomas tried to explain how she had come to pack Mr. Austin's things into the small bag.

XV

Mrs. Thomas had little capacity for feeling left. She had acted for Mr. Austin out of a sense of Christian duty. She felt no real anxiety as she sat in the hospital corridor.

Mrs. Thomas was fifty years old. She had buried a husband, but she was still dominated by her mother, Violet Effingham Crosby. Mrs. Crosby was a big woman and she walked with a cane. She gave the impression of being much fatter than she was. She had a big head and her shoulders and bosom were big. She was an ugly woman and she looked stupid but she was a woman of some intelligence and she was a self-indulgent woman.

Both she and her daughter were the victims of this self-indulgence.

Mrs. Thomas had never been free from her mother's domination. Even when she was married, her duties as a daughter took priority over her duties as a wife. She and Mr. Thomas had lived in the same apartment house as her mother and her mother had eaten dinner with them every night. And Mr. Thomas had learned to eat the things that his mother-in-law enjoyed.

When Mr. and Mrs. Thomas had gone on vacations, Mrs. Crosby had accompanied them. Mr. Thomas liked the mountains. Mrs. Crosby preferred the seashore. They went to the seashore. And when Mrs. Crosby was too ill to travel, Mr. and Mrs. Thomas stopped traveling too. Mrs. Thomas would not leave her mother. She did not want her mother to stay alone and her two sisters would not have Mrs. Crosby with them. Mrs. Thomas thought it unfair that she should carry the burden alone; her sisters should help. And so should her brother. She was willing to do her share, more than her share, but they should do something. They should not leave it all up to her. But that was what they had done. And what a burden it was. Her life would have been a lot easier if they had assumed part of the responsibility. But they hadn't and that was that. She didn't hate them for it. But only wished that things had been different.

Mrs. Thomas did not realize the depth of the bitterness in her.

XVI

Mr. Austin was given a sedative. He had insisted in telling Dr. Cleary that it was his stomach, possibly an ulcer. Dr. Cleary had told him that it was his heart but Mr. Austin would not accept this diagnosis. There was nothing the matter with his heart; there couldn't be. He had been taking good care of himself and had exercised regularly.

But he had to admit, he was tired. Very tired. Mr. Austin fell asleep.

Mrs. Thomas was told that the patient was resting comfortably but that his condition was critical. Mrs. Thomas said that all they could do was hope for the best. She told them that she would telephone in the morning to inquire about his condition.

Mrs. Thomas left the hospital. She took a taxicab home.

She was tired but she had done her Christian duty.

XVII

Mr. Austin was a man with a damaged heart but he would not admit this diagnosis. He adamantly insisted that his heart was all right, that the source of his pain was in his intestines and stomach.

He was in and out of the hospital three times. It was the last week in October. He had voluntarily returned to the East Side Hospital. He could no longer bear the pain. And he could no longer hold to his illusion about his heart.

He was sick, dying. He consented to surgery so that the doctors could insert a pacemaker. But the night before the operation was to be performed, Mr. Austin had his fourth and most serious heart attack.

The resident doctor was called in. In an instant, he realized that Mr. Austin was nearly dead. He called the nurse in to assist him and immediately prepared to do a chest incision so that he could massage Mr. Austin's heart, which seemed to have stopped. But the muscles in Mr. Austin's chest were hardened, his chest solid from the rigorous exercises of years. The doctor ordered the operating room prepared.

Mr. Austin died while the effort was being made to save him.

His face was ravaged from the pain he had suffered.

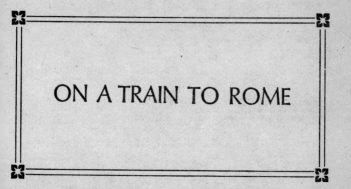

ON A TRAIN TO ROME

The train due to leave for Rome at 3:55 A.M. came into the station at Naples crowded, and people crowded to get on as it stopped. I was with a friend, Marie, who spoke Italian. We were lucky, and among the first to enter a second-class car.

On the left was a narrow aisle, and on the right were the compartments, each seating eight. Marie saw two people leave one compartment and immediately darted into it. When I followed, a grey-haired man in the compartment told her that only one seat was free. He pointed to a fat little boy of about eight and said in Italian (translated for me by Marie, since I understood only about thirty Italian words) that the boy's mother was coming back. I sat down to hold the one seat, and Marie was about to leave the compartment to search for other seats for both of us when a woman came in and spoke to her. Then Marie sat down too. I was confused, because I hadn't understood what had been said. There were now four men in the compartment, in addition to Marie and me, the boy, and the woman who had spoken to Marie.

The train didn't leave immediately, and I waited apprehensively, holding my small suitcase on my lap, fearing that

when the boy's mother returned I would have to stand up
and remain standing all the way to Rome. I was very tired.
The morning before, I had taken a long walk on Capri, where
I had been staying, and had come over to Naples on the six
o'clock steamer. It was the time of the Fiesta in Naples, and
no hotel rooms were available. I had tramped the streets looking for a room just for the night, and then, when it seemed
clear that no rooms were to be found, I had walked and
walked—to see Naples, the Fiesta, the crowds, and also to
pass the time until I could board the train for Rome. I had
fallen asleep in the waiting room and now I felt drugged and
exhausted.

Sleepily I looked at the other passengers. The grey-haired
man was seated opposite me by the window. Next to him was
a short youngish man in a cheap suit. Then the little fat boy,
who was dark and round-faced, his eyes fixed in a curiously
rigid focus. He was neatly dressed in a light red sweater and
grey trousers. The men on either side of me were young. The
woman was young but already beginning to get stout. She
had a very tired expression on her face, a look suggesting
weariness and hard work that I'd seen on the faces of many
of the women in Italy.

Marie finally told me in English, as the people talked, that
there were actually two seats, not one. She said that the grey-
haired man had lied because they'd wanted more room for
the boy, and that the woman in the compartment was the
boy's mother. I relaxed. I'd be able to keep my seat, and possibly to sleep on the trip.

There was noise and movement in the train and on the platform outside. A dwarflike monk, bearded and wearing a
bright red habit, came through the train begging. He carried
a big pocketbook for the money given him. He was badly
crippled. Just before the train had arrived, he had passed
along the station platform, holding his bag up before every
one in a kind of arrogance, waiting for alms as though they

were his natural right. Seeing him took me out of time; it was like watching a mendicant monk from the Middle Ages. Others went by in the corridor of the car, and there was more churning and noise outside. One of the men in our compartment turned out the light and closed the door. And finally the train began to move.

It was hot in the compartment, and I was so tired that I wasn't sure I could sleep. It was impossible to find a comfortable position; I could neither sit up nor lie down. There were small, restless, continual movements about me. The boy especially was restless.

I closed my eyes and tried to sleep, and wished that the train were already in Rome. I thought of Pompeii. I had been there two days before. For me there was something sad and awesome and fascinating in the ruins. One day, the town had been smothered in red-hot lava. The people had been going about their lives, occupied with their interests, their loves, their pleasures. They had been thinking of what would come next in their lives. Death had been unimportant, far away. There had been crowds in the Forum and chariots on the narrow streets. They had sprawled on the floors of their villas and eaten themselves into satiety. And then their city had been smothered in lava . . . My train was rocketing along.

I opened and closed my eyes in the darkness. To put myself to sleep, I tried to think about baseball, and all the players who had been in all the World Series games I could remember.

Suddenly the door of the compartment opened and a light flashed on, causing me to blink. It was the conductor, a small man in cap and coat. Everyone in the compartment had a different kind of ticket. Two of the men had to reach above them for their coats. The conductor punched each ticket. A few words were exchanged. The little boy said nothing and did not look at the conductor.

The conductor switched off the light and closed the door

of the compartment. Again I tried to fall asleep. I felt a cramp in my neck and tried to find a more comfortable position. I thought about the way Ty Cobb used to bat and finally fell asleep.

When I woke up, the light in the compartment was grey and bluish. Two of the men were gone and there was more room now. Outside, the day was beginning in the houses and fields we passed.

The boy was talking with the grey-haired man. I wondered what they were talking about. The grey-haired man was kind and sympathetic. He, and also the boy's mother and father, laughed frequently at what the boy said. The boy talked rapidly in the manner of one who is used to being the center of attention. And as he spoke, he kept reaching for his mother, putting his arms around her, and kissing her cheek affectionately. After kissing her, he would rub his cheek against hers. He kept talking. Several times I noticed his face. It was almost expressionless. There was no play or change of emotion on his features. And he did not look about much, nor at the person to whom he was talking.

It was getting lighter and brighter outside. One of the men who had left the compartment returned and sat beside me. Then the other came in. The boy chattered on. He spoke of America, and I was curious as to what he and the others were saying. He stood between the facing seats and talked, his eyes turned toward the windows of the moving train. His mother looked at him affectionately, and now and then she would pat and caress him tenderly. The boy seemed to me to be spoiled, too much the center of attention. He talked on and on, and even though I did not know Italian, it was clear to me that he was dominating everyone. All eyes were focused on him as he spoke nervously and continued to reach out for his mother, to embrace her, to kiss her, and again to rub his cheek against hers.

He stood facing me and talking. I looked at him and smiled

cordially. There was no response on his face. He looked at me and talked on as though I were not there smiling at him. And the others in the compartment continued to listen to him, and to laugh and to smile at what he said.

More and more he seemed to me a "mama's boy," and spoiled. As the train rolled on toward Rome, and as the day lightened, this scene continued. The boy's father now went out to wash up. The boy sat beside me. He stood up and talked with the grey-haired man. His hand touched mine and then he let it rest on my leg. As he went on talking, a bit rapidly and still nervously, he was heedless of me, even though he was touching me. The grey-haired man lifted the boy's hand from my leg. I tried to indicate to him that the boy was really not bothering me. The boy again reached out his arms toward his mother. She changed seats and now was riding backward. He kissed her noisily.

"Mama."

The man beside me took a holy picture of a saint from his wallet and handed it to the boy. There was talk, and I knew that it was about the picture of the saint. The boy held the picture in his hand and spoke. I thought he was reading the prayer or invocation that was printed on one side of the card. When he had finished, the boy sat down. He took out a small red wallet and let the wallet and the holy picture rest on his fat thigh. Then his mother took the picture and put it carefully in the wallet. She gave the wallet to the boy, and he put it in his pocket, and again hugged and kissed her.

Marie joined in the conversation, but she didn't translate for me. I kept watching and trying to catch the meaning of some of the words. The boy said something more about America. The boy's father returned to the compartment. He watched the boy tenderly.

Then we were in Rome. The other passengers hurried out of the compartment ahead of us. The father took the boy by the hand as they left.

We stepped off the train into a bright sunny morning in Rome. The little fat boy with the red sweater was ahead of us, walking between his parents. Each held one of his hands, each carried a suitcase in the other hand.

And Marie said: "The little boy is blind."

I was stricken with surprise.

And then she told me what she had learned. Suddenly, a year ago, the boy had gone blind, and now his parents were on their way to Milan, taking him to a specialist.

I asked Marie what they had said of America. She told me that one of the men had asked the little boy what he would do when he went to America. The boy had answered that he would work and send his mother twenty dollars a week.

I saw the brilliant sunshine over Rome in the early morning. I saw the boy, between his parents, disappear into the crowd on the station platform.

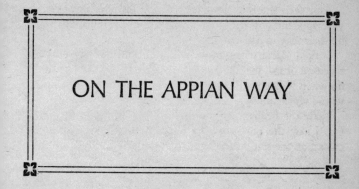

ON THE APPIAN WAY

The twilight hours are the most melancholy of the day. Even in the midst of noise, the world is quiet. The grey still air, losing color before the onset of night, invites brooding. It seems as if the world itself were brooding. And it was at such an hour that I rode along the Appian Way with my friend Jeanette. The day had been hot in Rome, but with the setting of the sun, it was growing cool. The traffic was heavy, pounding and confusing. Automobiles headed for Rome kept shooting by us, their blinding headlights glaring in our eyes. The road was cluttered on either side with Roman ruins, piles of stone, remnants of tombs and broken structures, and all of these were dark and gloomy in the grey-blue light. Along the way, there were houses, cafes, and gas stations; the past and the present stood jumbled together almost idiotically.

Where were all these cars going? Why so much speed, with cars crowding by one another, sometimes dangerously, along the old road where chariots once had rolled, and where the tombs of Romans had been built? Here and there was a slab with part of a Latin inscription. Piles of broken stone, a section of a foundation, shards of marble, the past, broken up and destroyed, left to lie as bleached bones might, mementoes of a way of life and of lives gone forever from this world.

It was a confusing ride. The heavy traffic was very disconcerting; the motorists bound for Rome kept switching their headlights, and this helped to create a feeling of imminent danger. Continuing on the road, seeing the incoherent ruins, made me feel a frustration and a hunger for the past. They were not too meaningful as symbols of an unknown world, forever dead; more than symbols, they were reminders. They were the bones of the decomposed body of history. Once, they had been part of tombs, and they had reminded Romans of distinguished families, of men and women of Imperial Rome who had gone beyond. Now, they were strung along this old route, senselessly. A deep feeling of depression came over me.

Jeanette drove on silently. She was too concerned with her driving, alert in the rush of cars, and the ever-recurrent switching of headlights—the code of the road in darkness. She had been over this road before and was less interested than I in the Appian Way. She had not found it especially interesting when she had first seen it. In the Forum at Rome, and even more so at Pompeii, the past had seemed different; it had not been disassembled as it was here. Piles of stone, fragments of inscription stone and marble that seemed meaningless except for the fact that I knew that once these stones and this marble had been part of a Roman tomb—all this represented the past as a tragedy of lunacy. Just as some lives seem to be such a stupidity, so did the Appian Way.

We drove on. Jeanette felt the strain of driving in the traffic. She was watching for something but would not tell me what it was. Finally, she found it, the dark ruins of an enormous tomb. I believe that it was the tomb of one of the emperors. Finding a place to park safely on the right side of the road, we crossed to the tomb. Three Italians stood talking in front of the opening to the ruins. Jeanette was frightened of them because it was now almost dark; she feared that they might be gangsters. She was quickly relieved when they crossed the road, got into a car and drove off toward Rome.

The inside was like a small courtyard. Three dirty little barefoot children, two girls and a boy, ran about; at the entrance to a room, a dark-haired woman held a baby. She was barefoot, and her dress was dirty. We approached her, and the three small children came and stared at us with awe and curiosity. The woman gazed at us, tired, disinterested, as though she were wearied of strangers coming to look at the ruins.

"It's the same woman who lived here when I was here before, three years ago," Jeanette told me in English.

Behind the woman, I could see that a home had been made out of what had once been a vault. The inside was damp and the room was furnished with a table, some wooden shelves, a bed, and a few old chairs. There was a similar room on the right. Another barefoot, tired-looking woman appeared in its doorway.

Jeanette said good evening in Italian, and the women greeted her listlessly. We stood before them for some moments, quiet, but they did not seem to resent our curious gazes, or to care.

Jeanette spoke again and, turning to me, said that they lived here. As they talked, Jeanette occasionally translated for me. One of them had said that her man was in Rome, but Jeanette added:

"They're deserted women."

I glanced again into the rooms. They were hovels. Had they been underground, they could have been described as caves.

Two of the children went to the first woman and clung to her skirt. Jeanette asked some more questions and the woman answered dully.

"Give them some money—they're very poor," Jeanette said.

I did. We left. It was almost totally dark. As we walked away, they all watched apathetically. We could have belonged to another species.

"They are both deserted women," Jeanette repeated. "They have lived here for four or five years. The men come and give them more babies and then go back to Rome."

We got into our car. Jeanette drove ahead until we found a place where she could safely turn around. Then we drove back to Rome along the old Appian Way. In the darkness, the stones looked weird and fantastic. The traffic was still heavy, and the cars zoomed toward us with their blinding yellow headlights.

Soon we saw, ahead, the lights of Rome.

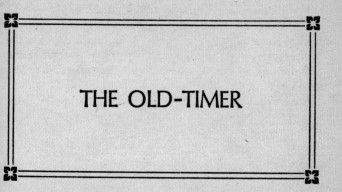

THE OLD-TIMER

I feel sorry for Willie Collins. The poor guy, he really is pathetic. It is hard to have to take the kind of come-down the company gave him, and he's never gotten over it.

Years ago, when I was young and on the extra list, I'd often get one of his gascars for special pickup loads. I liked it better when I got some other boss. Among all the bosses I ever had, Heinie Mueller was the best. The Dutchman was a prince, and he still is, but Heinie is old now and he got a raw deal. After forty-seven years as an express man, they retired him and he just makes ends meet. He always liked his beer and it was his only luxury but Heinie can't afford many luxuries now on his pension. He's aged and has a lot of trouble with his dogs. I'm having some trouble with mine myself. Working twenty-three years on the trucks in all kinds of weather isn't easy. The wear and tear gets rugged. At the end, before I was promoted to Route Inspector, I was beginning to feel it. It's been a little better since I was promoted during the War. My father got his promotion to Wagon Dispatcher—that's the same rank and pay as Route Inspector—back during the First World War.

I know from experience the difference between working on the trucks and supervising the drivers. That's why I feel sorry for Willie Collins. I'm not surprised that the little hair he's got left is grey. But so is mine and I'm younger than he is. I remember when Willie thought he was just about the best-dressed guy in the supervision. He was taken off a wagon and made a Dispatcher back in those dim old days of the First World War. He must have been about twenty-six then. When he was up in the Wagon Call Department dispatching special gascars, he used to call himself the Chief. And he sported fancy broadcloth shirts, striped suits, and loud jazz-bo ties.

You get a strange kind of feeling thinking of things like this when you've worked for a company for over thirty years like I have. I'm going on my thirty-sixth year. Willie has put in more time than I have. He's been in the express business now for about forty-six or forty-seven years. He's in his early sixties but he looks in good shape, better shape than most of the old-timers who are left. But I still feel sorry for him because he's been up and then went down and he never could accept this fact. It all happened years ago, but when I see him like I do some mornings when I am at the depot, getting my men off with their deliveries, he'll buttonhole me and tell me about the mistake Gumshoe Cooper made, and that Patsy McLaughlin never would have treated him that way, and that if Gumshoe Cooper only would have understood as Patsy did that he, Willie that is, was the best man in the supervision. And if the muckety-mucks on top now only knew this, they'd put him back on top instead of keeping him where he is, driving a tractor.

I've heard Willie sing the blues like this to me many more times than I can remember. I listen to him and feel kind of sympathetic because he was one of the men in the supervision in my own father's day, and most of those old-timers are gone now, and may God have mercy on their souls.

I do my job and go home and forget it. Every year, things get worse and they drive us to drive the men. It's business, pick up freight and no overtime. That's the bible of the company now and the morale of the men gets worse right along. But the few old-timers act like they was wedded to the company. They have a kind of faith in the company that I don't have. And I don't know where that faith leads them because I tell you, it's sad to see them go on their pensions. Saddest of all was Heinie. First they made him a second-class Wagon Dispatcher, which meant a cut in his pay, and then they retired him. There was a banquet for him but we all paid for our own dinner instead of the company doing it. They gave Heinie a lot of soft soap and sent him home. He gets about one-seventy-five a month pension and Heinie has tough going. His forty-nine years of service didn't mean much at the end except to be an occasion for soft soap. The big shots made speeches and praised him but you can't buy groceries and a can of beer with praise. Heinie didn't want to go and couldn't afford it but they told him to go. Well, he's aged but he's still with us and in pretty good shape considering everything. When they retire, the old-timers don't know what to do with themselves and they waste away. They don't get a good break. Take Simon Murray. He's seventy-five now, but he's in pretty good shape considering his age. I saw him at the funeral of Dago Belocki, an old driver. Simon was retired about four–five years ago, but he couldn't live off his pension so he supplemented it by getting a job as a night watchman. How can a man live on $109 a month? When I get my pension, I want to take it easy for the rest of my life, but I'm not going to be able to, I can tell you that.

I remember the night about five years ago that was my thirtieth anniversary working for the company. I don't think I'll ever forget it. Every night I take a train at the La Salle Street Depot and get off at Seventy-fifth Street, where I leave my car parked in the morning. I drive home. And on that night, I did it just the same as on every night. It wasn't much of a car I had then, a 1940 Chevy, but it ran and that's what counts. It had a lot of mileage on it when I traded it in and got a 1948 Chevy. I'm a first-class Wagon Dispatcher and at the time I was making $337 per month. Now, I knock down $449. I guess my work isn't too hard, except that they never let up on the overtime question. My old man had the same classification as I did when he died. Willie had it in those days but in the depression they bumped Willie, Simon Murray, and some of the other Route Inspectors and Wagon Dispatchers and put them back on the trucks. Well, when I went home that night that marked my thirtieth anniversary in the express game, I thought of things like this and I thought of a lot of other things. Thirty years, that's a long time to be working for one company. Now it's thirty-five. A lot of things happen to you when you go along over a period of time like that, and you don't think too much about how time is passing. You know it's passing, and someday you're going to get old, but you don't think much about it. You don't think of things like this any more than you have to.

After you have a family of your own, everything is different. You get ideas about lots of things in life, and especially you get some ideas about how your own father might have felt. I know I did, and I still think of him. He only lasted eighteen years with the express company and he didn't live long enough to retire on any pension. He wanted me and all of us kids to get ahead, and I guess he'd be proud of me and satisfied with what I've done and about all of us, his kids. He'd probably have no complaints. I got the same kind of a job now that he had and even if things could be better, they are a damned sight better over what they were like in his day. Of course, I only have one son and my mother had fifteen, but only six of us lived to grow up. I have a nice clean home and we eat good food and my boy went to the Sisters' school in our parish and now he goes to a Catholic high school. I paid his tuition and I even put by a little, a very little but something, for his college education. I wanted him to go to Notre Dame and become a Notre Dame halfback. He looked good to me when he was a young kid, but I guess now he's cut out for something else, and my dream now is to see him graduate from Fordham. It's a Jesuit school, and for my money, they're the best there is. If I can go along and not kill myself, and retire and take it a little easy when my time comes and see him grown up, a college graduate and a decent person, and feel that I really helped him to be better than I am, well, I'll be satisfied. Then when I'm called, I'll hang up my gloves, that is, figuratively speaking, and maybe I can honestly tell myself that I went along and did the best I could. But I was thinking on that day when I completed my thirty years of service, and I've often thought of it since that it has all turned out better for me than it did for Pa. He just about killed himself working. He had a stroke in his early fifties and already I have been lucky enough to live longer than he did. The work on the truck was starting to get me along about seven or eight years ago and my varicose veins would sometimes be a trial and I mean it. But then back during the last war, I was promoted. As I think I've said, my father was promoted into the supervision during the First World War.

I remember the day I got my promotion. It didn't come unexpected because for about five or six years Hiram Wolfe used to put me in as a substitute, working as a Dispatcher or Route Inspector to fill in at vacation time and whenever anyone was off sick. But when I got the news, I sure was happy. It wasn't only the extra money, which is always mighty useful in any man's life, but it was my release from some of those hard days at the wheel of the truck. As I say, I remember that day. It was a warm spring day. I was driving home thinking how it would be a happy occasion for us. And we were going to celebrate by going to see the girls' baseball game. I get a kick out of that, a bigger kick than I do out of seeing the Sox play. And some of them girl players are good, I mean it; they can play almost as good as boys their age. There was a team of them here in Chicago in the league but the franchise was withdrawn. Then there was girls' soft ball. I like that but not as much as girls playing hard ball.

Well, I was thinking that night at the game: I got no serious complaints or gripes. I get by and that's the most a lot of us can ask for. This isn't a bad country for us to live in and rear our kids. Things have sure gotten better than what they were like when I was a kid.

I can't see eye-to-eye with the old-timers. Maybe this is because I was on a truck too long before I got my promotion. You look at everything different when you're the man on the truck instead of the man who's telling the men in the trucks to go out and get it, pick it up, and no overtime, either. I remember those early days on the trucks. That was back in the 1920s. There was one Christmas season then, right after Pa died, when I slept in the garage for five nights straight. I got over two hundred dollars that payday, but I sure worked for it. Of course in them days, two hundred dollars was a lot more money than it is today, but I don't think I would say today that two hundred dollars is anything to look down your nose and sneeze at.

When I was on the trucks, I played some angles and didn't kill myself rushing. I guess I got about twenty more hours overtime that big Christmas week in the 1920s than I would have gotten if I had been a greaseball and just worked my you-know-what off for the company. Now it's different. If any of my men on the trucks gets overtime, I have to explain it on high. It's my responsibility and I get burned for it. Now, things are different and there's nothing to do about it, but I do think that I understand it.

As I say, I have nothing against the company. It pays me. I do my job. The company and the bosses have nothing personal against me. But I have no love for the company, either.

When I'm ready to retire, I won't be like some of the old-timers. I tell you, it's tough on them. It would break your heart to see some of them and listen to them when they went on their pensions. It was like the end of the world. I guess it was for many of them, because there aren't many of them alive now. That's why lots of old-timers don't want to give up and go on their pensions. Because when they do, they haven't got anything left in life. The company and their jobs, that's all they have got to keep them alive. Nothing else seems to matter to them and they become lost souls and just waste away. I sure am hoping with my fingers crossed, though, that this doesn't happen to Heinie Mueller.

That's the way they feel about the company. But does it think anything of them? A couple of years ago, Turk Neary went on retirement. Turk put in fifty years of service. When he started in the express business, driving a wagon, I wasn't even born. He was an express man before my old man was. Once, he worked with Patsy McLaughlin when Patsy was a young fellow on a wagon himself. Well, on Turk's last day, he had his time card punched at the garage, dropped it in the box, and walked away for the last time. Nobody said a word to him, not one word. He just walked off the same as he would at the end of any day's work. There was no difference, except that this day marked his anniversary of fifty years of service.

That's what I mean—there's no sentiment in the company or in the express business. And that's what I'm trying to get at about the old-timers. They feel this sentiment about their job and the company, but it doesn't pay them one cent or even get them an honest "Thank you," a word of praise, a pat on the back.

I guess it's all ignorance on their part, but I say this knowing that, after all, I don't have any education to speak of, myself. The old-timers didn't know nothing else but the company, I guess. But instead of my trying to figure it all out, let

me tell you what happened to Billy O'Brien. He was a
Route Inspector in the Loop when I started in as a kid, an-
swering phone calls in the old Wagon Call Department, and
then Billy was put Dispatching in one of the depots. I was put
in his place in the depot before they switched me and made
me a Route Inspector. Well, Billy, may God have mercy on
his soul, got to the point where he was too old to work and
too young to die. What was he to do? His wife was sick and
that took all his savings, taking care of her, and then she
passed away on him. That broke Billy up. His children were
married, and he was alone. It was pathetic. Billy was never the
same again after Mrs. O'Brien died. And then Billy had a
heart attack. He needed his pay to support himself, because
his son and daughter only get by, and he was too sick a man
to work. He was wasting away. And at home he was alone
with nothing to do. After that heart attack he never should
have come back to work. And when he did, he only lasted a
month. Then he had another attack riding home from work
on the streetcar and died. He just folded up and passed away
right there on the crowded car.

I remember him during his last days. He was so thin and
grey, such a shadow of a man. I'd try to remember him and
what he looked like when he was younger and strong and in
the prime of life, and it was hard for me to realize that I was
talking to Billy O'Brien. That's how much he wasted away.
Billy was always on the level. He wasn't one of those in the
supervision who rode his men. Whenever he could, he gave
them a break. I never drove for him, but I know a lot of fellows who have and nearly every one of them only had praise
for Billy as a boss. They would always speak well of Billy,
praising him.

I tell you, the first time I saw him back at work after his
first attack, I was touched. He looked so awful that if you
had known him before and if you saw him that day, it would
have made your hair stand on end. But he just had to come

back even if it was going to kill him, like it did. It wasn't right, and yet, what could he do or what could you say?

And then there was Shaughnessy. It was pitiful. Of course, what happened to Shaughnessy didn't have anything to do with the company, but it sure was a pitiful thing. He was another one of the old-timers. He just couldn't find the right wife, I guess. I know that one night when he came home from work, he found that his wife was gone. That was the first Mrs. Shaughnessy. She just left with another fellow, and when she did, she took every penny that poor Shaughnessy was saving so that he could buy a house. In those days, he was always talking about how a working man should own his own home, and he wanted that, I guess, more than he wanted almost anything else in the world. Well, his daughter was already married, and so he got a divorce and married another woman, and started saving all over again. But he never got that house of his own. He used to talk about it every time I ran into him. He planned to buy it out on the Northwest side, and in those days he would often go out on Sundays, looking at houses and planning and thinking of the day when he could buy that house. But then the second Mrs. Shaughnessy got sick. Every cent he saved after his first wife decamped on him went for the care of his second wife. It was pitiful, I tell you, yes pitiful, because Shaughnessy's second wife went out of her mind. The time came when she didn't even recognize him or know who he was, and he spent his second savings to have her taken care of. Finally, he couldn't afford to do this any more and he had to have her put in a public institution. Until this happened, he tried to keep up his courage and to be the same happy Shaughnessy that he had always been through the years he'd been working for the company. But this broke him, broke his spirit. It was then we began to see that he was a sick man, and that he was getting old himself. But he couldn't afford to retire, sick as he was in his last days. He would just about crawl down to work, and crawl home again every night. But like a lot of fellows said, what could he do. That was Shaughnessy, and he was also too old to work and too young to die, except that he did go on working. He must have had cancer. And just about the only merciful thing that happened was that once he started to go, he went fast. The second Mrs. Shaughnessy is still in a public mental institution, but I am told that she is so far gone that she doesn't even know that poor Jack Shaughnessy, her husband, is dead.

No, the old-timers don't want to retire. And it isn't just because of the money, even though that's important because most of them can't afford to live on their pensions. It's the sentiment. Listen to them talk, and you begin to wonder what's going to happen to the company when they retire. Why, you would think that each one of the old-timers is John Continental himself. Nobody says that any more, but back years ago when I was just a kid and just starting in the express business, they always used to speak of the company that way, as John Continental or Long John Continental. Yes, the old-timers are the company, to hear them tell it, the best men in the business, and nobody can touch them. I listen to them and I feel sorry for most of them. I'm getting old myself; but I hope to God that when I really am an old man, I am not like the old-timers I'm telling you about, an object of pity.

And it isn't only the old-timers in the supervision who are this way, either. A lot of the men are just the same. Take Pill Porter. Old Pill has about forty years seniority. He drives a tractor. And to hear him tell it, you'd think that nobody can drive a tractor as good as he does it. The way he tells it, if he knocked off a day of work, sick, the whole tractor-trailer service would fall apart. He is just the same as the others. And like I just said, what this is is sentiment. They feel that the company needs them because they need the company. I think that's it. I was beginning to feel a little that way myself back around the time my son was born. But his coming did a lot for me. It got me to see things different. As I said, I understand what I'm trying to say, but I don't know if I can explain it to make it all clear enough. But I'll try to and do the best I can with whatever the good Lord gave me.

Take a man, an average little man like myself. He's a young fellow, he started in working on a wagon; but he didn't think he was going to spend all of his life and every one of his best years with the company. He's going to work there on the wagon, or if it's now, on a truck, and get himself a stake. And then, something is going to happen, his ship is going to come home. He'll find a good wife and have a nice home and maybe get himself a business or something will happen. He's young and doesn't know what you get to know after you spend more than thirty years working for the one company. Well, he works year after year, and when he gets married, that's good, but he still has got to work, and kids come, and then one day he just wakes up in the morning and he tells himself, like it was something of a surprise, that he's going to spend the rest of his life working for the company, and that there just ain't no ship to come in that will put him on Easy Street for the rest of his life.

You tell yourself that you always kind of knew this but didn't think about it. Yes, you always knew that for you and all the other little people in the world, there ain't no Easy Street in life, and that all you can do is to try to earn your living. But I don't want to sound like I was kicking or complaining, because after all I want to earn my living, and I guess there are lots of worse and harder ways of earning a living than the way I do. And now I have the classification of Senior Dispatcher—Route Inspectors and Dispatchers are the same thing, and I am on a route instead of being in one of the depots. It isn't too bad, even though they are on my tail all of the time for me to keep down the overtime and to go out and get more business. But driving a truck was much harder and rougher on me. On real cold and raw days, I tell you, I feel sorry for a lot of fellows. It isn't easy handling a big truck on icy streets, and it can get on your nerves and shake you up. Then there's the lifting and sometimes that's rugged too. And to top it off, if the boss is on a man's tail, it can get you. Like I said, it was just about beginning to get me. Every winter, I started getting rheumatism. But there you are, this is all the work you've done all your life except odd jobs you had when you were a kid. What else can a man do but go along and make the best of it. And then if his wife goes off her head as a few of the wives of express men have, or if his marriage goes haywire, or if a man's kid turns out bad, where is he, what's he got? Ahead of him is his old age. And when things like these happen, then old age is a mighty bleak thing to look forward to.

I told you about Simon Murray, I believe. He had to retire at seventy, and now he works five nights a week as a night watchman because he can't live on his pension. So what I am driving at is this. What else is there but the company for many of the old-timers?

That's what I mean about them and about sentiment. Willie Collins is that way. Along with Simon and some of the other men in the supervision, he got a bad break years ago back in the depression. Simon, Willie, and ten others were demoted. Willie and Simon were put to driving tractors, and the others were sent out on the trucks or else put on tractors. And Willie never got over it. Once he was a boss, and he sat up in the Wagon Call Department, dispatching special trucks. We used to call them gascars in those days. He lorded it over everybody as if he was better than they. His title was Chief Wagon Dispatcher, but it didn't mean no more pay for him. It was an empty title, but Willie acted as if it made him better than the rest of the supervisors. I don't know how the Dispatcher in charge of special trucks got that empty title but what I think is that Gashouse McGinty, may the Lord have mercy on his soul, just appropriated it to himself. He was another one of those guys who tried to make himself more important than he was and he played big shot just like poor Willie Collins did. So when Willie got demoted, it was pathetic. He thought it was just temporary. As soon as things cleared up and there was a pickup in business, he used to say he would be back up there on top in supervision. Somebody had made a mistake and just didn't understand or else he never would have been demoted, depression or no depression. And if Patsy McLaughlin, the old Superintendent of the Wagon Department had been around, it never could have happened because he always claimed that he was Patsy's boy and right-hand man. This, of course, wasn't true, and Patsy was dead. I remember once not long after Patsy died when Willie said that Patsy must be turning in his grave because Patsy's ace Willie Collins had been put to driving a tractor. That was many years ago, but today he thinks and talks the same way. He's now been driving a tractor for over twenty years, but he still talks about how good he was as a Dispatcher and he's still waiting to be one again. He keeps complaining about it and explaining how they made a mistake in doing this to him, and he never changes his record or his tune. It would really be funny if it wasn't so pathetic. He takes a lot of needling on this. The younger fellows, in particular, laugh at him. One of them, Tom Jones, will talk to him deadpan, telling him that he was the best damned Dispatcher there ever was in the business and here they have him driving a tractor, and Willie will unburden himself and then Tom will go off and tell the story to his own cronies and they have a good time laughing at Willie's expense. Yes, I feel sorry for the poor guy. Even though he was hell to work for, still he did get a tough break and I don't like to see anyone get that. Nobody else's tough breaks do me any good.

It was ironic, too, what happened to Willie in the old days. He and Gashouse McGinty always hated each other's guts.

Day in and day out, when they both worked in the Wagon Call Department, they would be at each other's throat. There was no love lost between Willie and Mac, not them two. And then what happened to Willie when he was demoted but that he was put on a tractor and set to working for McGinty, who was on the tractor board in charge of the tractors and dispatching them. I still get a laugh out of this, and even though I don't like to laugh at someone who got a bad break, I still get a kick out of this when I remember it and think of Willie and poor old Mac.

Every morning, Willie drove his tractor from the garage into the Atlantic Depot and then had to call McGinty at the board in the Wagon Call Department for his instructions. And every morning Mac would order him to drive over and go up to the Call Department. Then Willie would obey his orders, troop upstairs to the Department, the same one where he had worked as Chief Dispatcher, and had tried to lord it over everyone.

"Hello Willie, how's the old lady," Mac would say just as if he cared.

"Oh, she's all right," Willie would say.

"I hear you sent her out doing domestic work for the guineas or niggers."

Willie couldn't come back at Mac as he used to when they were both in the supervision, so he would just clam up.

"What do you want me to do, Boss?" Willie would ask, but he would use the word Boss in such a way as to let McGinty know what he really thought of him.

And Mac would hand Willie the can and say:

"Here Willie, go out and get me some coffee."

That burned Willie up. But what Mac was doing was to treat Willie the same as the way Willie treated his clerks when Willie was a boss.

And after Mac got sick and couldn't work any more, then Casey got his place. That was even more of a humiliation because Casey used to be Willie's sheet clerk, keeping the records of the movements of Willie's trucks. And there was Casey, Willie's boss. When he was a clerk, Casey sucked up to Willie, but when the tables were turned, Casey treated Willie the same way as McGinty had, only Casey didn't kid him by making insulting jokes about his wife. But just like McGinty, Casey brought Willie over the first thing in the morning, and sent him out for coffee.

Only the other morning, I saw Willie. He comes up to me, and I heard his same pathetic refrain that I've heard from him for years.

"Say, I hear they're going to be making some changes."

"I haven't heard anything, Willie," I said.

"You haven't? That's funny because I hear that they're going to make some promotions."

"No, Willie, I didn't hear nothin' about it."

"Well they are, and I got it straight from the horse's mouth. Say, Bill, do you think I got a chance?"

"I don't know why not," I said to Willie, knowing full well that he has as much chance of being taken back in the supervision as I have of being offered a contract to play ball with the New York Yankees.

But who am I to tell him, and if I did, what good would it do? He wouldn't believe me and he'd only get sore or have his feelings hurt. All of these years he has gone on thinking that his demotion was only temporary and telling him otherwise and convincing him would be almost like seeing some kid on the street, sucking on a lollipop, and going up to the kid and snatching it out of his mouth.

"You know, Bill, it was a terrible mistake they made, knocking me off," Willie told me. "I was one of the best men Patsy McLaughlin had and if he had of still been Super, it never would have happened. But I ain't complainin'. I can take the good breaks the same as I take the bad ones. Only, I say, I've been in this business too long to be driving a tractor.

I know this business. You were around in the old days years ago and you know I was good, don't you, Bill?"

"Yes, Willie, I do."

It was like a phonograph record. In fact I hear Willie sing the blues like this so much, it sounds like a record, a cracked and scratched one.

"What do those high muckety-mucks they now got over us, what do they know? How could they know what a good express man is? Some of them are no damned good themselves."

By this time, I wanted to get away from him but he had me buttonholed.

"You remember me in them days, Bill. You remember I was good."

"Yes, Willie. And come to think of it, I think that there is going to be two Dispatcher jobs open. You know O'Toole and Doren are retiring. They're going on pensions."

He leans forward and looks up at me and gives me a shower bath as he asks me quickly:

"Do you think they'll take me back?"

"You can never tell."

"You ought to put in a good word for me, Bill. After all, you worked for me sometimes in the old days and you know what I am like. And I knew your old man. He was as fine a man as I ever knew."

"Of course, Willie, it ain't up to me. I only work here like everybody else."

"I know, but if you get a chance, put in a word, you know."

I felt really sorry for him. It seemed strange to me; here I was, a Route Inspector, and there was Willie, and he was a Dispatcher and in the supervision when I was a clerk and a young fellow on the extra list without enough seniority to have a truck myself. And he was asking me to put in a good word for him. I was too sorry for him to pull his leg the way a lot of them do. I watched him getting on his tractor and driving out of the depot. He looked like such a pathetic little guy. They used to say that if he was any smaller, he'd be a midget.

And I'm damned sure he had the same conversation with every Dispatcher or Route Inspector he could buttonhole. He doesn't hardly talk about anything else.

Willie takes it hard. And Heinie is taking it hard.

They're old-timers. That's what I mean about old-timers. I don't want to be like them; I don't want the same thing to happen to me that happened to them.

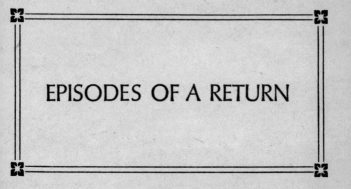

EPISODES OF A RETURN

I

—*Chicago*.

He was always returning to Chicago, Eddie Ryan thought, as he looked out of the window of the apartment on North State Street. And he always would be until . . . until when? One return would be his last. There is a last time, known or unknown to everything. But a man didn't have to be a slave to this fact. Until that last time, man was above death, free of it.

Eddie walked into the kitchen and poured himself another cup of coffee. Then he added cream and sugar and carried it back to the desk in the other room.

He stared at the paper in the typewriter. He was making notes for his speech tonight. The papers of Sherwood Anderson were being opened to the public and he had been invited to Chicago to speak at the ceremonies.

Back in the days when he had worked as a clerk for the Express Company, he had dreamed of coming back to Chicago a famous man.

Eddie typed a few lines and stopped. He leaned back in the

chair and sipped his coffee. He had written enough notes, the speech would go well.

He sighed and stared at the books on his desk. Thorstein Veblen. He remembered when he had first read Veblen. At the time he had been a student at the University of Chicago and working in a filling station. Veblen's book had stimulated him. He had been both outraged at the things wrong in the world and excited by the wonder of ideas.

Now Veblen was dead. But Veblen had been dead then. He himself was almost forty-five. He thought of death more often when he was in Chicago.

Tonight he would be paying honor to a dead writer. There would be a dinner at the Drake Hotel first and then his speech. His friends would be in the audience. And Olive. Pat Cullen would be there too.

—*Olive.*

He remembered last summer. He had been in Chicago for another speech. She had come to see him in his hotel room. He had kissed her passionately but had stopped because of Gordon. The next night they had sat next to each other in a group having dinner. She had pressed her leg against his.

He would be seeing her again tonight. Maybe they could come back here; he would be staying in this apartment for five days. It belonged to the library.

He felt a pang of guilt. He thought of Phyllis, his wife. And Gordon, her husband and his friend. But Olive and Gordon were almost washed up. Besides, there didn't have to be a permanent disruption. But after they went to bed, then what?

A shadow crossed Eddie Ryan's face. What if Pat Cullen saw them together? Eddie could hear him:

—Same old Eddie Ryan.

Clement Johnson would be there tonight with his wife, Patty. Clement had had two strokes and was paralyzed. Eddie had known Patty slightly, back in the old days. She was Beth Donovan's cousin. Eddie had suggested to Patty that she bring Beth along tonight. Years ago, he had been in love with

Beth but she hadn't even noticed him. He had asked her to go out with him once. She had laughed.

Why had he suggested that Patty bring her?

He glanced out the window. It was getting dark. He finished his coffee. It was cold. He got up, took the cup into the kitchen, and walked into the other room to get dressed.

II

Eddie Ryan looked around at the group in the private dining room of the Drake Hotel. His brothers Jack and Luke were there. They were both Route Inspectors at the Express Company now. Their wives, Molly and Florence, were with them. His sister, Clara, and her husband, Jack Boyle, were there. He saw Olive and Gordon. There were about twenty people seated at the table. Eddie sat next to a grey-haired woman. She was the wife of one of the trustees. She was talking to a bald-headed man on the other side of her.

He could hear laughter from the other end of the table.

"He is Gorgeous Jack," his sister, Clara, said in a loud voice.

A few of those at his end seemed to stiffen in disapproval. Eddie was amused; he could hear Clara laughing.

"I understand you are from Chicago, Mr. Ryan," said the wife of the trustee sitting beside him.

"Yes, I come from the South Side."

He could still hear them laughing and talking at the other end. Then Luke broke out in a loud laugh.

"You're seeing butterflies, Boyle," he said.

Eddie smiled; this was a family expression.

"I'm sure Chicago has changed a great deal since you lived here, Mr. Ryan."

"Yes it has; I left many years ago."

"But you keep coming back, Ed," Lawrence Ducket called over. He was head of the library.

"I enjoy coming back to visit, Lawrence."

"Of course you do; Chicago's in your blood."

There was another burst of laughter from the other end of the table.

"The vitality of your writing comes from Chicago, not New York. We'll get you back yet," Lawrence went on.

"Have you ever thought of returning to Chicago permanently, Mr. Ryan?" Hannah Slaughter, the Chicago *Choice* critic, asked. She was a plump, elegant woman in her well-preserved fifties.

"No, not seriously."

Eddie could hear the sound of talk at the other end of the table. He wished he had been placed down there.

"Do you get nervous when you give a speech, Mr. Ryan?" Hannah Slaughter asked.

"No, not any more."

"I suppose you've had a great deal of experience," the trustee's wife said.

"Yes, but sometimes I think I talk too much."

"Why, you've hardly said a word during dinner."

"Hey, waiter, bring us another pitcher of beer," Eddie heard Jack Boyle say. The family was having a good time.

"It's nice you could come speak," the trustee's wife was saying.

"I'm glad I could," Eddie responded politely.

He noticed Olive; she looked very pretty. Gordon was sitting next to her. He looked grey, his face wreathed in weariness. Olive looked up. Catching his eye, she smiled.

—She wants me as much as I want her, Eddie decided.

III

The applause was loud and prolonged. Eddie smiled shyly. After the applause had died down, a few people gathered around him. Others waited to speak to him in the hall. Many of his old friends were there.

On the back row was Clement Johnson and his wife, Patty, on one side; Pat Cullen on the other. Pat was still fat and his face wore the same beaming smile that Eddie remembered, except now there were jowls.

It took him about ten minutes to edge over to where they stood.

"Thank you, Eddie, for inviting us," Olive said.

"Yes, Eddie," Gordon spoke slowly, "it was good."

"You liked it?"

"It was wonderful. And thank you for having us invited to the dinner," Olive spoke in a low, quiet way.

"We'd like to see you before you go back if you aren't too busy, Eddie," Gordon said.

"I want to see you, too," Eddie answered. A flood of sympathy for Gordon rose in him. He looked at them, Gordon and Olive. They had trapped each other in unhappiness. Gordon was tired, worn out, from the battle of life and the age difference between them had widened.

"How about coming to dinner tomorrow night?" Gordon asked.

"I'm seeing my family. Why don't you come? You would both be welcome; it's just a family party."

"Gee thanks but we both can't come. One of us has to stay home with Morris. Olive can come though."

Eddie looked at her, a question in his eyes.

"I'd love to," Olive said.

Eddie set a time to meet her and then shook hands with Gordon, who said they had better be getting home. They lived way out in Evanston and he was pretty tired. Eddie kissed Olive goodbye. Then he walked over to Clement and Patty Johnson, and Pat Cullen. For a minute they all stood and grinned at each other; none of them knew what to say. Eddie hadn't seen Pat Cullen for over fifteen years. He had visited Clement and Patty last summer right after he had learned of Clement's stroke.

"I liked your speech, Eddie," Patty said, staring at him intensely.

"Thank you."

"We're getting ready to go. Why don't you come with us?" Pat Cullen suggested.

"Gee, I don't know; I half-promised to have coffee with my brothers and sister."

"Aw come on. Hell, it's been years since we seen you."

A tall chestnut-haired woman joined them. Eddie had noticed her earlier. He realized that she had been sitting beside Pat Cullen while he had been speaking; she must be his wife, he thought. Pat introduced her; her name was Edith.

Peter Moore, whom Eddie had known around Fifty-eighth Street, walked up.

Eddie decided to go out to Clement's with them. Peter said that he would come along too, he would follow them in his car. Eddie drove out in Pat Cullen's car. He found it strange to be with them after all these years. He remembered the fellow who had written him saying he had served in Arkansas with Pat Cullen during the war. The fellow had written that when Pat got drunk, he would say that Eddie Ryan was the best damned writer in the world.

"What happened to your brothers, Pat?" he asked.

"My kid brother's a lawyer; he's doing O.K. My older brother's doing all right, too. He's an executive. Mother passed away; I suppose you knew that."

"Yes, I was sorry to hear it. Clement and Patty told me last summer."

The car shot on. They talked of old times and what had happened to friends of high school days. Patty Johnson was sitting next to him. Her leg kept rubbing against his. He wondered if this were accidental. He thought of last summer and Frances' leg under the table.

"Remember this, Eddie?" Pat Cullen asked; they were in Jackson Park.

"Oh yes, I was out this way—I guess it's been about four years. I saw Laurence Reilly and Pat Devlin," Eddie said.

"You never looked me up," Pat said, an accusing note in his voice.

They were passing the Jackson Park bathing beach. The lake was rough. White-capped waves piled in against the snow-covered shore. Patches of snow looked blue under the glare of the full moon. As Eddie looked out, he felt the pressure of Patty's leg against his.

They drove on out to the large three-story building where the Johnsons lived. They lived in a large apartment on the first floor. Eddie noticed how Clement dragged his leg when he walked. Eddie remembered his visit last summer. He had sat for hours talking to them, mostly to Patty, because Clement had difficulty talking and could not always make himself understood.

Clement's family had been well heeled and he must have gotten a good inheritance from his father. They had had a family paper delivery business in South Shore which had been prosperous back in their high school days, and still was. Clement owned half of it but he wasn't able to do any work. He received enough income so that he and Patty could live according to the standard they had known. And thus they lived, while Clement waited to die. There were two boys; but death shadows stretched across their home. Eddie had sensed this last summer.

Patty asked what everyone wanted to drink. Eddie and Peter both said that they'd like a soft drink. The others asked for highballs. Clement said he might have one too since this was a special occasion. Patty warned him not to.

"Oh let him have one, Patty," Pat Cullen said.

She gave a slight shrug of the shoulders and went to mix the drinks.

"We've met, haven't we, Peter? Moore, isn't it?" Pat asked.

"Yes, years ago, with Eddie."

No one said anything. Eddie was quiet too, willing to let the others talk. He knew that any closeness he had felt to Clement and Pat had long since been washed away. Greater than the distance in time was the distance in thought. Clement and Pat both lived in a world which was a continuation of their old one.

Patty served the drinks. Her red hair was fading but it hadn't lost all of its glistening quality.

"Eddie?" Pat said, expecting him to say something.

"I'm glad we could all get together," Eddie said.

"Yyy-e-s. It's goood," Clement said in a halting way. There was embarrassment among them. The right side of his face was twisted. His withered right hand lay on his thigh, pitiful and lifeless.

"How have you been feeling, Clement?" Eddie asked.

"He hasn't been too well," Patty said.

Clement shook his head.

"All right," he managed to say.

Eddie thought of Clement wasting through his days from year to year, cared for like a baby. Sitting around, looking at television, listening to radio. Clement had said last summer that he didn't read much. He was devoid of inner resources and helpless in the face of his own tragedy.

"What I want to know," Pat Cullen said, "yes, what I want to know is this—what about Ryan's love life?"

Pat was watching Eddie closely. Eddie met his gaze head on. There was antagonism in Pat's stare.

"Not much to tell," Eddie said.

"Don't horse us," Pat said.

"Sorry, Pat, but there isn't a hell of a lot to tell."

"Aw, don't hand us that, Ryan," Pat persisted.

"Well maybe there isn't, Pat," his wife, Edith, said.

"He can't make me believe that. He's holding out on us." Pat laughed. His hostility seemed to have vanished.

"Tell me about yourself, Pat. What's happened to you during all these years?"

"I'm still selling oil for Rock Oil. I was promoted when I came out of the Army. I'm sales manager for this whole area now. I ain't doin' so bad."

"Where are you living?"

"Same place, Seventy-third and Jeffrey."

Eddie was silent. There wasn't much for Pat and him to say to each other.

"How did you like it in the Army?"

"Oh, it was O.K." Pat turned to his wife. "Wasn't it, honey?"

"I liked it but not as much as living here. But then who wouldn't rather live in Chicago than in Arkansas?"

"I imagine anyone from Chicago would find Arkansas pretty hard to take," Peter Moore said, obviously trying to make conversation.

"Sometimes I think any place, any place at all, would be a good place to go," Patty burst out.

Pat looked at her critically.

"Who wants another drink?" she asked, jumping up from her chair.

Pat held out his empty glass. He sat back in his chair, a contented beam on his face. Eddie remembered Pat, years ago, smiling in the same way.

"One thing I never liked, Eddie," Pat Cullen began.

"What's that?"

"All those stories about how poor you were when you were a kid. You weren't poor."

"I'm not responsible for everything that's written about me," Ed explained.

Patty handed Pat a fresh drink. He took a quick gulp.

"I was in your grandmother's house," Pat continued. "You weren't poor."

"I know, Pat. My father was poor, but . . ."

"You weren't poor and that wasn't any slum neighborhood we lived in."

"I never said that it was."

"I don't like stories like that. I don't like them at all." Pat's tone was belligerent.

"Tell me about your job, Pat," Eddie said, trying to change the subject.

"Oh, Pat has a good job," his wife said.

Pat finished his second drink. Patty jumped up to get him another one. The talk continued in the same vein. At one point, Clement mumbled something but no one could understand him but Patty.

"He's saying," she explained, "that he remembers Eddie's home and that Eddie wasn't poor."

"See, that's what I said," Pat declared.

He gulped down his drink and held out his empty glass again. He started talking about a gambling game he'd been in, in a hotel room on the Loop.

Patty brought him another drink. He took a big swallow.

A famous ball player who was retired had been in the game. He was in the Baseball Hall of Fame.

"He was chicken," Pat said, his voice thick. He told them how the ex-ball player had welshed. Then he mentioned one of their old classmates, Karl Rozinski.

"He was a furious Polish patriot," Eddie said, smiling.

"He borrowed five bucks from me and never paid me back. He tried to borrow from everybody in our class. I'm surprised he never wrote you for a touch."

"He didn't. I saw him once, years ago, on the I.C. right after our graduation, but I haven't seen or heard from him since."

"That sad-puss Brown; he's another one. Remember when

he was treasurer of our frat? The money was never accounted for."

"Yes," Eddie said.

"He came out to the house once," Pat said, turning toward his wife. "Remember, Edith?"

"I think so."

"I gave him five bucks but I knew I'd never get it back. And I didn't."

Pat Cullen was getting drunk.

"Ryan," he said, swaying in his chair.

"Yes?"

"Are you a Red?" Drunken anger was beginning in his voice.

Eddie raised his eyebrows and looked at him. Pat stood up, holding his half-drunk highball. He was swaying slightly.

"You are a Red, aren't you?"

"No, Pat, I'm not."

"Don't hand me that, Ryan."

Peter Moore stood up.

"You know, Ed, I've got to be going. It's getting late."

"I'll have to be going too," Eddie said. "Clement looks tired. It's been a long day."

They all got up and started saying good night. Patty brought their coats in. Clement sat, staring at them. Eddie wondered what he was thinking.

"Call me, Eddie, please," Patty said in a soft whispering voice.

"I will, Patty, and thank you very much."

The four of them stood for a moment on the sidewalk. It was icy. Pat's head was wobbling. Eddie looked toward the house. Patty and Clement were standing, looking out at them from their parlor window.

Pat gave Eddie their telephone number and asked him to call. Eddie said he would if he had a chance. He shook hands and turned to follow Peter Moore to his car, which was parked at the curb. As Eddie got in, he saw Edith take Pat's arm and lead him to their car. Peter started his car and drove Eddie to the North Side apartment where he was staying.

IV

The next night, after dinner, Luke and Florence had driven Eddie and Olive to the near North Side. They had chatted idly, riding in Luke's Chevrolet. It was a clear, crisp night. Eddie and Olive were sitting in the back seat; he held her hand.

Luke had suggested letting Olive off at Randolph Street where she could take the elevated train to Evanston. But Eddie had said no, that he and Olive would like to get a cup of coffee. There was a restaurant about a block from his apartment where they could get it; and she could take a cab home later.

When they reached the apartment, he and Olive had gotten out. No one said anything more about getting a cup of coffee. Eddie imagined that Luke and Florence had suspected.

This had been coming for five or six years; ever since he had met Olive. She and Gordon were married already and were living in New York. Olive had been working at night as a secretary for a motion picture firm. She was trying to raise money for Gordon's defense. He had been jailed as a Trotskyite on the charge of violating the Smith Act. Eddie had liked her from the very beginning.

Now, she and Gordon were living in Chicago and Gordon was a tired radical. His brothers had loaned him money to set himself up in a taxi-limousine business. But he was losing money and sooner or later he would either have to sell out or go bankrupt. He worked nights at one of the stands; and Olive stayed home alone, feeling that life was passing her by. She practically never went out.

Eddie had been surprised the first time she had spoken of her dissatisfaction in her life with Gordon.

V

Once inside the apartment, Eddie helped Olive off with her coat. He dropped it and his coat on a couch in the living room.

Eddie felt some guilt about Phyllis but his home was hell for him. Were it not for his son, he would have left long ago. All the way out to Chicago on the train, he had imagined being alone with Olive.

He walked into the kitchen, turned on the light, and moved toward the stove. Olive went to him with open arms. He kissed her, led her to the bedroom. They made love.

Later, they sat at the kitchen table, drinking coffee. Olive had put her clothes back on; Eddie sat with his shirt collar open. He puffed on a cigarette, content and quiet. She watched him, her blue eyes bright. It had been good between them.

He thought about Gordon. He didn't feel that he had betrayed a friend. Olive and Gordon were breaking up and had been for the last few years.

"You're very pretty, Olive."

"I'm too thin."

He smiled.

"Your smile. I love it," she said.

"I was smiling at what you said."

"Why?"

"A year ago, you wouldn't have discussed the subject of whether you were too thin or not too thin."

"I know." A shy smile broke across her face. "I didn't know if you cared."

"You knew I did. I knew you did."

"How?"

"Your letters."

"I feel good when I start a letter to you and type the words 'Dearest Eddie.' I felt the same way when I wrote you. And I knew that someday you'd hold me."

There was love in her voice. Love for him.

Olive spoke again.

"Do you feel guilty because of Gordon? Well, don't. There's nothing between us. He comes home and sits, tired out. He hardly even talks to me, much less takes me out."

There it was. The denunciation of Gordon. He had hoped he could prevent this.

"He's a hell of a nice guy, Olive."

"I don't say he isn't. He's too nice. He doesn't care any more."

"Maybe he's given up."

She sat up straight. Her face became thoughtful.

"Why do you say that?"

"Because I'm afraid he has," Eddie said.

"He doesn't look forward to anything any more, not with me, at any rate. I'm just there—his old carpet slippers."

Eddie didn't say anything.

"I don't know what I'm going to do. Tonight makes me afraid."

"Why? Don't be afraid. I would never run away from the consequences of what I do."

"It's not that. I'm just afraid."

"Why, dear? What are you afraid of?"

She didn't answer immediately. She fiddled with a cigarette for a moment. Then she put it in her mouth. He lit it. She took a deep puff.

"I'm afraid. I had thought that this part of my life was over —behind me. And now I know it isn't. What will I do?"

They sat, not speaking.

"That's why I've been so hesitant. I've been wanting to make love to you for a long time, darling," he said.

"And I wanted you to, Eddie. It was wonderful but . . ."

Reaching over, he touched her hand. Hers was thin, long, and very white. She squeezed his hand tightly for a moment.

"I don't know what I'm going to do. Tonight makes me afraid."

He looked at her. She was almost beautiful. She had such clear skin and lovely blond hair. He remembered Pat Cullen's question about his love life. He smiled.

"What are you smiling about now?"

"I love beautiful women."

"Many of them?"

He smiled at her. Her glance wandered. She saw snow fluttering outside the darkness of the kitchen window.

"Oh, it's snowing. It's night and it's snowing. We're all alone in Chicago. Chicago is asleep."

Suddenly, looking at her watch, she said nervously:

"I have to go, Eddie. It's almost two o'clock."

"I'll put you in a cab."

"You don't have to."

"I'm going to."

He pulled out his wallet and handed her three one-dollar bills.

"Is that enough for your fare?"

"Yes," she answered self-consciously. Then she smiled at him with affection.

"Thank you, Eddie."

They got up. Taking her in his arms, he kissed her again. No matter what happened, she had been his. And it had been clean and good.

"I have to go, Eddie."

"I'll get ready."

In a moment, he was ready to go out. He reached into his

pocket to be sure he had the key. They left the apartment quietly.

Snow came down, covering the dreariness of the decaying buildings on North State Street.

"It's beautiful," she said.

Tonight was important for them. This scene—the snow, the transformation of decay—it was part of the importance. The dark brick buildings, the stores with their old fronts, a flash of moonlight on exposed streetcar track, the white snow —some of the wet flakes hitting their faces, anonymous automobiles, silent falling snow, and the contented inner harmony he felt. All of this. Woman was the source and model of beauty. Olive had been for him tonight.

"It's so late, Eddie."

"Do you want me to go home with you?"

"Why?" she asked, surprised.

"In case Gordon is angry."

"Eddie, he'll be snoring. He won't even know what time I got home."

Eddie saw a cab and hailed it. They walked across the street, Olive clinging to his arm.

"When will I see you again?" he asked.

"I don't know."

"I'll phone you tomorrow."

She put her lips out to be kissed.

"Good night, Eddie."

She got in the cab. It was off, out of sight.

He stood there for a moment, feeling sad. She was gone. The scene was now wrapped in a soft strangeness. Big white flakes of snow covered the street. The buildings were thick black shapes. Through the swinging veil of falling snow, the sky was deep blue.

—Tell us about your love life, Ryan.

He could hear Pat Cullen's drunken voice.

He went inside, remembering how desperately alone he

had been here in Chicago, how he had wanted girls, and how he had been rejected by them.

And now?

Olive loved him.

But not forever.

He went to bed.

VI

Patty sat beside him at a round table. They were in a large restaurant and bar across from the library. It was dark outside.

Her face looked torn. Her lips were tight.

Eddie waited for her to talk. She had insisted on seeing him. He knew why. Her leg touched his. He allowed it to rest against his calf. His eyes wandered about the place.

"You didn't want to see me, Eddie," her voice was accusing.

"That's not true, my dear. I'm very busy."

"I go to bed with Clement. He's not impotent," she said tensely. Her voice throbbed with bitterness.

How grotesque Clement must be naked with his withered arm, his useless leg, his twisted lips, and his despairing soul. Reduced to being her baby and making love to her at the same time.

"I've thought of you a lot, Eddie, since you were here last summer."

She was upset. No, it was more than that. She was torn apart, reduced to a hunger which hurt her.

"Yes, of course."

When the waitress came, she asked for a martini. Eddie asked for a cup of coffee. They did not talk. Eddie could hear some men nearby talking about business.

"What do you think of me?"

Before he could say anything, she spoke again.

"Don't pity me."

"I didn't say I pitied you."

But he did. Patty was more trapped than Olive. Olive had trapped herself. She pressed his leg and looked at him with intense eyes.

"Could you love me?"

"No, Patty."

"Do you want to go to bed with me?"

"It wouldn't be right."

"I didn't say I would. I asked you if you wanted to. I get all I need at home."

Eddie didn't know what to say. He lit a cigarette.

"Well, why don't you say something?"

"I'm thinking. I want to be sure of what I say."

"Are you afraid to go to bed with me?"

He took her hand.

"Patty, it won't do any good. I have a wife. And children."

"So have I. And I'm a good wife and a good mother, too."

"I know you are, Patty. And I have an idea how hard it must be for you sometimes."

"What have I got to live for, Eddie?"

"Patty, there's nothing I can say. You've had a terrible thing happen to you."

"Clement's all right here," she pointed to her fading reddish hair.

"I know."

"He can't talk much but I can understand him. He was so excited the other night when you came out with Pat."

"I suppose so. Seeing Pat and me together probably brought back old days to him."

"Pat's different. Clement wants to get drunk with him but he's not supposed to drink. It raises his blood pressure. And he always gets sick the next day. I can't go out and leave him. His mother is with him now. She doesn't like what I do. What

I do! That's a laugh. I dress him. I undress him. I shave him. I do everything."

The bitterness in her voice was as understandable as it was terrible.

"I love him," she said but her voice contradicted her words.

"Patty, it's terrible that this happened to Clement."

"What about me?" she asked angrily.

"Both of you."

"I was young when this happened." There was no bitterness or anger in her voice now.

"I was a virgin when I married him. He was the most wonderful man in the world. When I married him, he wasn't a man, he was a boy. And what did I know?"

"Yes," Eddie said. There was little he could say.

"Look what happens to love." She was sitting stiffly.

"Overnight, he had a stroke. In a minute. Right on the street. They thought he was going to die. And five years ago, he had a second one. I had gone out. I went to see my mother. When I got home, there was an ambulance in front of the house. Now he sits around all day. I can't leave him alone. I'm afraid to. I'm afraid if I go out and there's no one there, he'll have another one. He could die."

Patty finished her drink. She looked at it.

The restaurant had become crowded. The sound of conversation was light and gay. A young girl wearing boots entered. Her youthful face was flushed from the cold. The part of her legs that showed caught Eddie's eye. The short fellow with her looked smug and confident.

"You aren't even interested," Patty said with despair in her voice.

"But I am, Patty. There's just nothing I can say."

She nodded her head but looked unconvinced.

"What do you really think of me, Eddie?"

"I like you, very much."

"Well, then, why wouldn't you go to bed with me?"

"It wouldn't help, Patty."

"You mean you don't want to."

"Patty, look at us, look at the circumstances of our lives." As he spoke, he remembered Olive telling him that she was afraid of the arousal of sexual desire. He had telephoned her today but she had said that she wouldn't be able to leave the house. Gordon wasn't home, Eddie knew this. Olive didn't want to see him again. He had been afraid of this.

"Patty, you could be hurt. It would solve nothing."

"What do you mean 'hurt'?"

Her face was bewildered and angry. There was nothing he could say to ease her hopelessness. Why shouldn't he take her back to the apartment? She was attractive. She appealed to him. And he would be leaving Chicago in two days. What would the circumstances be? What could they be? But he knew he couldn't.

"I'm not saying I would, Eddie. I'm merely asking. Would you want to?"

"It's impossible, Patty."

"Is something wrong with me? Am I ugly?"

"No."

"Then why, Eddie, why?"

"Patty, I know it must be hell for you. It must be a terrible problem."

"You're wrong, Eddie. I live a normal life. I told you. Clement sleeps with me."

He took her hand. She became calm. He realized that it was pointless to speak of the circumstances of her life directly.

"Clement's father had a stroke."

"Yes."

"He was always thinking about it. Even before he had one, he use to talk about it. I remember he talked about it on our honeymoon. We went to California. It's the only time

I traveled except when I went to college when I was a girl. But he spoke about it then, on our honeymoon."

"Can't he take training for the handicapped? There are plenty of things he could learn to do with his left hand."

"He can't."

"Why not?"

"He won't. He just doesn't feel he could. He can't concentrate except on baseball games or a television show, or poker. But when he plays poker, he drinks. He played about a month ago and came home drunk."

The bitterness had returned in her voice.

"I can understand . . ."

"Oh, sure, you can understand. Everybody can understand about poor Clement. But what about me? Can you understand me, Eddie, can you?"

"A little."

"Then tell me. Explain it to me. Why wouldn't it be right for us?"

"There could be consequences, Patty."

"You don't have to be afraid."

"I'm not afraid, dear. But what if we do? When I go away, then what? What about you?"

"I'm not asking you to sleep with me, Eddie. I'm only asking you if you want to."

"There's Clement."

Her face fell.

"Dear, you can't escape it, hopeless as it is."

"It's not hopeless," she said, her voice very low. He could hardly hear her.

"I'm not thinking of just Clement, Patty. You are caught. Caught by a tragedy. And I can't get you out, dear."

She was almost in tears.

"You'd sleep with anyone, an old whore even, but not with me."

He said nothing.

The glare in her eyes faded, and in its place, there was appeal.

"What am I to do, Eddie?"

"You'll go back home and take care of Clement and your family just as you have been. You'll go right on being the good wife and mother you are."

She didn't answer. She merely stared at him. He signaled for the waitress and paid the check. They walked out. There was a light snow fluttering in the air. The sidewalks were beginning to get slushy. Cars were lined up waiting for the Michigan Avenue light to turn green. Motorists jabbed their horns impatiently. People hurried along on the sidewalk. He took Patty's arm and guided her through the traffic, toward the Randolph Street I.C. Station. They stopped. He looked down at her, put his arms on her shoulders and kissed her.

"Goodbye, Patty."

She turned and strode away.

She was gone. A few snowflakes touched his cheeks and melted. He walked to Wabash Avenue. He walked slowly, thinking of the sad, tragic destiny of people.

Patty was going home, to a home that was a cemetery of love. And Olive was home, a seed of bitterness growing in her.

He lit a cigarette, and continued to walk slowly back toward the apartment.

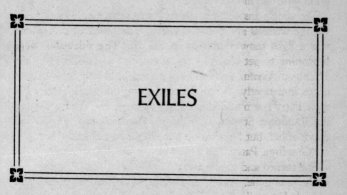

EXILES

Part One

It was a spring day in Paris. Tom Langley stood in front of the American Embassy, a gloomy look on his face. He took a package of Gauloises Jaune cigarettes from his pocket and lit one. Puffing on it, he watched a big black Cadillac with a C.D. license plate enter the driveway. He wondered who the big shot in the car was. A group of pretty young girls stood nearby. He heard one of them say in a gay voice:

"I know where we can go swimming right off the Rock of Gibraltar."

He smiled. He liked standing here listening to snatches of conversation in his own language. He didn't want to go back to the apartment, not yet. He didn't want to give Yvette the news. He was hurt. He knew that he should be angry but he was too hurt to be angry.

All of his hopes, his dreams—standing at the rail of an ocean liner with Yvette and pointing out the skyline of New York City, the Statue of Liberty.

—*Chérie*, this is my country.

Taking her to walk in Central Park as they had walked in the Tuilleries, the Jardin du Luxembourg, the Parc Monceau, introducing her to his friends, going on automobile trips across the country and discovering America together just as they had discovered so many places in Europe.

Tom Langley had come to love America since he had been living in Europe. He missed little things about it—hot dogs, baseball games, the slang, the nervous excitement of New York, even the bad cafeteria food, chocolate ice cream sodas, malted milks.

He lingered in front of the Embassy hoping that someone he knew would come by. There were people going and coming from the Annex next door; the PX was there.

He lit a second cigarette. He didn't want to go home; he didn't want to go any place; he didn't want to think. He stood, smoking and gazing about. Finally he walked away, turned the corner onto the Rue Royale, and wandered slowly away from the Place de la Concorde.

He dropped into a chair in a small cafe. He recalled the scene at the Embassy. He had walked down the long hall. Mr. Loring, the Vice Consul, had met him at the door; he had not invited Tom into his office. They had stood talking outside his door. Loring was a tall thin man beginning to get grey. Tom guessed that he was in his early forties but that was all he could make out about him. He would never be able to understand men like Loring, stiff, formal, and non-communicative. Loring had spoken in a monotone.

—Mr. Langley, no new evidence has been given us to warrant a change in my decision.

The scene stuck in Tom's mind—he and Loring standing in the long corridor, a corridor that seemed so clean, and so characterless. Tom's face clouded.

Loring had talked about the reasons that people were re-fused visas.

—According to the Act of . . .

Tom couldn't remember the year.

—And amended by the Act of March 1952, which makes citizens holding certain beliefs . . .

Again, Loring's exact words eluded him. Anyway, according to this act, certain people were ineligible. As a result, Yvette could not get a visa to visit the United States. He had to go back to the apartment and tell her. She was waiting. If he married her, it would probably be easier for her to get one. Why shouldn't he? They had been living together for over a year and they were happy.

His mind returned to the scene at the Embassy. He had tried to tell Loring that Yvette had never been a Communist.

—My conclusion is based on the information available, Mr. Langley.

—But it isn't true!

Tom had blurted this angrily. Loring had stood there, unmoved. In the face of Loring's impersonal manner, Tom had felt small and helpless. During the course of this case, Loring had at times given Tom the feeling that his love for Yvette was almost something to be guilty about, that love was a mark of personal weakness.

Tom sat, sipping coffee and smoking a cigarette. He looked out on the narrow street. Many people passed. Three girls walked by chatting gaily. One of them, a *petite* blonde burst out laughing; the other two joined her. They were obviously Americans. French pedestrians glanced at them as they walked on.

Idly, Tom watched the people along the sidewalk. It was as if he and the strangers he saw were together in a world of dreams. The street, the sidewalk, the cafe, he drinking his *café crème* which had become cold were all in a half-waking world. His mind was in a pleasant haze. He watched a little Frenchman in a shabby suit carrying a suitcase, two French girls in black suits with tight-fitting short skirts—one of them gesturing as she spoke. Another small Frenchman, this one wearing a suit jacket and trousers that didn't match, scratched his groin as he passed the cafe.

He should go back to the apartment. He didn't want to. The sun was warm. It was spring here in Paris, a beautiful spring. Yvette's fifty-five-year-old uncle had said the other day that this was the most beautiful spring he had ever seen in Paris.

It was spring in Paris and he and Yvette were in love.

What if he could never bring Yvette to America?

The question shocked Tom. For a moment he couldn't think. He could not believe this; he would not accept Loring's decision as final and irrevocable. There must be something he could do. This couldn't be happening; it was all a mistake. By some strange circumstances, he and Yvette were involved as victims in a Kafkaean world. But that was a world of fiction. These things could not happen in the real world. Kafka had not invented the American government.

He tapped a spoon against the glass to signal for the *garçon*. He paid for his coffee and walked toward the Madeleine.

II

Yvette was small and dark. When Tom walked into their apartment on the Rue de Bac, she embraced him tenderly.

"*Chéri, mon amour,*" she said softly, kissing him.

Holding her, he didn't know what to say. She drew away from him and looked at him closely.

"You look sad," she said, speaking in English.

"Kiss me, darling."

She kissed him again. They walked to the sofa and sat down, side by side.

"It is bad news, no?" she asked.

"We're out of luck."

"We are what?"

"Out of luck. Loring didn't even ask me into his office; he talked to me in the corridor. I might as well have been talking to a machine."

Her pretty face clouded.

"What did he say?"

"He gave me double talk."

"He gave you what?"

Tom hesitated for a moment; he was frustrated. He did not speak French well and Yvette's English was no better than his French. It was difficult to communicate. He was often aware of this frustration; there were so many things that they could not talk about.

"He spoke in the same way he writes letters. The answer is that you cannot get a visa."

"But what have I done, *chéri?*"

Tom shooked his head.

"He won't listen to me. No matter what I say, he remains unconvinced," he said.

"He is a beast-man, like the Nazis."

No, Tom thought, Loring was not a beast-man, nor was he a Nazi. He was merely a bureaucrat seeking a better post, a higher diplomatic rating, and he was afraid to take chances.

"He is a beast-man," Yvette repeated bitterly.

Tom reached out and took her hand.

"But what did I do, *chéri?*"

"It isn't you, darling."

"But I have always been anti-Communist. I was anti-Communist as a student; I am anti-Communist now. Everybody who knows me knows that I am anti-Communist and that I was, even before Stalin and Hitler, they make the pact."

She spoke as though she were trying to convince him. Didn't she know that he believed her?

"I know, *chérie.*"

They sat on the sofa holding hands. The room was quiet.

They did not hear the noisy sounds of Parisian traffic from the street.

"Oh *chéri*, why won't your . . . your government believe me?"

Tom didn't know how to answer her. They lapsed into silence again.

"Now you will not love me, perhaps," Yvette said.

"Don't say that, *chérie*. I will always love you, *toujours*."

But a doubt crept into his mind. If they were married she could probably get a visa. *Toujours*. Always. Why did he resist a permanent involvement with her? He had never loved anyone else the same way.

III

Tom thought of himself and his motives. He was thirty-six years old, taller than average, and good-looking. His father had been a dealer for a car company in Detroit, Michigan. Tom had worked for him after he had graduated from the University of Michigan, before he was drafted during the War.

He had been stationed in Texas. Florence Cather, the girl to whom he was engaged, had sent him some books by André Gide as a present. Gide had influenced him, influenced him as no other writer had. Tom realized that he was not adequately conscious of himself, of life.

By the time Tom Langley was released from the United States Army, he knew that he wanted to become a writer. He had alternating periods of self-confidence and of despair. There were times when he seemed to have two attitudes about every vital question that concerned him. But the intense desire to write was fundamental in his nature.

He had not been back in Detroit long when he realized that he did not want to marry Florence Cather. She was not sympathetic when he spoke of wanting to write. She was afraid to share the risks that he would have to take. He began to feel uneasy about her. Even when they made love, he felt this way. She was too middle-class, too conventional-minded, he thought, even though she had not hesitated to have a sexual relationship with him. He could not make a commitment, a permanent one, now. He had to learn more about himself and about others so that he could write.

Tom didn't know how to tell Florence that he wanted to end their engagement. He shrank from being blunt; he didn't want to hurt her.

He spent the entire morning brooding. He held imaginary conversations with her. He became depressed. What if her life were ruined? But what about his own life?

Tom and Florence quarreled the next weekend.

She began by accusing him of not appreciating her and what she was doing by going to a hotel with him. He lay beside her, stunned.

He could use this as an excuse to break the engagement. No, he couldn't do that. She was feeling guilty about their relationship; it was her conventional values. Tom tried to mollify her by being affectionate.

"Don't paw me," she said coldly.

He was hurt. She told him that he was selfish, that he thought only of himself.

". . . and you act like a pig at times," she had ended.

They had lain side by side, silent. The room had become oppressive. Tom had wanted to say something but he couldn't. Finally Florence had spoken.

"Tom?"

"Yes?"

"Let's make up."

She had cried. They had kissed and embraced. But Tom's hurt has remained.

Three months later, Florence abruptly ended their engagement. She told him that she loved someone else. They had been sitting in a restaurant after seeing a movie. Tom had had no forewarning and although he knew it was for the best, the immediate effect of her words had been almost shattering.

Tom had brooded for several weeks. He tried to write a story about himself and Florence but he couldn't. He sank into daydreams in which he became a great writer, proving to Florence that she had made a serious mistake.

One day, Tom Langley woke up.

—I'm being childish, he told himself.

A month later, he went to New York.

New York fascinated Tom; he had been to the city before but for only a week and he did not remember much from that visit. He thought of the writers and the would-be writers who had come here, high in hopes. He was following in their footsteps. He was making the same kind of struggle that they had made. He did not like to admit that he was excited; he tried to convince himself that he was blasé. And he tried to think of himself in terms of Freud, for this was the basis for the prevailing enlightenment.

Tom Langley was self-conscious and defensive about his ambitions. He wanted to dedicate himself to his writing but he masked his sincerity.

He settled in a small apartment in Greenwich Village. He wanted to start work immediately on a novel but he was unable to concentrate. He was lonely. In his loneliness, his self-confidence sank to a low ebb. He would take long walks and gaze at people, streets, and buildings. He felt removed, a stranger without roots.

Sometimes, at dusk, he would walk uptown. He wandered into Central Park or along the edges of the park. The buildings against the dramatic twilight sky were dark and towering, their shapes changing in the shifting light like a world of make-believe. A hunger for life and love would spring up within him; at times it was agony. But sometimes he would become so enraptured that he would lose awareness of the immediate world and feel an inward calm. He might as well have been in a quiet cathedral as in one of the noisiest cities of the world. Self-doubt, loneliness, a bitterness because of Florence's rejection—all had shaken his faith in people and in life. But the vista of buildings with sparkling lights against the dark, mute, and immobile stone gave him a restored, even though passing, faith.

Sometimes he would stare at the crowds on the street and daydream, making up stories and giving imaginary histories to the people who happened to catch his attention. Tom believed that he saw them with fresh eyes and insight but he was not able to articulate what he saw or what these insights were.

Lonely as he was those first days in New York, Tom had a feeling of freedom and hope. He was without ties. He could do what he wanted, write as he wished. There was for him a future filled with promise. He was already thirty-four years old but even so, there was time ahead for him. He was resolved not to waste this time.

And yet, he was not making progress with his work. He was alone too much. Tom Langley yearned for companionship.

Then, he began to meet people. There were others in New York who wanted to write. Some of them had already been published. And there were girls, girls who lived alone or with other girls. There were parties. And life. Tom fitted in with this life. It was different from the Bohemianism that he had heard of. Most of the people he met had jobs and some of them earned good salaries. Many of the girls worked in publishing offices or advertising agencies and they made enough money to dress well. He met one young writer who had gotten an advance of two thousand dollars for a novel.

Tom started going with Rose. She as a big, well-built, red-haired girl. Tom had met her at a party. It was on a Friday night. He had been brought to the party by a young critic named Michael Kartman. Kartman had a six-month-old son. Between exchanges on Freud and Marx, Kartman would remark that he might sound bourgeois, but he found his son interesting and liked to take the baby out on Sunday.

Tom did not know many of the people at the party, although he had seen a few of them before. He felt shy. Many of them seemed to have read a lot and he hesitated to say much lest he appear ignorant. The party was being given by a young couple in an old three-story brownstone house that they had rented in the Village. The crowd kept growing and getting noisier. Conversations were begun, interrupted, and left unfinished. Many of the people to whom Tom was introduced would ask him what he did. Out of shyness and a feeling that he had accomplished little, he would answer by saying he did nothing. This produced banal replies. He had been at a loss, not knowing what to say. The growing noise had begun to drum in his ears. He wanted to leave. He didn't belong here. He didn't belong any place.

"You look out of place," a girl had said to him.

At first Tom was surprised but he was glad that she had spoken to him. He had been aware of her standing nearby; she was a damned good-looking girl.

"Do I? I don't feel out of place."

"Well, you look lonely and sad. Why would you feel sad at a party?"

"I was just observing, quietly."

His remark sounded false and silly to him.

"The quiet type," she remarked.

Then she smiled. There was something in her smile that puzzled him.

"I don't know many of the people here," he said.

"Shy."

"I'm not shy," he said, feeling foolish.

"Aren't you enjoying yourself?"

"Of course I am."

They faced each other. Again her puzzling smile.

Tom offered her a cigarette and then took one himself. He lit a match. As she leaned forward for a light, her hair brushed his cheek. Tom had felt a tingling excitement. This had been his closest physical contact with a girl since coming to New York.

"What do you do?"

"Nothing but . . ."

"How can you get away with doing nothing? I wish I could."

"I was going to say that while I do nothing, I do . . ."

"You're the first man I've met who does nothing in I don't know how long. Doesn't it give you guilt?"

"No, not at all," Tom answered.

People were still milling and talking noisily all around them. They could hear the sound of jazz being played in another room. They drew back in a corner.

"You fascinate me," she said.

Tom had started to say that while he did nothing now, he intended to write. But her remark had given him a role in her eyes. He let himself slip into this role.

"You must not have had a Puritan childhood. Did you have a Puritanical upbringing?"

"No," he said.

"You don't know how lucky you are. Perhaps you won't end up on an analyst's couch. Are you in analysis?"

"No, I'm not; are you?"

"God yes, I go four times a week."

It had occurred to Tom that she was a bit screwy but then she was damned attractive and he was only talking to her.

"It's doing me good but right now I have a mad on against my analyst."

Tom looked at her. Would she let him? A warning came to mind; there was something about her. What was it? She was smiling at him again. It was her smile, that was it, her smile was puzzling to him. He smiled back.

"You have a nice smile," she said.

Tom threw caution to the winds. He took her home from the party and kissed her good night.

Three nights later, he took her to dinner. It was a spring night. Tom was filled with hope and the desire for love. He had taken Rose's arm as they had walked across the Square. They did not talk much; he couldn't think of anything to say. He gave up trying; they could talk later when they were in the restaurant. As they walked across Washington Square, he glanced at the Arch. He thought of the Arc de Triomphe. He had seen pictures of it. Some day, before he was too old, he would like to go to Paris.

The restaurant was crowded. They sat in the corner. Both of them liked the atmosphere of the place. They ordered martinis. As they sipped, they talked casually about the restaurant, the weather, and the party. Then they ordered dinner. As they ate, Tom told Rose that he wanted to write.

"Maybe I'll write some day too," she had said.

Tom thought of the two of them, having an affair, maybe falling in love, and beginning their literary careers together.

"Of course I would have to make more progress with my analysis first. Maybe analysis would help you write, too."

"I don't have any deep-seated problems," Tom said.

"Everybody has, nobody knows anything about themselves."

This depressed Tom. Suppose she was right?

"How long have you been going to your analyst?"

"A year."

"You ought to be through soon."

She gazed at him with contemptuous tolerance.

"I haven't scratched the surface of my unconscious."

"It must be a terrific expense."

"It's worth it. I was in a frightfully neurotic state when I went to Dr. Kreiker."

"You seem normal enough to me," he said.

"No I'm not, nobody is."

They spent over two hours eating, talking, and sitting through spells of silence when Rose's face would become expressionless. She seemed sad in these periods and Tom was touched.

He began to see Rose regularly. Sometimes she would kiss him and allow him to embrace her passionately but she refused further intimacies. He would walk home at twelve o'clock, one o'clock, two o'clock, tired and frustrated. He would get angry and decide never to see her again.

At times she would not want to be kissed at all.

"We don't have to do that, not tonight," she said one night as they sat on their sofa.

Rose liked to talk about her analysis. She told Tom that all her trouble stemmed from the death of her father when she was three. She couldn't remember him and her analysis, to date, had not brought forth any memory of him. Tom was certain that she discussed him with her analyst. This made him uneasy. A third person, unknown to him, was involved in his relationship with Rose. Eyes, unseen by him, peered at them as they lay in one another's arms and kissed; and other ears heard him when he excitedly pleaded with her to say yes.

Sometimes when he thought of this, he would become angry. She was using him. He was merely material for her, he angrily thought one night while he paced his room. A few moments later, as he sat in a chair smoking a cigarette, he wondered if he might also be using her as material. He was far from certain about his own sincerity. He should give her up.

The next day he phoned her and asked her to dinner. They

ate in an Italian restaurant. Later, they walked back to her apartment. She played *Don Giovanni* for him on her record player. He kissed her.

"Let's go to bed," she said.

IV

The next morning in his own apartment (Rose had not wanted him to spend the night) Tom had awakened at peace with himself. Lying in bed in a languorous mood, he thought of how much better he had felt with Rose than he had ever felt with Florence. He was glad that he had not given her up.

He continued to think of her as he ate his breakfast. It was as though last night had not ended; it continued to glow. He felt fulfilled.

All morning, Tom felt this way. He did little else but think of himself and Rose.

V

Rose became even more puzzling to Tom than she had been. He became, if anything, less sure of her. She was contradictory. One time she would respond passionately to his kisses; another time, she would be cold and aloof. He tried to understand her but his early doubts about her returned. He knew that they could not establish a stable relationship. Eventually they would have to break off.

He began to want a change; he thought of Paris. But he worried about leaving Rose. He didn't want to hurt her; yet he wanted to go alone. He decided to wait a little while and see what happened.

VI

Tom had not meant to say it. He had blurted it out impulsively.

"Let's go to Paris, Rose."

"I'd love to."

Instantly he was sorry. They had made love and were sitting in her living room having a drink.

"I always planned to go there some day," Rose said.

"When can you leave?"

"I don't know," she said.

"I'm fed up with New York; I think I'll write better in France."

Rose said nothing for a moment, then:

"But my analysis, I can't give it up now."

A vague smile crossed her face. Impulsively Tom leaned forward to kiss her.

"Let's not go into that again," she said coldly.

He felt awkward and clumsy.

When he left her apartment that night, Tom walked aimlessly for blocks. He thought of the two of them in Paris. They would sit in sidewalk cafes and they would see the art of the old world. They would walk in parks like the Luxembourg Gardens; he had heard so much about this park. He tried to visualize Paris and to see himself and Rose against the background of buildings, but it was difficult. And yet he didn't want to go without her. He had been lonely in New York and Rose had ended his loneliness. No human being was perfect. She through analysis and he through his efforts to write were both trying to change, to become better. Better in the sense of being more human and more true to themselves. Perhaps they could have a rich relationship.

VII

Two weeks later Rose ended their affair. He had tried to kiss her but she had stiffened up in his arms.

"I don't want to."

Excited and breathless, he had gazed at her. Her clothes were in disarray; her hair mussed. Calmly she rearranged her skirt and blouse, and then smoothed her hair.

"I understand myself better than you do, Tom. You aren't stable, we can't get married. I want to marry but I won't marry anyone who hasn't been analyzed."

She looked directly at him, her eyes probing.

"Are you hurt?"

Her question surprised him.

"No, I'm not precisely hurt."

"Good, then we can remain friends."

"Yes," he answered.

He wanted to get out of her apartment.

VIII

Five weeks later, Tom Langley sailed for Paris. He was eager and expectant. He would find himself. He tried to convince himself that he was as indifferent to Rose as he had been to Florence but Tom was hurt, and he was angry. Neither Rose nor Florence would ever know that he had rejected them first.

His week on the ocean was slow. He danced, played shuffleboard, flirted, read, and somewhat self-consciously played bingo at nights. He enjoyed the trip.

His first sight of Paris and its grey buildings was disappointing. It was different from what he had expected. It was confusing. And he felt so helpless when he tried to speak. He had studied French in college but he could not make himself understood. Nor could he understand anyone. This made him shy; he had to force himself to venture forth. He didn't know what he wanted to see and he didn't know what to think of what he did see.

One spring morning at the end of his first week in Paris, he was walking along the Left Bank. Ahead of him in the sunlight was the Cathedral of Notre Dame.

—It's beautiful.

Tom meant the city of Paris.

He lived in an inexpensive hotel on the Rue Jacob. Gradually he fell into an easy way of living. His writing improved. Florence and Rose both seemed to be part of a remote past.

Tom soon discovered that being lonely in Paris was different from being lonely in New York. Here he could sit in sidewalk cafes and stare at people and become dreamy. Time passed easily and slowly.

Then he began to meet people. He visited the St. Germain *quartier* where he met other Americans. A number of them were eccentric; many sported beards. How foolish he would feel wearing one, knowing that the only reason he did was because others did. He wondered what their beards meant to them. Did beards have a relationship to the existentialism which they always talked about?

The first bearded chap that Tom met was a tall young man named Joe. He was wearing dungarees and a khaki shirt open to expose an unusually hairy chest. His soft brown beard was full and bushy. He had small, dark eyes. There was a strange expression in them that Tom found disconcerting. Joe had overhead Tom asking for his bill at the Café Royal St. Germain. He had known that Tom was American and had walked over and sat down at the table. The first thing that Joe had said was:

"The French bourgeoisie is sabotaging a Customs Union in France. That's what the crisis is all about."

Tom was flabbergasted.

"It isn't the Russians; it's the French bourgeoisie," Joe went on.

"What?" Tom asked, not able to follow him.

"They are against a Customs Union and America supports them. That's behind the Cold War. The French bourgeoisie was gleeful that Wallace wasn't elected last year."

—He's a screwball, Tom thought.

Joe was interrupted by several others who joined them. A pretty girl named Ruth sat next to Tom. And there was a couple, both of whom wanted to write. The husband, David Steffel, was the son of an eminent Harvard professor. His wife, Dey, was plain-looking. They both kept saying that conditions for artistic creation were better in Paris than they were in America.

"You die spiritually in America," David said angrily.

"How is the novel coming along, Dave?" someone called out.

"I finished another chapter last week."

"What do you do?" Tom asked Ruth, ignoring the conversation of the others.

Tom waited for her to answer. She was the first girl he had spoken to in Paris.

"I'm a refugee from an analyst's couch," she said flippantly.

Tom thought of Rose. He wondered what she was doing. Just before he had sailed, he had learned that while she and he had been going together, she had also been having an affair with a young man who aspired to become a scenic designer on Broadway. There was a surge of bitterness in him but it passed almost as quickly as it had come.

"The French bourgeoisie . . ." Joe was saying.

"Do you speak French?" Tom asked Ruth.

"They do what the Americans tell them to do because the

Soviet Union isn't capitalist. It's Wall Street talking," David Steffel said, interrupting Joe.

"I only speak a pidgin taxicab driver and waiter's French," Ruth answered, laughing strangely.

"Are things as awful as ever in America?" an effeminate young man asked Tom.

Tom was taken aback. He didn't answer immediately.

"I have nothing to go back to, nothing but an analyst's couch," Ruth said, laughing strangely again.

"I don't know that things are so awful," Tom said to the effeminate young man.

"Look what they did to Wallace," a newcomer said.

"Why did you come here?" the effeminate young man asked Tom.

"To see France and Europe."

"I love Paris; it's wonderful," a blond girl said. She was small and boyish and she wore bluejeans.

Tom looked at Ruth intensely. She touched off desire but Tom decided that they were all screwballs. He rose, excused himself, and walked away. He wandered for blocks, lonely and reflective, wondering what he would find here in Paris. Later he sat in a cafe on the Boulevard St. Michel in the warm sunlight watching students pass on the crowded sidewalk. What did he expect to find in Paris? He wasn't sure that he knew. America seemed far away. The past became less vivid to him; he was entranced with Paris. He saw the harmony and beauty of the city. He thought of it as a monument that men had built over the course of centuries. There was a melancholy in the background of its passing, day-by-day, life.

One day, wandering about on the Right Bank, he came to the Parc Monceau. He walked in it. It seemed to belong to Paris. The park, the people, the buildings flanking it, the soft light of the afternoon—they all belonged together as parts of one composition. He sat on a chair and read. Then he put his book in a pocket and looked about. There were a number of mothers, grandmothers, and nurses with young children. The children were plump and obviously well fed. He remembered going to a party with Rose one night and listening to a friend of hers talk about the change in the children in Paris since 1945. Rose's friend had said that the children had been thin, underfed, and pale. When she had returned to Paris four years later, the children had looked different.

Tom thought of how France, and the French, had suffered during the War. He wished that he had been part of the liberating army which had entered Paris. Such wishes were vain. He watched three young mothers, all of them well dressed. One, a dark-haired girl with fine and sensitive features, was knitting. Hopelessness seemed to rest on her pretty face. He looked at the children. They were more quiet and more obedient than American children in a park. The women chatted in French with their children. He resolved to try to learn to speak the language. Why did these young mothers look so tired? Why did they sit with sorrow on their faces? Was this the result of the War?

He rose and left the park.

Tom met other Americans. One of his uncles had a friend, a man named Allison Brock who was in his fifties and who held an important post in E.C.A. administering the Marshall Plan. Allison Brock's liberalism had horrified Tom's father back home.

Tom went to see him one day in his office in the Hotel Talleyrand.

"Tom, what are you doing over here!"

Tom was too shy to say that he had come to try to learn, to find himself.

"I wanted to see what it was like."

"I could have told you on a postcard; it's a rat-hole," Allison Brock said.

Tom said nothing.

"Listen, Tom," Allison Brock continued, "our forefathers

left this place in droves, and for good reason: Now we're back, pouring everything we've got right down the drain. And what are we accomplishing? Nothing. Not one God-damned thing. Every single one of us ought to get out of here as fast as we can."

"Won't the Communists take it if we do?"

"So what? The French don't care; they don't care what happens to them."

Tom remembered the despair on the faces of the young French mothers in the Parc Monceau.

"Let me tell you of just one thing to give you an example. They, and by they I mean the Frogs, were giving a recep-tion for our new Ambassador . . ."

Tom half-listened as Allison Brock went on to tell how the American Ambassador had been virtually snubbed and left to stand in a corner at the reception that had supposedly been given in his honor by French officials.

"I've had all I want of this rat-hole, Tom. I'm ready to pack it and go home. You'll come to the same conclusion, wait and see."

Through Brock, Tom met young Americans working for the American government. One of them, a bright, extremely good-looking young man about thirty named Caleb Ashborn, was married to a quiet, dark-eyed girl from New York.

They invited Tom to dinner. The Ashborns lived in a large apartment on the Left Bank. Caleb had worked in a public relations firm in New York City before working for the government.

Another couple, the Boyds, was present. Boyd was from the American trade union movement. His wife had been a social worker.

The Ashborns and the Boyds represented a new world to Tom Langley. They talked of politics, of international affairs, trade unions, and the economy. Tom had read of these mat-ters; and having come from Detroit, he knew of the American trade union movement but he had never spent an evening with people who talked of these things.

"Are you with the government?" Boyd asked him.

"No I'm not."

"What do you do?" Mrs. Boyd asked.

"I'm trying to write a novel."

"Hell, I hardly ever get a chance to read a book any more," Boyd complained.

"I wish Caleb had time to write," Mrs. Ashborn said.

"What's this I hear, Caleb?" Boyd asked, turning to him.

"It's true; I once had literary ambitions," Caleb said.

Boyd laughed. "I guess that won't be held against you in the government but it would be a real drawback in the C.I.O."

"Is it easier to write in Paris? Is that why so many American writers come here?" Mrs. Boyd asked Tom.

"I don't know . . . I'm just finding out," Tom answered.

"Do you like Paris?" Margaret Ashborn asked.

"Oh yes, I do, and until I came here I never realized the charm of Paris."

"It gets nearly everybody," she said.

"There's no charm in its politics or its economic situation, not to mention the condition of the labor unions here," Boyd said.

Later, over coffee and brandy, they talked about the French people.

"I haven't really met any yet except for waiters and others who work at my hotel and I wouldn't exactly say that that was meeting them," Tom said.

"Wait until you do," Boyd said ironically.

"Why Boyd, you sound anti-French," his wife exclaimed.

"I'm not, not yet I'm not; but if I have to work here much longer, I might become anti-French, I'll tell you that much."

Caleb turned to Tom and spoke:

"Paris looks different when you're a tourist but when you try to get a job done over here, you end up tearing your hair out."

"But they've suffered so much," Mary Boyd said.

"I know that but the question is, do they want to go on suffering?" her husband asked.

"They draw such a line between their business life and their social life. I've been here for over a year and I have yet to be asked into a French home," Margaret Ashborn said.

Tom said nothing. He had nothing to contribute to the talk. His impressions of Paris were personal and subjective, relating more to himself than to Paris and to the French. He liked it here, he knew that.

"Tom here is still new to Paris; let's hear what he thinks," Margaret Boyd said.

"I don't know—other than that I like it. I find it different from America," Tom said, a little surprised by the question. "The pace is a lot slower."

"You can say that again; try to get something done," Boyd said.

"They probably criticize us as much as we do them," Margaret Ashborn said.

"We've got a job to do over here," Boyd said. "And we aren't getting much help from them. Right now, for instance, we're releasing funds—a hundred million francs. The French want to use this to electrify the railroad from Paris to Lyon. Have you ever heard of such nonsense in this time and age? This is the age of the Diesel engine, for God's sakes. So I went to some of the F. O. leaders. I talked to them; I told them that some of us are against the plan for electrification. I explained why, that this is the age of the Diesel engine. I asked them if they had a counter plan. I said that if they did, we would support them. Do you know what they told me—'We're not competent.'"

Tom listened. He thought how far he was from so much of the world. He wasn't touching the roots and basis of modern society. How could he write without knowing these things? He felt inadequate.

Boyd went on:

"I've told the non-Communist unions that they have got to strike if they want anything. They say they can't strike against the government. If they do, they'll weaken it and the Communists will gain. They keep giving the ball to the Commies. How can they build non-Communist unions if they won't strike? Hell, the French worker is getting gypped. No one is leading him; he isn't getting his piece of the pie. And some of our policies aren't helping him either. The smart boys from the Treasury Department and Chamber of Commerce economies aren't going to revive France."

He turned to Caleb.

"I didn't tell you, at that policy meeting a couple of days ago with some of the big shots from Washington, I put it on the line. I asked them if they expected the French workers to fight and die for the slogan 'Balance the Budget.'

"When I came here, I never expected to find it this way. Last week, I needed some statistics. I went to the union and asked for them. They didn't have them—so do you know what they did? They invented them!"

Boyd shook his head.

"If this keeps on, we're going to get nowhere fast. The situation is damned serious. There's nothing exaggerated about the Communist danger."

The doorbell rang. They stopped talking as Caleb got up, walked over to the door and opened it to another young couple.

IX

By now, the Ashborn living room was full of Americans talking about France and the French.

"Buchet is one of the best of the non-Commie trade union leaders," Boyd was saying. "He came up from the docks; he has genuine working-class origins. We were discussing the situation and he said, 'The French worker wants a revolution but he doesn't want anything changed.' And that's just about the size of it. A friend of mine, a steel worker named Pat Kiernen, was over here for a few days. Pat's the kind of worker who's the backbone of the union. He saves his money and every two or three years he takes a trip to Ireland to see his relatives. He flew over here to Paris to see me. He said that he guessed that the French workers had organized into unions in order to disorganize themselves."

Boyd looked around the room, waiting for the others to comment, or laugh.

Caleb passed out drinks.

"Let's face it, Boyd, you don't like the French."

Tom hadn't caught the name of the tall man who said this when he had been introduced.

"I don't know if you're right or wrong, Hal. I'm not thinking of the question in those terms; I'm thinking of the job we've got to get done."

"But if we push them too fast, we won't get anywhere," the tall man said.

"Push them too fast?" Boyd asked, almost snorting. "We've got to have viable economies and stronger non-Communist trade unions over here, and we've got to do the job fast. We're not getting it done."

"I know that," Hal said.

"This is all we ever talk about when we get together—the French situation," a plump woman said.

"That's what we're here for—to help change it," Boyd said.

They went on discussing the French situation.

X

Tom Langley would sit at his desk every morning and try to write. As he worked, sometimes slowly and painfully, he sensed a feeling of exile, both past and present. He was feeding on emotions and memories of the past which he was expressing in his novel in progress. And he fed these emotions from his feelings of the present.

His surroundings were still new to him. This helped him retain the sense of making a beginning, a fresh start. He awoke every morning expecting something to happen. When he went out for breakfast, it was as though he were bound on an adventure.

The streets of Paris fascinated him. He watched people and speculated about them in a way that he had rarely done in America. He found a distinct pleasure in being in Paris. There was charm everywhere—the *quais* along the Seine, the parks, the narrow streets of the Latin Quarter, the Boulevard St. Michel, the Champs Élysées.

Again and again, Tom would go out hoping that this time he would meet a girl, a French girl. French life seemed closed to most Americans. Tom often wondered what their lives were like in their homes.

Tom met American girls, some who worked in government agencies, others in the St. Germain *quartier*. They made it clear that they did not want permanent attachments. This was the reason they gave for rejecting him.

Cecilia Worth was a striking blonde. She was a secretary in a government agency and owned her own car. On Sunday night, they had a date for dinner. She picked Tom up early and they drove through the Bois de Boulogne. The park was crowded. The sight pleased Tom and he was especially happy because he was with a girl. He had looked forward to this date all week.

Cecilia talked mostly about herself. She had been in Paris for over two years and she couldn't make up her mind about staying on.

"I have to go back sooner or later," she said.

"Why?"

"I don't know; I just do. Sometimes I feel guilty about living such an easy life over here. Don't you ever feel that way?"

"No I don't; that's why I am over here, to see and learn. But I expect to go back eventually," Tom said.

"When?"

"I don't know—maybe when I finish the book I'm trying to write."

They decided to take the boat trip along the Seine and to eat on board. The sun was just going down as the boat pulled out. They sat, eating, and looking out at Paris and at the trees along the banks. They saw the day turn into night with a full moon reflected on the water. The dark shadowy lines of shrubbery, the houses framed in the shrubbery, the lines of black trees, the river banks, the odd shapes of the moonlight on the dark shifting water, the smell of the water, the vast sky overhead—at moments, the scenes took their breath away.

Tom felt a sudden impatience for the trip to end so that he could be alone with Cecilia and make love to her.

"When I go back to America, I'll have to leave all this," she said.

"But you will have seen it." Tom wanted to say more but he didn't.

"The French know how to live better than we do, don't you think?" she asked.

"Then we should learn from them."

In the darkness, Tom saw a quizzical expression on her face. It quickly passed and her features grew impassive. They remained that way as she gazed out at the water and at the slowly changing banks of the Seine. Tom wondered how he could reach her.

When they were back in her car, he tried to kiss her.

"Don't spoil it, Tom," she said.

He wanted to ask her why she thought the evening would be spoiled by a kiss but he didn't.

Later he learned that Cecilia had, just before he had met her, been jilted in a love affair.

There were other girls whom Tom took out but there were always problems—broken love affairs, a desire for marriage, guilty feelings about living so well in Paris, doubts about readjusting to America and routine jobs as secretaries.

One girl had come to Paris to break up a love affair with a newspaper reporter in Washington. She told Tom how horrible the affair had been and how she had not been able to get rid of her lover in any other way but to leave. Periodically she would get a letter from him and become panicky that he would come over to Paris. She would tell everyone that even if he did come over, she would not marry him.

The second time that Tom took her out, he put his arm around her.

"Let's not have any of that," she snapped.

At times Tom was amused, at other times depressed because of his experiences with American girls in Paris. He felt an emptiness. He didn't only want a girl; he wanted a companion.

XI

Tom first saw Yvette at the Jeu de Paume Museum. He had decided that he was seeing too little in Paris. He thought of some of the Americans he had met and some of the girls who worked for the government agencies. They were making too little of the opportunities afforded them in Paris. He did not want to make the same mistake. He did not want to return to America with regrets about wasting his time in Paris. He was seeing too much of Americans, too little of the French. And he was exploring Paris less than he had planned to.

Tom knew little of art. He did not often visit museums and

galleries. To know and feel more of the world of art was one of his unrealized ambitions. He had liked what he had seen of French painting. The ones he was most familiar with were those of Cézanne and Van Gogh.

Wandering about the rooms of the Jeu de Paume, Tom was absorbed. He almost believed he was participating in French culture by looking at the paintings. This visit would help him understand more of French life, he thought. He peered at Degas' dancing girls. He wished that he had lived in Paris then and had known them . . . to see them practice, to watch them sit down tired and perspiring after practice, to see them go out and become lost in the crowds on the streets. The circus, the theater came to life before his eyes as a painted world of color and movement. He thought of the observation that had gone into these paintings, the noting of details.

And Tom was struck by Manet's portraits. He wished that he could have known these people.

He wandered about fascinated.

Looking at the Cézannes he found himself standing near a small, extraordinarily pretty girl. He guessed that she was French. She went from picture to picture, looking quickly but with concentration. She didn't seem to be at all aware of him. Tom was so struck by her that he could no longer look at the pictures with the same interest and absorption.

Then, they happened to look at each other. They both smiled. She spoke in French.

"*Je n'ai pas parle Français bien*," Tom said haltingly.

"*Vous parlez bien*," she said, smiling again.

He shook his head.

"Do you speak English—*parlez Anglais?*"

"A little but very badly," she answered.

He was relieved. Trying to speak French was a strain for him; he was painfully self-conscious about it.

"You are American?" she asked.

"Yes, and you're French?"

"*Oui.*"

At a loss for what to say, Tom smiled. He wanted to know her better. Suddenly he started talking; he was relaxed and at ease.

"I never realized before how fine French art was. I had known Manet and Degas only as names. They are wonderful painters."

"Yes," she said but there was bewilderment on her face. Tom realized that he had spoken too quickly, that she had the same difficulty in understanding English that he had in understanding French.

In a few moments she left the gallery. Tom wanted to follow her but he didn't. The spell of the paintings was broken. He tried to go on looking at them but it was a meaningless effort. He left the gallery. The sunlight was momentarily blinding. He stood in front of the museum, glancing about, hoping that she would be in sight. She was gone. He had a feeling of emptiness as he walked off. He would never see her again. It would be foolish to even think of her.

But Tom did think of her. He imagined meeting her again and talking to her. When he went to other museums and galleries, he would hope to see her. But even if he did, what would he say to her? There would be no basis for anything between them. The barriers would be too great. The experience of an affair with a French girl would be valuable to him, but he couldn't think of it as permanent. Suppose she should?

"Hell," he told himself laughing, "the girl doesn't know me from Adam."

Tom was sitting in the sun in a small cafe on the Boulevard St. Michel watching the crowd pass by. He sat a little longer. Then he left the cafe.

At about this time, Tom met Thelma Constable at a small gathering. She was from California. She was escorted by a young French lawyer, a man in his thirties, who spoke English. Tom rather liked her and wondered what her relationship was with this Frenchman, René.

Their hosts, an American professor and his wife who were on a government assignment in Europe, were talking of an experience they had had with the concierge in the building. The concierge had come in to wash the windows; they were French windows. He had fallen off his ladder, crashing into an expensive marble-top table that had split in two. When Carolyn, the professor's wife, had returned to the living room, she had found the broken marble and the concierge on the floor bleeding profusely. The concierge had lost two front teeth, cracked a rib, and suffered bruises and contusions.

"René, darling," Carolyn said, "you are different, of course, but . . . it's . . . it's the way many Frenchmen are."

"Concierges, they are the lowest type," René said.

"Ever since Fred and I have come here, we have had one headache after another."

"Carolyn, things would be easier for you if you would learn French," said her husband.

"I'm not good at languages, Fred, and you know it. You can't teach an old horse new tricks."

"But he is not talking about old horses, he is talking about charming women," René said.

"René, you are a darling. If all Frenchmen were like you, I'd be a confirmed Francophile."

"Carolyn misses Minneapolis," her husband explained.

"I most certainly do."

They spoke again of the concierge. He was covered by social laws and had been compensated for his injuries. But they were afraid that when their lease expired, the landlord would hold them responsible for the table.

"And prices are frightful. Why it costs as much to live over here as it does in America," Carolyn said.

"Dear, prices are high but they are not as high as they are back home."

"They are frightful. Every time my maid, my *femme de ménage*, comes back from the market, I am appalled at how much things cost."

"You must watch her, perhaps she cheats you," René said.

"*C'est possible*," Fred said.

"But what about the table," Thelma asked them, "what will you do?"

Fred told her how he and Carolyn had searched extensively in stores and had not been able to find a replacement. They had not found another table exactly like the one that was broken but they could tell by looking at similar tables that it would be expensive. Of course, Fred added, he could hold the concierge responsible but he didn't want to do that. He would rather pay for the broken marble than make the concierge pay for it even though it was his fault.

René examined the table and said that they could probably get away with having the marble glued. He knew of an expert who could do the job so well that the landlord probably wouldn't notice it—at least not until it was too late and they were back in the States.

The conversation turned to other subjects—food, market prices.

In a moment of lull, René began to talk of love, religion, and mysticism. He liked to read philosophy, he said, and he had read a great deal. This had led him to see the higher values and the higher meaning of life, which was love. Tom was surprised to hear a Frenchman talking this way, especially an educated one. He wondered again about the relationship between René and Thelma. Two or three times during the evening she had spoke of René and herself as "we."

At first Tom listened to René, curious to know what René had to say when the word "philosophy" was used. But René did not go into specific details; he kept insisting that the highest form of love was spiritual, not material.

"I don't think so," Tom said.

"Then what is there in life?" René asked.

"Whatever we find in it and whatever we make of it."

"Have you found it?" René asked him.

"Have I found what?"

"What you say you are searching for?"

"I haven't found much yet, not very much," Tom answered, shaking his head.

There had been too little of emotional content in his life, he thought. He had not been conscious of himself and of the world. Were these people here any more conscious? He at least was trying to do something about it. He had broken away from his past and had come here to Paris. He had become an exile.

Tom sat, listening to the conversation. René was talking again; his enthusiasm did not seem genuine to Tom. René kept asserting that the spirit was higher than matter and that the higher love was to be found in the spirit.

"I see you are skeptical," René said looking at Tom.

"Of course I am."

"But my friend . . ." René repeated what he had said.

Thelma and Carolyn paid no attention to him, they were talking about clothes and dressmakers. René was directing his conversation toward Tom.

"I'll never agree, I'm a hard-boiled naturalist. You won't convince me so let's talk about something else," Tom said.

"I guess we Americans are too pragmatic for Europeans," Fred said.

"But then what is life? What is man without love?" René asked.

"He is lonely," Tom answered.

Thelma heard Tom say this. Her eyes met his in a sudden glance of understanding.

XII

It was late; there was a slight chill in the air. Tom and Thelma sat outside a small cafe on the Champs Élysées. René had had to leave early for an appointment. Thelma had driven him but then she had returned. Later, she had offered to drive Tom home. He had suggested that they stop and have a cup of tea.

"My relationship with René is platonic, we are friends," she was saying.

Tom did not comment but he was glad. But suddenly he wondered why.

"I've learned a lot from him, he's a dear," Thelma went on.

"Did you like him?" she asked, after a short pause.

"Yes," Tom answered slowly.

"He's charming."

Tom nodded.

"But I don't agree with him and I lost interest when he was trying to talk about philosophy."

"I mean he's personally charming."

Tom nodded again. He looked out on the sidewalk. An American sailor walked by aimlessly.

"Poor fellow," Tom remarked.

"Why?"

"He's all alone on the Champs Élysées late at night. He hasn't got a girl. What else is there for him to do in Paris at this time of night but find a girl?"

"I suppose so," she said.

Then, turning to him, she asked: "Do you like it here?"

"Very much."

"I suppose it's different for a man living alone."

"I get lonely at times too."

"Oh, I'm not particularly lonely. I have friends over here now and I've met some French people through René. I was talking about some of the other American girls. You should have dinner at the Hotel Wagram some evening and see them eating alone."

"Can't they find boyfriends?"

"Most Americans over here are married. Of course there are the transients who come and go but most girls don't want that. I know I don't."

Tom suddenly thought of the French girl he had seen in the Jeu de Paume.

"Sooner or later I want to settle down, don't you, Tom? May I call you Tom?"

"If you'll let me call you Thelma."

"Why of course, please do."

They didn't speak for a few moments; then Tom said:

"I do get lonesome at times and pretty fed up with this kind of life."

"What do you mean?" Thelma's voice was sympathetic.

"I presume the phrase is 'settle down' but that's not precisely what I mean, not in a bourgeois or conventional sense."

She was easy to talk to, Tom thought.

"But what do you mean by a bourgeois or conventional sense?"

Then, as though it were an afterthought, she added:

"I guess I'm bourgeois and conventional."

This was probably so, he thought, and yet he found she had a growing appeal. She was sympathetic; this more than any other trait was the basis for her appeal. Rose had never been sympathetic; neither had Florence.

"Bourgeois is an overused word," Tom admitted.

"I hear it flung around all the time and I'm not always sure what people mean."

"What I meant," Tom said, "is that by settling down you

don't have to go to sleep. You don't have to lose your curiosity, your"—he searched for a word—"your zest. You don't have to lose your zest for life."

"Of course not."

Here they were, he thought, two strangers far from home, sitting in the calm and beautiful Paris night, fumbling toward knowing each other.

"I'm always surprised at what happens to me. I'm constantly finding myself surprised that I'm here in Paris."

"I'm used to it but I still like it. I'll be sad to leave," Tom said.

Suppose he never did?

"I know that I will leave eventually. I like my life here, too, but I want to get married sometime."

"You're different from many of the American girls that I've met over here."

She gave him a questioning look.

"Some don't seem to want permanent attachments," he said.

"All girls do," Thelma said.

"Maybe, subconsciously."

He thought of Rose. That was the decision that she seemed to be coming to as a consequence of her analysis, wasn't it?

"I do," Thelma added.

He offered her a cigarette.

"Here, take one of mine," she offered.

"I will since it's American."

"I'll get you some if you like; I can on my PX card."

"Thank you, I'd appreciate it if it's no extra trouble."

He lit her cigarette, then his own, and took a sip of tea.

"Sometimes I think I would like to go back and study," she said.

"Where did you go to college?" Tom asked.

"I didn't; I went to high school and then to secretarial

school. That's why I wonder if I should go back and get a part-time job so that I can take some courses."

"Do you want to?"

"I'm not sure. Sometimes I feel satisfied over here but the way I live now isn't permanent."

"It's the same with me," Tom said.

"But you're a writer."

"I have to prove that still; and maybe I never will."

"Oh I think you will, you give the impression of knowing where you're going."

Tom smiled at her.

"Don't you feel that way about yourself?" she asked.

"Not always, it's more the way that I want to feel than the way I really feel."

"How do you really feel?"

"Determined. At least most of the time I do."

It was late. Reluctantly they left the cafe and walked to her car. Tom wished that the drive to his hotel were longer. The Place de la Concord was brilliant but deserted. The Boulevard St. Germain was deserted also; the Café de Flore and the Deux Magots were closed. There were still some people at the Café Royal St. Germain.

They arrived at his hotel. Thelma gave him her card with her home and her office phone numbers. She told him to be sure to call her. He promised to do this soon, thanked her, and said good night. He pushed the button of his hotel door. Slipping inside, he heard the motor of her car as she drove off.

Was Thelma the one?

XIII

The next morning, Tom had difficulty concentrating on his work. He kept thinking of Thelma. Several times he started to phone her but he didn't. Hours passed. He was not working well. At about three o'clock he went out for a walk.

As soon as he was outside, the charm of Paris seduced him. He forgot his dissatisfaction with his work. There had to be days like this. He had had them before, all writers did, even great ones, he guessed. He walked to the Luxembourg Gardens. He would bring Thelma here sometime. He sat in a chair in the sun, lit a cigarette, and looked around. The people seemed relaxed; they were at home here. He wasn't. But he had felt the same way in America. Was this what Thelma was trying to describe last night? Perhaps they were both homeless and looking for the same thing. He imagined being married to Thelma and living here in France. He had daydreamed like this when he was engaged to Florence. Waking up together on Sunday, having lazy Sunday morning breakfasts after making love, making love again, and then taking walks. Thelma was different from Florence. And from Rose.

A young couple walked by, locked arm in arm. He wanted to walk that way in this park.

Restless, Tom got up and wandered about. The flowers, the sun, the trees, the soft light—he had never seen a park more beautiful. He wanted to cry. And to make love. Anyone who lived in Paris and didn't fall in love on a day like this was a damned fool.

He walked back to his hotel. He telephoned Thelma and asked her to have dinner with him that night. She said that she couldn't, not for six days, she had previous engagements.

XIV

Tom had thought of taking Thelma for a boat ride on the Seine but it was too chilly. They found a restaurant on the Rue Jacob. There was a piano up front. The food was good. Tom ordered wine. Tom had been depressed when he had met Thelma because his work had not been going well. But once they were in the restaurant, he forgot this. There was an atmosphere of gaiety. All about them, French people were talking excitedly. He and Thelma both liked it.

They talked about how much they liked Paris, how there couldn't be another city in the world like it. Tom spoke of his work and what he wanted to do. He tried to explain his need to be more conscious so that he could be more articulate. He told her that he thought others felt this need too. Thelma was not certain that she understood what he meant. He was disappointed but he made an effort to explain what was in his mind. It wasn't only, he said, what something meant that was important, it was how you felt about it. Thelma thought that she understood him better.

Shortly after they started eating, the entertainment began. The performers received no pay; they tried out in the restaurant and hoped that they would go on to other jobs where they would be paid.

Tom and Thelma ate slowly. They sat back to listen and watch. Tom felt frustrated, he could only catch the meaning of a few words. Thelma knew a little more French than he did but not enough to understand. One singer followed another. A plump woman of about thirty-five started to sing.

"This is '*La Seine*.' I like it," Thelma said.

Tom liked the song too. He listened, trying to understand the words. He thought of the boat ride he had taken on the Seine. He and Thelma might take one. He turned to glance at her. She was absorbed in the song and looked pretty. Perhaps he would fall in love with her.

Elle roule, elle roule, elle roule . . .

When the song ended, there was a burst of applause. Tom turned to Thelma and smiled. She returned his smile.

"Only in Paris can you find anything like this," she said.

"I like it."

The entertainment went on for another hour.

Tom and Thelma left a few minutes before eleven. They drove to the Deux Magots and sat outside, drinking coffee. When Tom left Thelma shortly after midnight, he still did not know if he wanted their relationship to get serious.

XV

Tom had told Thelma that he would meet her at the Café de Flore. He didn't know why, he didn't like the cafe. He felt out of place there.

He had finished his writing for the day and had read for a while. Then he had dressed and had walked slowly to the Rue St. Benoît and Boulevard St. Germain. It was sunny and warm, he looked forward to the evening. He had been alone for the last four days, he needed company, the company of a girl.

He found a table up front. Most of the tables were filled and the cafe was noisy. There were quite a few Americans. He saw some familiar faces, people he had seen around but whom he didn't know. He heard a woman behind him say:

"I just got here yesterday and I love it already."

"How long are you staying?" someone asked her.

"Only a week."

It was pleasant here today. Tom ordered a beer. He was glad he was early; he could sit and watch. The conversation around him was loud. He could single out a few words of French here and there. Would he ever learn the language? He should study it more systematically. But he had to finish his book. Would it be published? Would he become a writer, a great writer? Every writer must dream of becoming a great writer, he thought.

He looked around the cafe. Thelma would be here within a few minutes, it was still early. He thought of her. She was warm and outgoing. She didn't withdraw the way Rose did, her face blank when he tried to talk of his work and the future. Thelma was more sympathetic than Florence. And she was good-looking.

Tom grew impatient for her but it was still early. He glanced about. Two tables away from him, sitting alone, was a beautiful girl. She looked familiar. Yes, it was she, the French girl he had seen in the Jeu de Paume. She was looking in the other direction. Would she remember him? She was glancing about as though she were waiting for someone. Would she look in his direction?

She turned. For a moment, there was no light of recognition on her face. Tom smiled. She returned his smile with an expression of bewilderment.

"Hello," he called.

She paused a moment.

"Hello," she said tentatively.

"Don't you remember me?"

She looked confused.

"I spoke to you one day at the Jeu de Paume."

Tom had walked over to where she sat.

"*Vous ne parlez par Français?*" she asked.

"*Un peu—très mauvais.*"

"My English, she is very bad."

Tom wished that he weren't meeting Thelma. This French girl was beautiful. He stood looking down at her. She smiled weakly.

"*Asseyez-vous, s'il vous plaît.*"

He raised his eyebrows.

"I . . . sit down, please."

He sat down.

"I only have a minute," he said.

"Have I meet you . . . someplace?"

"I spoke to you one day at a gallery . . . Jeu de Paume."

"Oh yes, I remember now."

Tom asked her to meet him at the Deux Magots the next afternoon. She hesitated but then said that she would be there. Just then Tom saw Thelma walking toward the cafe. He excused himself and went to greet her. Thelma had parked her car across the street. They walked to it. After they had gotten in, he asked:

"Where would you like to eat?"

"You pick the place, Tom."

He couldn't think of a place. He was self-conscious because Thelma had come along while he had been talking to the French girl. He did not explain anything to Thelma.

"I know a place on St. Michel," he said.

It was an expensive restaurant and cost more than he had planned to spend.

"Whereabouts on St. Michel?"

"Right by the Seine."

"Oh I know the place, it is a good restaurant. It's . . . I can't remember the name of the place."

"Neither can I."

Thelma started the car.

"That French girl I was talking to . . ." he began.

"She's a very pretty girl."

"I happened to speak to her once about some paintings; I met her at the Jeu de Paume."

"Isn't it a wonderful museum!"

"We'll have to go together sometime," Tom said.

"I'd love to."

Thelma didn't seem jealous and yet Tom felt nervous. His feelings about Thelma had changed. He wished that he were with . . . , he didn't even know the French girl's name.

"Did you get some good work done?" Thelma asked, driving along the Boulevard St. Germain.

He didn't answer for a moment; he was absorbed in his thoughts.

"Yes, yes I did. And you? What kind of day did you have?"

"Oh, my days aren't very exciting; I'm only a secretary."

Thelma parked the car and they walked to the restaurant.

"This is an excellent restaurant," Thelma said as they walked upstairs. The headwaiter, in tails, led them to a seat against the wall. Sitting back, Thelma sighed. Tom didn't have anything to say. He was thinking about the French girl. He would see her tomorrow. Thelma chatted about Paris. She had gotten up early and had taken a walk before going to work.

"Since I got my car, I haven't done much walking and one should walk in Paris. There are so many things to see."

"I agree. *D'accord.*" He hesitated a moment. "We'll have to take some walks together."

"I'd like to, Tom, anytime you want to."

"Paris remains an unexplored place to me."

"How long have you been here, Tom?"

"About three months."

"I've been here for almost two years; long enough to get home leave. I get it in three months."

"Are you going back?"

"I don't know; I can't make up my mind. I don't know what it will be like, going home after two years."

Tom nodded. America did seem far away. He didn't think about it too often. Yet in a way, it was always with him; he was an American.

"You never get away from America," he said.

"What do you mean?" Thelma asked.

Tom knew what he meant but he didn't know how to explain it.

"I don't want to get away, not permanently. Do you?" she asked.

"No, that's not what I meant."

He was trying to find himself here. Why? So that he could

return to America and be recognized. What else? But was that all he wanted? Tom knew that it wasn't. He knew that he was searching for love, and recognition would help him to find it. He thought of the French girl again.

After they had eaten, Tom suggested that they go dancing. They went to a place on the Boulevard Montparnasse. The dance floor was surrounded by tables. The orchestra was good. The waiter put a bucket containing ice and a bottle of champagne on the table. Tom decided to take it. He raised glasses with Thelma.

"This is the first champagne I've had in France," he said.

"I haven't had it often but I like it."

For a while they sat and watched the dancers. Then they got up to dance. They both enjoyed it. A crooner sang in English. Tom listened to the music without paying attention to the words. It was like so many songs he had heard over the years. Dancing on the crowded floor, Tom was surprised when he heard French being spoken. Listening to the crooner sing an American song, he had imagined that he was in America. He had forgotten that he was in Paris, dancing with a girl he had known less than two weeks.

They returned to their table and sipped champagne. Tom could not help but notice how sweet and easy it was to get along with Thelma.

Tom was still curious about the relationship between Thelma and René. She had mentioned him several times. She, René, and a few friends had spent the weekend in the country at the little house of a French friend. It was near Chartres. She had planned to go see the Cathedral but once she had gotten to the country and into old clothes, she had changed her mind and had just sat in the sun and read. They had all talked and had eaten wonderful meals. Everyone had been congenial; it had been a lovely weekend, restful and relaxing. Maybe the next time they went, Tom would like to come? Tom said he would but he was not sure he would if René were going to be there.

Tom asked Thelma to dance again.

All during the evening, Tom was undecided about his feelings for Thelma. He knew that he liked her. And he was getting tired of taking one girl out once or twice, then another girl, and going through the same process of being undecided, and of not knowing how far she would go. It wasted time, energy, and money. And it was childish. Tom knew that his evening with Thelma would have been different if he had not seen the French girl. He had believed that a good relationship was possible between Thelma and him. He had started looking forward to it. But now, he was marking time, thinking about tomorrow evening when he would see the French girl again. Thelma was second choice. He had kept the date tonight simply because he had already made it.

They stayed out late. Then she drove him to the door of his hotel. She said good night in a friendly manner. Tom said he would call her and she told him to please do this. He watched her car drive off. He turned and rang the bell. There was a buzzing sound and the door opened. Tom stepped inside. He was tired, he wanted to get to bed. He had not kissed Thelma. He thought of the French girl.

XVI

Tom was nervous. She was fifteen minutes late. He tried to read but he kept looking out on the sidewalk, watching for her. He had looked forward to this meeting all day. Where was she? Tom smoked nervously. He kept watching the sidewalk. Suppose she should stand him up? What would be lost? How disappointed could he be; after all, he didn't know the girl, he didn't even know her name. Nervously he kept watching the sidewalk. He looked at the clock over the door of the Abbey of St. Germain des Prés across the street. She was twenty minutes late. It seemed as though he had been waiting much longer. How long should he wait? Tom was angry for a moment. He kept watching the sidewalk.

There she was! Tom relaxed. Then he became anxious again. What would he say to her? She was looking around. She saw him and walked toward him, smiling. He stood up. She was beautiful.

She spoke to him in French. A blank look crossed Tom's face.

"I am sorry, very sorry, to be late . . ." she said.

"That's all right."

"Did you think that perhaps I shall not come?"

"No," Tom lied.

She smiled.

"I thought that because I do not know you, it might not be correct to come."

"I don't bite."

She didn't understand him.

"I have never done such a thing before, made a rendezvous with a stranger that I have not met properly."

"You can meet me now," Tom said.

She smiled again. Tom asked her what she would like; she asked for an apéritif. They were still shy with each other. Finally, Tom started to talk. He told her that he liked this section of Paris. She said that she lived on the Right Bank, in the 16th Arrondisement, and that her name was Yvette Mangan. He told her his name.

"You work here for the Americans?" she asked.

"No."

"You are here on holiday?"

Tom shook his head. "No, I'm just here for a while."

"You do nothing? You are a rich American?"

"No, I am trying to write."

Tom had wanted to say, "I am a writer," but until he was published he couldn't call himself a writer.

"You are a writer? Maybe I can read what you have wrote. No, that is not correct, what you have written."

"I am only trying to write."

"You are modest."

"No, I'm just telling the truth."

His self-consciousness vanished. It was easy to talk to her; he felt he knew her.

They sat for some time, talking casually. He asked her to have dinner with him. She agreed. They left the Deux Magots and walked along the Boulevard St. Germain. The sun had gone down. The atmosphere was lazy. People sauntered by.

They went to a small restaurant on a side street. It was almost empty. After they were seated, he said:

"I hope you'll like this restaurant."

"It looks all right."

"It is not very gay but the food is good."

She smiled.

They ate slowly, talking intermittently. Tom soon realized that she could not understand him unless he spoke simply and slowly. She tried to speak French to him but he could not understand her. The language barrier between them emphasized the fact that they were strangers. If they couldn't communicate, how could anything develop between them? It was a strain to talk but he had already invested so much emotion in her.

They finished eating. Their eyes happened to meet and they smiled self-consciously.

"What would you like to have?" Tom asked.

"*Rien*, I will take a *café* only."

"I don't want any dessert either."

Tom signaled to the waiter with his head. He didn't want to call; he pronounced the word *garçon* so badly.

XVII

Tom had heard about this *bal*. On an impulse, he had suggested to Yvette that they go dancing. He had brought her here. There was a bar in front. The stools were covered in red plush. There were also small tables. In a corner, an orchestra of three was on a dais. The dance floor was small and there were only a few couples dancing. They were all French. Yvette had thought that the girls were either domestic servants or textile workers.

Couples whirled around as the orchestra played a fast waltz. Tom had difficulty because the floor was uneven and slippery. He held Yvette closely and said nothing. When the music ended, they walked back to their seats.

"You have never been to the *bals* in the 20th Arrondisement?" she asked, as they sipped cognac.

"No."

"You should; it is a popular *quartier* and they are more interesting."

He was disappointed.

"Isn't this place interesting to you?"

"Oh yes."

The music played again. They watched couples dance.

"They seem to enjoy it," Tom commented.

"Yes."

Tom watched them. They were spinning in another fast waltz. The proprietor was dancing with a fat woman, whirling and spinning her around. They talked steadily as they danced. There were two girls dancing together. One was a good-looking blonde; the other, a haggard, sharp-nosed girl. Their faces were expressionless as they twirled.

When the music stopped, he sat back and turned to Yvette.

"If you don't like it here, we can leave."

"I like it but it is hot."

"We'll go."

"No, we stay for a little while more," she said, touching his arm.

They danced again. As they did, the lights were suddenly turned out. The proprietor blew a screeching whistle, red lights flashed on and off. Some of the dancers were frightened. Tom drew Yvette closer to him but she wasn't frightened. When the lights were turned on again, she smiled.

They left shortly after and walked to the Seine. Strolling, they stopped to gaze at the Cathedral of Notre Dame in the moonlight. Tom paused at the sight of the series of flying buttresses. He always felt a thrill when he saw them.

"It's magnificent," he said.

He had wanted to say it in French, "*C'est magnifique*," but he had been too self-conscious.

The Cathedral had stood, as it was now, for centuries. It spoke of the ages, of centuries gone by, and of the aspirations of dead men. It seemed endowed with a voice and meaning wrenched from time. The white stones were clear in the moonlight. The dark front with its two symmetrical towers, the dark ensemble of the Cathedral, had stood against the ravages of time, a thing of peace. He would never attain the peace which he saw in the stones of Notre Dame that were half-lost in the night.

Tom put his arm around Yvette's waist as they stood looking. Suddenly he turned and kissed her passionately.

"It is an American blitzkrieg," she said, surprised and breathless when he released her.

XVIII

The next Sunday, they walked to the Bois de Boulogne. It was a little after five o'clock. The sun was warm; there was a lazy, Sunday atmosphere. The park was crowded.

"I make myself a promenade here every day, it is good for the health."

"You walk here?" he asked.

"I speak English very badly," she said.

"I speak French worse."

"You must try."

"I have a terrible accent; it is midwestern."

"*Non.*"

She seemed more feminine when she spoke French; her voice sounded softer.

They walked on, going into the wooded section of the park. They were alone. The sun was going down. The sounds of the park seemed far away. They walked slowly along a footpath in single file. When they came to a clearing, Tom stopped, turned around, and put his arms around her.

"You will make a scandal."

"Is such a scandal possible in Paris?"

She smiled. "*Oui.* You are a bad boy, from the Middle West."

He tried to kiss her. She shook her head.

"*Non.*"

He didn't know what to do; what did she want?

She took his arm.

"We will find our way back and take a *café.*"

"And then?" he asked.

"And then you will return to your work."

Her eyes were playful; she took his arm and clung to him. But when he tried once more to kiss her, she said, "*Non.* You want to scandalize me."

"No, I want to love you."

"But Tom, you do not know me."

It was the first time she had called him by name.

Later, they sat outside of a restaurant called *Chez Pyrénées.* It was almost dark. All about them other diners were eating and talking. They had both ordered chateaubriand. Tom could not eat; he had no interest in food. But it was more than this. So strong was his desire and immediate physical need for this girl that he could not think of anything else. He was weak from the force of his desire. He said nothing. He made an effort to eat, trying to mask his feelings. Never had he felt this way about a girl. He looked at her. Yvette wasn't eating either.

"Aren't you hungry?" he asked.

She shook her head.

"Neither am I."

He wanted to ask her to leave with him, to go back to his hotel. Instead, he repeated:

"I'm not hungry either."

She smiled at him. Her face had changed; it seemed more beautiful. Her eyes were brighter. Tom sensed that she felt as he did.

"Yvette," he spoke softly.

She waited for him to go on.

"Come with me."

She said nothing.

"Come with me to my hotel."

She said nothing. He waited, taut.

"Do you want to?" he asked.

"*Oui.*"

"Then why?"

"I should not. When you leave Paris, I will be hurt and I will be sad. It is not a question of morals. Me, I am not a moralist."

She spoke with strain.

"But I don't know when I will leave Paris."

"You will leave. You are an American and you will leave and I will be hurt."

"And I might be hurt too."

Her manner changed. She tried to eat but he could see that she had no interest in the food before her. He cut a small piece of his steak, stabbed it with a fork, and put it into his mouth. He chewed, not tasting anything. They looked at each other. Her eyes were very bright. Her expression had melted into softness. He had never seen a girl so beautiful.

Tom decided that she was telling him with her expression. He signaled for the waitress.

"We will go," he said.

She did not speak but continued to gaze at him with the same soft expression. Tom signaled again but the waitress was busy, coming and going with plates, and she ignored his wave. Impatiently he rapped a knife against his glass. The waitress still did not respond. Yvette continued to gaze at him. He reached over and took her hand, squeezed it. She squeezed back.

"We will leave now."

"I cannot say no," she answered.

He tapped his glass again.

XIX

Outside the hotel, Yvette took his arm. He was thinking that the emotions of sex were very delicate. It all boiled down to how you felt afterwards. And he felt clean, fulfilled. Yvette took his arm. It was a submissive gesture. He had often seen French girls clinging to the arms of men this way. They turned on to the Rue St. Benoît. As they approached the Boulevard St. Germain, the streets became noisy. The sidewalk was jammed with people. Tom and Yvette, like others, stepped out onto the street to walk, Yvette still clinging to his arm.

The passion he had felt a little while ago with her in his hotel room, his new sense of her, of her body, lingered in his mind.

They turned left and walked slowly through a crowd of

milling people. They found a table at the crowded south terrace of the Deux Magots.

"We are back where we met tonight," he said.

She smiled but her smile was different.

"You have uncombed me," she said lightly.

"With your collaboration."

"*Non.*"

For a moment, Tom felt uncertain but then he realized that her talk was the banter of love.

"The woman, she is always getting combed, and the man, he is always uncombing her."

"And she likes to be uncombed."

"*Non, non.*"

There was a playful gleam in her eye as she spoke.

Never had he felt as he did now, Tom thought, not after Florence or Rose. Never.

The waiter came and they ordered beer. While they waited for him to bring it, they sat quietly. There was a bounce to the noisy conversation all around them. Talking, sitting in this cafe on such a night appeared to be a very important act. As Tom glanced around, he felt her lips brushing his cheeks. He was grateful.

"I will scandalize you in the public," she said.

"Please do."

The waiter brought their beer. He raised his glass.

"*Pour l'amour.*"

She smiled tenderly. No girl he had met seemed more feminine than she did at this moment. And she loved him. Did he love her?

He had not believed in love. This was clear to him now although it had not been before this moment. There had always been some question in his mind about girls. When he had been engaged to Florence and while he had been having an affair with Rose, doubts had risen in his mind at moments. And there had been the curious feeling that they had been sharing some secret guilt, some collaboration in shame. He had no such feelings now.

They sipped their beer. Words were unnecessary.

Tom saw Yvette almost every day after that.

All Paris—his work, his life—they were all different to him. There was a glow to everything. Paris seemed to shine; Yvette and the city were bound together in his mind.

He met her the next day after that Sunday, in a cafe on the Boulevard St. Michel. She had suggested meeting him here rather than at his hotel.

They walked in the Luxembourg Gardens. Tom felt as though his life were changed. His contentment from the night before had lingered all day. He had sat at his little desk in his hotel room, too dreamy to work. Several times he had stretched out on the bed and thought about Yvette. But by the time he went out to meet her, he had become unsure of himself. What would she think?

The way she had said "*chéri*" when they met reassured him.

They walked aimlessly in the park. Its beauty seemed a perfect backdrop for his feelings. As they wandered in the shade, he put his arm around her. She asked him what he was thinking.

"Anyone who comes to Paris and doesn't fall in love is a fool."

"And you, are you in love?"

"What do you think?"

She looked at him flirtatiously.

"You Americans," she bantered.

"What about Americans?"

"You come to France and take all the French girls."

"I don't want all French girls; I just want you."

"To make me uncombed."

"You're so pretty today. I want to muss you up."

"That's the man; he always does that. And the woman . . ."

"She runs France; that's all she does."

"What is that?" Yvette asked him.

"I was talking about politics."

"Politics," she said knowingly.

They strolled on and stood watching some young boys sailing boats in the pond. Tom remembered when he had walked here alone, not so long ago. He looked at Yvette. She asked him if something were wrong.

"I was merely watching you."

She smiled.

"I used to come here with my brother," she said.

"Did you sail a boat?"

"No, but I wanted to. I wanted to do the things he did but he, he would not permit me. He is older than me."

"What does he do?"

"He is a businessman—pharmaceutical business."

"Does he live in Paris?"

"No. Lyon."

"What does your father do?"

"He is dead. He died in the war. We were in the Free Zone but he was here. We do not hear from him for months. The Germans, they kill him."

"Why?"

She turned to look at him in perplexity. He grinned apologetically.

"My question was foolish; I am sorry, dear."

"He was in the Resistance. He help many people to escape. He save many people; he keep them at our home. One day the Gestapo, they come and they take him away. We never hear from him again."

Tom had often tried to imagine Paris with the Germans in the city. Germans in uniform sitting in cafes, taking tours, sightseeing, approaching French women, being picked up by prostitutes. He had tried to think of what had gone on in the minds of French people during those days.

As he and Yvette took chairs in the fading sun in the Jardin du Luxembourg, Tom thought of this again. He was quiet for some moments. Yvette sat next to him.

"I like this park," he said pensively, still thinking of Paris and the days of the Occupation.

"How did you feel when Paris fell?" he suddenly asked.

She didn't answer right away. He watched an old Frenchman walk by. Had he been in the First World War? In the Battle of the Marne? He knew so little, almost nothing, of this land and its people. And he was falling in love with this French girl. She was a stranger to him, and he to her. Yet, he was falling in love with her.

"I was too busy trying to escape," she answered.

"Did you feel sad about leaving?"

"No, I feel almost nothing. It was no more Paris, not with the Germans coming. It was different, not the same. My English, she is so bad, I cannot say. It was not Paris any more."

"When did you leave?"

"The day before the Germans arrive."

"Were you afraid?"

"No, it was a *crise*. You had to save yourself, there was no time to think. I drive the car. It was slow; there were many cars, and people with wagons. The German *avions*, they bomb us."

"Did you know that France was falling?"

Tom looked around. German troops must have come and walked and sat here. They must have talked with French girls here. The Park had been as peaceful that spring as it was now. Children must have sailed their boats. Students must have strolled. Tom was overcome with wonder.

"What is it you mean?" she asked him.

"Did you, when you fled from Paris, did you know that France would surrender?"

"No, we knew nothing. We never think that the German will come to Paris. We think, like the last war, the other one before, that our army will stop him. Our army will stop him on the Marne. When we go from here, we think our army will stop him on the Loire. Or stop him somewhere. We do not think that the war will be over and that France will be beaten. In Bordeaux, I hear the news. Then we learn that the German, he will come to Bordeaux. We go there because in the other war, the government, she go there. We leave again. We do not know where to go; it was terrible, *terrible*. We were afraid the German catch us. After I finish my studies at college, I write articles. I am anti-Nazi. I am afraid that the German will take me. It was *terrible*. And we have no food. Some French, they collaborate with the Nazis, but most of us, we suffer. It was *terrible*."

Tom was touched. Yvette went on.

"There is no water for the bath. We can cook once a day only. There is no milk for the babies. People do not know where to sleep. I have one friend, he sleep in barn. We share but we have nothing to share. I was hungry; I remember, I am so hungry all the time. You in America, you do not know it. It was *terrible*."

He turned to look at her with sympathy. Her expression was vague for a moment and then she smiled. What, he wondered, did she think of him? Did she love him? They were far away from one another. And yet last night; her body, her kisses. All this was so new, so unexpected. And it was different from his dream of finding a French girl. It was more.

"Now I think of it, it was—what do you call it—*la nuit blanche?*"

"What?"

"White night; you do not sleep, you have bad dreams, very bad."

"Nightmare."

"Yes, nightmare," she said.

They looked at each other. Their expressions were tender. Then, with desire, they went to his hotel and made love.

Later, they strolled about the streets of Paris. It was a lovely night.

XX

Tom was swept off his feet by Yvette. He was totally absorbed in her but he did not think of marriage. He told himself that he could not live permanently in France and he did not believe that she could uproot herself and live in America.

They lived in the present. They talked little of the future. Tom thought that she, as much as he, realized that theirs could not be a permanent relationship.

In the beginning, they had only been able to communicate with a few words.

"I must say to you everything with one thousand words," Yvette had said to him one day as they had strolled.

Tom had been troubled. There were many times when he had felt frustrated because of the language barrier between them, times when they had had to stop talking and just sit in a cafe, or stroll in silence, because it had been too difficult to talk.

XXI

After Tom met and fell in love with Yvette, his thoughts of America became poignant. They would, one day, have to part. She was French, he was American.

And the problem of language remained a barrier although Tom had learned much more French. He still hesitated to speak the language. He would become self-conscious. Yvette could not understand him because of his pronunciation.

He came to know Yvette slowly. She was never on time for engagements. And she had a strong desire to cultivate herself. She read a great deal and she attended lectures. Her attitude toward sex was frank and natural. One day, they were in a cafe. They had just left his hotel.

"Can I speak vulgar?" she asked.

"Why not?"

"You . . . you satisfy me."

"That is not vulgar," he said.

"Tell me about American girls," she said.

"I don't like them any more, I like you."

"That's *blague*. That is the word we say in French for what you are speaking but I like you to say it."

"I would not trade you for American girls."

"You must know many of them."

"No."

She laughed.

"Am I different from the American girls? They look so pretty and they dress well."

"When they aren't wearing bluejeans," he said.

"What?"

"Bluejeans."

"How do they make love?" she asked him.

"I haven't had a great deal of experience," he said.

She looked at him and laughed again.

"You like American girls?"

"I love you."

She grew serious.

"*Je t'aime . . . beaucoup, beaucoup, beaucoup.*"

XXII

Tom sat gazing at the papers on his desk. He was in a low mood; he had awakened questioning himself and everything he was doing. All morning he had thought of America. He had taken his own country for granted. When Yvette asked him questions about the United States, he realized how little he knew of its history, its industry, politics, its culture, morals, and manners. Yvette knew so much about France.

He went to the Deux Magots for coffee. An intense longing came over him, a longing to go back. Behind him, a couple spoke in French. The sound of the language made him lonelier. Had he run away? If he had, he still didn't know what he had run from.

In Paris he had gazed at shop windows, looked at merchandise, noticed prices. He had observed the clothes that people wore. He had asked himself questions about different aspects of French life. He had not done this in America, at least not much of it. Books, and mostly contemporary books, had been his absorbing interest.

Looking back, he saw how much he had missed. He knew in a more intimate and personal way now what he had meant when he had said that the level of consciousness in America had not been sufficiently developed. He had said this of himself as well as of others. He had wasted years during which he could have been developing. Now, he was seeing more and feeling more. But what could he write of here in France?

His coffee was cold. He signaled the waiter and ordered a fresh cup. He did not want to return to his room and to his work, not yet.

Suddenly he thought of Thelma. He felt a slight twitch of guilt. She had phoned him once and had invited him to dinner but he had told her he couldn't make it. She had asked him to call her. He had promised that he would but he never had. He had become totally absorbed in Yvette. He must have come to Paris looking for something, something that he couldn't find anywhere else. He was less anxious here. He worried less. And he didn't feel as resistant to his environment as he had back home. He didn't have to fight the same things. He didn't have to think of television, the movies, former friends, of his mother and uncles in Detroit who were disappointed in him because he had tossed aside a career in business to try to become a writer.

He hadn't realized it before but he had felt a pressure in America, a kind of pressure that he did not feel here in Paris.

XXIII

He lay beside Yvette calm and wearied, falling asleep. He felt empty. He reached his hand over and touched her flesh. He felt a great tenderness.

And yet, they were still strangers.

Yvette touched him.

"*Mon amour*," she said softly.

He felt grateful and gratified. He smiled to himself. Through the window came the noises of the Paris streets.

They lay side by side, drowsy and half asleep. Again he thought of the two of them as strangers. He would go back to America some day. This would end; he would leave Yvette here. How would he feel, remembering moments like this? He found himself wishing for the time when he would be back home remembering. He turned and gazed at her. Her face was calm, her eyes bright. Contentment shone in her face because of him. He was proud. He bent over and kissed her lightly. She smiled tenderly.

He dozed off but even as he slept he retained a vague awareness of her beside him. He woke up, surprised for a moment, blinked his eyes, and touched her. She lay quiet, her eyes fixed on the ceiling. He turned and kissed her hungrily.

XXIV

"You ravished me and uncombed me," she said facing him across a table.

"You look abused," he teased.

A frown crossed her face, she did not understand him.

The waiter brought their food. They were both hung and ate heartily, neither of them speaking. For a moment, I thought he should say something; he tried to think of som thing but he couldn't. Then he realized that there was nothir he needed to say. Their eyes met and they exchanged smile His mood was one of tenderness. Would he ever find anyor else who would please him as much? Love him as much? (satisfy him as much?

"My darling, are you *triste?* Sad?" she asked.

"No, not at all, I'm tired."

She formed her lips in a kiss.

"That is because you should behave. You are a bad boy, *polisson.*"

"What's that?"

"You."

"Do you want me to be tired?"

"Yes," she answered with a grin.

"Why?"

"Because you do not behave and you make me uncombed.

"You're combed now."

"*Oui*, but I have a fear that you won't let me stay combed.

"Do you want me to?"

She answered with an inviting smile.

What if he married her?

It wouldn't work; he didn't think it would.

She kicked him lightly under the table. He looked at he surprised. She laughed. "That is because you are a boy wh does not behave."

"Paris has done that to me."

"Did you behave in America?"

He nodded.

"I do not believe you."

"From now on, I will behave here in Paris to convinc you."

She made a face at him.

"Don't you want me to behave?" he asked.

"The woman always she wants the man to behave. He should behave well in public and behave not so well at home."

They both smiled.

Part Two

I

Tom was going back to America. Alone. He was leaving Paris. And Yvette.

He had planned to spend a year here, he had stayed two. Six months ago he had thought that he would take Yvette back with him. She would enjoy visiting America. They could explore his country together just as they had explored France.

Visa trouble.

He had not expected it. The first time he had visited Loring's office he had anticipated no problem; it would be simpleminded routine.

But it had not turned out that way.

He and Yvette were sitting in the Deux Magots. He could understand the French spoken around him. He gazed at the Romanesque tower of the Abbey of St. Germain des Prés. He would miss Paris. But he wanted to get back to America.

He and Yvette were silent. Her eyes seemed darker than usual tonight. There was a different kind of glow in them, the glow of unshed tears.

—Goddamnit!

He would miss her, he knew this. He had never before felt

so close to anyone. But that was not the reason he had sworn to himself. He had sworn to himself because he was not sure that he was sorry to be leaving her. He wanted to go back and the sooner he was on his way, the better. He was being foolish to feel guilty. He would have shoved off two months ago but for Yvette and the visa matter.

He was going home. He was leaving a Paris that was almost *fini*, that was becoming another, different Paris.

He looked at Yvette. He wanted to cry. But his life was across the Atlantic. Home, home in the land of the skyscrapers and . . . and what?

II

Looking down on the garden, Tom had seen the coming dawn, black with rain. The time for leaving had come. Yvette would drive him to Le Bourget. They would be leaving in another half hour. He drank more coffee, waiting for her to get dressed.

It was difficult to concentrate on anything. His restlessness was mounting. Emotionally, the adjustments to his departure had been made, not by an act of will but in the way that feelings, deeply planted, manage to come to resolutions.

He was leaving Paris. He was going from the old continent of Europe.

He was an American. Europe was not his home and never could be. But he could not tell Yvette this. It pressed too closely to the differences in them and in their past.

They had never discussed the future in terms of permanency. He had waited for her to speak of it but she never had. And were he to have done so, it might have produced scenes. He had learned that Yvette was strong-willed and often became angry and accusatory when her wishes were crossed. Her suspicion would overcome her logic and good sense.

It was raining heavily now. He hoped that the flight to Stockholm wouldn't be canceled. Waiting another day would be anticlimactic. It would give him another day with Yvette but, even so, he would rather be off. He poured more coffee. Time was heavy in moments like this. His interest in Paris was dying, or at least going to sleep. But underneath his impatience, there was sadness and melancholy.

He was aware of time passing in sheer waste. But he was in no mood to work. In a few minutes Yvette would be ready. They would be off. He lit another cigarette.

"We might miss the plane," he called to her.

"Don't be nervous," she answered in English.

Just then she came out, looking very pretty.

The porter helped put his luggage in her car. Tom said his final farewells, shook hands with the porter, and got into the car. It was still raining.

"Don't be so nervous, *chéri*, we will be there on time," she said as they drove off.

They swung around the Étoile. The traffic was heavy. He had explained this to her last night and she had agreed to be on time. But they were off to a late start. There was no sense in getting angry about it, all he could do was hope that she would get him to Le Bourget on time.

"You are a nervous man, *chéri*."

He said nothing. The rain was still coming down and the darkness of the morning cast a veil of gloom over Paris.

"In twenty minutes we will be there," she said.

He did not answer. He looked out the window and watched the people hurrying along the sidewalk in the rain. She glanced at him quickly, a puzzled look on her face.

"Just do the best you can, my darling. If we miss the plane, I will get another one," he answered.

"We have plenty of time," she said.

But progress was slow in the cluttered traffic. Frequently she had to stop. They were both silent.

"Is something wrong?" she asked, keeping her eyes ahead.

"No, nothing is wrong."

"You are silent for so long."

He did not know what to say. If he showed any desire to be off, she would be offended. He did not want to offend her; they had been too close. And yet he did have such a desire. This led squarely into all that he had never said to her and never could say. They had known such intimacy and yet they were still strangers.

"Such a day. I would have liked a better day for leaving," he said.

"When you return, we will give you better French weather, *mon chéri.*"

"Yes."

She had never been to America. She knew nothing of his life there. He could sense more about her past than she could about his. Again and again this thought had been in his mind.

They were held up by traffic again.

"This traffic, it is *impossible*," she exclaimed.

He had known that there would be heavy traffic and that was why he had stressed the importance of getting an early start. He did not say anything but he could not curb his anger, not entirely. Why had she ignored his urgings and taken so long to get dressed?

"I never expect such traffic in the morning," she said.

He slumped back in the seat. There was nothing he could do. He might as well accept the fact that he was likely to miss his plane.

"I am going to miss you, *chéri.*"

Her words struck him.

"And I will miss you," he said.

They were silent for some moments. They were outside Paris now. The rain had let up.

"You will not be late. I am sure."

But they were. The propellers of the Air France plane were

turning when they arrived at Le Bourget. It took about an hour to change his tickets and get booked on a Scandinavian plane departing at five o'clock. Tom was annoyed but decided that there was no use in saying anything.

They had had another mishap.

Yvette's car had stopped with engine trouble. Fortunately it had happened in front of a garage and they had been able to get a cab to Les Invalides Air Terminal.

"I am sorry; it is my fault," she said as they walked out of the airport entrance. "But we could go back, it is a long wait for your plane. We could have lunch at home."

"Let's have it out; I think it will be better," he said.

She took his arm as they walked out of the terminal.

"It has not turned out badly, missing the *avion*."

"No," he said.

They walked away from the terminal. The sun had come out. It was warm with autumn in the air. It would be a beautiful day. He grew moody. Once, on autumn days, he had yearned for love. Now he was on the other side of such yearnings.

"We have seen many places together," she said wistfully.

They passed a young couple kissing on a bench.

The thought came to Tom that this could be the end.

"You seem sad," she said.

He hesitated to answer. His need to leave was compelling but he did not want to say so. She would be hurt. A love affair like theirs could not last. There was more than the Atlantic Ocean between them; there were things she could not know or understand. And there were things that he could not know or understand.

They had walked for several blocks. They passed a bistro. It began to rain again.

"Let's have coffee here," Tom suggested.

He noticed a clock.

"It's almost twelve."

They sat down and ordered *café crème*. Next to them sat several working men in blue overalls drinking wine and talking volubly. Other working men entered and stood at the bar. The bistro became lively. Tom could understand little of what was being said.

"They drink too much alcohol," Yvette remarked.

Through the opened door, Tom could see that the sun was shining. It was going to be one of those Paris days he loved. He had loved Paris. So much had happened to him here. But his thoughts were contradictory; he could only know them clearly at some time in the future. Paris was a beautiful city. To him, the most beautiful city in the world.

They finished their *café crème;* Tom paid and they left. The sky was clear. A cab passed, he hailed it. They went to a restaurant right off the Champs Élysées. They had eaten there before. It was crowded and, like all crowded French restaurants, noisy with conversation. Tom looked around. A period of his life was ending. But he shouldn't be sad, he was going back to his own country. Turning toward Yvette, he saw a soft tender smile on her face. That look in her eyes had often aroused him. It still could.

"What are you going to have, my darling?" she asked.

He didn't care much what he ate even though he was hungry.

"Chateaubriand."

She studied the menus. He quickly shot his eyes around the restaurant again. It was large and rectangular. Waitresses in black dresses with white aprons were hustling back and forth. The headwaiter, clad in black with a white tie, was here and there, his manner one of completely assimilated *savoir faire*. Most of the customers seemed to be French businessmen, middle-aged or old. One grey-haired man wearing a dark suit sat with a woman whose hair was platinum blond. She was elegantly dressed and sat, listening intently, while the man spoke in a steady, quiet tone of voice. Four men, two in dark suits, one in grey, and the fourth in a black jacket with grey trousers, were laughing and talking.

"What are you thinking of, *chéri?*"

"Oh, I was just looking at the people here, wondering about them, what they do."

"They do not look interesting; they talk of business."

The waitress, a pretty girl, came for their order. Yvette started ordering. Tom wished that she had let him do it. He had intended to order in French. But he said nothing. The waitress wrote. Yvette reached across the table, took his hand and squeezed it. A slow smile came across his face. He remembered the first time he had made love to her. They had gone to eat in a restaurant on the Boulevard St. Germain. There had been the same soft look on her face. Had it been love, or desire, or both? It was merely a question of definition, he thought. But he remembered; neither of them had been able to speak or eat. They had left the restaurant and gone to his hotel. Afterwards, they had strolled and Yvette had taken his arm. It had begun then. It was ending now.

"You look sad, *chéri,*" she said.

"I don't mean to."

"I am sad. I will look at the postcards with the pictures of the places where we have seen."

The waitress brought their soup.

"Don't eat so fast, *chéri,*" she said.

Tom slowed down.

After they had eaten, they took a cab back to the air terminal. Tom stared intently at the Arc de Triomphe as they had swung around the Étoile. He had seen this monument daily. He had come to take it for granted. It was graceful, yet magnificent in the strength that it embodied. France was a living nation with a continuity of history going back to the days of Napoleon and even before that epoch. But she was a nation whose grandeur was faded and tarnished. The weak-

ness of modern France seemed to be mocked by the strength
in this monument and by the power, glory, and victory that it
represented.

They passed on out of sight of the Arc de Triomphe. Soon
they were on the Avenue du Président Wilson with its grey
buildings, big doors, and its air of bourgeois comfort. Then
the bridge, the Seine. Soon they were back at Les Invalides
terminal. It was too soon to board the bus for the airport.
They sat in a waiting room. There were many people there.
Now and then announcements of bus departures came over
the loudspeaker system.

These last minutes with Yvette should be spent in talking,
Tom thought. But he was experiencing a flood of feeling and
emotion, and he could not give voice to these feelings. He noticed a line of people with their baggage beside them check-
ing in at the KLM counter. Already, he was half out of Paris.
The air terminal was a kind of border between France and
the rest of the world, a door through which one came or
went. He looked at the clock. It was only three-fifteen and
the bus would not leave until four. Time spent with Yvette
had always seemed to sweep by but now it crawled.

He and Yvette had both had dreams to live. They had lived
some of them with each other. There were many kinds of
love, many emotions which became tangled and intertwined
with that of life and with the physical desires which love
aroused and kept alive. These could be wrapped up in dreams.
One day, though, while the love of two people was wrapped
up in a dream which each was living, there could be an
awakening. There would be for him and for Yvette. His
had been a dream of his youth. And her dream? He was not
certain.

Finally they boarded the bus which took them to Le Bourget. It was almost full and Tom noticed that there were several different languages being spoken by the passengers. The

bus went along a route he knew. He had ridden this way in reverse when he had arrived, lonely and uncertain. And then he had met Yvette. Now?

She held his hand.

"I am sorry you are leaving."

He checked himself from explaining why he had to leave.

The bus moved slowly. Yvette looked at him. They arrived at Le Bourget. He was quickly hurried through customs. Their farewell kiss was brief and quick.

III

He was alone. Yvette would be driving back now. It would be a long slow ride in heavy traffic.

Soon the call came.

He picked up his coat, briefcase, and typewriter and walked slowly through the gate.

There she was, on a step to his left, waving and blowing him kisses.

Tom put his things down and blew kisses to her. She looked lovely in the sunshine; he could feel himself choking up.

He picked up his things and walked to the steps leading to the door of the plane. Again he stopped, set down his things, and turned to wave at her.

He picked up the typewriter and briefcase and walked up the steps.

In the plane, Tom could not get a seat on the side where he could see Yvette. He sat, fastened his seat belt, and tried to read. Life was full of farewells, he thought. And one farewell would be the final farewell.

Suddenly Tom unfastened his seat belt, got up from his seat and crossed the aisle. Apologizing to a man sitting there, he leaned toward the window hoping to get another glimpse of her. But Yvette was gone.

Tom returned to his seat, refastened his seat belt, and started to read.

A NIGHT
IN NEW JERUSALEM

I

"What are you doing tonight, Eddie?" Pete asked.

"Nothing, I'm tired; I'll probably stay in and work."

"I have a date," Pete said.

"With the same girl?"

"No, but she has the same name—Judith," Pete answered, laughing.

Eddie Ryan had thought about making a date for the evening but had finally decided not to. Eddie's decision was as much a matter of habit as it was of conscience; his work was almost a compulsion. And besides, he hoped to sell whatever it was he wrote; he needed the money.

Suddenly Eddie felt sad. He did not want to go upstairs and write in a lonely hotel room. He looked around the hotel dining room. On the dairy side, he noticed a plump, greying rabbi wearing a skullcap. He was with a woman, obviously his wife, and a young man about twenty who was growing a beard. The young man was wearing a skullcap also. There were not many people sitting on the dairy side.

But on the meat side where Eddie and Pete sat, there were

many people. Most of them looked like tourists recently arrived from America.

"Where did you go this time?" Pete asked.

"The Galilee."

"Kinnert?" he asked.

"There were incidents there," Eddie said, "there are incidents everywhere I go, either a day or two before I get there or the day after I leave."

Pete shook his head.

"There are two sides of the story, Eddie. Have you talked to any of the military people?"

"No, I haven't."

"You ought to. Some of these kids are as rambunctious as our marines. You can't blame the Arabs for getting jittery about them."

Pete was a tall young man and, even though there was something strained and taut in his manner, he was charming. He worked for an American magazine and they had sent him over to the Near East. He had been in Israel for over a month before Eddie Ryan had arrived, and he had spent three months in the Arab world before arriving in Israel. He had already sent back several short pieces and one long one from "the other side." That's how he referred to the Arab world.

"Hell," Pete went on, "those guys go right up to the border with their guns pointed just like this." He sat up and, leaning forward, pointed an imaginary gun in Eddie's face. "This is how they do it, they go right up to the Arabs and point their guns. Then they turn around. They keep doing this. Naturally the Arabs get jittery. Who wouldn't? So they open fire on them. And then the Jews plaster them."

Eddie didn't say anything for a few seconds.

"But Pete, the Arabs have more arms, and they're doing a helluva lot of infiltrating. Why, every place I've gone to has had incidents—shootings and shellings of cows or goats."

"Oh, I'm not saying the Arabs are right, Eddie. I'm disgusted with them. I think the Jews ought to declare war on them right now. It's their best chance."

"But most Israelis want peace. I'm convinced of that, Pete."

"They say they do, but why don't they make a gesture?"

"Make a gesture and die?" Eddie asked.

"That's what the Cabinet Ministers of Government told me when I asked them the same question."

Eddie was troubled. The Middle East situation was serious; it could explode. He wondered if there were any solutions; if only he knew more about the problem. Pete had been out here longer than he had but Pete wasn't of too much help when Eddie asked him specific questions; Pete sympathized with the Arabs.

"You're really pro-Arab, aren't you, Pete?" Eddie asked.

"No, but I feel sorry for them."

"What about the Jews? Do you feel sorry for them?"

Pete seemed to think for a moment before he answered.

"No, not in the same way. They're top dog over here."

"But with Egypt's arms superiority and the fact that there are forty million Arabs against a million and a half Jews . . . ?"

"The Jews won't make a gesture, Eddie. Hell, I met an Arab in Jordan, in Amman, to be exact. He's in the Jordanian government and he told me honestly that he's for the dam."

"Can you quote him?"

"Of course not, he can't say it in public. And he can't do anything, either. None of the moderate elements among the Arabs can speak out. This man told me that as long as they have a crackpot visionary at the head of the government here, he can't do a thing, none of the moderates in the Arab world can, not as long as they keep the old man they've got here in power."

"Be reasonable, Pete, you don't think that the Jews should let the Arabs tell them who to pick as Prime Minister, do you?"

"You know I don't. But I will tell you one thing; there is something that's happening in the Arab world and the Jews don't know what it is."

"It works both ways, Pete."

"What do you mean?" He looked bewildered as he asked this.

"The Jews aren't sitting still; they're making progress, too."

"Sure they are. That's why I say if there's going to be a war, the Jews had better attack now. The sooner they do, the better chance they have."

"Do you think that war can be avoided?"

"Most of the time, I don't, Eddie. How about you, do you think it can?"

"I don't know. It looks bad; it's a rotten situation."

"I guess so."

A tall, pretty girl walked up to the table. Pete introduced her to Eddie. It was Judith, Pete's date for the evening. She sat down.

"You're American?" Eddie asked.

"Yes, I'm here on loan. What do you think of Israel, Mr. Ryan?"

"That's what we've been talking about," Pete said, laughing.

"I like it; I like Israel," Eddie told her.

"Why?" Judith asked.

"The effort they're making. The gallantry of the people."

"Yes, it is gallant," she said. For a moment she seemed solemn, but then she laughed.

"What's the joke?" Pete asked.

"I was thinking of something that happened to me last Shabbath. I was hit on the neck by a stone. Fortunately I wasn't seriously hurt."

"The fanatics from the Hundred Gates?" Eddie asked her.

"Yes."

"I'd like to stack them up against our Howling Methodists and Holy Rollers. They'd hold their own, I'm sure of that," Eddie said.

"You've seen them then?"

Eddie nodded, grinning. "You ought to sell them to the Arabs."

"The Arabs wouldn't want them," Pete said.

"I sometimes wonder what the Arabs do want," Judith said.

"You people on this side don't understand the Arabs," Pete told her. "The Arabs are afraid of the Jews; they won't attack."

"But they are attacking, every day. What would you call what's been happening along the Jordanian border?" Eddie asked.

"I know that there are skirmishes but the government makes so much about them in the papers."

"They have to publish it, the people know that it's happening," Judith explained.

"But it's making people so jittery," Pete argued.

"I don't think the people here are so jittery." She turned toward Eddie. "Do you?"

Eddie shook his head.

"Well, they are," protested Pete. "I was in Tel Aviv and I watched people when they bought the morning papers. You should have seen their faces."

"But they go about their business. Even when they know it's dangerous, they go on. There are far more incidents than the ones that get into the papers."

"I know that, Judith," Pete said, "but my point is that by publicizing these incidents, they are making the public jittery. It's bound to build up even more hostility and there'll never be any hope about talking to Arab moderates then."

"What Arab moderates? Where are they, Pete? Do they have anything to say?"

"There are Arab moderates; I was there; I talked to them. They can't say anything publicly, not now with the situation the way that it is."

Judith gave him an impatient glance.

"It's true, Judith. And I'll tell you honestly, I'm not pro-Arab but I feel sorry for them."

"You can feel as sorry for them as you wish, Pete. As for me, I would be more inclined to sympathy if they'd call off their infiltration."

"I know it's a bad situation, Judith. But come on, we'd better be leaving or we'll be late for *Mr. Roberts*."

Pete turned to Eddie. "We'll discuss this more tomorrow, Eddie, if you're free."

II

Eddie sat in the lobby with a cup of coffee. He had had a cup in the dining room with Judith and Pete earlier, but because the restaurant was kosher they had served it to Eddie black. And Eddie liked milk in his coffee. He was drinking it the way he liked in the lobby. He looked around at the other people.

"I'm not opposed to religion or to observance," a stout, grey-haired woman was saying in a loud voice. She wore a floral printed dress cut very low in front. She looked over-dressed. With her was a young rabbi and two elderly tourists who looked American.

"People see things differently," the young rabbi commented.

Eddie turned in the other direction. Near him sat a middle-aged woman with two young army officers. Eddie had seen her before. She was the wife of a Canadian officer who had stepped on a mine on Mount Scopus earlier in the week. Eddie had heard that he had been very seriously wounded.

"He'll be out of commission for a long time," one of the men was saying.

"Yes, it will be quite some time," answered the officer's wife.

A tall man came out of the hotel dining room. He looked around in the lobby. When he saw Eddie, he walked over to where he was sitting.

"You play *echec*, chess?"

"All right."

"One minute then."

The man turned and hurried over to the steps, beside the elevator that led to a bathroom. Eddie took another sip of coffee. Eddie had met the young man before but knew little about him. He was a relative of one of the hotel owners. He had been born in Hungary and had emigrated to Palestine in the early 1940s. He spoke English poorly but he had tried to explain to Eddie how much he liked working outdoors. Before the War of Liberation he had been on a kibbutz but then he had been wounded. The wound had destroyed some nerves in his left arm, partially crippling it. Because he could not work, he could not return to a kibbutz.

The Canadian officer's wife was explaining what the doctors had told her about her husband's condition.

The overdressed woman was saying that she had spent a day in Galilee the week before and was going to Beer-sheba tomorrow.

Eddie yawned and looked toward the door.

A couple entered the lobby. The man was in his thirties; he was dark-skinned and could have been taken for an Arab. The woman was tall and had a good-looking, youthful face. As she walked, she swished her skirt.

They walked up to where the overdressed woman was talking to a group.

"Here, my dear friends, my very dear friends. Come and buy. I have jewelry, beautiful jewelry, that will make you beautiful. Wait, you will see such earrings. They are so beautiful and they should be worn only by a beautiful woman," the man said. He directed himself to the lady in the gathering.

"You are charming," she answered coyly, "even if what you say is not the truth."

"No. But maybe I can go to school and not go into the army so soon."

It was clear to Eddie that she did not relish going into the army.

III

Eddie sat in the bar. It was quite large. A small square area had been set aside for dancing. An orchestra was playing "Danny Boy." The violinist, speaking with a thick accent, had announced that the song was being played for Mr. Ryan. The orchestra played badly but Eddie didn't mind. Hearing this song in Jerusalem touched him. He thought of Chicago, his youth.

As a boy, he had dreamed of seeing the world. And he had seen much of it but the world was different from those romantic dreams of his.

The music stopped. The violinist looked over toward Eddie.

"'Kathleen,'" he announced.

Eddie grinned self-consciously. The song was a tearjerker but it always got to him. He thought of Ireland, his dead grandmother, his wife, of the girls he had loved, and the girls he might have loved if he had ever met them. He felt as he had in his youth, he was waiting, waiting for a girl with a sense of love. And yet he knew that what he dreamed could never be.

The music stopped. Eddie took a drink of his beer and looked around. It was a slow night; the bar was almost empty.

The violinist grinned over at him.

"Thank you," Eddie said, lifting his beer in salute.

"Anything for you, Mr. Ryan."

The three musicians left the dais and sat at the bar. The place seemed dead. Eddie knew he ought to go upstairs and go to bed, or else read. But he sat there drinking beer. He dreaded the idea of that hotel room. It was so empty. Suddenly, he wished his trip were ended. It would be at least two weeks before he got back to New York, maybe three. He finished his beer, signaled the waiter, and ordered another. He was going to relax now and drink a few. He wouldn't get drunk but there was no point in his going up to that lonely room. He looked around the bar again. He couldn't help but think that he could be any place, even in a small town in America. Bars were pretty much alike, all over, he thought. So were hotels.

The waiter brought over a second bottle of beer. Eddie took a drink. The orchestra started playing again.

Two couples got up to dance. Eddie looked around. More people had arrived. Eddie saw Moshe and his wife with Shosheneh and a short man about thirty, walking into the bar. They sat down at a table. When they saw Eddie, they waved for him to join them. He carried his beer over to their table and sat down.

"I would like to go swimming," Moshe's wife said. "Do you want to go swimming later? I went at two o'clock last night."

"No, I don't," Eddie said, shaking his head.

"Oh, I love to swim late at night, at two or three in the morning. It's wonderful."

"Go swimming now," Moshe said. "Tomorrow you will go to Tel Aviv early to make money."

"I'll be there. I love business, too," she said.

Eddie was bored. The conversation tired him. He had to

get up early the next day; he was going to visit Arab villages in the Triangle. It would be a long, hard day.

"I will make money tomorrow," Moshe said.

Shosheneh turned toward Eddie:

"When will you be returning to America?"

"In two or three weeks."

"Will you be glad to go?" asked Moshe's wife.

"Yes, I've been traveling long enough."

"It won't be bad for you in America; you aren't a Jew," she said.

"Or a Negro," added Shosheneh.

"Jews are persecuted in America," Moshe's wife said.

"That's not true. There's some anti-Semitism there but many Jews do well in America," Eddie protested.

Moshe's wife stared at him, unbelieving.

"Maybe there is not so much prejudice against the Jew, but what about the Negro?" Shosheneh asked.

"There must be prejudice against the Jew. There is everywhere; there was in Vienna—everywhere except here in Israel," Moshe's wife said.

The orchestra started to play another song. Shosheneh and the young man got up to dance. Eddie asked Moshe's wife if she cared to dance. She said yes. She danced well, holding herself close to him.

"How can you understand Jews?" she asked him.

Before he could saying anything, she added:

"After all, you're not a Jew; you're a *goy*."

"What's that got to do with it?"

She didn't answer but danced more closely against him in silence.

IV

"I don't like the Jew, I like the Arab," Moshe said. "The Jew . . ." He made a face.

"And rabbis," he went on, his voice full of sneers, "I hate them."

"Suppose they buy something from you?" Eddie asked.

"Then I love them. I love anyone who buys something from me. But I hate rabbis. Hypocrites!"

"The rabbis from America are the worst," his wife said. "One of them kept trying to get me to go up to his room."

"See? Hypocrites. I wish I was Arab, not Jew."

Moshe was denouncing rabbis and Shosheneh tried to talk about the color question. The young man was trying to get her attention. Eddie wished he had joined a more interesting group.

"There they are," Moshe's wife suddenly interrupted the conversation.

They all turned. A couple had just walked in. The girl was about twenty-five, very thin, with short red hair. Her face was pretty, but lifeless. The man with her was dark and very broad, almost fat. He had a small mustache. He stared directly ahead, his expression somewhat forbidding.

"It's time for the show," Moshe's wife said.

"She's too skinny to wear an evening dress like that. She would look better with more clothes on."

"They're not very friendly. I have never seen them talking to anyone in the hotel," Eddie said. Then, "Couldn't the hotel get a better show?"

"They're *goy*. The hotel owes them money, that's why they're still here. Their contract is over but they're waiting for their money."

"I thought the hotel was making money; it charges enough," Eddie said.

"They have invested too much. Everyone is grumbling. And those two, they are very mad. They come from Switzerland."

"I don't like their show; I don't see why the hotel engaged them," Shosheneh commented.

"If they were not engaged, this would not be a night club," Moshe's wife said.

"But why does it have to be a night club?" Eddie asked.

"You have to have a night club in a hotel if you want to attract Americans."

More lights went out, drums banged, and a fast waltz was struck up. The couple moved out onto the floor. The man started spinning and whirling the girl around.

Their dance ended. The man sat down. The girl did a dance alone.

"Do you like her?" Moshe's wife asked Eddie.

He shook his head. "It's a combination of stiff ballet and night club."

The girl was awkward. In a little while, she removed her skirt. She moved off to the side. When she reappeared, all she was wearing was a silver G-string and a silk brassiere. She went through a routine of leaps and turns in a stiff, disinterested way. The dance ended. Her face remained listless as she bowed to applause.

Next, she and her partner did an acrobatic routine.

When the act ended, Eddie noticed the fatigue on her face.

"She's too skinny," Moshe's wife said, "she looks better with her clothes on."

"I like her," Moshe said.

"Oh, stop it," his wife said.

"Any girl's more interesting without clothes. I love girls. Come, we go home."

"Don't you want to stay and go swimming?" his wife asked.

"No, we go home. Tomorrow you go to Tel Aviv. You make me money."

"I make you money?"

"Yes," he said, signaling for the waiter.

The music started again and Shosheneh and the young man got up to dance.

Eddie finished his beer. He was tired.

V

The others had gone but Eddie Ryan had sat down with Major Calverton. The bar was deserted except for the bartender, a waiter, and the violinist.

"I'll have one more, then I'm calling it a night," the Major said.

"I'll have another one with you."

"A second officer was wounded today."

"Yes!" Eddie was surprised.

"In Galilee. Maybe you've met him; he's a Swede, Captain Sundquist."

"No, I've never met him. Is he seriously wounded?"

"In the leg," Major Calverton said.

"The situation's getting worse every day, isn't it?" Eddie asked.

"No, I wouldn't say that."

"You don't think there'll be war?" Eddie asked.

The Major shook his head. "No, I don't think so. It'll go on just the way it is until you and I are dead, and our grandchildren are grown up."

The waiter brought the beer.

"Sometimes this job gives me the creeps. Have you been in the Gaza Strip, Ryan?"

"No, I've been in Arab refugee camps but not there. I couldn't get there."

"I'm sometimes afraid to go in there and I fought in Korea. We can't carry arms; all we can carry is a little white flag."

He shook his head.

"That mob, I'll tell you, Ryan, it's something. I'm afraid of it. Anybody could stir them up in a half hour and they'd stone you to death. They did stone some of our officers a couple of years ago. They can be incited at the drop of a hat."

"You find the same kind of unreasoning violence in India and in other parts of Southeast Asia," Eddie said.

"I guess so, but these would stone you and not know why. Once they've been riled up, they'd stone anybody to death."

"The violence of frustration," Eddie remarked.

"It doesn't matter what kind of violence you want to call it if you're the guy on the receiving end of it."

"I guess not. Do you think there's much hope of improving the situation?" Eddie asked.

"I'm here on a tour of duty but it won't be much longer. I'm going to be sent to school. I'm up for promotion to the General Staff. Maybe I shouldn't be telling you that."

"I've already forgotten it," Eddie assured him.

"You know, Ryan, I've been in the army for eighteen years. I've worked hard for this promotion and I have to be careful what I say. We can't associate too much with either side. If I say too much, I'd be sent home with a bad record. It happened to a captain. He was called home."

The Major went on.

"Neither side likes us. Every time we reach a decision, we have one or the other sore with us. You sit out there in a hut on the Gaza Strip and every time you hear a mortar go off, you put your fingers in your ears. Later you go out to see who shot it."

"I guess you'll be glad to get your other assignment."

"You can say that again. But I'm a soldier; I go where I'm sent. But this isn't the best spot for a soldier, especially when all he can carry is a little white flag."

"Is the Israeli army good?"

"Yes it's well officered but they're a bit rambunctious. They've gotten the Arabs jittery."

"Do you think they could win if there's a war?"

"Probably."

"It's too goddamned bad that there can't be peace." Eddie's voice sounded angry.

"Yes, but I see this going on and on. Like I said, Ryan, it's going to be going on when our grandchildren are old."

"But there must be something that someone can do. What about the Suez problem? Maybe there will be a war now."

"I don't know, Ryan. The Jews have a good army; they could take care of Jerusalem."

"But if there's a war, the whole area will be set back."

"Take a look at the Gaza Strip and you'll ask how they can be set back."

"Christ, I'll be glad to get home."

"When are you leaving?"

"In another couple of weeks."

Neither of them spoke for a while; they sat and drank their beer. Eddie was too tired to talk any more. Finally the Major spoke:

"I'm going to turn in. I'm on duty tomorrow."

"I hope it's quiet."

"If it's quiet tomorrow, it won't be quiet sooner or later."

Eddie finished his beer.

They both stood up, paid their checks, and said good night.

Eddie walked up the stairs to the main floor. He got on the elevator and went to his room. He was depressed. So far he had not talked to anyone who thought that there could be any solution to the problem. What would happen to Israel? He looked at the bed. He could not answer this question tonight. He was tired. Slowly he got undressed and fell into bed.

ONLY TOMORROW
AND TOMORROW

I

There was something in his makeup that chilled them away from him, and made them say Mr. Eliot instead of Bill. There were bigger barriers between him and the wagon men, between him and everybody than was the case with the other Route Inspectors and Wagon Dispatchers. Sometimes he was satisfied with this, even proud of it. Why the hell should he care about knowing all the muttonheads and clodhoppers in the Continental Express Company? What did their opinion of him matter? But at other times, it left him keenly sad with a sense of loneliness and isolation. Well, he might as well shrug his shoulders, and let it go at that.

Freight was piled all around Bill Eliot on the platform. There was an early morning autumn snap coming in from the open runways. He gave orders curtly and mechanically. There were so many loads sorted out, and he pointed them out to his men. He had to get all of this delivery freight loaded and his chauffeurs had to be off and at their work. He was as little interested in it as they were. He and they had to help to do the work of the world, he told himself ironically.

"Cripes, Mr. Eliot, that's pretty stiff, and I got them three new concerns on my route that are shipping heavy these days," Louis Cordozza, a lanky teamster, said.

"There's the freight," Bill told him, and Cordozza slouched away, a sulky look on his face.

Bill felt quick regret. He didn't like to be so curt, but goddamn it, he knew all those things, and there was the freight. The freight must go out. That was the way the business was run. One of the arteries of the great nation, don't you know? The freight must go out.

Mike Mulroney, a cigar in his fat face, passed by and waved a patronizing greeting to Eliot.

"Heavy today, ha ha!" he added, turning around, and taking the cigar out of his mouth.

Eliot nodded to his fellow Inspector. He walked over to Spiegel's wagon. He liked young Spiegel, a decent sort of kid.

"Say, Spiegel, what the hell is this kick that is always comin' in from the Consolidated. I got another letter from Patsy McLaughlin."

"It ain't my fault, Mr. Eliot. It's the way they pack their stuff. They pack it in cardboard cartons and boxes, and half of the time it's fallin' apart. I can't take that. I keep tellin' them, but it ain't no use."

"I guess I'll have to go see them," Bill said.

"I wish something could be done. Every day I got to battle with 'em, and turn down their stuff. Then they start burnin' up the wires. The shippin' clerk and traffic manager there are the kind of guys who ain't got any consideration for nobody."

"All right," said Eliot.

"Here's your load, Mike," Bill then said to Mike Sporney, who had just approached him.

"O.K., Mr. Eliot."

He walked back along the noisy platform among the assorted loads. They were all set. He'd have to hang around now until the men got off with them. He stood off by himself, watching his wagons being loaded. He was bored, heedless of the tremendous clatter.

Autumn! And outside the sunny autumn mornings. Other autumns! Autumn football back in those days. But he had never liked football. He had dragged his can out to practice on weary dull days. Some fellows had gotten a thrill out of the glory and a muscular exhilaration out of the sheer contact on the field. Not him. He had never done anything he wanted to do, even then. There were many classmates of his, fellows who had forgotten him, undoubtedly, fellows who were writers and editors and businessmen and even a few football coaches. He wondered how they felt now as they began to be submerged in the heaviness of middle age? All life narrows down to one mortal career, and all the many promises of youth prove to have been illusions, not promises.

He moved about the freight. The thing to do was to find some kind of forgetting thought or activity for every minute of the day. Years ago, he had read Walter Pater. If they knew this at the Express Company, they'd laugh at him behind his back even more than they did now.

"Good morning, Mr. Eliot," said Billie O'Brien, the new Wagon Dispatcher at the depot. He wore an old blue suit, a blue sweater, and a grey cap slanted to one side of his head.

"Hello, O'Brien," said Eliot.

"Listen, how about sparing me one of your wagons. I just got in a rush delivery I have to shoot out right away. I could call up the Dutchman at the Wagon Department, but it would take maybe a half hour or more to get one of his wagons here. This has to go out quick."

Eliot shrugged his shoulders, and looked at his wagons.

"Hey, Joey!"

Joey McNeil rushed over.

"Get that stuff off, and take a load here for O'Brien. Then go on your route."

"Yes, sir."

Eliot worked with several of his drivers, rearranging the load Joey had, sorting it among them. It kept him busy for a while. Then, he stood back, and watched his wagons draw away from the platform.

He jumped off the platform and strode out of one of the runways. He wanted to avoid having to walk over to the Wagon Call Department with Mike Mulroney or any of the other Route Inspectors. He was in no mood to listen to them talk this morning. He knew that they considered him queer, and that they resented him as a high-hat bastard and college graduate, but he could not bring himself around to talking with them and simulating interest. He had never been quite able to mask his feelings, and he was aloof in their presence. That was why he always hurried away from the Call Department after routing his calls.

He walked along business streets, with hulk-like factories lining both sides. He had a half hour or an hour to kill before going to the Call Department to help sort the damn overtime tickets, and he didn't know what to do. He walked about, aimlessly. He noticed some strike pickets in front of a wholesale clothing house, two thin little fellows, marching resolutely to and fro with boards flung over their shoulders:

FINKELSTEIN AND WEINER
UNFAIR TO ORGANIZED LABOR

He experienced a feeling of union with the pickets, and he had an impulse to speak with them, but he didn't know what to say to them. A sentimental phrase came into his head, *Humanity*. He wanted to feel himself part of Humanity, absorbed in its purposes and aims. He wanted to share in the common feelings of men, and he knew no door by which he might enter and share. The pickets tramping slowly backwards and forwards before the red brick building stirred up these impulses, energized them with life, and left them objectless and unrelieved.

He went on, and slipped back into a mood of cynicism. He thought of how many of the men at the express company described with doting details, their bedroom lives with their wives, and of how the young and unmarried fellows on the wagons talked with relish of their experiences with pickups and whores, going over them detail by detail. And their jokes, particularly their ideas of the humor to be found in any re-mark about homosexuality. None of them was overtly in-clined that way in the least, but it was a subject that caused loud and raucous guffaws, the same as did the mere mention of the word queer. He thought of their work. Most of them hated it but accepted it in a grumbling way. He understood their almost general attitude of dislike for work, and their desire to stall. The most common working experience in the company seemed to be that of getting out of something, of putting something over on the boss. There was no common experience of work to link them together, no common feel-ing. At times, it seemed as though a liking of dirty jokes was their only common link, and this was a slender one at best. The ideal of service, of moving the freight of the nation, did not touch and fire him, and it seemed to touch and fire almost no one else, except possibly the editors of the company mag-azine, *The Continenal Expressman*. But few people in the company seemed to read the magazine with any seriousness. From top to bottom, he was getting to hate American life more every day. The country was being ruined by the slobs of service, and nobody seemed to care. He wondered why he should, how he could, and what it would mean if he did care. For a brief period in France a few years ago, a very, very brief period, he had felt some thrill at being American, and at being a small part of the power of a great nation. It had been, however, a final rationalization against the crush-ing power of a military organization upon his own personality, and that thrill had subsided quickly into silent and cynical resentment. In a twisted, bitter, almost pathological mood, he quietly sang to himself: *My Country 'Tis of Thee*.

He noticed that he had gone far out of his way. He traced his steps back to the Wagon Call Department.

II

"Porky's off work today," said Mike, as they sat around the table sorting overtime slips in the big Wagon Department office of Patsy McLaughlin, the Superintendent.

"What's the matter now?" asked Cole.

"Same thing, trouble with his wife. You know, she found some Merry Widows in his pocket, and she raised holy hell with him. Jesus, he was weeping on my shoulder the other day. Ha! Ha!"

"Leonard's getting tired of Porky layin' off. I heard him talking the other day. Porky better start watching his step," said Emmett Carr.

Bill Eliot quietly sorted tickets, bored with their conversation, anxious to get the goddamn job over with.

"Did you hear about McGinty this morning?" asked Sam Benton, a new North Side Route Inspector.

"No," said Cole.

"He's got piles again, goddamn bad."

They laughed.

"Say, Ben, how's Bones McNeill workin' under you?" asked Kane.

"He's no goddamn good to me. Christ, is he a stalling bastard," said Sam.

"He was a good worker when I had him on one of the electrics," said Bohunk August.

"Well, you can have him back," said Sam.

"Say, Frankie Noonan is gettin' worse and worse. You know he's dumb, and he's afraid the Jew clerk will get his job, and he doesn't do nothin' but jaw at him all day," said Emmett Carr.

"We'll have to kid him," said August.

"Why should anybody worry about a job? Worry about a job? Ha! Ha! Ha!" jeered Mike Mulroney, flashing a roll of bills.

Bill Eliot was glad to get up, with the tickets sorted, and to go into the Call Department to route his calls.

III

Bill went on his route, which was the north end of the Loop. He met four of his wagonmen in an alley off Randolph Street, and gave them their calls. He told them to phone the Call Department back about three o'clock, and that he would call the Department at a quarter to four. He knew where each of them would be at four-thirty, or where messages could be delivered to them, and at that time he would give them any further instructions.

He went up to see the Consolidated fellow. The shipping clerk was a stout man named Cohen. Surrounded by boxes, he was busy ordering two girls around.

Cohen bowed him in.

"What's the trouble?" Eliot asked.

Cohen had a long, involved, and bewailing story about how the wagonman Spiegel would not accept their goods.

"He'll accept them if you pack them better. We can't be accepting badly packed packages. They're liable to come apart, so that goods will be lost, and would be liable for claims."

"What you call not good packed?"

Bill pointed to some loosely tied cardboard boxes.

"Do you call that packed well?"

"Good enough!"

"Listen, you'll have to pack them better. We won't take them and you can beef all you want to. It won't do you any good."

Cohen brought out the traffic manager, and Bill was involved for almost an hour in a stupid argument. He walked out on them, telling them finally that their goods would not be accepted unless they were put up in stronger and more tightly tied packages. The goddamn stupidity of the whole business enraged him. He stopped in a restaurant to get a cup of coffee and to quiet his nerves.

He felt like just sitting in the restaurant. He did not see how he could go on with the damn work, seeing shippers, phoning for his calls, distributing them, listening to his men complain about loads that were too heavy, hearing the crap some of them dished out so that he wouldn't know they were stalling. He arose, paid his check, and went back on the route.

He phoned the United Pencil Company and vainly tried to persuade the shipping clerk and traffic manager to get their shipments ready an hour earlier in the afternoon. He began to strain more at the leash. While arguing with them, he had felt as if he were divided into two parts, and as if the part of him that talked and listened to their repetitive commonplaces were one person, and that another and more internal *he* stood apart and listened to this, laughing, sneering, revolting.

He phoned the Wagon Department, got his calls, and looked up his men to give them to them. Then he was finished. He only had the long evening to get through now; after that and sleep, only tomorrow, tomorrow and tomorrow.

IV

Riding home on the streetcar to his room in a West Side boardinghouse, he thought of how ever since he had been demobilized out of the army in January 1919 life had been empty. He had gone on day after day for over five years, fighting this emptiness. Why? What was the use of it? Why should he still hate his rich father, and the memory of his dead wife? Why should he go on boiling about his college days when he was a rich boy and a star football player? Why should he be this way?

He noticed the other passengers on the crowded streetcar. Many of them looked tired and dull. They were stupefied after their day's work. Many were just ordinary working men, like his own teamsters and chauffeurs. There was a working man in overalls, clutching a strap near him. The man was getting old. His face looked so calm, but his eyes were sad. And a girl, good-looking, with a cold, empty face.

Why hadn't he remarried? Why hadn't many things happened?

The car started, stopped, started. The car gradually emptied. Bill found a seat.

He got off the streetcar at his stop, and walked three blocks to his boardinghouse in the dusky early autumn air.

He let himself in and looked at the table by the hall tree for mail. He did this almost every night, but there was rarely mail for him. It was a private ritual he performed with himself. He expected something he would never get. He waited for news that wouldn't come.

Bill slowly went up the carpeted steps. The boardinghouse was quiet, and had a musty smell.

His room was big and clean but disorderly. He had a few books on a small shelf, and magazines and newspapers were stacked in corners, unread.

Bill sat on the big bed.

He would spend the evening alone as he had many other evenings. And tomorrow he would go to work, hating it.

He heard footsteps in the hall outside his door. He heard a door closing.

This place was full of lonely men like himself.

He sat for a while. Then, with a slow and cold deliberation, he got up and pulled two old suitcases from the closet. He packed all his clothes, still in a mood of calm deliberation. Pulling on his coat and hat, he quickly left his room, and went downstairs with the grips. No one saw or heard him.

He laid his key on the table and left. He hurried to the corner, turned it, and then he walked slowly with a grip in either hand.

He would take a streetcar down to the Loop and go off somewhere. He didn't care where he went. He would just go.

Bill Eliot was never heard of again by the men at the Continental Express Company. To them, and to all who knew him, he became a man who had disappeared. He became a lonely, wandering, bitter man, going from job to job, forever hating his youth, his past, his education, his rich father and his dead wife. He drifted about from city to city across the American continent, retaining his bitterness and his loneliness, slowly sinking deeper and deeper into middle age. He went on from day to day, continuing to see life as merely one empty tomorrow after another.

TOM CARROLL

Part One

I

"Tom, when Bill comes to dinner tonight, please don't start any political arguments with him."

Tom Carroll looked toward his wife from a darkened corner of the living room. At first her request surprised him. Then he became irritated. He watched her move across the room to switch on a lamp.

Ruth Carroll pressed a button. The light gave the room an instant brightness.

Tom Carroll did not show his irritation. He was a slender man in his early fifties with a thin, sensitive face. He was a handsome man with attractive features but there was an unhealthy pallor to his skin.

"For my sake, Tom," Ruth urged, her tone pleading.

She was a well-preserved blonde who looked much younger than her forty-seven years. Her face was almost beautiful and her full figure was still youthful. Ruth Carroll looked her best in the stunning black suit she was wearing.

"Tom?"

"All right, I heard you, Ruth. If he doesn't start an argument with me, I won't with him. It's usually the United Front of my family that brings on these rows."

"Oh Tom, why should something—or anything for that matter—that's happening in Moscow, thousands of miles away from us, come between a father and his son? It's so senseless," Ruth paused, "and if you only knew how distressing it is to me."

"Why should anything happening in Moscow affect a twenty-five-year-old young man who claims that all he wants is to become an artist? And why should this affect his mother? Who, incidentally, also wants to be an artist."

Ruth sat down near her husband.

"Tom, you used to be liberal."

II

The Carroll living room was large. The walls were lined with books. The furniture was simple in design and comfortable. Two oil paintings by Georgia O'Keefe were hung on opposite walls.

Tom and Ruth were having cocktails.

"Two weeks ago, Bill told me the same thing—that I used to be liberal."

There was irony in Tom Carroll's voice to cover up his hurt.

Ruth didn't say anything. She took a sip of her martini. She had a thoughtful, reflective air. Then she spoke.

"Why have you changed?"

"Have I?"

"I don't mean only about politics, Tom. That's not the most important thing in the world. I mean in everything, Tom, in almost every way."

Tom was silent. His eyes were directed upon his drink. Ruth's words had hit his sensitive spots. He had not been feeling well lately; he had had severe stomach aches. And he felt unduly tired much of the time. He had been depressed. Yes, he had changed, he thought. In these ways he had changed. But Ruth did not know about these changes. He had not said anything to her, nor did he intend to.

"After a man and woman have been married as long as we have, Tom, and have lived together for so long, romance goes out the window. We both know that."

Ruth paused.

"But we can and should be friends."

"Aren't we friends?" Tom asked.

He looked at Ruth closely. How sincere had he been in asking that question? Precisely what was his feeling about her? Ruth was still a desirable woman and she knew it. Men younger than she found her so. He shouldn't be jealous. And he wasn't.

He became saddened that he could feel no desire for her. Something had worn out between them.

And once—once he had adored her.

III

His attitude toward Ruth was a mixture of sympathy and boredom. Actually they had nothing more to say to one another. All that needed to be said, or could have been said, had been spoken. He had given her all the love that he could give any woman but now his love was gone. It had vanished, disappeared.

"You used to be so patient, Tom, so tolerant. You were always calm and serene but now you're so irritable. You seem so annoyed sometimes."

Tom almost winced in shame, but then he felt a stir of anger. He said nothing.

"The last time that Bill was over here, you all but jumped

down his throat. And, Tom, do you really think that a father ought to tell his son that he's a damned fool?"

"Someone ought to tell him something," he said.

His remark to Bill must have really hurt her, he thought. She probably suspected that he frequently thought that she was a damned fool too.

Ruth sat in silence.

Tom looked down at his drink. He lifted the glass to his lips. He knew that he concealed the pain he felt. Ruth had no idea how much he suffered because of the damaged relationship between his son and himself. He had loved the boy. He still did, and he feared for him. But how could he express his love and quiet his fears?

—How can I help my son?

He had sat up late, night after night, asking himself this. He had walked the streets in brooding loneliness. He had tossed in his bed, tormented. Again and again, he had come to feel that it was all in vain.

Ruth set her glass down on a small table beside her.

"Bill is an idealist, Tom. You were once one."

"What am I now? A cynic? What do you think I am now?"

Tom knew that if she were to say what she thought, the words that she would throw at him would be:

—Reactionary!

—Fascist!

He suspected that hurting him was Ruth's strongest motive in defending their son.

"You're the one who taught him to be liberal, Tom. You're the one who talked to him about being reasonable, tolerant, and open-minded. Now you've turned on him, you walk roughshod over reason and tolerance."

Tom controlled his anger; he didn't speak. He had to curb his tongue. Most likely she would twist anything he said. He wanted to maintain his self-control. It was better when he did.

"What I'm saying, Tom, is . . ."

He interrupted.

"I tried to instill a respect for truth in Bill. I tried my best."

He had spoken with more intensity and emotion than he had wanted to. He had not been able to keep his anger in check.

Ruth gave him an impatient glance. But then her vain pretty face with so little of the years written on it became lost in an expression of confusion. She was irritated with Tom, really irritated with him, but she was at a loss for anything to say to him. Looking at him, she was aware that he was getting grey. He looked thin. He was pale, too, and there were a number of little wrinkles around his eyes.

Oh, how she had loved his eyes. They had been sharp and penetrating; and yet they could be soft, soft and gentle. Or full of twinkling humor. But now? Now they were just sad and tired, the eyes of a man growing old.

She had drifted away from him.

But he had drifted away from her first, hadn't he?

Many women had been in love with Tom Carroll. And she had. But she no longer loved him. It was his fault. There was a wound deep inside her, and he had caused this hurt. She had never told him; he didn't know that he had opened this wound in her.

And there was yesterday. Yesterday! She didn't want to think of it now. Walking in the twilight along Fifth Avenue. Proud, fully proud of her figure and of her youthful appearance. The joy, the rejoicing. To know that she could still find love and fulfillment.

—I'm an adultress!

She had called herself this in a silly moment of happy pride. She had immediately felt foolish. This was dated, as dated as Ibsen's doll, Nora. She was being old-fashioned. And she was a modern, a free, spirit. Tom had always used to talk about being free spirits.

Suddenly Ruth started. Something of her thoughts and feelings may be showing on her face.

Her expression became bland.

IV

Ruth and Tom were still sitting in the large living room. It was dark outside now.

Bill would be joining them for dinner tonight. Her son. She loved him. He was so handsome and so talented. She was proud of him. Bill had taken her to many political meetings and dinners. Sometimes standing by her side, he would introduce her to people who could hardly believe that they were mother and son.

Tom scoffed at Bill's political interests and activities. He laughed at them.

—Truth.

What was the truth? Why did Tom think he and he alone knew the truth? Why had he turned against his own son? And why did he laugh at her? Ruth looked at him, bewildered and resentful.

"I'll fix you another cocktail," he said.

"You're tired, let me do it."

She rose and went to a tray on a small table where there were bottles, glasses, and a bucket of ice.

Tom leaned back in his chair, took a cigar out of his waistcoat pocket and lit it. As he took the first few puffs, he felt an uncomfortable pressure in his chest. Heartburn? He shouldn't smoke.

Ruth was mixing martinis. Tom saw the pride in her face. She took pride in mixing drinks for him and in ordering for him in a restaurant.

The drinks mixed, Ruth served him one. She poured the other one for herself. Just as she sat down, the telephone rang. Ruth set her drink down carefully on a table beside her chair, and rose. She picked up an opened package of cigarettes and a book of matches, took out a cigarette, lit it as she went over to the corner table where the phone was.

"Hello," she said into the mouthpiece.

Ruth was nervous.

"Someone had the wrong number," she said, walking back to her chair. Tom wondered if it was her latest lover. Did he know him? Did Bill know about him? What did he think?

Ruth picked up her drink.

"Tomorrow—Sunday. I dread Sundays; they're such a bore."

Tom didn't say anything.

Years ago, on Sunday morning, they used to stay in bed and make love.

Why had he thought of those disappeared Sunday mornings? He couldn't remember how he had felt, only that he had been happy. He knew that Ruth was not to blame, nor was Bill, for the coldness between them now. And even if there were someone to blame, it meant very little to do any blaming now. Their relationship was meaningless. The differences between them were irreconcilable.

"Tom, what is it?"

"What?" he asked, feigning ignorance.

"You're different."

She had the quick fear that he was ill.

"Am I?"

"You were so spirited, such a fighter. Why, everybody knows you as a fighter, a man who fought for what was right, for the oppressed, for lost causes. You had such spirit, such intelligence, such wit; but now . . ."

Ruth rose and took a few short nervous steps to the center of the room. She turned toward him.

"Now you're so different."

Tom noticed how nervous her movements were.

How much had he changed, he wondered.

"A man can't reach the age of fifty-three and retain the illusions of youth," he said.

"That's part of what I mean, Tom," Ruth said, sitting down again. "You talk like an old man. You aren't that old."

There was a nervous twitch of her lips.

If Tom were getting old, so was she. And if he kept talking about his age and started acting like an old man, where would that put her? He was a constant reminder to her, and to everybody else, that she was no longer young.

"I don't know that there's much sense in my saying anything, Ruth."

"No," she agreed.

Through the big window, Ruth could see the day ending. The patch of sky above the red brick house across the street was dark. When a day ended, especially as this one had, Ruth felt melancholy. To say that a day had ended carried an undercurrent of sadness.

But there had been yesterday. She had been in Harry's arms. She had never felt anything like this. She had made love, not because she loved him but because for the time that it lasted, she felt younger. When they made love, she thought that time was standing still, or moving backward.

She felt strange. Sitting here in their living room, talking to Tom, and thinking like this.

She didn't really love Harry. Did she still love Tom? She didn't know; she knew she didn't hate him. But there was more than that.

"I never said that life was a good bargain," Tom said.

He sighed.

"Nor did I ever say that marriage was."

Ruth agreed with him but it was Tom's fault that their marriage was not a success. And it wasn't. It was nothing more than a formality now. She wondered why they stayed together. Did he ever wonder about this? Strange that this question should hurt. She had wanted it to be different. She wished, she wished her whole life had been different. This was why she sympathized with the Russians and the Communists; they were trying to change their lives; it wasn't only because of Spain that she cared.

But Tom didn't care.

Last night, after she had come home and gone to bed, she had tried to remember how she had felt when she and Tom had first been in love. She hadn't been able to bring back, even in memory, any feeling.

Here they were, the two of them—she and Tom—sitting and having a drink while another day of their lives drifted away.

"Oh, I almost forgot to tell you. I'm going to that meeting on Spain tomorrow evening," Ruth said.

Tom silently sipped his martini.

"Will you be there?"

Tom shook his head.

Love and politics, he thought. He was bitter. And yet he shouldn't be. It was in violation of his own philosophy to be bitter now. It was inconsistent with his belief in freedom.

—Free spirits.

This phrase had once meant so much to him. His youth. How the world had shone. The future had been full of every kind of promise. Now, day by day, that promise seemed to be denied on every side. He and Ruth had been the children of rich promise. And now? He looked at her.

A guilty look vanished from Ruth's face. She smiled quickly and took a sip from her drink.

"I suppose you disapprove of my going to the meeting to help the Spanish Republicans?"

"What right have I to disapprove? Besides, what difference would it make?"

"Oh, Tom, if only you hadn't changed."

He sat, bored. He found himself unable to speak. It was

tiring, too tiring, to search for banalities. He idly ran his hand over his face; he felt a slight roughness. His beard was getting coarser, harder to shave. And it was turning grey.

"I was thinking, I'd like to go to Europe again, Tom."

"Why don't you?"

He wondered if she had some special purpose in going to Europe.

"Do you ever think of our two trips, Tom?"

He raised his eyebrows. He fought the rising sentiment within himself. It was useless to be sad over all that had gone in time.

"Yes, of course I do, Ruth."

She finished her drink, rose and walked over to the table where the bottles and ice bucket were.

"Want another drink, Tom?"

"He shook his head.

"No . . . no thanks."

—Did he ever love me?

One night in Venice, she had watched the sky turning pink. She had wanted to cry with joy and feeling. In Venice, he had held her in his arms. In Venice, she had cuddled against him in a gondola one night. She had thought that no other woman could ever have been as happy as she was.

"I'll go back and see Europe, visit Paris again once more before I die," Tom said reflectively.

Why did he have to say things like that? It was because he was old, an old man, she thought. That was why he was against Russia. That explained it. And that was why Bill resented him so much. Well, she wasn't an old woman, not yet she wasn't. Biologically she was much younger than . . . she didn't want to say it, not even to herself, she didn't want to think it even, she was years younger than . . . than forty-seven.

"Tom, you're beginning to talk like an old man," she said, her voice sharp.

"I'm not a spring chicken," he remarked with a trace of irony.

"One would think you were really old. You talk like you've given up, like there's nothing worth fighting for, or aspiring for. That's what Bill has against you, he said that you had become cynical and that you don't believe in anything any more."

The words had rushed out. She sat back, looking at him. She had not meant to tell him what Bill had said.

Tom was hurt. It wouldn't matter if others had said this, but Bill. He had been aware of the rift between them but still he was hurt by what Ruth had just said. A deep frustration came upon him. They misunderstood him. More important, Bill misunderstood. Bill misunderstood politics and he misunderstood life. He was playing with dangerous people.

Tom looked closely at Ruth. Was she so silly as not to see? He thought of how he had loved her.

"I think I'll go get dressed for dinner."

She rose and walked slowly out of the room. As she reached the door, she turned.

"Tom, please don't fight with Bill tonight."

She was gone before he could reply.

Tom turned and gazed out of the window. A soft rich pink filled the sky. It was full of a remote and empty beauty. The beauty of life was gone from him too.

V

Tom was still sitting alone. A copy of *Spoon River Anthology* lay open in his lap. He had admired this book and had gone back to it many times. Now, as in the past, it filled him with disquiet. It was filled with a bitter kind of truth. He wouldn't say that it was disillusioning—that wasn't the word. It represented a feature of life which he knew to be true. It told stories which rang with truth and there was such sadness in this truth.

What would he say when his time to die came? If he could express himself about life from the grave, what would he say of it?

He picked up the book. Thumbing through it, he came upon the poem:

ANNE RUTLEDGE

Out of me unworthy and unknown
The vibration of deathless music;
"With malice toward none, with charity for all!"
Out of me forgiveness of millions towards millions
And the beneficent face of a nation
Shining with justice and truth
I am Anne Rutledge who sleeps beneath these weeds,
Beloved in life of Abraham Lincoln,
Wedded to him, not through union,
But through separation.
Bloom forever, O Republic,
From the dust of my bosom!

The poem touched him. It brought to his mind the image of Lincoln. He often thought of Lincoln and he was shy because he liked to think of himself as like Lincoln. He put the book down and continued to sit, almost immobile, his eyes turned toward the window. The pink was fading from the sky; it was getting dark.

He had nothing to do now until dinner.

What would happen when Bill came? How had it happened with his son? In college, the boy had seemed uninterested in politics; he had taken literary and English courses. He had changed only in these last couple of years. Would he change again?

Tom's mind traveled back to when Bill had been a small

stocky boy of eight. Tom had read him Kipling and Mark Twain. Bill would sit beside him, quiet, his round face alert, his eyes wide with curiosity. He would sometimes ask the boy:

"Do you understand?"

"Yes, Dad."

He had thought of the time when his son would be grown. He had wanted that time to come. He had imagined how his son might be proud of him. He had been in many fights and struggles. He had, in the 1920s, been something of a hero to radical and liberal youths because of his stand on the War. He had been a professor at Wilmington College in Ohio. And he had been kicked out because of his opposition to the War.

He remembered one Saturday morning. Bill had been only a kid. He had come in crying. Ruth had asked him why but Bill had refused to answer her. Instead, he had turned accusing eyes on his father. He had gone over to the boy and put his hands on his shoulders but Bill had turned away from him. He had gone and put his little arms around Ruth's thighs and had sobbed with all of his body. Tom had stood there feeling helpless. He had been troubled by the sight of his son sobbing. Ruth had finally gotten out of him why he was crying. The other boys would not play with him. He remembered Bill's bewilderment and hurt.

—Charlie Spoon says my daddy is for the Kaiser.

He had acted, he believed, the only way that he could. Some of those nights had been terrifying. And he had been afraid. He recalled how he would, during those last days at Wilmington, sit alone in the parlor trying to read. Would they come get him? Would he be lynched? The mood of the country was such that there were grounds for such fears.

He remembered the night when the students had burned him in effigy. The howling mob on the lawn in front of his little house. And Ruth in terror, looking at him for protection. The cries had sounded like the yells of savages. The

eeriness, looking down from their darkened bedroom, seeing
the mob move like shadows in some strange land. Watching
the flicking red and gold flames of the fire, the shadowy
forms, their howls and insults.

Ruth had clung to him. He had said in a low voice,

"Let them howl."

He was proud that he had shown courage. Now, years
later, he was more proud of his courage than he was of the
views he had held in those days. And he had thought that
when Bill grew up, Bill would be proud of his courage.

And now, Bill was grown.

That night, when they had burned him in effigy, he had
had a fierce desire for Ruth. He had wanted her, wanted to
spend himself, and then, in exhaustion, go to sleep. But Ruth
had been afraid. She had remained cold all through their love-
making. Later, she had cried herself to sleep. He had been
unable to sleep. The darkness, the quiet of the night, the
sudden movement of the wind in the tree outside their window, Ruth's breathing, the sigh escaping from her as she
turned in her sleep—all of this and the realization of an emptiness at the core of life. Never before, or since, had life
seemed so empty. Never before, or since, had he felt as alone
as he had on that night.

Why was he remembering this now?

He lit a cigarette. Puffing on it, Tom knew the answer.

There was the ring of the doorbell.

Tom got up. This was his son. He stood, tense, waiting for
him.

VI

They were eating. Tom said little. He remained inwardly
tense but he did not reveal this.

Bill Carroll was short and slightly plump. He had his mother's features, there was a softness in his face. He had brown hair, brown eyes, and his mother's pug nose. He wore a spotted grey suit. His hair was long, it looked dirty. His tie was carelessly knotted. There were several stains on it.

"Bill, let me give you more," Ruth said. "It's good, isn't it?"

She turned to Tom.

"Don't you think so, Tom?"

"Yes, it is," Tom answered in a measured tone of voice.

They were having roast beef, baked potatoes, and broccoli.

Tom was not able to finish his portion. His stomach felt full but he tried to conceal his distress. This was happening fairly often of late. Could it be something serious?

"Bill, do you know what?" Ruth asked eagerly.

"What?" Bill asked without looking up.

"I've finally been able to start reading Marcel Proust."

Bill said nothing. Ruth's face clouded in disappointment.

"Ten years ago Proust was all right to read. But now, in the kind of world we live in . . ." Bill didn't finish his sentence. He went on eating.

"But the feeling in Proust!" Ruth exclaimed.

"What good is feeling in a world like this?" Bill asked in a cold tone.

"You like Proust, don't you?" Ruth asked, turning toward Tom.

Tom nodded.

How could he reach his son? How could he penetrate the wall that stood between them? He had not liked Bill's remark, not because of what Bill had said about Proust but because of what he had said about feeling. There was a growing coldness in his son.

"With the Civil War in Spain, I couldn't sit down and read Marcel Proust," Bill went on.

"I know, dear, I must confess that I feel a trifle guilty myself reading him," Ruth paused. "Bill, you're not thinking of going to Spain to fight, are you?"

Her question surprised Tom but he retained his appearance of calm. The few moments which elapsed before Bill answered were long and dramatic for him.

"What gives you that idea, Ruth?"

"I know how brave you are and what a healthy hatred of fascism you have," she said, an embarrassed smile on her lips.

"If they want me to go fight, I will," Bill answered.

"It isn't because I'm your mother; I couldn't think of the fight against fascism in such a personal way. It's just that, well, everybody can serve in a different way. You wouldn't know how to fire a gun. You never were practical. I remember when you were just a little boy six or seven years old, I used to say to your father that you were born to be a poet, an artist."

What would he do if his son did go to Spain? Bill had said that he was ready to fight if "they" wanted him to. What did he mean by "they"? Troubled, Tom wondered if Bill had joined the Party.

"And you are doing work for the Spanish Loyalists," Ruth went on.

A cold look settled on Bill's face.

"Oh, Mother, that reminds me. I brought two tickets for the dinner we're running to get aid for Spain," Bill said.

"Good. When is it?"

"The thirty-first. I thought that you and Tom would come."

"I'm sorry; I'm busy on the thirty-first," Tom answered.

Bill looked at him, disbelieving. His eyes narrowed.

"Couldn't you change whatever engagement you have? This is for a good cause. Even you admitted that you wanted to see the Loyalists win against the fascists. It's little enough for us to do, Tom."

Bill had his eyes fixed firmly on his father.

His son's stare was troubling.

"I'm sorry, I can't," he said quietly and firmly.

"I told you, Mother."

Disappointed and confused, Ruth looked from her son to her husband and then back at her son. The least Tom could have done was agree to attend. He could have done this much. Bill had told her that Tom wouldn't but she had hoped that he would.

"If I ask you especially, as a favor, would you come, Tom?" she asked.

If he would appear with her at the banquet, all of the people who criticized him and talked about his being a tired and old radical would see that they had been wrong. And many of them would assume that this had been her doing. For over a week she had imagined herself attending this dinner with Tom. Bill could probably arrange it so that they would sit on the dais. And Tom would have been introduced, and there would have been a bombshell of applause. Everyone would be excited about welcoming someone like Tom Carroll into the fight. The applause would have gone on and on. She had bought a new dress for the occasion; she had bought it at de Pinna's the other day.

Tom and Bill were staring at each other.

She gazed at her son. What would he say if he knew that she had been in Harry's arms yesterday? Harry was a Party leader. She flushed with guilt. What a thing to think of now. The way they were looking at each other; they would fight. Of this she was sure. Oh, she couldn't bear it. Why was Tom so stubborn? Why did he do things like this? He was hurting her.

"I knew you wouldn't come," Bill said disdainfully.

"You should have," Tom answered quietly.

"Well, you aren't my responsibility."

Tom didn't say anything. Was he responsible for Bill? Was it his fault that Bill was turning out this way?

"I'll never sell out," Bill added, a sneer in his voice.

"What does that mean?" asked Tom.

"Let's forget politics for our dinner," Ruth suggested.

"Everybody has to take sides in this war," Bill declared.

"But Bill, your father isn't on the side of France and the fascists."

"No, he's just neutral."

"How in hell would you know what I am? You never listen when I talk, or, for that matter, when anybody else does."

"Tom, dear, you don't always listen, either," Ruth said.

"What's the use of fooling ourselves. We're on opposite sides of the barricades," Bill said.

"You've got barricades on the brain, boy," Tom said.

"I suppose there aren't barricades in Spain."

"I wish you would listen to me, Bill."

"Yes, listen to the siren songs of reaction."

"Why do you talk like that?"

"Because it's the truth. This is no world for fence sitters. Fence sitting is reactionary; it aids and abets reactionaries. And you're a fence sitter, Tom."

"Listen, Bill, you're my own son," Tom began.

"Here we go again," Bill said, the sneer back in his voice.

Tom looked at him. How could he reach the boy? He didn't like what was happening to his son. He was troubled by the note of cruelty and the air of intolerance which accompanied what Bill said. He was concerned with what was happening to his son's character and personality.

"All right," Tom said curtly.

—There's no use, he told himself.

The three of them ate in silence.

VII

"Harry Helmholtz is one of the great men of our time," Bill said.

He and his mother were talking over coffee and dessert. Tom sat quietly.

"Do you really think so, Bill?" Ruth said.

She noticed Tom. He was like a foreign presence here. Was he disapproving? Or was he envious because she and Bill belonged some place where he didn't belong? Well, he could belong if he weren't so stubborn. Did Tom suspect that there was something between her and Harry Helmholtz?

"You know him, don't you, Tom?" she asked.

"Just by name. I've seen his name in *The Fist*."

He spoke the name of the Communist newspaper with contempt.

"I only subscribe to it to help; I don't read it; it isn't written for people like us; it's written for workers," Ruth said.

"I read it," Bill said challengingly.

"You have to because of your work with the Loyalists. Besides, you're a writer. A writer should read everything," Ruth said.

Was his son a writer? Would the boy ever develop? What had gone wrong between them?

"I'm writing a novel, Mother."

"Oh, tell me about it. When can I read what you've written?"

Bill didn't answer. He sat impassively while she gazed at him waiting for his answer.

Tom wondered if he would be a character in the book. He said nothing; he felt like a stranger here with the two of them.

"I can't talk about it," Bill finally said.

"Not even to us?" Ruth asked.

She glanced quickly toward Tom. He seemed calm but she knew that he was disapproving.

"No, no one."

"What's it about, darling? You can at least tell us that much."

"The problems of the day."

"Oh. I'm sure it will be a wonderful novel," Ruth said, speaking now only to make conversation.

"I hope you'll keep politics out of your book, Bill," Tom said.

Bill glared at him.

"But Tom, surely you don't believe in the ivory towers?" Ruth asked.

Tom looked at her. Could she really be so blind to what was happening to the boy? Couldn't she see that he was getting himself involved in something dangerous?

"Politics is the only subject for a novel today," Bill said.

There was a bewildered expression on Ruth's face.

"What about love? Beauty? Friendship? What about the things that great writers from the days of the Greeks to our own times, what about the things that these writers have written of?" Tom asked.

Bill warned himself to be careful before he answered his old man. He remembered the talk he had with Harry Helmholtz at lunch. Harry had given him some sound advice.

"Carroll, your old man was once a hero and a great historian. We Communists honor whenever honor is due. We honor what your old man was, not what he is. He is a tired radical. But you and your mother can win him over. If you help him, you help us. If you help us, you help the future."

These hadn't been Harry's words exactly but they contained the sense of his words. And he was not following Harry's advice. He didn't know what it was but whenever he saw his father, something happened to him. He'd show him, all right. He remembered how, even as a boy, he had thought of what might happen when his father died. His father had been a hero. He had been burned in effigy for what he believed. And Bill had been proud of him for a while. Then he had envied his father. And later, his envy was mixed with anger. Look at what Tom Carroll had been. See what he was now. A reactionary. Yes, his old man was reactionary. Reactionary and weak. His old man was old. And he was young. He had written a poem the other day. It had begun with the lines:

> *I shout the voice of the Future.*
> *You whine the voice of the Past.*

Still, his old man could be of help. Harry had made this clear. Suddenly Bill was all mixed up. What sort of concession should he make to his father?

"You might be right, Dad," Bill said, smiling affably.

His change of manner surprised Tom. Tom's eyes lit up.

Bill floundered for a second. What would he say next? He wasn't too good at sparring with his old man; his father knew so much.

Ruth smiled at her husband, a smile of justification. It was as though she were telling him:

—See you were wrong about our son. He isn't a fanatic.

"I don't believe in the excesses of the left critics. They don't understand literature," Bill said.

Was Bill beginning to understand? Tom hesitated before speaking. Normally he spoke honestly and directly, but with his own son some barrier had come up.

"That's what I think too," Ruth said. "I couldn't write proletarian literature if my life depended on it."

The old dream awoke in Tom, that of helping his son and guiding him.

"If you want me to read what you've written, I'll be glad to," Tom said.

"It's not in good enough shape yet," Bill said.

What would his old man say if he saw that first chapter? Would he be hurt?

"Who will have more coffee?" Ruth asked.

They both shoved their cups toward her.

"How do you find the time to write with all the things you're doing, darling?" Ruth asked Bill as she poured coffee.

"I make the time. But if necessary, I would sacrifice my writing," Bill said.

Tom leaned forward, put his elbows on the table, and said, speaking slowly and with great sincerity:

"You know, I'm fifty-three now. I've seen more than most people have, and I have had a fair amount of experience."

Bill tried to look interested.

"At one time, Bill, I tried to do some of the things that you're trying to do. I suppose you can say that it's an effort to affect and influence history; to awaken the people to truth and justice. I boiled with the desire to do this."

—The old man's a romantic. Bill told himself this, half in admiration, half in contempt.

"We know that, Tom. Bill doesn't want to hear you tell the story of your life all over again."

"That's all right, Ruth," Bill interrupted. "I'm interested."

Ruth's interruption cut the flow of Tom's thought. He had suddenly seen clearly what it was he needed to say to his son. He had started to speak with confidence and with the hope that what he would say would penetrate. Tom felt shy as he spoke. He was not merely trying to impress the boy; he was trying desperately to help his son.

"I had something to do with the radical movement even though I was never an extremist. I knew Jack Reed. I met many of the figures of the radical world."

"Tell me about Jack Reed," Bill said.

"He was a fine type, brave, idealistic and spirited," Tom said.

"He knew where the future was to be found," Bill stated.

"He died disillusioned. He was changing his mind. If Jack Reed had lived, he might have told different stories," Tom said.

Bill frowned. But immediately he remembered what Harry had said. He knew that it was important to get Tom to say something in favor of the Soviets about the Moscow Trials. Bill remembered joining a group at *Mass Action* a year ago when Smathers, who had done a biography of Reed, had admitted that he felt that he would be justified in neglecting evidence about Reed if it conflicted with the position of the Party. But his old man wouldn't be able to see that. His old man was a sentimental liberal. It was no wonder he had ended up a reactionary. He was an old-fashioned liberal, a tired radical. Suddenly a feeling of sympathy came over Bill. He liked his old man. But he pushed his sympathy back. Sympathy was a weakness when history was marching with seven-league boots. Sympathy could lead you into detours and blind alleys of reaction. Just because this man was his father did not mean that history would give him any special consideration. Tom Carroll was one more man. He must either be on the side of history or he must be against history. And if he took a stand against history, he must be crushed. Bill looked at his father. He believed that he was stronger than his father had been. He listened.

"I risked my neck for my beliefs once," Tom said shyly.

"Yes and that will never be forgotten." Bill said.

Bill's concession was warming. It brought a smile to Tom's lips. Perhaps he had misjudged his son.

"Yes, you were brave and noble, Tom," Ruth said, having taken the cue from her son.

"I don't know; I thought that it was my duty. I thought that I was right. I remembered my father. You never saw him, Bill. He was a fine man. He took a stand against imperialism during the Spanish-American War. I remember how he talked of William James. Such enthusiasm. His example inspired me."

Tom stopped. Would Bill take this to mean that he was asking Bill to follow his example?

"And I remember how excited we were when we heard the news of the Russian Revolution."

He halted again. He had almost mentioned Trotsky. He didn't want to introduce anything that would jar on the evening.

"God, it seemed to be the hope of the future," Tom went on.

"Isn't there still hope in Russia?" Ruth asked.

"I wish there were," Tom said.

"Who's going to fight if Hitler starts a war?"

"If I were convinced that the Russians would fight with us and not against us," Tom started.

Horror came instantly on the faces of his wife and son.

"What do you mean?" Bill demanded.

"I mean," Tom said, measuring his words carefully, "I mean that Hitler and Stalin might get together."

"Oh Tom, you can't believe that," Ruth said, laughing nervously.

"That's a reactionary belief," Bill shouted, pounding his fist on the table.

"How can you say such a thing, Tom?" Ruth asked.

"I mean it. I mean it as much as I mean anything that I have ever said."

Ruth turned to Bill, waiting for him to speak. Bill sulked in anger.

Tom went on:

"The great tragedy of our lifetime, the great tragedy of the twentieth century is to be found in Russia. It is what happens when love turns to hatred and when good turns into evil."

Bill continued to smirk.

"Can't you see it? My God, they've killed the very men

who founded the state they rule. They made them confess to sordid and impossible lies. They've torn truth into shreds. How can it be good? Don't you see what it means, what it will do to you?"

"What?" Bill asked, his voice tense.

"It will poison you. It will poison your mind, your life."

"What about fascism?" Bill asked, the smirk back on his face.

"If fascism is red or brown, the color makes no difference."

"Heil, Hitler," Bill sneered.

"When we were young, we didn't have your insolence," Tom said, now sharp and curt.

It was too late, he thought.

Behind the grin which Bill gave his father, Bill was shaken. His father knew so much.

"I don't believe in indulging in personalities," Bill Carroll said.

"Yes, Tom, you do engage in personalities," Ruth said.

"How?" Tom asked, relieved that Ruth had spoken. This might reduce the chance of a bitter argument with Bill. He didn't want this to turn into the same kind of bitter argument that had occurred the last few times that he had seen his son.

"Well, yesterday I was talking about Spain and you told me that I didn't know what I was talking about."

Bill remembered his father saying this to him.

"Saying that someone is insolent doesn't answer questions, Tom. Calling me insolent doesn't help in the fight against Hitler and Franco," Bill said.

Ruth looked at her husband with resentment. She knew that he had not taken her seriously, he had dismissed the things that she had said. She felt close to her son. There was a bond between them. It wasn't, she assured herself, merely the fact that they were mother and son. They were friends, companions. She turned from her husband, whom she had looked at with eyes of resentment; her eyes softened and filled with love as she regarded her son. He was nervous, she could tell, because of Tom. Tom should not have said what he had said.

"Bill, you're making a mistake and I hate to see you doing it. If you want to write, the people you are running with cannot be of help to you. They corrupt and destroy people. Why do you think I talk about the Moscow Trials the way I do? It's because they prove everything you need to know about these people. They are destroyers, the destroyers of humanity and of the human spirit. You're my son . . ."

"But I can stand on my own feet. I don't need a speech like this," Bill interrupted.

"What I'm trying to tell you is to rely on your own mind. You come here and give me arguments which I know. I can read them in *Mass Action* or *The Fist*."

"I won't discuss anything in this vein," Bill said angrily.

He rose.

"I'm leaving," he said.

This came as a shock to Tom Carroll. He had not expected it. For a moment he was in a state of such surprise that he had no thoughts. He stared at his son.

"Bill!" Ruth burst out, her voice frantic.

"I'm leaving. I did not come here to accept reactionary personal insults."

Ruth ran to his side and put her arms around his shoulders.

"Please, Bill, don't go."

"Mother, I have nothing against you," Bill said, adopting a formal manner, "but I must leave."

He did not give his father even a backward glance. He left the room.

Tom heard the front door close. He sat still.

—I've lost my son.

Ruth came back into the room with anger flashing in her eyes.

"You didn't have to be so mean to him."

Tom looked at her; she was a stranger to him.

"You drove your own son out of your home with insults," Ruth accused.

"I did like Hell," he said. He spoke curtly but not angrily.

"I asked you, Tom Carroll, I pleaded with you. I begged you not to ruin this evening, but did you listen? No! You don't care about me."

She paused.

Tom guessed that she did in order for him to say something. He did not speak. It was more the other way around, he thought, she didn't care about him.

"And you don't care about Bill. It doesn't matter that you don't care about me, but your own son! What's happened to you, Tom? You weren't like this. What has happened to you?"

She grabbed a cigarette, lit it, and started puffing rapidly.

Tom waited briefly, then he asked:

"Do you know what you're saying, Ruth?"

"More insults! How dare you imply that I don't know what I'm saying. What makes you so certain I don't have a mind? Oh I could scream."

"Why don't you?"

She glared at him.

"Because I'm civilized. I hate scenes and I won't make them. But to witness my son driven out of his own home by you, his father. To think that we should come to this."

"If you love Bill . . ."

"Why, you, you would question my love for my own son?" Her voice was sharp.

"If you love Bill, you'll worry about him, not me," Tom said calmly.

She stared at him, speechless, but for only a second.

"Tom Carroll, your behavior was shameful, perfectly shameful. I'm glad that there was no one here to witness it. It was not only what you said but the way you said it. You were cold and cruel. I never realized before what a cold and cruel man you are."

"Oh for God's sake, Ruth, stop talking nonsense. Sit down and let me talk to you."

Ruth paced around the table. Finally she sat down, her face vacant.

"Bill is making a dangerous mistake. I can't reach him. If he believed what he thinks he believes, he wouldn't have walked out. Years ago when a gang of students burned me in effigy, did I walk out? Did I . . ."

"Go ahead, brag. Brag about what you've done. As if anyone cares about what you did twenty years ago. Go ahead, brag like an old man. Kill the spirit of youth."

"It's clear that I can't talk to you either."

"Why should you want to? You never loved me."

"Ruth, you know that's not true," he said. He had suddenly become very gentle.

"Don't you dare pity me, Tom. Oh stop. Stop or I'll scream, I tell you, I'll scream."

"All right, scream. Go ahead. What you say to me doesn't matter. It doesn't matter what you think of me, Ruth, I'm too old to be hurt by it. But if you want to help Bill, you'll have to do a little hard thinking."

"Tom . . . Tom, you've become a spiteful and mean old man."

"And you, Ruth, have become a frantic woman so jealous of youth that you're jealous of your own son."

Ruth gasped. She stared at him.

She rose and walked out of the room.

Tom Carroll sat, troubled. His stomach felt heavy. His heartburn had come back. He heard Ruth's door close. He rose from his chair and went into the living room.

He sat with a Scotch and soda on a little table in front of his chair. He ought not drink it. He would sip it slowly. One lamp was on.

Ruth had been cruel, calling him an old man. But it was true; both of them were starting to get old. Aging was on Ruth's mind a lot, he knew this. She would get flustered, then pleased, whenever anyone, particularly a man, complimented her on her youthful appearance. And she became downright silly when people told her that she and Bill did not look like mother and son.

And she had changed during the last ten years. She was thirty-five when she had decided to write. He had not taken her seriously, he realized this now. He should have but he hadn't. He had never displayed any enthusiasm for anything she wrote. But Christ, how could he? Her writings were consistently shallow. She tried so hard to be clever and Ruth was not a clever woman. And now she was confronted with the problem of growing old. If not this year, next year, or the next. She would see a grey hair; a wrinkle would come. Little crow's feet would appear.

Sympathy for his wife flooded out his anger and contempt. It would be hard for her, much harder than it would be for him.

Tom Carroll took another sip from the tall glass which held the Scotch and soda.

VIII

He had been sitting for a long time; he did not know for how long. He had finished his first Scotch and had mixed himself another one which he was now slowly sipping. He was pretty certain that Ruth had gone to bed by now. He had heard her moving around a little earlier.

He had been thinking of their long years together. There had been a slow and imperceptible ending of their love. A night had come when he had not wanted to make love to her. A night had come when he felt that he should out of a sense of duty. And a night had come when he was going to make love to her out of his sense of duty and she had turned to him and had said coolly that she felt too tired "for that."

Tom Carroll had turned to other women.

He sipped his drink.

He remembered one night when Bill had been an infant. Ruth had put Bill to sleep and they had both stood over the cradle watching him. Later, he and Ruth had sat, smoking cigarettes, and talking about their son.

Meaningless now to wish back moments from that night. Those days had long fallen away into the past. There was no use in thinking about them.

—Tom, I want our love to be the most romantic love in the world.

Ruth had said this. Her eyes had glowed with love as she spoke. He had looked at her tenderly.

—Yes.

He had shared her wish. He had spoken his "yes" with love.

It had been an April night. They had been living on Central Park West at Ninety-fifth Street. Ruth had gone to bed first. He had stayed up reading. He couldn't remember the book but he had read it until very late. Then, he had put the book down and had walked across the room to the window. He had looked at Central Park. The scene was blurred in his memory. The park had been dark and the trees had seemed small and black. The lights of passing automobiles and the patches of light from the building across the park gave off golden touches. He had thought of what Ruth had said. And he had thought of his son. He had speculated about what his son might become, what he would be like when he grew up. The days that he had wondered about were these days. In those days, he had thought about what was now. And now, he was thinking about what was then.

He was not the only father who had experienced this disillusionment. It was not rare; it happened often.

Tom sat in his chair in the dim living room, brooding, remembering.

Tonight Ruth had said, her voice gripped by fear, that she was afraid for Bill.

—Too damned bad, he had thought.

Ruth was worried; he could see that she was. Finally she had told him why she was beside herself about their son. He might go to Spain.

—A lot of those fellows of the right persuasion get trips to Spain.

Tom had said this to Ruth.

She had said that he had not understood her. Would he do her the favor of listening, please? Bill, his son, and her son, might go to Spain to fight.

Tom did not think that Bill would volunteer for the Lincoln Brigade. Bill wouldn't do anything like that. But if he did? If he did, and were killed?

A chilling fear had struck Tom.

Bill wouldn't go. He wouldn't. And if he did? Bill was a grown man. Whatever he did was his own business.

Tom Carroll was sleepy. He did not want to sit here and think thoughts that led nowhere. He heard the noise of automobiles from down below. Sounds of no interest, heard briefly, and then dying away.

Sitting in shadow in the living room, Tom Carroll looked profoundly melancholy. But he did not know this. He only knew how he felt.

IX

Tom Carroll frequently reflected that his life had not turned out as it might have. In the main, his life had been a simple one of work, of study, of writing, of lecturing and teaching. For a moment, his life seemed to have been empty, meaningless. But Tom knew that this was not true. His books —*History of American Culture*, his biography of Walt Whitman, his *History of the United States*—they were good books and they would last. His years of patient and lonely work were not in vain. He was a man with a celebrated and honest reputation. He had earned the respect of many people of worth and intelligence. He had lived a life of honor.

But why was he sitting here thinking about it and giving himself this reassurance?

He knew why—it was Bill. Bill had no respect for him. While Bill was growing up, Tom had thought that he was working for his son. He had imagined that when Bill was an adult, that he would understand what his father was doing, what he was trying to do, and would respect him. He had hoped that he was handing something on to Bill and to Bill's generation. He had often spoken of this hope in lectures—the hope that he was helping to preserve a heritage and pass it on.

Was there much of a heritage to pass on?

The question saddened him.

X

Tom Carroll was still sitting in the shadowy darkness of his living room. The trend of his thoughts had changed. The world was one of power and might. Day after day, as he read the morning newspaper, he could see how changes were coming about. He could perceive the growth and spread, the serious prevalence of violence in the world. He had read of events which had within them the menacing trend toward catastrophe. This had been particularly so during the last four years. There had been the rise of Hitler in Germany, the

Italian invasion of Ethiopia under Mussolini's direction. And the war in China. And now the civil war in Spain.

This violence was far away from the United States, but America was not immune.

The war in Spain. No American was immune from that war. America was not immune to the changes being wrought in the world. This was obvious; Tom Carroll knew this. But go tell the obvious to Americans. Most of them would not believe you and some would even dispute you.

Tom grew more melancholy. Was Western Civilization rotting at its very roots? It was as if it were a great cathedral on a foundation about to crumble away. Tom thought of cathedrals he had seen in Europe—the Cathedral of Notre Dame of Chartres. Saint Serena in Toulouse. The Cathedral of Toledo in Spain. Saint Zeno in Verona. Imagine one of these on a crumbling foundation, wavering, and then crashing down into dust. This is how it seemed to him. Day by day the foundations were softening. They would get softer and softer, until one day the great and grand edifice would sway, waver, and then topple over in a thundering crash. The dust would fill your nostrils and choke you. Dust, broken stone, smashed glass. All that had been beauty would collapse. Dust, the dying screams of those crushed to death beneath the falling stones, hopeless moans. The end. It could be.

He remembered the ruins of ancient Rome. Ruth and he had walked through the ruins of the baths of Caracalla. It had been a sunny morning. They had listened to their guide, a shabby little man with a mustache who spoke with an accent.

Ruth had called the trip their second honeymoon. In a way it had been. Bill had been a little boy then and was staying with Ruth's mother for the summer.

They had been happy in Rome. He remembered something of that happiness but the feelings were gone from the memories. He had new feelings substituted for the old ones; feelings of regret and of bitterness. It was as though he saw these remembered scenes on a screen. They would become vague and blurred.

About a year ago he had been in a theater on Broadway which showed only newsreels. One of the items on the news had been the fighting in China. He had seen Chinese men, women, and children shot down, killed, and wounded. But what he saw on the black and white screen with the routine voice of the announcer had not seemed real to him. He had tried to share their pain and agony as their bodies were ripped by bullets. But he couldn't feel very deeply. There had been no horror evoked by the scenes on the screen. There had been almost no horror in death as it was caught by the camera. Death had seemed unreal.

It was only after he had gone outside and let his own imagination review the scenes that he had known the horror of the helpless pain he had seen.

His memories of love with Ruth were like this except that they had left a residue of nostalgia. Even with the bitterness, contempt, and regret that he could now feel for her, he wished these moments back. Yes, he and Ruth had been happy in Rome. He wanted that happiness back again.

He wanted to love again as he had once loved Ruth. He wanted to feel young and creative from love and from its fulfillment. It was over for him and Ruth; he could understand this. It didn't even make sense for him to live with her. This was not a new thought. He had, in fact, thought of this many times; mostly when he was annoyed with her. Now and then he and Ruth had quarreled but this was not very often. They had come to be somewhat tolerant of each other but he had perceived that their mutual affection was wearing out. The only bond between them was the product of their having lived together for so many years. This bond owed some of its strength to the passion that they once had shared. It preserved some of the memories of their early days, the struggle when they had been, if not poor, possessed only of very moderate means. And the bond had been cemented because of Bill.

Now, tonight, Tom Carroll believed that this bond had been broken.

It was all over.

Tom walked out of the living room. The sirens faded away. There was a dull pain in his abdomen. He went to bed.

XI

Tom Carroll awoke in pain in the darkness. For a few seconds, the pain was not real. It was in the same area as the lesser pains he had had, on and off, all evening. But this time the pains were sharp and intense. He lay quiet, as still as he could. He knew where he was. He had been having a strange and disquieting dream but the content of the dream had already slipped away from him.

The pain came again; he almost groaned aloud. He didn't want to awaken Ruth. After the scene tonight, he did not want her to see him like this. He lay open-eyed in the darkness. He stretched his legs and then he pulled his knees up. He held his arms rigidly against his sides and clenched his fists. There was perspiration on his face. Maybe if he relaxed, it would be easier. He unclenched his fists.

What time was it? He could hear the clock; the sound of its tick was eerie.

Another pain. He clamped his lips together to prevent himself from moaning aloud. Oh God.

He thought of Abraham Lincoln. What was Lincoln's last conscious thought before his mind slid into the darkness? Was he dying?

Again, pain shot through him like flames burning him. He belched. Ebbing flames now. Was it the dinner? The Scotch? It must be a digestive disorder. Senator Tom Walsh had had a digestive attack and had died on the train returning to Washington for President Roosevelt's inauguration. Walsh had died in his berth. Or was it a compartment?

Once more pain burned his thought out of his mind.

He tossed. This might be serious; he might be ill. God, suppose this was the real forewarning of death and he should die with Ruth at his bedside. Ruth was like a stranger to him now. He might be dying and he had no one.

What had been Senator Walsh's last conscious thought?

—Alabama casts twenty-four votes for Underwood.

He had to be stoic. He lay, stretched out in a relaxed position, and pulled the cover over him. He would think of something—Abe Lincoln. Walt Whitman.

When lilacs last in the dooryard bloomed . . .

The funeral train going slowly across a new and virgin America. Mourners crowding the stations and along the way. Puffs of smoke from the chugging engine. Thaddeus Stevens in a field giving a last salute as the train proceeded slowly through Pennsylvania.

Tom pressed his hands against his stomach as the pain gripped him again. He would have to bear it until morning. He should not have had that second Scotch; he had known that his stomach had been getting nervous these last few days.

Pain burned inside him.

He would concentrate on something. Gibbon. Gibbon finished *The Decline and Fall of the Roman Empire*, and late that night, he had stood outside his home in Geneva feeling empty; feeling that there was nothing left.

Was there anything more for him? Would it matter if he did more work, or if he didn't? His youth, his dream of immortality. As a historian he had made himself a keeper of immortality. Those remarks of Lord Balfour on immortality. You are cold and insensate and the world goes on. The ruins of the Colosseum in Rome. Looking down at them with Ruth at his side, he had thought of the lions roaring into the arena. Ruth had been bored. Man, not nature, not time, had destroyed the Colosseum.

He tossed with pain. The spasms were regular now. The clock ticked. Ruth was sleeping, breathing easily. Would he ever again sleep in the same bed with a woman at his side as he had with Ruth? Some thoughts for a man of fifty-three who might be seriously ill.

The pain rose in intensity. He gritted his teeth.

What had he been thinking of? His mother? She had died when he was twenty-two. Or was it twenty? He had married Ruth shortly after his mother's death. He remembered her, grey and thin and tall.

How slow time was on this lonely night of pain. It had seemed so fast when he had looked at Hadrian's villa.

He moaned.

XII

"It's just a bellyache," Tom said.

In her red kimono, Ruth stood over the bed, looking at him apprehensively. Her hair was disordered.

"You should have awakened me sooner, Tom."

He looked up at her. He wanted her sympathy but he could not ask for it. He felt humiliated, weak and powerless. He didn't want to be this way in front of her.

"I'll get you a hot-water bag," she said.

She hastened out of the room.

Tom lay quietly. What idiocy it was for him to feel humiliated.

The pains continued in rhythmic succession. He was tired. His thin body was tired. His eyes were tired; his head was tired. Where was Ruth? The hot-water bag should help. It would soothe his pains and put him to sleep. That was all he wanted now, sleep, sleep without pain. He wouldn't mind dying if he could just fall gently asleep and never wake up.

Pain gripped him again.

Where was she? Why didn't she hurry?

Was there anything as humiliating to a man as pain? Pain was a symbol of man's biological tragedy. How much pain had Lincoln suffered that final night? And Whitman—sick and crippled—living out lonely years, not given his due?

He closed his eyes. The pains came again but he lay still.

Ruth was back. He looked at her with gratitude.

"Here, Tom, this will help. Now I'll go telephone Dr. Gladman," she said. There was a restrained sympathy in her voice.

"Do you remember what Ben Gladman says about undertakers?"

"What?"

A look of annoyance crossed her face. He was ill and he was talking this way. She was jittery inside. Tom was old and he was a sick man.

—I once called him My Tom, she thought.

"He says he hates undertakers."

"Tom, this is no time for jokes."

He caught the nervous annoyance in her voice. She was frightened. Was she frightened for him or for herself?

"Well, I don't hate doctors even though I hate their function."

"I'm going to call him; you might have appendicitis."

"I probed myself, my abdomen is soft. I've never been atypical about anything else so why should I have an atypical case of appendicitis?"

A sick feeling came over him. Suppose he should be rushed to the hospital and have to be operated on? He had once been given gas. He had borne it well but it had been a kind of sick intellectualized feeling that he had had.

"I've just got a bellyache, Ruth. You can't live fifty-three years and not have some goddamned thing go wrong. Call him."

The hot-water bag was soothing. He felt sleepy. He watched Ruth pick up the telephone on the stand between their beds. He could see the book she had been reading before she went to sleep. *The Coming Struggle for Power* by John Strachey.

The death of love is far worse than a physical death, he thought. He heard the clicking of the telephone dial. He closed his eyes. The heat was helping.

Part Two

I

Tom had been drunk only a few times in his life. He had had a couple of hangovers. That was how he felt, as though he had been drunk the night before. He had a hangover feeling.

He sat at the desk in his study with paper before him. His typewriter was on one side. Sometimes he wrote in longhand and then copied his writing. He looked up at the picture of Abraham Lincoln hanging on the wall. He had had a picture of Leon Trotsky hanging there. One morning he had taken the picture down and had replaced it with this one of Lincoln.

His mind was sluggish. He had been a damned fool last night. Ruth had spoken to Bill on the telephone this morning but she had not told him what Bill had said.

She had been a little aloof today. She had gotten him his lunch of tomato soup and soft-boiled eggs herself.

Ben Gladman had told him that it was probably colitis and that he need not worry. He had given him phenobarbital to take, one before each meal. And he was to rest before his meals, take a nap in the afternoon, work less for a while, take it easy, and try not to worry.

He felt no pain now. In fact it seemed to him that the

agony of last night had been part of his imagination. But he knew that it had been real.

It was difficult to work; he could not think clearly. The phenobarbital was making him sleepy. He ought to finish this book review. It was of a biography of Robespierre written by an Englishman. He could not complain of the man's scholarship, but he had interpreted Robespierre as a liberal, like English liberals. Tom leaned his elbows on the desk. Once he had admired Robespierre. He had talked himself into accepting a doctrine of historical necessity. And he had been impressed by Mathiez. But the Moscow Trials had caused him to question himself deeply, profoundly.

There was nothing wrong with changing his mind, in recognizing that he had been wrong. This book review represented that change of mind; it was a recognition of error.

How often did we make mistakes?

His mistake on Robespierre had been an intellectual one that was removed from his personal life.

Had he made a mistake in marrying Ruth? No, he didn't think he had. But both he and Ruth had probably made a mistake in allowing the marriage to go on so long.

Bill? How many mistakes had he made with his son? Parents should bear some responsibility for their children, should they not?

He thought of last night.

If he left Ruth, where would he go? Live in a hotel? Give up the comforts of his home? Find another girl? Would he divorce Ruth and marry someone else? A young girl perhaps? How often had he longed for some young girl he had seen? But to marry one now and have her nurse him? It could be hideous. And unfair to the girl. What young girl with brains would want him?

Would he live out his last years alone?

He had known all along that this might happen. He had thought about it even in his days of youthful hope and idealism. He would tell himself that it would be different for him but he had known that it could happen. He had beaten his lances against windmills. In his own way, he had played Don Quixote.

Tom picked up a pencil. Work was its own justification. He started writing, his mood one of deep personal disillusionment.

> *Robespierre was not a liberal in the modern*
> *sense of the word. Robespierre was a fanatic.*

II

Tom sat in his chair. His weariness made him look older than he usually looked. He looked gently and with understanding at the baby-faced young man who sat before him talking. The fellow's name was Joseph Benton. He was from the Trotsky Defense Committee. He was probably a Trotskyite. Tom had seen his name somewhere but he couldn't remember just where. He wondered if Joe Benton knew Bill. Or knew of him.

"I admire you, Mr. Carroll, as one of the outstanding American historians and liberals," Joe Benton said. He spoke with somewhat of a Harvard accent.

He paused. Smiling, he went on.

"We honor you for your sentiments. The day will come when you and everyone else who takes a stand against the Moscow Trials will be honored far and wide."

Flattery was pleasing and did no harm as long as it was not confused with fact. Men might not be honored one day for denouncing the Moscow Trials. They might be killed, murdered like Kamenev, Zinoviev, and the others. Stalin might win. Did Bill realize that totalitarian politics was a business of life or death? How did Bill compare with this young fellow? If both of them had their way, they would fight a life-and-death struggle.

No, Trotskyites would never be that important.

"I needn't tell you, Mr. Carroll, that world opinion is revolted by these shabby frameups."

"It's not as revolted as you imagine," Tom interrupted. "I remember the struggle to defend Sacco and Vanzetti."

"Yes, I know, Mr. Carroll. You were one of the defenders of those martyrs."

"There was indignation on then, world-wide indignation. Men, strong men, wept," Tom said, a trace of passion in his voice. His own feelings were rising. He no longer seemed tired.

"I remember the picket line around the courthouse and I remember the way people felt. They felt as though the execution of Sacco and Vanzetti meant the end of the world. I don't want to sound like a lecturer. Christ knows, young fellows don't want to be lectured to . . ."

A twinkle came into Tom's eyes. Joe Benton cut in on him.

"I am pleased, in fact, honored to listen to you, Mr. Carroll."

"I don't know why. I'll help you on this Moscow Trials fight anyway."

"You misunderstand me," Joe Benton said quickly. "I wouldn't think of doing anything so unprincipled as flattering you. It is a question of principle here. The Moscow Trials are cognate with the Sacco-Vanzetti case, the Dreyfus case, all of the great cases for freedom and the right of asylum in history. They are more enormous than any of these other cases."

"Yes," Tom said.

"Well, I don't want to take up your time. What I came to see you about, Mr. Carroll, is this. Our Committee has organized a meeting for the thirty-first of next month. We have rented the Hippodrome and we are certain to pack it.

We have made arrangements for Leon Trotsky to address the meeting . . ."

"How can you get him into America? And if you got him here and he speaks in public, there might be a riot. He might be assassinated."

"America is not yet free enough to give asylum to Leon Trotsky. You must know the chapter in his autobiography, *The Planet Without a Visa?*"

"Yes, I know it."

"Trotsky is going to speak over the telephone. His voice will be carried to the meeting."

"Won't the Stalinists sabotage it?"

A grin spread across Joseph Benton's face.

"We think we know how to fight the Stalinists. They'll be furious. They'll rage. They'll pour filth on us when we make our public announcement."

"It'll be a coup. That they won't like," Tom said.

"But we're not afraid of them. With this meeting, we will drive telling blows against the liars and the frameup masters of the Kremlin."

Venom came into his voice as he said this.

"Will you be one of our speakers, Mr. Carroll? If you accept our request, we will feel highly honored. This is going to be a meeting which will go down in history. Trotsky, in his own words, will answer his accusers. He will hurl the lie back into their teeth."

Ben Gladman had warned him about excitement. Ben would not approve of his speaking at this meeting. Anything could happen. And Bill? Bill would be enraged. And Ruth would be gotten to work on him. Last night, he was certain that Bill had been given some kind of instruction to work on him. And today, this young fellow had been sent here to work on him.

"As a historian, Mr. Carroll, you can appreciate the fact that this meeting will be historic."

Tom nodded. He had already made up his mind; he needed no urging.

"I'll speak."

"You won't regret it, Mr. Carroll."

Tom looked at him. This young man believed in victory. His son probably did, too. Was this young man idealistic or fanatic—or both?

"The exposure of the frameup of the Moscow Trials can be the most deadly blow struck at the Kremlin," Joe Benton said.

Tom smiled.

"They'll survive it."

"They are rotten at the roots and this will be a seed of their decay," Joe Benton went on.

Tom shook his head.

"Politics isn't as simple as that. Passion plays a bigger role in it than reason. I've seen the way things have gone. I've seen the way politics can generate passions. And I have seen the death of many hopes in my time. I guess I am not an optimist; I don't have your fighting faith," Tom said.

"I think I could convince you of our ideas," Joseph Benton said.

He had heard all this before; it was, in a sense, where he had come in.

Joseph Benton looked at Tom Carroll. He noticed how tired he looked. Here was an honest liberal, an honest intellectual. Joe Benton had become a Trotskyite because he believed that the life of the world was corrupt, rotten, filthy; and the most rotten, corrupt, and filthy of any group in the world were the intellectuals. But he made an exception of Tom Carroll. He had read Tom's books while he was in Harvard. He had quit Harvard to work in an advertising agency in New York. At the time, he had been a devotee of the philosopher Whitehead, and he had objected to Tom's liberalism and pragmatism. But later he had ditched Whitehead or Marx; and now, his opinion of Tom Carroll was that he represented the best liberal tradition in America. But sitting here, talking with him, made him feel sorry for him, superior to him. At the same time, there was some fear. He would not want to lock horns with Tom Carroll. Tom knew more than he did about history, but then the man should. It was his business. But like other liberals, even John Dewey, he did not understand the laws of history.

Suddenly Joe Benton was moved. He didn't know what to say. He had accomplished his mission. Tom Carroll had agreed to speak at the meeting. The old man had needed practically no persuading. Perhaps the fire of the Tom Carroll he had read about, the Tom Carroll of the days of the World War would flame again.

"I'm writing a book review of the new biography of Robespierre by that Englishman . . ."

"Oh yes, I must read it. I've read Mathiez. Robespierre was the great figure of the French Revolution. But then you know that. I recall an article you wrote on Robespierre years ago."

Tom was pleased that Benton remembered the review. It had appeared some years ago in a historical journal.

"It was a review of Mathiez's *History of the French Revolution,*" Tom said.

"Yes, I was working one night in the library when I came across it. That was how I became interested in Mathiez; I had never heard of him.

"I've changed my mind about Mathiez and Robespierre since then," Tom said.

The young Trotskyite paled. He was taken aback.

"Don't you see any connection between the Bolsheviks and the Jacobins?" asked Tom.

"Yes, the Jacobins are the historic predecessors of the Bolsheviks. Both Trotsky and Lenin had said that."

Tom noticed that Benton had said Trotsky before Lenin.

"We think that what has happened in the Soviet Union is a parallel to the Thermidor."

"Violence begets violence. Fanaticism begets fanaticism. Once you allow violent men in power, there is no end. I hailed the Russian Revolution. I remember those days." Tom's eyes were bright as he spoke. "God, it was like a new day. A rotten autocracy was toppled. The people, the workers had asserted themselves. They would move into a free society. The world was ravaged by the bloody war, and I was against it—then."

A sense of triumph rose in Joseph Benton. He derived a sense of comfort from what Tom Carroll was saying. With his liberalism, his tolerant ideas, Tom Carroll was helpless to see the world. He was denying his youth. This was pitiful. But Joe Benton lived in a stern inner world. There was a right and a wrong in history. He was right. And Tom Carroll telling him that he had changed his mind about Robespierre, about the Jacobins, and about his opposition to the War was convincing him that he was right.

"Nobody will win in history or any other way if Hitler and Stalin win," Tom said.

"That's true."

Tom raised his eyebrows. This chap was too certain. Bill was that way too. Tom remembered his own youth, his uncertainties. How could they be so sure?

Joseph Benton felt sure that the meeting would revive Tom Carroll. They could work on him, convince him. If Tom Carroll would go to Mexico and talk with Trotsky, the Old Man would convince him.

But anyway, he had accomplished his purpose. Tom Carroll would speak at their meeting. The Stalinists would' froth at the mouth. Let them. Carroll's son was a Stalinoid liberal or a fellow traveler. He had no use for Carroll's son. One more mediocrity making a career out of being Stalinoid. The old man was better than the son; he was one of the best of the

iberals. And look at him—one of the best. Think of the difference between him and Trotsky.

He listened as Tom explained how and why he had changed
his mind on Robespierre. He reminded himself that Tom
Carroll was a historian lacking in historical insight. But he had
redeemed himself by agreeing to speak at the meeting. Maybe
it would do something to reinspire Carroll. Maybe Trotsky's
voice would awaken sleeping memories of his heroic youth.
How sad to see a hero looking so tired, talking so weakly,
and denying his once sound ideas. It was a lesson.

Tom finished talking.

They sat for a moment. Tom wanted Benton to go now.
He wasn't much impressed with him. He was a tight-minded
young fellow.

Joseph Benton rose.

"If you'll excuse me now, Mr. Carroll . . ."

Tom rose.

"Write me a letter and send me the details of the meeting."

"I will; and you'll never regret what you're going to do."

"No I won't," Tom said, not knowing what he, himself,
meant.

They shook hands, said goodbye, and Tom watched the
young man walk out of the room.

III

"Who was he?" Ruth asked, coming into Tom's study.

"A Trotskyite," Tom said very casually.

She tried to mask her displeasure but he caught it. He had
enjoyed saying this to her.

"What did he want?"

"He asked me to speak at a meeting."

"I hope that after what Ben Gladman told you that you
said 'No.'"

"I said that I would."

She gazed at him, bewildered, uneasy.

"Hell, I think the trials are a bloody frameup. I might as well say so in public."

"But after the pain you suffered last night, what about your health?"

He wondered if it were truly his health that caused her not to want him to speak at the meeting.

"I'll be feeling much better by the time I have to speak. It's the thirty-first of next month."

"Oh that's the night of the banquet for Aid to Spain," she said.

"I wasn't going to that banquet anyway."

"I had hoped that you would—but what I hope means nothing to you, Tom," she said dispiritedly.

"Ruth there's no use in you and I talking politics," he told her.

Was there any use in their talking of anything?

"I . . . no, I won't say anything," she said.

She half-turned to face the door.

"Go ahead, Ruth."

"No, you're not well. I'll try and take care of you. Let's not argue."

"Oh, one of these days Hitler and Stalin will put their arms around each other's shoulders or something will happen, and you'll say that you were fooled."

"Tom, that's ridiculous," she said.

She was angry. He wasn't taking her seriously. Had he agreed to speak at this . . . this Trotskyite meeting just to shame her? She had told him about the banquet. She had asked him to go.

"Do you want something?" she asked, determined to control herself.

"No thanks, Ruth," Tom said, rising. "I'll take a nap."

"Are you too sick or too tired to see my guests tonight?"

"Oh, I'll see them for a little while," he said.

"Come lie down," she said, trying to sound sympathetic.

She looked at him. He did look tired. Ben Gladman had said it wasn't serious, but suppose it were.

She followed Tom out of the room.

Tom was sick, something was happening to him. What he'd said about Hitler and Stalin. If people heard him talk like that, they'd think he was crazy.

She felt nervous. Oh, she wished that their life had turned out differently.

She watched him disappear into their bedroom. She went into the living room and looked out of the window. Tom was getting old. She never wanted to get old. Life was becoming interesting for her now. But Tom. He would become more and more of a drawback to her. What should she do about it?

Oh, she felt sorry for Tom. She only wished that he were different, that he weren't changing the way he was.

She turned from the window and wondered what she would do with herself for the next half hour or so. She decided to have a cocktail.

IV

Tom and Ruth ate alone. Ruth was having roast beef. Tom had mashed potatoes and baby food before him, and a glass of milk by the side of his plate. He ate slowly, without appetite. He noticed the relish with which Ruth ate. For the third time, she said to him:

"This wine is excellent. It's a pity, Tom, that you can't drink any of it."

"It makes no difference," Tom said.

"Oh, I forgot to mention it—I also invited Jack Eichorn tonight. He's coming with Sarah, remember her?"

Tom didn't answer. Memories rushed into his mind.

"What happened between you and Jack? Once he was your closest friend," Ruth said.

"Nothing. I like Jack."

"Yes, but you never see him any more. Why, ten or twelve years ago, you two were inseparable."

Did Ruth suspect anything about him and Sarah? He wondered.

"He's one of the most charming men I know," she added.

Tom repressed an impulse to grin.

"I was surprised to hear that he's coming with Sarah," Ruth said, cutting another piece of roast beef.

Tom took a spoonful of the pureed peas.

"I wonder if he has gone back to her?" Ruth asked.

"I haven't seen Jack in years, except for a casual meeting on the street about six months ago."

"You had a crush on Sarah, didn't you, Tom?"

"Yes, I suppose so."

And now he was indifferent.

"Jack is a very influential man in Washington these days," Ruth said.

"Yes, he's a braintruster," Tom said, taking a fork full of mashed potatoes.

"I never could figure out why you didn't do what he did. You should have gone to Washington," Ruth said. Suddenly she changed the subject.

"Oh, I'm so sorry, Tom, that you can't eat more. This roast beef is delicious."

She wondered what Tom and Jack would say to one another. She knew the entire story. Sarah had been Tom's mistress and Jack had taken her away from Tom. Oh, the pain she had felt in those days. She would be civilized tonight, but God, she hated Sarah. She wondered if Sarah had begun to show signs of age.

Sarah. Love grown cold just left one indifferent, Tom thought. And yet, he had loved Sarah even more than he had loved Ruth. Would he ever love again? Sarah would see him tonight, looking fatigued. And Ruth would talk of last night. Why had Ruth invited them over? She must know something.

"Did you and Jack ever quarrel?" Ruth asked.

"No," Tom said.

"Did you grow away from each other because of political differences?"

"I like him. I'm glad to see him so successful."

Tom took another spoonful of peas.

"Jack isn't a fellow traveler," she said.

"I know that, Ruth."

"I'm glad," she said.

"Oh, drop the irony. Ruth, if you want to disagree with me, go ahead. You're free, white, and twenty-one."

He had never loved her, or he wouldn't say that. Saying it now did not hurt her. But when they were young and she had loved him, he had told her that she was free. And she had been hurt. Had he ever loved her? Had he ever loved anyone but himself?

"Well, no fellow travelers are coming tonight so you need not worry about getting overexcited and having a relapse. We'll have a quiet, civilized evening. And Jack ought to be able to tell us what's going on."

Tom took another spoonful of baby food.

V

Ruth's brother Alvin and his wife, Louise, sat in the drawing room with Tom and Ruth. All except Tom had drinks in their hands.

"I don't know why so many businessmen complain about Roosevelt," Alvin was saying. "God, I remember when he took over. I was heading for the same place that the whole damned country was—the rocks."

"You both must come out and see our new home," Louise said.

"Yeh, it's quite a layout," Alvin said.

"And we want you to recommend some books for us. We have so much wall space," Louise said.

"Yeh, only don't pick out a lot of pink books for us. Hell, it's bad enough out there in Westchester County if I say that Mr. Roosevelt isn't a sonofabitch. If they find me with a house full of pink books, I don't know what they'll think of me," Alvin said.

"But they are nice people, even if they are Republicans," Louise said.

"Tom," Ruth said, looking at her husband and ignoring her sister-in-law, "Tom isn't a radical any more."

Tom frowned but before he could say something, Alvin grinned.

"I always said that Tom would mellow. You were sure a firebrand in your day, Tom. Well, we all get over our youth." Nostalgia crept into his blue eyes. "Hell, I remember the way we used to paint the town red when I went to college."

"Yes, Ruth, Alvin is even becoming a moderate drinker," Louise said.

Tom listened, somewhat bored. When would Sarah and Jack arrive? How would he feel when he saw her?

"So you're not pink any more, Tom?"

"I don't know a thing about politics," Louise said.

Tom smiled ironically at Alvin. He never had taken the fellow seriously, but he liked him. He was kind and decent; he just lived in a totally different world, that was all.

"Alvin do you want to fix more drinks? Tom can't drink because he's got colitis. But I'm glad it's that and not an ulcer," Ruth said.

"I'll fix the drinks," Tom said, rising.

"Oh, but Tom, you had a bad night," Ruth said.

Tom went to the table and mixed the drinks while they

talked. Alvin spoke of business. He was in the real estate business in Westchester. He had just sold a house that had been a white elephant.

"Tell us about it," Ruth said.

Tom passed the drinks and sat down. He lit a cigarette as Alvin talked.

"Didn't I ever tell you the story about Mr. Yarnell?" he asked.

"Alvin you must have. I have heard nothing but Mr. Yarnell for days now," Louise interrupted.

"I haven't heard it," Tom said.

Louise sulked a moment, grinned and took a sip from her glass.

"Yarnell doesn't have to do anything to make money. It just rolls into him. He was in the clothing business, had a big job and a lot of stock. He decided to retire and sold his stock. Two days later, it was Black Friday on Wall Street."

"An unforgettable day," Ruth said.

"Yes, I lost everything but my shirt. The only reason I didn't lose that was because I was wearing it," Alvin said.

"I warned Alvin about his investments, but what husband listens to his wife?" Louise asked.

"Did you lose any money on the market then, Tom?"

"No, I never played the market."

"A man like you, Tom, ought to have some investments. I tell you that not only as a friend but as one of the family."

"Tom never takes advice," Ruth said.

"He's just like Alvin," Louise said.

"But I want to know about Yarnell," Ruth said.

"Come on, Al, tell us about Yarnell," Tom urged.

"I told you that Yarnell was in business, and he closed out; that is, he retired," Alvin said.

Tom found it difficult to concentrate on what his brother-in-law was saying. He was anxiously awaiting the appearance of Sarah and Jack. He had thought that the whole painful episode was behind him but now, suddenly, it rose out of his memories. Touches of all of his old emotions flickered like feeble candle flames, and then popped like firecrackers in his mind.

Alvin was still talking. Tom half-listened.

"Yes, he retired," Alvin said. "He had a lot of stock. He is rich, but you wouldn't know it or believe it to hear him talk. He was a Horatio Alger boy. He actually shined shoes when he was a kid. He worked his way up the ladder." Alvin turned to his sister, and again, as had happened several times during the evening, an expression of apology came upon his face. "You have to give him credit, Sis. Of course he isn't an intellectual like you and Tom, but he suscribes to the Book-of-the-Month Club, and he goes to the theater. He loves the theater." He turned, almost defensively, toward Tom.

"Hell, I haven't got anything against him, Al, I don't even know him," Tom said, his mind now on Sarah. Did Sarah ever think of him any more? What a meaningless question. There was the vanity of a man.

"Alvin, don't have an inferiority complex," Louise said.

Her remark embarrassed Alvin.

"I only meant that you got to give Yarnell credit," he said apologetically.

"Well, I think you're probably right. But tell me more about him. He fascinates me," Ruth said, thinking that she might get a *New Yorker* story out of Yarnell.

"Well, I told you he retired. When he retired, he sold his stocks, and the stock market crashed. He made a lot of money. He's been doing that for years. Take his house. I never dreamed I could sell it."

"I told you you could. I'm the one who met Mrs. Brady, the wife of the man who bought it, at my bridge club," Louise said. "Remember, Alvin, I brought them to the house? I invited them for tea?"

"Yes, honey, you were a pearl, a pearl. You were a mighty important help.

"Anyway, that's the story. I sold this Mr. Brady the house. He's in the distributing end of the movies."

There was a silence after this remark of Alvin.

"Tell me about Mr. Brady," Ruth said.

"I really don't know much about him but . . ."

"His wife is *nouveau riche*," Louise said.

The doorbell rang.

They were here. Tom was tense and expectant. He had never expected this to happen in this way.

VI

Jack Eichorn was forty-eight years old, a stocky, well-dressed man. He seemed to be as likable as ever. Sarah was short and slender, and still beautiful. Her strawberry hair had begun to lose some of its once fine texture, but it was still beautiful. She greeted Tom with a warm but aloof friendliness. Jack had put his arm on Tom's shoulder, shaken his hand warmly, asked him how he was, told him that he was looking good, and had turned to everyone and had said:

—I love this man as much as ever.

The doorbell rang again. Others came in. Will Ackers, a lawyer, his pathetic looking wife, Bertha, and Fred Lens, an advertising man and a bachelor.

Sarah and Jack sat on the far side of the large living room. Tom wondered if this had been purposeful. He heard Ruth telling Sarah that Tom had been ill.

"Tom, you must take care of yourself," Sarah called across the room.

He smothered an impulse to self-pity.

"Don't worry, I will," he said, and turned back to listen to the story that Will Ackers was telling him.

Ruth and Sarah went on talking, and Jack spoke with the others. Tom heard him mention the names of Roosevelt, Hull, an Admiral, Harry Hopkins, Thomas G. Corcoran, and Ben Cohen.

Tom had heard Ackers' story before. He listened out of politeness, and because it was easy to listen and to think. He had a need to remember. The appearance of Sarah and Jack had awakened his sleeping memories. They were painful, but he was glad that this had happened. Perhaps he might understand something that he hadn't understood before about this triangle of the past.

"I had to act the way I did. I didn't sell out the workers the way Moses Kallisch and the others say, and *Mass Action* had no right to attack me. Why they practically called me a fascist," Bill Ackers was saying.

Tom's eyes happened to rove. He caught Jack smiling. Jack's smile was as charming as ever.

Bill Ackers went on to explain the situation. Two years before, the Communist writer and editor of the weekly magazine *Mass Action*, had organized a strike in the publishing house of Gibbons and Company. Moses, at the time, had been editor, and he had organized the office employees in a local of the Office Workers Union.

"The Party controls the union, you know that, Tom. Everybody does," Will told him.

Tom nodded in agreement.

"Tom you old so-and-so, I never hear from you," Jack called over to him, grinning with geniality and affection.

Tom put his hand up toward Jack, and continued to listen to Will.

"I was retained by Gibbons. And after all, a lawyer has an obligation to his client. And I was working on Gibbons himself to get a good settlement. I told Moses this, and I explained to him that Gibbons was bewildered and surprised.

There never had been a strike in a publishing house before, not to my knowledge," Will said.

Tom recalled that Bill, his son, had picketed in the strike, and had made a fiery speech on a soap box. His picture had been taken just as he had made a sweeping gesture, and copies of it, along with pictures of other writers who picketed and made speeches, had been sold, autographed for twenty-five cents a copy at the Communist book store. Bill had given Ruth a copy of the picture. She was proud of it. She'd been disappointed when he hadn't reacted with pleasure. She and Sarah were still talking.

An uneasiness came over him.

"Lorette loved Harold Brooks," Ruth was saying.

Tom caught this. Lorette, now fifty, and Harold Brooks, a book reviewer in the twenties. He had died last year of a heart attack. Lorette was married now to an advertising man. Both of them, the looks in their eyes one night in a speak-easy in the twenties, the way they had sat in a corner, ignoring everyone at a big party for a famous European writer. That had been back around 1925 or 1926. And now. Ashes. Disintegration. Change.

"Tom, you know I wouldn't be against the workers?" Will Ackers asked.

Tom stared at him. Why was a successful theatrical and literary lawyer talking this way?

"I was working for a decent agreement. What the hell, Tom, fifteen employees of a publishing house, led by Moses Kallisch, aren't going to set up barricades on Fourth Avenue and win the Revolution. Did you see how they attacked me in *Mass Action?*"

"No, I quit reading it a long time ago. If I want to read what the Russians think, I'll read the Moscow dispatches of the New York *Times*."

"I can't find out who did this dirty hatchet job on me," Will said.

"It's an honor to be attacked by them, Will. Don't let it disturb you," Tom said.

"Oh, it doesn't disturb me," Will said.

But Tom could see that it did.

"The hatchet job was written by someone named Carvell Takiss. Have you ever heard of him?"

Ruth happened to hear this remark of Will's. Her eyes lit up with interest and she looked across the room at Will and Tom. Tom noticed this. Carvell Takiss, his initials turned around. Bill must have written it.

Ruth saw him staring at her, and she quickly went on talking in a rapid but low voice to Sarah.

"What do you think of it?" Will asked.

Will was asking him what he thought of what his own son was doing? Tom was almost overcome with humiliation.

"I tell you, Tom, not one line of that stinking article is true, not one line. This punk wasn't present when I sat in at the negotiation and he must have gotten his dope from Moses Kallisch. Why I am attacked more than Gibbons. And they made demands that they knew Gibbons can't meet. Hell, a publishing house is not the United States Steel Corporation. They knew it. Moses Kallisch does. And he shook hands with me at the end of the meeting, and thanked me for what I said. He said I was a great help. But they must have told this punk Takiss a different story. Now, Gibbons is sore. He won't budge. The picket lines in front of the building on Fourth Avenue, the attacks on him—and yes, the attacks on me as his stooge. Why I was called 'the slimy stooge of Gibbons.' All of this hasn't done those kids any good, they're just being manipulated. Tom what do you think?"

Ruth was listening again. He could tell.

"It's rotten," Tom said.

Did that mean that his own son was rotten?

"Another drink?" Alvin asked, appearing over them.

He seemed ill-at-ease in the group, and he had kept himself busy serving drinks.

"I'll take one, thanks," Will said.

"You can't, can you, Tom?"

Tom shook his head.

"My heart goes out to you," Alvin said sympathetically.

Tom wished the evening were over. He wasn't enjoying himself.

"Good old Tom," Jack said, giving him an affectionate pat on the back."

Tom said nothing.

Jack sat down beside him.

"I miss seeing you," Jack said. "You know I love you."

"I keep up with you through the newspapers, Jack. I'm glad to see that you're doing well and that you've gone up."

"But it's never sure, I can be out tomorrow. Nothing is sure in politics. But then, is anything sure anywhere? I miss those old days when we used to see so much of each other, Tom. We used to have good conversations in those days. In politics, the talk is different."

"By necessity, you develop partisan thinking," Tom said.

"That's why we need men like you. You gave me great help six or seven years ago. You should have gone into politics. It's not too late, Tom; I could get something fixed up."

Tom recalled the time in his youth when he had dreamed of a life of politics. The example of Woodrow Wilson had moved him. Then the bitterness and the feeling of betrayal when the United States had entered the war. To this day, it was hard to think of Wilson without his personal feelings intervening. That was why he had put aside the biography of Wilson that he had started.

"It might be good for you, Tom. That last book of yours— I didn't like it. We're close enough friends for me to tell you what I think, aren't we?" Jack said.

"Which one was that?" Tom asked.

"What did you say?" Jack asked. His face looked bewildered.

Out of the corner of his eye, Tom was watching Sarah. He remembered how she had walked with a kind of womanly pride, naked, into bed with him. But to make love to her now would be grisly. It would be a way of playing with ghosts. There was no going back. And sitting here talking to Jack; they were ghosts of friends talking.

"I asked which book you meant."

"That last one, the last one you wrote. What was it called?" Tom smiled.

"Oh thanks," Jack said as Alvin appeared and pressed a drink upon him.

"You're not drinking, Tom?" Jack asked.

"I had a goddamned bellyache last night."

"I'm sorry. Well, Tom, here's to you. You know, I've always looked upon you almost like a father," Jack said, raising his glass.

He took a sip and then looked around the room.

"Sarah still looks beautiful, doesn't she?" Jack said.

"Yes," Tom said somewhat indifferently.

"But so does Ruth," Jack went on.

Tom couldn't think of anything to say. He could not summon up any interest in Jack.

"Are you two talking politics? Give us the benefit of your wisdom if you are," Mrs. Ackers said, joining them.

"If any," Jack said, smiling charmingly.

"Jack, don't be so modest. You are one of the men who shapes political affairs," Ruth said.

"I only wish I did," Jack answered, his tone still modest.

"I always think what a pity it is, Jack, that you aren't a Congressman or a Senator," Ruth said. She looked at Tom. "Don't you, Tom?"

"Yes, Jack would make a damned good Senator."

"Why don't you run? You could, with your connections,

e nominated. And with the prestige of Mr. Roosevelt, why a
Republican wouldn't stand a chance here in New York City,"
Ruth said.

"And in my neck of the woods, you wouldn't win for dog
catcher if you are a Democrat," Alvin said, turning from the
table where he was preparing more drinks.

There was laughter.

"I would never be able to run for office in this country,"
Jack said.

"Why?" asked Ruth.

"I'm a divorced man."

"Nonsense, we don't live in the dark ages any more."

"This is politics," Jack said, smiling boyishly toward Ruth.
"And I am supposed to be an expert on politics."

"You are, aren't you?" Ruth asked.

Jack laughed self-deprecatingly.

"My father here," he said, nodding toward Tom, "I wonder if he thinks I'm an expert on politics."

"You know you're a smart guy," Tom answered.

"Thank you, thank you," Jack made a mocking bow to
Tom. "Tom and I love each other."

"I'm serious when I say that this is still a highly moral
country, almost puritan, about the men in government."

"I can't believe it," Ruth said.

"They aren't that backward in Westchester. Maybe they
voted for Landon, but they don't care what you do with your
wife, or with somebody else's wife," Alvin said, moving
away from the table with a tray full of drinks.

"They might not care when they're talking with their
friends at cocktail parties or at dances, but they care when
they get in that voting booth. The results have shown how
much they care."

"Jack, I never could understand why you never married
again," Ruth said.

"Well, I have given it some thought," Jack said.

They all looked at Sarah.

"Don't look at me," Sarah said calmly. "Jack is Washington's most eligible bachelor."

Jack was both embarrassed and pleased. He liked the fact that the conversation had turned on him.

"Maybe he has too much sense to get married," Tom said.

Jack watched Tom. He was not sure what Tom meant by this remark. He thought again how glad he was to be seeing Tom. He didn't think that Tom knew how much he admired him, how deep his affection was. They hadn't seen each other for years but his affection and respect had remained.

"Jack is a born bachelor," Sarah said.

"When I see how lonely my bachelor friends are, I wonder if a man's a fool to remain in a state of blessed bachelorhood," Jack said.

"But, Jack, do tell us how it feels to be a braintruster," Ruth said.

Jack grinned boyishly again.

"It's hard work. The era of Tammany politicians is gone. Politicians today have to work. And their staff works. I work sixteen hours a day. The pressure is killing. I did get a two-week vacation last year; it was the first one in years. I've had none this year."

"That's not good. Every year, Louise and I go away for two weeks. We forget the real estate business. We forget the world," Alvin said.

"Don't you believe him," Louise said. "When we were away last summer, Alvin never stopped fretting about his business."

"That's not true, honey. I did worry about that Yarnell deal but it wasn't closed then. That's all I thought about," Alvin said. He looked around. "Anybody want another drink?"

"I'll take one," Jack said.

He enjoyed being in this atmosphere, away from politics

with its pressures, its handshakings, its narrow range of talk, and its daily demands. He thought of the old days when Tom was important and he was just another newspaperman. A sudden nostalgia came upon him. Sometimes he would like to be back on the old *Chronicle,* writing his daily story, enjoying his cynicism, being free to criticize and to dislike at will, standing in the bar at the end of the day, talking with other reporters in the National Press Club in Washington, guessing and second-guessing, wondering what really was going on in the White House, beefing.

He remembered the joy he had gotten with his first byline. Well, someday, he would write a book. No one knew it but he kept a diary. He looked at Tom again. Tom wrote history while he was making it. The thrill of this was something he couldn't convey. To be telephoned at six in the morning, to get out of bed, shave, grab a cup of coffee, and hurry to the White House, to know that you had a hand in world events even though your name did not appear in the newspapers. There was a thrill of power. It was a narcotic.

But he sometimes yearned for recognition. Tom had this; his name was on his books.

"You're one of the most important men in America today," Ruth was saying, "and you're so modest."

"Darling, I'll give you a bouquet for that compliment but don't exaggerate my importance. My head could fall at any moment."

"I don't understand why you don't become a Senator," Ruth said.

Maybe he should, he thought.

"Would you vote for me, Tom?" he asked jokingly.

"That would depend on your Russian line. If you hated Russia enough, Tom would vote for you, wouldn't you, Tom?" Ruth asked.

Jack's smile disappeared. He looked surprised.

"We're going to need Russia," he said.

"Do you really think there's going to be a war? Tell us what you know that we don't," Ruth said.

"Nothing. Anyone can see the way Hitler is moving," Jack answered.

"Tom here says that Hitler and Stalin are going to get together."

"Why, Tom!" Jack burst out in a laughing affectionate tone of reproof. "It must be your old sense of humor at work."

The room became still. They all looked at Tom.

"All I say is that don't be surprised if it happens. Stalin is not killing the old Bolsheviks as German agents for nothing. And God knows there are no principles that would prevent its happening on either side."

"But with fascists?" Will Ackers asked.

"Red fascism, white fascism, black fascism, brown fascism —they can unite and if they ever do, we will fight for survival," Tom answered.

"Jack, you're in a position to know what's going on in Russia," Ruth said, appealing to him for support.

"Tom has always been a passionate man. But I think your passion has carried you away on this. I know of nothing to support what you say; I'd have to see it happen to believe it."

"We are standing by while the world changes and formations of power are growing that can destroy every value we cherish," Tom said.

"But, Tom, no one disagrees with you on that point." Ruth interrupted. She turned to Jack. "But a war. I can't imagine it; it's too horrible."

"It's going on in Spain," Jack said.

"And what are we doing?" asked Fred Lens.

"Yes, it's a pity we can't do more," Ruth said.

Jack shook his head.

"Our hands are tied. The country would be in an uproar if we intervened."

"We're all getting old and the world has changed on us. All that we believed in our youth is being torn to shreds. It is being undermined. Day by day, the world we know is being broken and a new one is being formed. A new world of terror and brutality," Tom said.

"Don't be so downhearted, old man. That used to be my privilege. I was always the gloomy one," Jack said.

"Jack, you never were a pessimist," Ruth said.

"If Jack weren't a pessimist, he'd never get anything done. In order for Jack to do something, he has to have a fit of gloom," Sarah said, her smile softening the words. "Once he thinks that the situation is hopeless, he goes into action."

"Well, at least he acts, that's what counts," Ruth said.

Tom knew that this was directed at him. He said nothing. His eyes fell on Sarah. She smiled.

"Tom, the next time I get down from Washington, we've got to have a long lunch and a good old-fashioned bull session," Jack said.

"It would be good for Tom," Ruth said.

"It might be good for me too," Jack said.

"Anybody want another drink?" Alvin asked.

VII

As they sat side by side, a thousand unspoken memories hung between them.

"Jack hasn't changed, has he, Tom?" Sarah asked.

"No," Tom said.

"He still has great respect for you, Tom."

"I have for him."

How much talk was empty talk?

"So have I," she said.

"I want you to, Sarah. It makes me happy to know that you do."

"I do, Tom. I always did."

Was there, he wondered, any love for him remaining? There must be. Love never died, it only dropped down to another level and lay there, sleeping and lost.

He looked at Ruth. Then at Jack. He was aware of Jack's mannerisms. His modest boyish smile, his politeness, his ways of flattering, the way he held his hands.

"I think we can have complete trust in Roosevelt," Jack was saying.

"I hope so," Ruth agreed.

Suddenly she leaned forward. "Jack, did you write that speech, the one in Chicago about quarantining the aggressor?"

"I honestly wish I had. No, I didn't. But I share those views. If we don't adopt that policy, there's no chance of avoiding a war."

"There can't be, there just can't be a war. Of course, Hitler is a madman," Ruth said.

"Mad like a fox," said Fred Lens.

"Tell us more, Jack," Ruth said.

"You are as beautiful and as gracious as always, Ruth."

"Jack, you are a diplomat; you should be made an Ambassador, but thank you, Jack darling."

"Don't thank me for telling the truth. You know I always loved you and Tom. If you weren't Tom's wife, I could say more."

Sarah was watching Tom intently.

"Tom, I'm very sorry that you were ill. Are you taking care of yourself?"

"I obviously had not been but I shall, Sarah."

Did he look ill? Is that why she had asked this? He felt better now than he had earlier in the evening; his pain was gone.

He smiled at her; she smiled back.

"There is not a lot to say, is there, Tom?"

He looked at Jack.

"We'll have lunch some day and talk," he said.

"I'd like to, very much."

Her voice was wistful, caressing. He turned to look at her. She was still so lovely; she was over forty now, forty-three, he thought. They had been in love ten years ago. But she could still look at him and give him the feeling that she had eyes for no one but him.

"I'm getting my divorce," she said.

The news surprised him.

"I'm sorry."

"Are you really sorry, Tom?"

"Yes. How does Charlie feel?"

"He's hurt. He cried when I told him but I can't help it. I can't live a lie all my life."

"You had affection for Charlie."

—But you loved me, he thought.

Could they go back, find what they had once had? He knew that it was impossible.

"What are you going to do, Sarah?"

"Write a book."

"You gave up writing."

"Yes," she said, speaking in a low voice. "I couldn't write with Charlie. I never had peace of soul with him. I had it once, for a little while."

He knew what she meant. Fragments of memories came into his mind. Walks in Central Park, the Italian restaurant in the Village, hotel rooms, a taxi ride in the daytime when he had kissed her passionately and drivers going by had honked their horns, when he had gotten out of the cab at Eighth Street and Fifth Avenue, his face smeared with lipstick, a cop had grinned at him.

"Do it in private, Mister," he had said.

"We may be able to avoid a war," Jack was saying.

"I'm glad to hear you say that, especially since it comes straight from the horse's mouth," Alvin said.

"I think of you often, Tom," Sarah said.

Once he could have said the same thing. But lately he hadn't. Indifference had crept into his spirit like fog on a sunny day.

That look in her eyes. Her beautiful eyes. She was as much as asking him why he had done it. Could he, should he, try to explain? There had been days of silent agony for him. Days of struggling to be fair, to calm the anger and jealousy that threatened to sweep everything else from his mind. It was strange to look at this part of his past now. Love had turned into indifference.

"Jack, it isn't too late for you to marry," Ruth was saying.

"Perhaps no one would marry me," Jack said with modesty and a touch of lightness.

"Oh, don't tell me that."

"I mean it."

Tom and Sarah exchanged looks.

"Who wants another drink?" Alvin said.

"I could stand one. You know, you can drink nowadays, thanks to the President. I'm glad we don't have to drink the stuff we drank in the twenties," Jack said.

"But those were wonderful days. We were so innocent; we just lived then," Ruth said nostalgically.

Tom felt himself growing tired again.

"We'll have lunch next week," he told Sarah.

"Please call me."

"I will."

"When I was a newspaperman in those days, I never imagined that I'd be where I am today. I never thought that I'd become a politician," Jack said.

"You wanted to be a writer, didn't you, Jack?"

"Don't embarrass me with memories. I have enough to embarrass me as it is," Jack said.

"You don't write now, Mr. Eichorn?" asked Mrs. Ackers.

"I do, but I don't sign my name to it," Jack said.

"But you're doing so much, Jack," Ruth said.

"I don't know that I am. The President gave me an autographed picture of himself and he said I was doing a lot. But I wonder sometimes; I'd like to get out of it. But what could I do?"

"Get out of it? We need you. If I had my say, you'd be a Senator," Ruth said.

"We'll organize an Eichorn-for-Senator Club right now," Will Ackers said.

"Will you vote for me, Sarah?" asked Jack, looking across the room at her.

"I would with pleasure," she said.

A smile played on her lips.

"And you, Tom?"

"Maybe you could fix it up for me to vote twice for you," Tom answered.

VIII

"It was a pleasant evening. Are you feeling well, Tom?" Ruth asked.

They sat in their living room. The ashtrays were full. A faint smell of alcohol and vague clouds of cigarette smoke hung over the room.

"You were cold to Jack. And he admires you so much," Ruth said.

"I don't think I was cold to him."

"Well you were, Tom. Everyone knew it even if you didn't."

Had he seemed cold? He hoped not, he found Jack somewhat boring but he did not dislike Jack.

"You've written books with warmth. You wrote of Walt Whitman with love. Whenever you write of Lincoln there is warmth. But people can only get so much out of a book, Tom. They can't get the warmth of a man out of his books. They must get it out of him."

There was an angry sincerity in her voice. She meant what she was saying.

"I don't know what you mean," Tom said defensively.

"Tom, do you love Sarah?"

Her remark hit him hard, and brought utter surprise onto his face.

"No," he said.

"Tom, I never told you but I knew. A wife can tell when her husband is unfaithful. But I hate that word, unfaithful," she said.

"What should I say now of the past?" he asked, speaking as much to himself as to her.

In his work, he labored over and lived in the past. He dredged it from pieces of paper, and out of this there rose living beings in his own imagination. He wrote of this with power and sincerity. He had reached the point of looking backward, not forward. He looked back on what was lived, and he no longer faced the future with open-eyed confidence and courage. Was he only half-living?

"Tom, you might as well know. I was hurt. I loved you. There were nights when I cried myself to sleep. Many nights."

He had never wanted to discuss this with her.

"Ruth, I loved you too. But I never promised you eternal fidelity," he said.

"I know. I know, Tom. Life isn't a bed of roses. Romantic love doesn't last. All men are the same. Take Jack. I like Jack, but a woman can tell in no time that he is a philanderer. Tom, a woman wants to be loved deeply. Do you remember when we were married?"

"Yes," he said, deciding that they must now face the wreck of their marriage and all that it meant.

There was guilt and regret in him. Once, yes, once he had

wanted their love to be different from other loves. Once, and despite all of his talk of freedom, the modern spirit, the free man, the free woman, he had wished that he and Ruth would live in fidelity for their entire lives. He had tried. For years, he had tried. And then, Sarah. But he couldn't tell her this.

"Did Jack take Sarah away from you?"

"Ruth, I thought that we had come to a tacit understanding to go our own ways," he said.

"Tom, I'm not criticizing you. I'm not even angry. I was sure that you and Sarah were having an affair. Did I behave badly?"

"No, you didn't."

"The first time that a woman discovers that her husband has slept with another woman, it cuts like a knife. When we were married, I thought that no girl, no woman could ever come between you and me. I thought that mine was a happiness that I didn't deserve. And do you know one of the reasons I was so happy?"

"Why?"

"I remembered myself in my bridal gown. I was a virgin. I was trembling—afraid and eager. I looked at you. You were so tall and wonderful, so handsome. And I thought to myself, 'He's mine.' And I told myself, 'We'll always be in love, we'll always be together.' Do you remember when I cried after the ceremony? You were annoyed."

"I couldn't understand why you cried."

"I cried out of happiness. They were tears of joy. Oh, is there any use in talking of all that now? We've changed, Tom, you and I. There's never anyone to blame. Is there?"

"That time with Sarah, it meant no rejection of you, Ruth."

"Oh, Tom, this isn't logic. You're so logical. There's no logic in the human heart."

"I gave up Sarah," he went on.

"Maybe you shouldn't have. Maybe you weren't fair to

her. She is getting divorced now. Are you sure that you don't love her, still?"

Tom shook his head.

"You don't love anyone, is that it?"

"I have an affection for you, Ruth."

"Tom, let's be honest and not fool ourselves. You no longer love me."

"You no longer love me either, Ruth."

She looked, for a moment, as though she would burst into tears.

"I wanted to love you. I tried."

"Do you think I didn't try?" he asked.

"I suppose you did."

The past. The memory of lost ecstacies. He felt sad and foolish.

"We've grown apart." He spoke calmly. There was no trace of the melancholy he felt in his voice.

She looked at him. She was winning her silent battle with herself not to cry. Tom, there. Grey. Thin. In pain last night, moaning in pain. She had lived with this man all of her life. At times it seemed as though she had lived with him forever. Her life began with him. She had moaned and cried out in the arms of Harry Helmholtz, but her cries had not come from the depths of her being. Once, she had cried out in Tom's arms. She had moaned and sobbed and cried out, and the cry had been a cry of joy from the center of her, from every part of her. That was gone. She no longer loved Tom.

He felt a nervousness in his stomach. For a moment he was afraid. Would he have another attack?

He was tired.

"Romanticism is a lie, Ruth."

"Oh, Tom, all the hopes of youth are lies."

"Ruth, don't cry," he said gently.

"Oh, Tom, I'm crying about life. I'm not hurt. Tom,

you can have your mistresses if they give you what I can't give. It's not that. It's life. It betrays us. That's why I want the world new. That's why Bill . . ."

She stopped, and ran the back of her hands over her eyes. She smeared her face with her own tears.

Should he remind her of her own lovers? But to tell her now would only hurt her more.

There was nothing to say.

She stood up.

"Tom, shall I get you the hot-water bottle for your stomach?"

"No thank you, Ruth."

"There's nothing more to say, Tom. It turned out different from my dreams."

"I had dreams too, Ruth."

"All right, Tom. Our dreams."

He rose.

They went out of the room. She switched out the lights.

The past. The deaths a man dies before he finally goes. No, there was nothing to say. Now, he and she would undress in front of each other. Their naked bodies would mean nothing to one another.

Would he awake in pain again tonight?

And Sarah. He remembered once, when he lay in bed with her, it had been wonderful. He had told her that. And she had said that it had been magnificent. And he had said:

—Sarah, I want to spend the rest of my life with you.

That was years ago.

He turned the light on in their bedroom. His pajamas lay by the pillow. Ruth had placed them there.

He began to undress. She began to undress. They undressed for bed in silence.

He noticed her naked body. It was still soft and youthful looking. He felt infinitely sorry for her.

The past. That day in Pompeii. The past of every man was a Pompeii.

As he got into bed, he said gently:

"Good night, Ruth."

"Yes, Tom," she said, pulling a pink nightgown over her naked and still beautiful body.

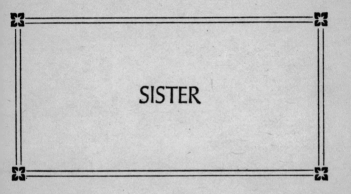

SISTER

I

n my seventh-grade year, we had Sister Battling Bertha.
t was a bad year for me. I lost interest in my school work,
nd my marks were lower than they had been in any year
during my whole period in grammar school. Sister Bertha
vas quite hysterical. She had taken a dislike to me early in the
ear. My averages—over eighty in sixth grade—had sunk down
nto the seventies, and as the year had gone on, I had gotten
only passing grades. In the spring I had not even been sure
hat I would be promoted to the eighth grade. I hadn't been
ble to arouse my interest even though I had not wanted to
emain two years in the same grade. Many times Sister Bertha
ad made me leave my seat to stand or kneel in the front of
he room. Sometimes she had hit me. She used to hit the boys
ften. She had screamed and shouted at me more often than
he had at most of the other boys in my class. I don't know
ow many times she told me that I was no good for nothing
ut fighting.

I went back to school in September of 1918, dreading my
eighth grade year. I expected that Sister Bertha would be our

teacher again. I didn't like her. Scarcely any of the boys in our room, consisting of the seventh and eighth grades, liked her. Except for a few of the boys who always had a high average, she treated all of us in the same unpredictable manner. None of us knew when she would descend upon us, when she would give us a tongue-lashing or even hit us. I had lost confidence in my ability in the classroom, and even in myself. My seventh grade year had been a poor one. I went back to school on that first day of my eighth grade year, in September of 1918, expecting a repetition of what had happened in seventh grade. I was convinced that Sister Bertha didn't like me. There was nothing to look forward to but trouble with her for one whole year, and perhaps I wouldn't be able to graduate.

When I walked into the classroom that sunny September morning, I was instantly relieved. Seated at the desk, there was a strange nun I had never seen before, but who couldn't be worse than Sister Bertha. No matter who she was, I could make a new start. However, I feared Sister Bertha might have told this new nun all about me and she might be down on me.

Sister was tall. She had dark skin, unhealthy, sallow and swarthy. There was a touch of dark down on her skin. Her eyes were brown. She wore glasses. She spoke that first morning. I can't recall what she said, but I do remember that she left with me the impression that she meant business, and that she wouldn't tolerate much fooling around in class. After she spoke to us, we were dismissed for the day.

In the days that followed, it became clear to me that she was not going to be like Sister Bertha. I got off to a good start in her class. I did my homework regularly, and I discovered that I was able to keep up with the class. I had thought that I wouldn't be able to because of my poor seventh grade year. During the last months in seventh grade I had done as little studying and school work as possible. When

got my first report card for the new year, I saw that my
verage was ninety.

Sister Magdalen talked to us so much differently than had
Sister Bertha. She told us about some of her experiences at
other schools, and about boys she had taught. She came
from Indiana, and told us something about herself, and the
small town from which she had come. It was easy to sense
very quickly that she was not like Sister Bertha. I wanted to
get good marks and to win her approval. I wanted her to
like me. When I realized that she did like me, I tried to do
better work. Within a few weeks of the school year, I was
a different boy. I wanted to go to school, and I looked forward to each morning. The hours in the classroom didn't
drag. I did less vain daydreaming. I began to care about my
marks and about being right and having the correct answers
when I was called upon to answer questions or to recite.

Sister alternately heard the lessons of the seventh and
eighth grade boys. While she gave the lesson to one class, the
other class was supposed to study. I used this time for studying. With Sister Bertha I hadn't done this. I hadn't cared.
I began to think of Sister Magdalen not as a mere teacher
and a nun, but also as my friend.

Sister Bertha had never talked to me, told me things in
private about myself, or showed that she had much interest
in me. She used to bawl me out in front of the class, but this
was a kind of honor. It would set me up because if you got
bawled out by Sister Battling Bertha, that was something to
brag about. Sister Magdalen was so different. Early in the
year I told her that Sister Bertha hadn't liked me, and she
apologized for her predecessor by saying that Sister Bertha
was old. She asked me if I knew why I hadn't gotten along
with Sister Bertha. I didn't know why, except that I thought
that she didn't like me, and used to tell me that the only thing
I could do was fight. Sister Magdalen told me that I was
loyal. I never imagined that I was, but I began to try to be

loyal. I didn't quite believe her, and I sometimes imagined that I was fooling her. At other times, I would be troubled thinking that I was not living up to her idea of me. I would be troubled, but I would try all the more to be the kind of boy that she thought I was. Likewise she told me that I had perseverance and stick-to-it-iveness. She often used that word. I tried to be more persevering.

A number of us liked to stay after school to help Sister do odd things in the school room, to clean the erasers, rub off the blackboard and to put things away. I had never stayed after school to help Sister Bertha. I liked staying to help Sister Magdalen. This was considered a privilege. Sometimes I would stay alone, and other times there would be a group of us. She would talk about the school, about herself, and the other nuns, about other schools, or about us. I liked to hear her talk, and many of the other boys did. From the very first day of the school year, she had command of the class, and she never lost it. Her command, however, was not merely based on her authority, which she would use if she deemed it necessary. Her command was fixed on her personality, her interest in us, and the way she talked to us.

In the eighth grade I rose from a boy whose averages were just passing to one who was among the top boys in the class. After the first month, my averages were always above ninety. I wanted to please Sister Magdalen and to win her approval, and I studied harder to do this.

Before, we had looked down on boys who were too smart or whose marks were too high. But with the boys in Sister Magdalen's classes, this wasn't the case. Good grades didn't make you out to be a sissy. The atmosphere of the classroom was so different from what it had been under Sister Bertha.

I liked Friday afternoons in class especially. Of course, this meant the end of the week, but that year I often left school on Friday afternoon looking forward to Monday morning. During the last hour on Friday, there was a let-down. We had our weekly lesson in Bible History. We began each day with a catechism lesson. The year before, when we had Bible History with Sister Bertha, I used to daydream and I would always be impatient for class to end, freeing me for the weekend. Sister Bertha made us recite; the lesson would be dull. But Sister Magdalen would make the lesson alive.

I sat in the row nearest the door. I can recall myself, seated in the middle of the row, looking up at her desk on the opposite side of the rather large room. I would listen with all of my attention. She talked in a firm, steady voice. She told us of the Twelve Apostles as though she had known them personally. Sister was especially fond of St. Peter, and she had more to say of him than she had of any of the other Apostles. She described St. Peter as loyal and fallible, temperamental and impulsive, a man, not a saint. I could easily visualize him and feel that I knew him. I remember, on a number of Friday afternoons, listening to her talk of St. Peter and wishing intently that I had been him. Sister was particularly absorbing when she spoke of how St. Peter had acted at the time of the Crucifixion. She explained that St. Peter was hot-tempered, and he became even more human to us.

Sister seemed to have a particular interest in me. In return, I responded to her eagerly and enthusiastically. I believe that she achieved similar results with other boys in the same way. I kept trying to live according to the standards and virtues of which she spoke.

I sometimes had talks with her in the classroom after school. She believed that my folks were richer than they were, and used sometimes to speak of how well off my grandmother was, and how much my grandmother cared for me.

All year she talked of the scholarship examinations for Catholic high schools which were held every spring. She wanted some of us to win a scholarship, and quite early in the year she picked a group for special training, with the hope that one or more of us would be successful. I was one of the boys in this group. This gave an added spur to my studying and made me more eager to get good marks. After a month or so of the school year, I was one of the eighth grade boys who was sometimes given the seventh grade homework papers to correct and mark. This was another honor. It further built up my confidence in myself.

Sister had a way of talking to us as though we were her special confidants. She would try to find out more about what we did away from school. In the middle of the school year, she surprised the class one afternoon by announcing that she knew that some of the seventh and eighth grade boys and girls were going to moving picture shows together on Sunday afternoons. She treated this as though it were bad, or at least dangerous. She asked all who were among the group to speak up. Billie Morrie, Dick Buckford, Glen Squires and some of the other boys, who were doing this, admitted that they had been in the group. It was the same as confessing to a sin.

I was not implicated. I would stand well in her eyes as a good boy. I wanted this. But the boys and girls who were going to Sunday movies were in my own group. They were the kids I played with. And the fact that this harmless action and flirting was going on was also a painful discovery to me. I was being left out of something. I derived no pleasure by going free of the reprimand given to the boys I played with. I was hurt. I knew that if I had only had the opportunity, I would be standing up with them receiving a lecture.

I had a boyhood worship and love for one of the girls in the eighth grade class, Roslyn Hayes, and she was one of those who had been going to Sunday movies. I didn't want Sister to know how I felt about Roslyn. I wanted no one but Roslyn to know. I didn't want to be laughed at. But on that afternoon, I sat in the classroom, knowing how I hadn't been wanted by Roslyn and others of the group.

Not Sister Magdalen alone, but practically all of the nuns at the school treated association between the boys and girls of the school as though it were a sin. Perhaps this was why the boys and girls were separated after second grade. Two classes of boys and two classes of girls occupied the same classroom.

Just about midyear, I was alone with Sister Magdalen in the classroom after school. She had asked me to remain after classes because she wanted to talk with me. Sister was very serious. She told me that she had heard that the seventh and eighth grade boys and girls were violating the sixth commandment, and she wanted to know if I knew anything about such goings on.

I didn't.

I am certain that no such thing was happening. Most of us were very innocent, far more innocent than we should have been at our ages. Of the girls, the most we spoke of was their legs. And at the few parties I had attended—I had not always been invited—I think there had always been the question as to whether or not there would be kissing games. Sometimes we played kissing games and sometimes we didn't.

When I answered Sister by saying that I knew of no such conduct, I did not have to conceal anything. But her manner and her seriousness gave me the impression that it was a very grave matter. Sister Magdalen told me that Sister Bernadette, the principal of the school, and the teacher of the seventh and eighth grade girls was also concerned. And Sister must have questioned other boys as she had me.

On another occasion, some of us arrived in the classroom ahead of Sister and before the bell had rung for the afternoon session. We shared a narrow dressing room with the girls. But it was so timed that we never were in the dressing room at the same moment as the girls. On this particular afternoon the doors of the classroom were opened. We were talking with the girls. Sister caught us.

She was angry and ordered the girls back to their room and told us to go downstairs until the bell was rung. We were further punished by being kept after school. But we weren't questioned about what we had been talking about with the girls. The conversation had been utterly innocent. The mere fact that we had been talking with the girls had been treated as bad.

II

Sister Magdalen's attitude toward the boys fighting was much different.

Across the street from us, there was a Greek Orthodox church and school. There was friction between us and the Greek boys. The danger that this would result in fighting was constant. One noon hour there was almost a gang fight. In the midst of it I had challenged the leader of the Greek boys to a fist fight. He was supposed to be their best scrapper. We had squared off with clenched fists when Sister Magdalen appeared. She ordered us back to our own grounds.

That afternoon, she spoke to me, but in a most understanding way. She explained to me that she knew how boys sometimes got into fights, but added that I should try to control my temper. I wasn't punished. I would have been by Sister Bertha.

There was another incident concerning fighting. Toward the end of the school year, we were rehearsing for our class play, which was to be put on for one night, near the time of our graduation exercises. A group of us were taken to be fitted for our costumes at a theatrical costume establishment near the North Side of Chicago. While we were there, two boys from another school happened to come into the place. One of them was a stocky boy of about my own size and weight. He and I took a quick dislike to one another. He spoke in a loud, surly, and bullying tone. I felt impelled to speak out.

"Who talked?" he asked like a bully.

"I did," I said.

Sister intervened and prevented a fight.

Again, she talked to me instead of yelling and bawling me out as Sister Bertha would have done. Her reaction to these incidents gave me the feeling that I was close to her. She was my friend. While I knew that she didn't approve of my fighting, I sensed that she understood why I sometimes got into fights with other boys. I didn't start the fights; but, in certain situations, I would feel a need to defend and uphold myself. It was a question of my desire to take the lead among my companions. I must be the leader, I felt. And I wanted to stand out and act like the hero of the bunch. Sister's treatment of me and her attitudes toward this conduct of mine didn't violate or run counter to needs which I felt with depth and urgency. This strengthened my reliance in her. I trusted her. I believed that she trusted me. And more than reliance and trust, there was approval. She approved of me. She knew, in some ways, what kind of a boy I was. She had told me she understood how I had almost become involved in fights. And particularly in the case of the strange boy at the costume establishment, she had seen what had happened, and known that I hadn't started it. And yet, she would tell me:

"Daniel, you have the germs of destruction in you."

She said this to me a number of times during the school year, both in class and when we were alone talking. To this day, I am not sure that I know what Sister Magdalen meant. She didn't say this to the other boys, at least, not in class.

I have often pondered what Sister said to me about the germs of destruction. I began that eighth grade school year a very troubled boy. There was very much of which I was ashamed. At times, and especially in my seventh grade year, I felt that I was an outsider. The boys with whom I played would sometimes ditch me. One boy had been ordered by his mother not to play with me because there was drinking and cursing in my home. I wasn't happy, and couldn't be. I had little reason to care about many things. And I didn't. I half gave up.

I was a nervous boy, probably more so than just normally nervous. It was very difficult for me to sit still in class. I used to turn about and squirm in my seat a good deal. I bit off the erasers of the pencils. I chewed my fingernails. I know now that it was partly in reference to this nervousness and these habits that Sister said that I had the germs of destruction in me. She had in mind, particularly, my chewing pencils. But, also, there was a general carelessness in me about books and about things in general.

But I have several times posed the question, did she mean more than this? I am certain that Sister sensed some unclear feelings of disturbance in me. What she did for me was to help me to have more confidence in myself. This, over the years, has been a decisive, saving force for me.

My penmanship was sloppy. Every year, the boys submitted all of the exercises in the Palmer Method book, which was one of our text books. Every afternoon, we spent the first half hour of class practicing writing and exercising our arms in accordance with Palmer Method instructions. Every year the exercises submitted were sent to the Palmer Method officer to be considered for the granting of Palmer Method diplomas. I wanted to receive one, so that I, like nearly all of the others of the graduating class, would, at the exercises on graduation night, receive two diplomas. I worked hard and diligently, writing out all of the necessary exercises, but despite my serious effort I turned in sloppy papers. I had no hope of winning a diploma for writing in the Palmer Method. One day, Sister told me that I had been awarded a diploma, which I would, of course, be given on graduation night. She, also, told me how she had spent some hours, cleaning up my exercise papers, and erasing ink blotches from them. This strengthened my belief in Sister as a friend.

III

Earlier in the year, Sister introduced an innovation which I liked and accepted with enthusiasm. The sidewalk space, fronting the school, church, and parish property covered more than a long block. The art of shoveling the snow off of this sidewalk space was significant for Father Gilhooley, our pastor. In the late fall, Sister spoke of this, and on a volunteer basis, she said that she would organize the seventh and eighth grade boys into snow brigades to come and shovel snow off of the sidewalks in winter. As a reward, those of us who belonged to the snow brigade would, in the spring, be given the afternoon off, to attend the opening day of the baseball season, of the White Sox or the Chicago Cubs. I volunteered, and Sister appointed me as a marshal of the snow brigade. I accepted this as an honor.

But at home, when my Uncle Ned heard of this, he became angry. He claimed that Father Gilhooley and the nuns were cheapskates, and that they were getting us boys to do work that should be done by men, and paid for. I tried to convince him that it was work we should do because it was for the Church, but my effort was hopeless. I couldn't say more; I couldn't tell him that Sister wanted me to do it. I couldn't explain to him that I considered myself honored. I resented my Uncle Ned's criticism, and when he told me that I shouldn't go to shovel snow for nothing, I told him that I had to. He asked me why I had to. I didn't want to tell him that it was for Sister. I answered that I'd given my word. He told me to give him my word that I didn't have to do it. I wouldn't do this. He pressed me about why I believed that

I had to go. I burst out that I'd do anything for Sister Magdalen. My Uncle Ned was both surprised and sarcastic. He clucked his lips, and laughed in bewilderment, and asked me what that Sister was doing to me. He said that I was being used. I didn't change my mind and I still resented what he had said. He didn't understand.

When the first Saturday snowfall came, I went to the school, was given a shovel, and shoveled snow. Only two other boys in the snow brigade showed up.

On the White Sox opening day, Sister gave the entire seventh and eighth grade classes the afternoon off, despite the disappointing turnout for the snow brigade.

IV

Another incident of that year concerned Limpey Sweeney. Limpey was in our class. He was a pleasant, sweet, likable boy, new to the school and to the neighborhood. He was nicknamed Limpey because of a slight limp. He had had tuberculosis of the bone in his right leg. It was thinner than his left leg. His father was either dead, divorced or separated from his mother, who worked. He was less well off than most of the boys in the class. As the year progressed, most of us got to like Limpey. He smiled a lot, he had a friendly disposition, and he was witty.

When parts were assigned for the school play, Limpey was given one of the best and biggest roles, that of an Irish servant named Tighe, a Handy-Andy, stage Irishman type of character. And from the first day of rehearsal, Limpey was very good in the part. Everyone expected him to do well on the night when the play would be staged. And Limpey was enjoying playing the role of Tighe. He blossomed, feeling a new importance, and he became friendlier, smiled more. It was the one time during the entire school year when he stood out. He became more popular, too, with all of the kids in the cast, and this consisted of practically every boy in the eighth grade class. We all liked him doubly as Tighe.

When he performed in rehearsals, we laughed. These were, to us, the brightest parts of the play, and of the rehearsals. And we thought that he was one of the best of all of us on the stage. Sometimes at play, or coming to or going away from school, we would call him Tighe, instead of Limpey. We all felt that we had gotten to know him better, since he had become Tighe in the play. He was a damned good kid, and we were sorry that he had that thin right leg and the limp.

About three weeks before the end of the year, Limpey got into some kind of trouble with Sister. I forget what it was exactly but I remember how I felt about this, and how I was saddened by the outcome. At the time I didn't think that what Limpey had done was a matter of great importance. But anyway, Sister took him out of the play and assigned the part to someone else.

Limpey was very hurt. During the last weeks of the school year, he was a very saddened boy. He smiled less. He had very little to say. He didn't complain because he was being so severely punished, but to him this was a very severe punishment. It practically ruined the entire school year for Limpey. The one chance he had had to stand out, to shine, to be important, had been snatched away from him.

V

I felt that Sister had been unfair. For about a week I kept hoping that he would be restored to the part of Tighe. But Sister was unrelenting and severe. She wouldn't change her mind. She didn't explain to us, either, why she had done this. The qualities that many of us had sensed in her on the very first day of class were revealed in this episode. By the spring of 1919, the previous September, when our school year had begun, seemed far away. Much had happened to us, and most of us had had a good year, the most interesting of our whole eight years in school. September was very distant. Sister had given me, or, at least, helped me to gain an entirely different feeling about myself. But she had inspired not only loyalty, ambition, respect, and perhaps even love; she had also inspired fear. From the very beginning we all sensed, knew in some way, that if we disobeyed her in any serious way, we would be punished. We knew that we wouldn't get away with anything on her. We couldn't put anything over on Sister. If we tried, we would have received a punishment as drastic as Limpey's. Not for as little as one minute during the entire school year did her classes ever get out of hand. We were afraid of Sister.

My own relationship with her—and, I suspect, that of many or at least some of the other boys—was more complicated or complex than this, but of course I was too young to be aware of it completely. I needed someone to help me gain greater self-confidence and Sister had given me that help. She became a figure in my life and in my mind. She gave me the impression that she was genuinely interested in me, and that I was in her confidence. I believed that she wanted me to win a scholarship, to do well in school and in life. And she wanted to help me to save my soul. I was one of the oldest boys in the class. I had not been started to grammar school until I was seven, going on eight, and I had passed every year. In my eighth grade year, I was fourteen, and then fifteen. My development had been slow in some ways, and I was naïve.

Because of early experiences with death in my own family, and because I had been sincerely and deeply influenced by my catechism lessons, the eventual salvation of my soul was a matter of utter importance to me. This question penetrated all of my problems. And I saw in Sister someone who would help me, not only in this world, but in the next one too—in eternity. In the back of my mind, and not always in the back, all during my boyhood, there was fear of Hell and the sense of death. When I felt that I was bad, it was not merely a matter of being bad in the eyes of my own folks, or of priests and nuns; it was being bad in the eyes of God. Sister, like all priests and nuns, was good in the eyes of God. I believed this firmly. Sister was going to Heaven.

All during the year, and especially as the school term drew to an end, Sister spoke about Catholic high schools. She wanted us all to go to Catholic high schools. She was certain that I would attend one and made no special effort to convince me, or to get me to convince my folks to send me to a Catholic high school instead of to one of the public schools. She believed that my grandmother was rich. She saw no problem of tuition fees, as would be the case with some of the boys. My folks weren't rich, but they were comfortable. The folks of the boys I played with were all better off than mine were. When Sister frequently told me that my grandmother was rich, I was pleased. This was a lie and I was allowing her to believe in this lie, but it was not an important or a sinful lie. And it covered up, at least in her eyes, one of the areas or spots of shame which sometimes troubled me. And as far as Catholic schools were concerned, my folks were sufficiently well enough off to send me to one. But if my folks had objected to this, or even if they couldn't have afforded it, Sister's influence on me would have been strong enough to have impelled me to take a stand, and to have argued with my folks to send me to a Catholic school. And I would have been sunken in shame if I had felt that I would have to go to a public school. Mixed up here with religion, however, was the aspect of social snobbery. The snobbery of some of the boys I played with affected me.

VI

It was very much due to the influence of Sister that I was more religious and more pious during my eighth grade year than I had been during any other year of my grammar school life. I went to Mass almost every morning during Lent. I received Holy Communion on the nine first Fridays of the month. Sister approved of this, and I prized her approval. But my motives were mixed. Every time I went to church, just as every day I went to school, I left home with the hope and expectation that I would see and talk to Roslyn Hayes. She was in my mind almost constantly, no matter what I did. I thought of her knowing about what I did, just as I thought of Sister in the same way. In my imagination I did more things and performed more feats to impress Roslyn than I did to impress Sister. I knew that it was not mere love of God and the desire to save my soul which were my sole motivations in becoming so religious during this last of my years in grammar school. I did this, hoping to meet Roslyn, and to walk home from church with her. But if I did see her, I was usually so overwhelmed with my own shyness that I couldn't speak.

After several months of the school year has passed, Sister began to talk about vocations. She usually spoke on this subject on Friday afternoons. After a few of her talks I began to think that I had a vocation. I told her this and she believed that I probably did have a vocation. I then experienced torment and sadness. My two great dreams for when I grew up were to become a star big league ball player and to marry Roslyn Hayes. And were I to become a priest, I would have to abandon both of these dreams. As the months of the school year wore on, as spring approached, I began to feel more strongly that I should become a priest. I sometimes imagined myself as one. But these were sad imaginings. These were day-dreams which depressed, whereas my daydreams of baseball and of Roslyn exalted me.

VII

On some Friday afternoons Sister spoke of the early Christian martyrs. Under her influence, my idea of religion became one of sacrifice and martyrdom. I was struggling with myself to be sincerely and honestly religious. I was trying hard, seriously hard, to be a good Catholic boy. But for me, in those days, there was no joy in religion. It was solemn and serious. It called for sacrifice. It deepened the sense of death which was latent within me, and which had been strongly planted in my feelings for some years, since the deaths of my grandfather and one of my aunts. To be good and holy meant, seemed to mean, to be joyless, to give up, to abandon the world, and all of the things in the world which one wanted and could expect one day to have. To be a good Catholic was bound up with the idea of sacrifice, even of martyrdom. Holiness, piety, was a form of sadness. I didn't, however, reason this out. I felt it. The church services which appealed to me most were those around Easter time, with the Good Friday services. The black on the altar, the sense of a pall hanging over the church and the world, the Friday afternoon Stations of the Cross in the church decorated in black, all of this affected me. The story of Christ's Golgatha and His Calvary became more painfully real. I felt within myself the world become dark and sunless at three o'clock on Good Friday, the time of Christ's death on the cross.

VIII

Now, looking back over a span of years, and trying to remember my relationship with Sister, it seems to me that she helped to make religion seem more joyless. And yet, she was a positive, not a negative person. Excepting for the relationship of boys and girls she always showed that she wanted us to have fun. She took an interest in our play, in my interest, for instance, in baseball. She reacted differently than Sister Bertha did, when we got into fights, and she brought to life our notions of saints and of figures in the history of the church. With all that can be said positively, it still remains now, as I see it looking back, that she didn't really make religion something of joy.

This was important. Her influence on me, in the period when I believed that I had a vocation, was paramount, decisive, and my future, in this short-lived period, seemed to be joyless. I thought of entering the priesthood only in terms of sacrifice, of giving up, and what I believed that I would be giving up were my two fondest dreams.

But more must be said here, if I am to make more full my portrait of Sister, and my account of my own relationship with her.

To me—and to many of the other boys also—a nun was an object of awe. A nun was only slightly less awe-inspiring than a priest. This was an attitude which grew into me, and into many parochial school boys of my own generation. It seemed as natural as the air which we breathed. The awe with which nuns and priests were enshrouded deprived them of their humanity in our sight. They were not quite human beings. They stood above us, and above our parents, our aunts, our uncles, our grandparents. They were holy. They walked this earth as the representatives of God. They didn't sin as we did. We knew very little of sex and the emotions, and feelings of physical love were then incomprehensible to us. Sex was a bad thing to us. It had never been explained to us. But it was bad. And a bad act had been performed in order that we could be born. My mother and my grandmother were not virgins. Nuns were virgins. Their bodies were covered with long black flowing robes. We saw only their hands and a part of their faces. We saw their feet encased in black shoes. Their habits were so full that the feminine outlines of their bodies were concealed. The outlines of their breasts, for instance, were lost in their full, flowing garments. The fact that they, like all human beings, performed natural functions was startling to us. Thus, one day Sister said in Billie Norris' presence—he was one of my eighth grade companions—that she felt constipated and needed to take a physic. Billie spoke of this to us. It was strange for a nun to say such a thing to a boy. It was almost like dirty talk about sex. It was an example of extraordinary frankness. It embarrassed Billie, and had I been present when Sister had said this, I should, likewise, have been embarrassed. I felt sorry for Sister that she had a body, subject to the laws and necessities to which all human bodies were subject. Women and girls were mysterious to me, and mystery of woman, represented in the figure of a nun, was a mystery much compounded.

A nun then, and Sister in particular, was a special type of human being. She was a holy virgin. Often at home, over the course of the years, I had heard my grandmother refer to nuns as "those holy virgins." Any kind of revelation, on the part of a nun, which indicated a common humanity, came to me as a startling surprise. A personal revelation of feeling and emotion, separate from us boys, was equally surprising. Once when Sister told us of a party she had gone to as a girl, before she had gone into the convent, I was surprised. I couldn't think of Sister Bertha, or of some of the other nuns with whom I had come in contact, as having been girls who had gone to parties. I couldn't think of them as ever having been anything but nuns. It was difficult, when Sister told us of this party, for me to visualize Sister as having been young, and going to a party.

All of this affected me. That so awesome and holy a person as Sister should like me was more than a surprise. For me to be able to say that she was "my friend" was a great honor. After this particular talk with Sister, I was troubled. I had very divided feelings. There was a conflict of needs within me. I needed to persist in all of my feelings and daydreams of romantic love. And I needed the attention and friendship I received from Sister. I knew that my romantic love and worship of the girl, Roslyn Hayes, was neither sinful nor wrong. I feared that Sister, however, wouldn't approve. I was hiding and hugging to myself all of these feelings. If Sister should have found them out, I'd have been deeply embarrassed and chagrined.

And my divided feelings and conflicting needs were further complicated by my conviction that I had a vocation. Sister influenced me in a developing belief that I did have a vocation. And if this were so, then I should have to give up all of my hope of winning the love of Roslyn Hayes. I should have to abandon the daydreams which I nourished day after day. I couldn't wake up each morning with the hopes that the particular day would be the one during which I would see Roslyn, when she would talk to me, and my daydreams would begin to come true.

Sister told me what was right, what she said to me was what God wanted and expected of me. And if Sister found out that I did have such a worshipful love of a girl, I had not the least doubt as to what she would say to me. She would tell me that I must give it up. And her telling me that would have been almost tantamount to God having told me that.

Thus did I become burdened. However, I think I should add here that most children are not burdened with problems and inner conflicts as adults are. Boys can more easily forget their burdens than men can. There were many hours of play, of baseball, and of fun when these burdens did not lay on my mind in any conscious sense. I did not drag them with me, minute by minute through my school days and the times when I would be playing. But I came back to them.

As the school year drew to an end, I came, increasingly, to believe that I had a vocation. I told this to Sister. She was glad. She told me that if ever a boy had a vocation, I did. My decision, my growing belief in the trueness of my vocation, did not bring me happiness. In my mind, it took on the character of a sacrifice I would have to make. I would have to give up what I most wanted and cherished in the future.

I felt, during this time, closer to Sister. My daydreams persisted. My worshipful feeling for Roslyn Hayes did not die out. But I believed that I had made my choice. I could look Sister in the eye and believe that I was being truthful with her.

It was good to be an eighth grade student with graduation approaching. It was spring. There were those lovely, sunny days. The air, the sun seemed pregnant with the future. There was so much to look forward to. There was all of life to look forward to. The gloom I felt about what I believed to be my vocation only came upon me at times. Spring and hope took that gloom away. Those weeks of spring were good weeks. There was less school work. Now and then, we eighth graders had afternoons off. Some of us still had special work to do in preparation for the scholarship examinations. But school life was easy. And we eighth graders felt very important. We wore ribbons on our coats or shirts, and the girls wore their ribbons on their dresses. These were our class colors, and signified that we were graduating. We were proud of our ribbons and of our school. Sister had stimulated this pride in us. Rehearsals for the class play went on, almost daily. This took us away from the classroom. There were the scholarship examinations held at schools all over the city. And those of us selected to take them, went in a group. We had the streetcar ride, the strange and new sights of other parts of Chicago, the tense excitement of the examinations, the competitive zest which they roused in us, baseball, the White Sox getting off to a good start in the season with their stars back in the lineup after the War and promising to bring the team to another pennant—these and many other things made the springtime wonderful. The world was opening up for me. I would soon go into a larger world. High school would be exciting. There would be new subjects to study, and there would be athletics. I was interested in becoming a high school baseball and basketball star. There was a sadness in leaving grammar school, and in leaving Sister. Sometimes it came upon me. But the possibilities of the future, the joy of growing up—there is joy as well as all of the confusions and doubts of puberty and of early adolescence—outweighed my moments of sadness.

Everything considered—that is everything essential of that school year which I can remember—it was a good school year. And Sister helped make it so.

On graduation night I was sad about the end of my grammar school life. I graduated believing that I had a vocation. This and my sadness were more superficial than the simple and instinctive forces of growth in me. A few days after graduation we had a class picnic in Jackson Park. Sister wouldn't have approved of this. Roslyn didn't come. But we played kissing games. I remember kissing a seventh grade girl, just after she had been eating candy. Her lips were red and sweet. That kiss was more powerful than all of the words of Sister during the entire school year. It troubled me and also enthralled me. The lips of a girl could be so sweet and so red. One could have more kisses. Life was wonderful. I was troubled by this—because I thought of Sister. I still thought that I had a vocation. But that kiss sealed the end of Sister's influence on me.

During the summer I picked another Catholic high school, rather than the seminary. I gave up my resolution to be a priest. I was interested in baseball, in my daydreams, and in a future that was throbbing with excitement and possibility.

During my first year in high school, I saw Sister a few times. I went to the convent or the classroom after school to see her. She was pleased that I was in a Catholic school but disappointed about the change in my resolution to be a priest. The old ties were snapped. Life had moved me a stage forward. She was beginning to become a memory. She was fading into what she now is—someone in my past.

Between then and now, much has happened to me. I do not know what happened to her. She is dead or she is an old woman now. I came to reject all that she believed in. But the warmth of my memories for her, my gratitude to her has never dimmed. Sister didn't know it but she was freeing me from and for more than she imagined. There is an irony in all of this, but life is rich with ironies.

And these few pages, I have written as a recollection and a tribute to her memory.

A Murder: Love Story

WILLIAM S. RUBEN

A story for every man who ever dreamed of having a mistress and for every *other* woman. To end a tender love story, Paul contrives a most reasonably perfect murder: but the question was, whom shall he kill, his mistress or his wife?

15238—$1.50